Steel

The dust, the heat, the fear and the humour, and the pervading smell of cordite make this book a riveting read. The complex weaving of the story as seen by both sides of a conflict will have wide audience appeal; but it is also a fitting tribute to those who were privileged enough to have played some small role in this great adventure. The characters are so well portrayed that the ghosts of the real soldiers who took part can be felt peering through the veil of fiction. It is a story of tough men and boys spurred to great heights by an overwhelming bond of comradeship. - John Smith.

This is another exciting read and a fine follow-up to the author's prizewinning first novel 'A Skirmish in Africa'. It's in the same vein drawing on first-hand experience as well as detailed knowledge of Southern Africa. - Jeremy Martineau

This dynamic, action packed, novel weaves in historical events of the Rhodesian Bush War when young and committed combatants found themselves undermined by the machinations of Cold War era politics and espionage. The soldiers receive difficult or impossible warfare assignments, cooked up by their political masters playing power politics in the presence of double agents and moles. I could not put it down. - James Knox.

A stirring account of the men in the Rhodesian Bush War in their fight for survival against the combined power of the communist backed Liberation movements. The story gives a fascinating insight into the struggles for leadership supremacy amongst the Freedom Fighters, both the winners and the losers. A must read book for anyone interested in a better understanding of how Zimbabwe arrived at the point it is at today. - Philip Morgan

Daryl Sahli was born in Bulawayo Zimbabwe (Rhodesia) and attended Hillside Junior School and Gifford High School ('Tech'). After completing A-levels, he, like all other young men at the time, was called up for national service. The bush war was raging as 163 intake arrived at Cranborne Barracks in Salisbury (Harare).

Daryl, together with a hundred other hopefuls travelled to Llewellyn Barracks outside Bulawayo for the Officer Selection Board (OSBs) and was duly sent to the School of Infantry in Gwelo (Gweru) for training (Inf26/163(D)). After completing training he was posted to 4 Independent Company (RAR) based at Victoria Falls where he completed his national service.

Daryl completed a B.Comm LLB degree at the University of Natal (Pietermaritzburg) and worked at both Ernst & Whinney (Young) and Arthur Andersen in Johannesburg. After immigrating to Australia, Daryl completed an LLM degree at the University of Queensland. Today Daryl works as a management consultant in his own practice in Brisbane. Daryl is married to Karen (nee Young, born in Ndola, Zambia) with two children Megan and Jason.

STEELY-EYED KILLERS

DARYL SAHLI

MyStory
PUBLISHING

Northlands Business Consultants Pty Ltd
ABN 75 091 308 146 Trading As

MyStory Publishing
P.O. Box 5336, West End, QLD, 4101, Australia
www.mystorypublishing.com.au

Copyright © Daryl Sahli 2012

The right of Daryl Sahli to be identified as the moral rights author of this work has been asserted by him in accordance with the Copyright Amendment (Moral Rights) Act 2000 (Cth).

This work is copyright. Apart from any use as permitted under the Copyright Act 1968, no part may be reproduced, copied, scanned, stored in a retrieval system, recorded, or transmitted, in any form or by any means, without the prior written permission of the publisher.

National Library of Australia Cataloguing-in-Publication data:

Sahli, Daryl
Steely-eyed killers / Daryl Sahli

ISBN: 9780987156426 (pbk.)

Southern Rhodesia. Army. Selous Scouts - - Fiction.
Southern Rhodesia. Army. Rhodesian Light Infantry - - Fiction.
Zimbabwe African National Liberation Army - - Fiction.
FRELIMO - - Fiction.
Civil war - - Africa - - Fiction.
Zimbabwe - - History - - Chimurenga War, 1966-1980 - - Fiction.

A823.4

This book is a work of fiction. Names, characters, places and incidents are either the product of the author's imagination or are used fictitiously and any resemblance to actual persons, living or dead, business establishments, events or locales is entirely coincidental.

Cover design by Despina Papamanolis
Maps & Contact Diagrams by Daryl Sahli
Author photograph by Jason Sahli
Typeset in 10 / 13.2pt Palatino
85gsm creme

My thanks to Lt M. L. (Mick) Walters RLI, Course Officer Inf/26(163)D and WOII K. M. (Keith) Bartlett RLI, Course Instructor Inf/26(163)D, for getting me through the School of Infantry and subsequently my national service in one piece.

We should always be in that number ... when the Saints go marching in ...

I wish to thank my wife Karen for her wonderful support and her ability to take a 'MSWord' document and create, as if by magic, the thing you are now holding in your hands. She is truly amazing.

To my unpaid and overworked editorial panel; Ian Livingston-Blevins, John Smith, James Knox, Tom Dawe, Phil Morgan, Jeremy Martineau, John Bucknell, my Headmaster from Gifford High School, Mr Harry Fincham, and my beautiful daughter Megan, thank you. Your enthusiasm is truly inspirational.

'My friends are the ones who bring out the best in me.'
Henry Ford

Map 1: Southern Africa circa 1975 - Country names (colonial names) [year of independence]

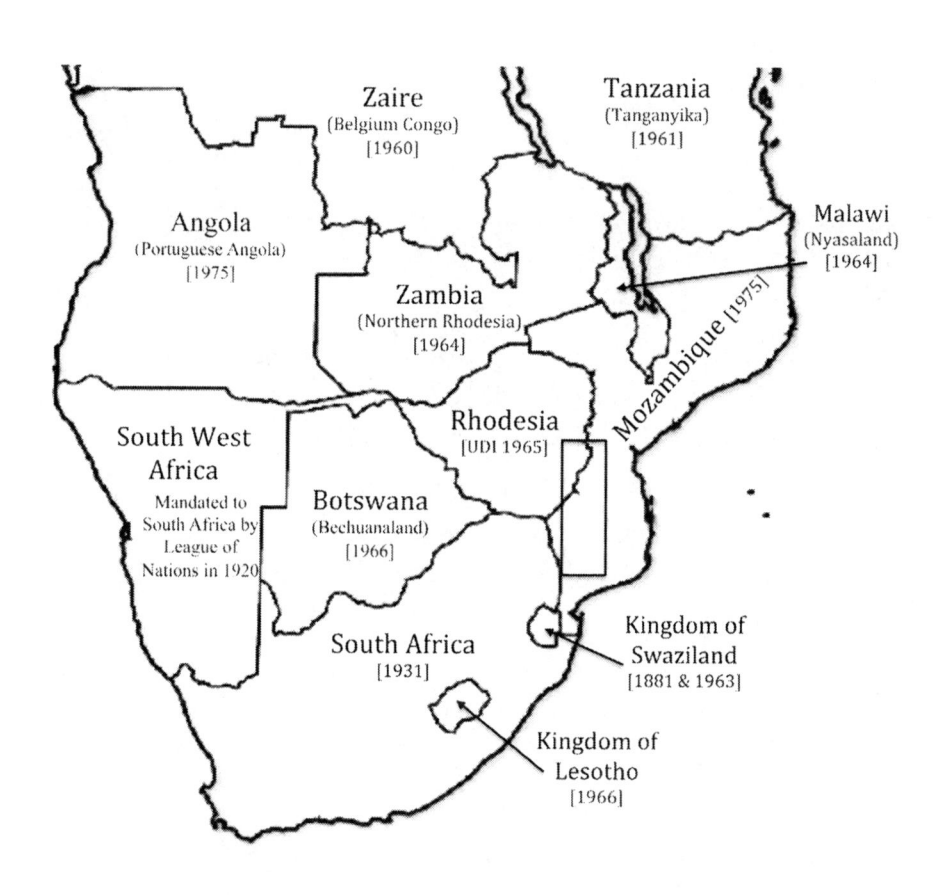

Map 2: Operational Areas for Rhodesian Forces and the Patriotic Front (ZIPRA, ZANLA)

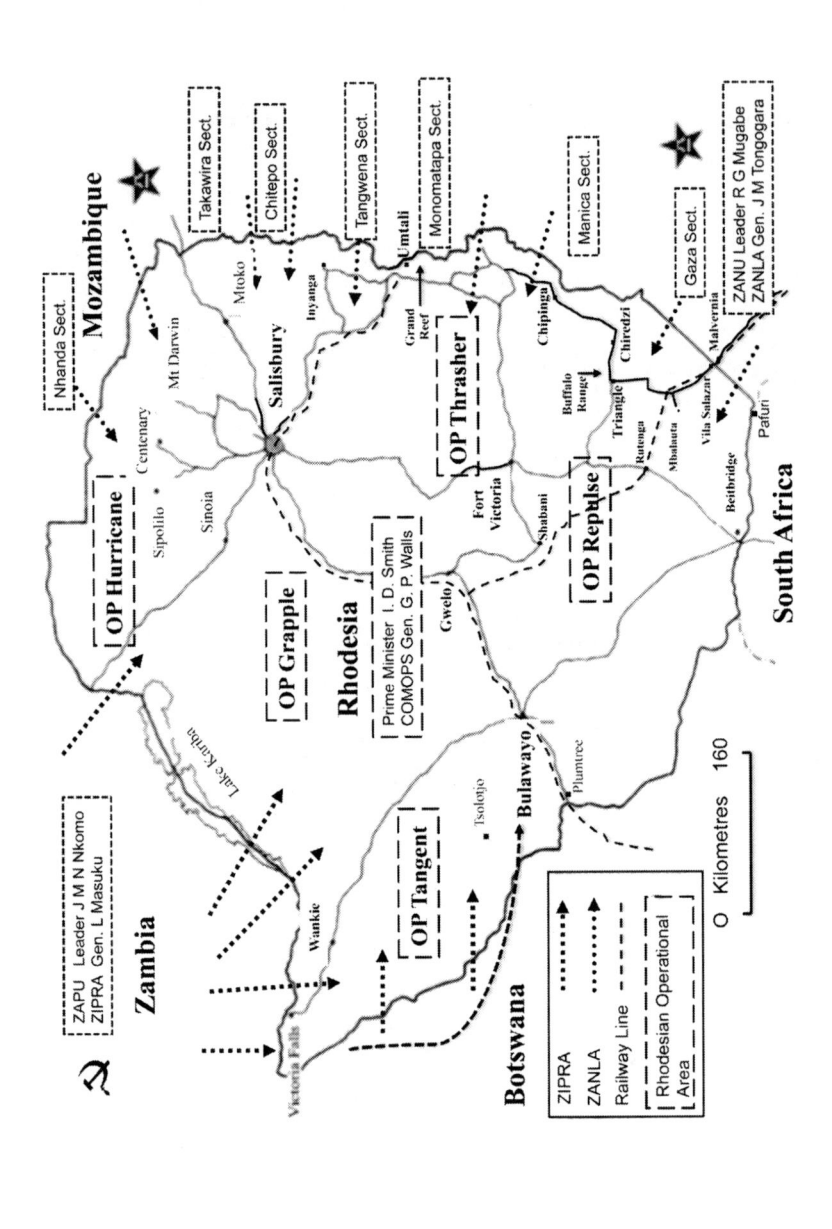

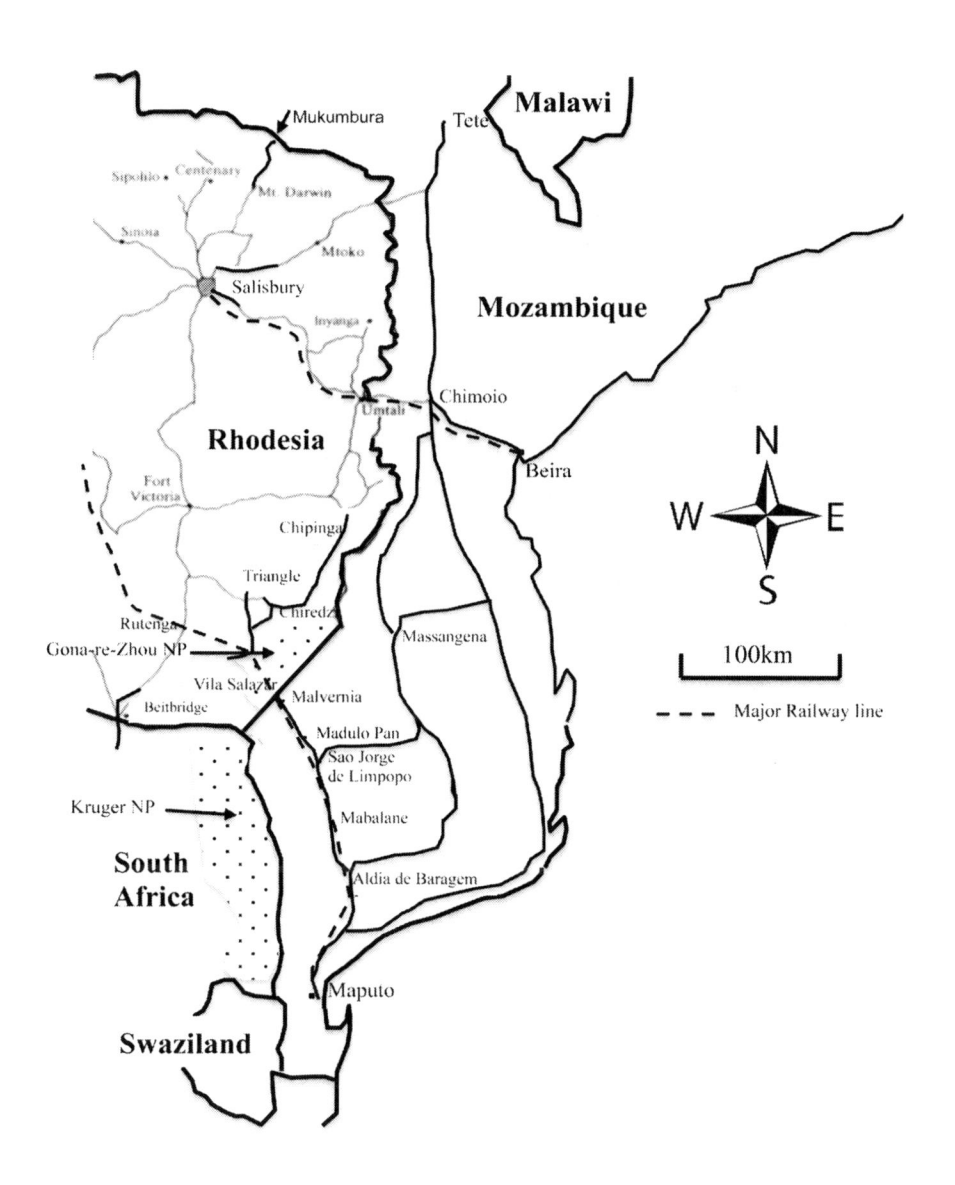

Map 3: Eastern Border of Rhodesia and Mozambique

Map 4: South Eastern Boarder of Rhodesia and Mozambique, where most of this story takes place

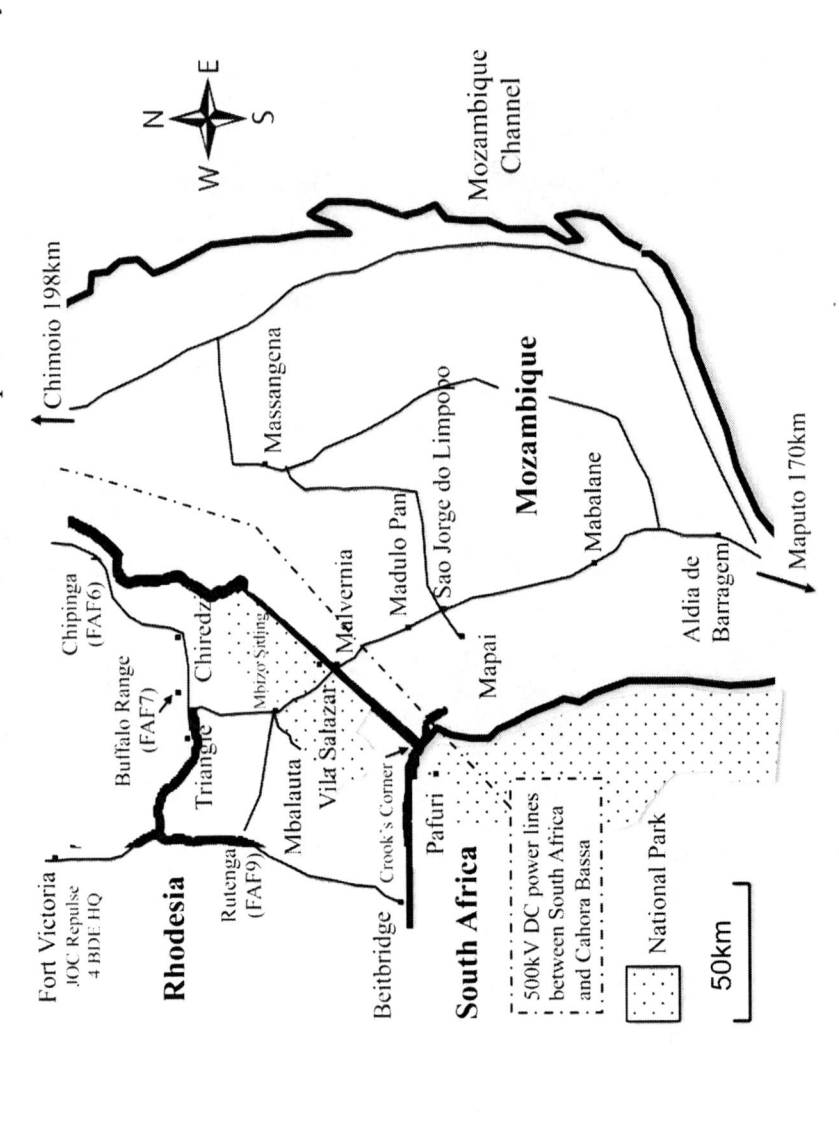

Glossary

2IC	Second in Command
A63	Small VHF radio, carried by Section and Stick commanders. Also referred to as the "small-means".
AGL	Above ground level.
AK	AK-47, Soviet Union, (or Kalashnikov), selective fire, gas operated, magazine of 30 rounds, 7.62×39mm assault rifle
AKM	An upgraded version of the AK-47 assault rifle.
Avtur	Aviation fuel – turbine
AWOL	Absent without leave
BCR	Bronze Cross of Rhodesia, awarded for valour in the face of the enemy.
Big-means	The nickname for the TR48 HF radio.
Bivy	Short for bivouac, a plastic sheet used for creating shelter usually by being strung between trees, low to the ground.
Blue Job	Air force
Braai	Barbeque
Brown Job	Army
BSAP	British South Africa Police was the name of the Rhodesian Police Force, a hang over from the pioneer column of the 1890s when the British South Africa Company supplied the police. The British South Africa Company was the company set up by Cecil John Rhodes to exploit the riches of South-Central Africa.
Call-sign, c/sign	Call-sign, Rhodesian voice procedure, the name or number given to a unit, large or small. Personnel issued with a radio would automatically be allocated a c/sign. A c/sign was a vital element of voice procedure.
Call-up, continuous call-up	The call to active service for territorial and national service personnel. The continuous call-up in the latter stages of the war was "six weeks in and six weeks out" and affected most territorial soldiers in the age group 18 to 35.
Canberra	The English Electric Canberra B2, twin-engined, light bomber, supplied to the Rhodesian Air Force in 1959.
Casevac	Casualty evacuation
Chilapalapa	Hybrid language, developed by the earliest settlers, miners, traders, hunters and farmers to assist with communication with the African tribes of Southern Africa. Words were taken from seShona, siNdebele, Afrikaans and English. The language was in daily use and played a vital role in improving communication between the races.

Glossary

Chimurenga	The liberation war. The ZIPRA called the First Chimurenga the Matabele Rebellion of 1890, ZANLA referred to the First Chimurenga as the Shona Rebellion of 1893, while the Second Chimurenga is believed to have started, by both ZIPRA and ZANLA, with the battle of Sinoia on 28 April 1966 in which 21 Freedom Fighters were intercepted by Rhodesian Forces and killed.
Chopper	American slang - Helicopter
Choppertech	Rhodesian slang, field maintenance technician and gunner on Alouette III G-cars and K-cars.
Civies, civy-street	Civilian clothing, anything other than the army uniform
Combined Operations, COMOPS	The organisation lead by General Peter Walls to co-ordinate the activities of Air Force, Police and Army. COMOPS were also responsible for planning and executing External raids.
Contact	An encounter with the enemy. A battle.
Cordon Sanitaire	Border minefield. These were laid in a number of places around the country. In the Op Repulse, area the minefield stretched from Crook's Corner on the South African border, past Vila Salazar, for 162km to the Sabi River.
CQMS	Company Quarter Master Stores
Crow	Rhodesian slang, woman
CSM	Company Sergeant Major, in the RLI Commando Sergeant Major, Warrant Officer 2nd Class.
CT	Communist Terrorist, most common voice procedure term used to describe insurgents.
Culling	Rhodesian slang, killing – derived from the term used for reducing the number of large game animals like elephants in national parks.
Dak. Dakota	Douglas DC3, military transport version C47, also Paradak for delivering airborne troops.
Donga	Eroded river or streamline, normally dry but a rushing torrent after a rainstorm, often steep sided and boulder strewn with sometimes very thick vegetation along the banks. Most often caused by overgrazing and deforestation.
External	An attack outside the country. Rhodesia raided insurgent training and logistical bases in all neighbouring states, even as far as Angola and Tanzania.
FAF	Forward Airfield, FAF 1 was at Wankie, FAF 2 Kariba, FAF 3 Centenary, FAF 4 Mt Darwin, FAF 5 Mtoko, FAF 6 Chipinga, FAF 7 Buffalo Range, FAF 8 Grand Reef, FAF 9 Rutenga and FAF 10 Gwanda.

Glossary

Fire-fight	A battle.
FLOT	Forward Line of Own Troops, the line demarcated with smoke grenades or mini-flares to mark the position of ground forces to allow for safe airstrikes.
FN	*Fabrique Nationale* (Belgium), self-loading rifle, magazine 20 rounds, 7.62×51mm intermediate (NATO) round.
Follow-up	The process of tracking and following insurgent groups.
Four-Five	Mercedes Benz 4.5 ton 4×4 chassis with a steel, V-shaped, armoured body for mine and ambush protection.
Fran, Frantan	Frangible tank napalm bomb.
FRELIMO	*Frente de Libertação de Moçambique*, Liberation Front of Mozambique, founded in Dar es Salaam Tanzania in 1962 to fight for the independence of Mozambique. After the withdrawal of Portugal from its African colonies following the Carnation Revolution in Lisbon in 1975, the movement/party has ruled Mozambique from then until the present day, first as a single party, and later as the majority party in a multi-party parliament. At its 3rd Congress, in February 1977, it became a Marxist-Leninist political party and its official name became the Frelimo Party *(Partido Frelimo)*.
G-car	Aerospatiale Alouette III, helicopter troop carrier, mounted twin .303in Browning MkII machine guns on the left, cyclic rate of fire 1,200 rounds per minute. 'G' referred to General Purpose, capable of carrying four fully equipped soldiers, plus the choppertech and the pilot.
Golf Bombs	Rhodesian made, 460kg pressure bomb.
Gomo	seShona, hill or mountain. The air force may have used the word to describe major navigation landmarks like the Chimanimani or Vumba mountains while flying into Mozambique.
Gook	American slang from Vietnam, adopted by Rhodesians to describe insurgents.
Hondo	seShona, war.
HQ	Headquarters
Hunter	Hawker Hunter FGA9 Mk IX, ground attack fighter, delivered to Rhodesia in 1963.
Indep Co	Independent Company, six in all, part of the Rhodesia Regiment, after 1977, transferred to the Rhodesian African Rifles (RAR).
Intaf	Internal Affairs

Glossary

JOC	Joint Operations Command, the JOC for Operation Repulse in Victoria Province was located at Fort Victoria (Masvingo).
K-car	Aerospatiale Alouette III, helicopter gunship, mounting one French Matra MG 151 cannon on the left, cyclic rate of fire reduced to 350 rounds per minute, high explosive incendiary shells. 'K' referred to killer, carried the gunner or choppertech, the pilot and the Fireforce Commander. Cannon calibrated to 800ft AGL.
KIA	Killed In Action
Koppie	Afrikaans, hill, koppie is a small hill, words used interchangeably.
Locals	Local villagers, tribes-people.
Lynx	Reims-Cessna FTB 337G, twin-engined, push-pull aircraft, used for close air support, carried mini-golf bombs, 37mm SNEB rockets, Frantan canisters and twin roof mounted .303 Browning machine guns. These aircraft were smuggled into Rhodesia from France in 1975.
LZ	Landing Zone
M962	Fragmentation grenade
MAG	*Fabrique Nationale* (Belgium), *matirueurs a gas*, 7.62×51mm (NATO) round, belt fed machine gun, cyclic rate of fire 650 rounds per minute.
NCO	Non-commissioned Officer
NS	National Service
OC	Officer Commanding
OP	Observation Post
Ops	Operations, Operations Room.
Paradak	Douglas DC3 converted for delivery of parachute troops.
Patriotic Front	Formed in October 1976, after sustained pressure from the Frontline States (Zambia, Tanzania, Malawi and Mozambique), the Patriotic Front was an alliance between Joshua Nkomo's Zimbabwe African People's Union (ZAPU) and Robert Mugabe's Zimbabwe African National Union (ZANU). The purpose of the alliance was to focus on the common enemy the white minority government instead of fighting amongst themselves.
PATU	Police Anti-Terrorist Unit
Pom, Pommie	Colonial slang, person from England, can be a term of endearment or derogatory, believed to derive from Prisoner of Mother England - convicts transported to Australia.

Glossary

R&R	Rest and Recreation (recuperation)
RAR	Rhodesian African Rifles
Repulse, Op Repulse	Operational Area – most of the Province of Victoria in the southeast.
Revved	Rhodesian slang, attacked or shot at, also applied to being mortared.
RIC	Rhodesian Intelligence Corp
RLI	Rhodesian Light Infantry, one regular battalion, made of four airborne commandos including a Support Commando, HQ and Training Troop. The unit exclusively white specialising in Fireforce operations and major external raids, mostly regular soldiers but in later years included national servicemen to boost numbers. The unit included many foreign volunteers from the Commonwealth Countries (United Kingdom, Australia, New Zealand and Canada) but also South Africa, France, USA (Vietnam veterans), Holland and Germany.
RPD	A light machinegun, Soviet Union, 100 round segmented belt in a drum container, 7.62×39mm cartridge, cyclical rate of fire 650 rounds per minute.
RPG-7, RPG	Rocket Propelled Grenade, Soviet Union, hand-held, shoulder-launched anti-tank weapon capable of firing an unguided rocket equipped with an explosive warhead, fired both anti-tank and high explosive/fragmentation warheads.
RR	Rhodesia Regiment.
RSM	Regimental Sergeant Major, Warrant Officer 1st Class.
RV	Rhodesian voice procedure, rendezvous, also RV Point
Saints, The Saints	The RLI were called the Saints, it was a nickname that arose out of the Regimental March, *When the Saints go marching in …* adopted by the men soon after the Regiment was formed in 1960. A bagpiper, L.Cpl. 'Mac' Martin, had played the tune on his pipes during early route marches. New words were added to the tune in later years.
SB	Police Special Branch. BSAP Special Branch.
Scene	Rhodesian slang, a contact with the enemy, a battle
SF	Rhodesian Security Forces
Shumba	Shona for lion, used to describe Lion Lager beer.
SInf	School of Infantry, Gwelo (Gweru). Also Hooterville and College of Knowledge.

Glossary

SKS	Semi-automatic carbine, Soviet Union, 10 round internal box magazine, 7.62x39mm.
SNEB	Lynx carried Matra 37mm SNEB rockets, Hunter Matra 68mm SNEB rockets.
Stick	A group of 4 men in full operational kit, the maximum number that could be carried in a fully armed Alouette III troop carrying helicopter, G-Car.
Stop, Stop Group	A group of men used to block the escape of insurgents after a contact. In a Fireforce, stops were numbered Stop 1, Stop 2, Stop 3 etc. A Stop Group could be made up of more than one c/sign, as in the case of troops deployed by parachute.
Subbie	Regimental Subaltern, 2nd Lieutenant, one pip.
Sunray	Rhodesian voice procedure, Commander, or senior officer.
Sweep, sweepline	The process of spreading out attacking forces in line abreast to flush out insurgents, sometimes in thick bush.
Terr	Rhodesian slang, terrorist
TF	Territorial Forces
TR48	HF radio, the big-means
TTL	Tribal Trust Land
Two-Five	Mercedes Benz Unimog, 2.5 tons
UNHCR	United Nations High Commissioner for Refugees
US	Unserviceable
Vlei	Afrikaans, marshy, low-lying area.
White phos	White phosphorous delivered by hand grenade or rifle grenade.
ZANLA	Zimbabwe African National Liberation Army, military wing of ZANU. Leader Josiah M. Tongogara
ZANU – (PF)	Zimbabwe African National Union – (Patriotic Front alliance after 1976), Robert Mugabe became the leader of ZANU after the death of Herbert Chitepo in 1975.
ZAPU – (PF)	Zimbabwe African People's Union – (Patriotic Front alliance after 1976), Joshua Nkomo was the leader of ZAPU from its inception in 1961.
ZIPRA	Zimbabwean People's Revolutionary Army, military wing of ZAPU. Leader Lookout Masuku.

Foreword

Steely-eyed Killers is a story set in the time of the civil war in Rhodesia (now Zimbabwe) in the mid-1970s. The 'Bush War' between the liberation movements and the Rhodesian regime started in 1966 and ended with the independence of the new Zimbabwe in 1980.

This was a time of considerable upheaval in post-colonial Southern Africa with liberation struggles taking place in South West Africa (Namibia), Rhodesia and South Africa. In addition, there were superpower-sponsored civil wars taking place in the ex-Portuguese colonies of Mozambique and Angola and in the Belgian Congo (Zaire). The liberation struggles provided fertile ground for the extension of Cold War influence by the major powers. China was supporting regimes in Tanzania and Mozambique while the Soviet Union, together with its communist ally Cuba, were active in Angola, Zambia and South West Africa. The USA were supporting opposition movements in Angola and Congo and providing tacit support for South Africa in its war against the South West African People's Organisation (SWAPO) and the Cubans in Angola.

The liberation movement in Rhodesia, an alliance called the Patriotic Front, consisted of two very different organisations split mainly on tribal lines; the liberation movement led by Joshua Nkomo (Matabele), the Zimbabwe African People's Union (ZAPU) and the movement led by Robert Mugabe (Shona), the Zimbabwe African National Union (ZANU).

Britain, as the ex-colonial power in Rhodesia, maintained economic sanctions and an arms and oil embargo. Sanctions were a response to the Unilateral Declaration of Independence (UDI) declared in 1965 by the Rhodesian Government led by Ian Smith. Britain was anxious to ensure a path to black majority rule in Rhodesia but was strongly resisted by the white 'rebel' government. Feeble post-UDI British foreign policy regarding its rebellious colony, plus internal pressure caused by the civil war in Northern Ireland, a struggling economy, labour strike action and the oil crisis, left a political vacuum where the so-called 'Rhodesia Question' became a Page 5 story.

The United Nations, the Organisation of African Unity and the Commonwealth Heads of Government placed considerable pressure on Britain to negotiate a settlement to the Rhodesian Question. The Commonwealth crafted a set of principles that targeted both Rhodesia and South Africa, tarring them both with the same brush.

The United Nations Security Council Resolution 277 of March 1970 confirmed the legitimacy of the armed struggle conducted by the liberation movements to secure their rights as set out in the UN Charter. Article 4 of Resolution 277 placed the obligation on Britain to secure the freedom of the 'the people of Zimbabwe'. Rhodesia was also designated as a threat to world peace. The resolution called for the complete isolation of Rhodesia from all international organisations. Article 14 of Resolution 277 urged, *Member states to provide moral and material assistance to the people of Southern Rhodesia in their legitimate struggle to achieve freedom and independence.*

The UN's active call for support for the armed struggle effectively legitimised the intervention by the Soviet Union and China.

The United Nations Security Council Resolution 415 of September 1977 called on the President of the Security Council to, '*Enter into discussions with the British Resident Commissioner designate and with all the parties concerning the military and associated arrangements that are considered necessary to effect the transition to majority rule'.*

During the crucial 1974 – 1978 period, weak Labour Government in the UK under Harold Wilson and James Callaghan, made half-hearted attempts to negotiate a settlement between the opposing parties. All failed. Various Commonwealth leaders, who had already made up their minds on who should rule the new Zimbabwe, placed pressure upon the British Government. Malcolm Fraser of Australia, Pierre Trudeau of Canada and General Olusegun Obasanjo of Nigeria (himself a military dictator), openly backed Robert Mugabe, while Kenneth Kaunda of Zambia (a one-party state), Julius Nyerere of Tanzania (a one-party state) and Sir Seretse Khama of Botswana (for all intents and purposes a one-party state), supported Joshua Nkomo.

The Soviet Union had taken the decision, as early as 1961, to support the liberation movement led by Joshua Nkomo, ZAPU. The Soviets trained freedom fighters in bases in Zambia, Tanzania and Angola while the most promising leaders were sent to the Soviet Union for training.

Considerable strategic, philosophical and tribal differences existed between Soviet-supported Joshua Nkomo, ZAPU, and the movement led by Chinese-supported Robert Mugabe, ZANU. The differences between the liberation movements spilled over into a series of internal revolts and leadership purges. These revolts and purges occurred both within each organisation and against each other. The UN-sponsored alliance in 1976 between Nkomo and Mugabe (The Patriotic Front), however, allowed the two movements to suppress their differences to focus instead on the common enemy, the white minority government.

On the opposite side of the political divide lay Ian Smith and the white Rhodesian electorate. Initially intransigent, the pressure of the war forced Smith to make secret approaches in order to negotiate a settlement with Joshua Nkomo, his preferred partner. All were rebuffed. As the war continued to escalate and casualties mounted, Smith finally realised that a political settlement was vital. He began a negotiation with internally based black leaders Ndabaningi Sithole and Bishop Abel Muzorewa, the so-called 'internal settlement'. The prospect of an internal settlement, with the potential to be internationally recognised, spurred the Patriotic Front to even greater violence.

The apartheid regime in South Africa was desperately trying to prop up their position in South West Africa and Rhodesia, the 'Buffer States'. The Prime Minister of South Africa, John Vorster, publicly supported Rhodesia but in actual fact, was more focussed on his relationship with the USA and currying favour with Southern African leaders. His successor in 1979, P W Botha restored Rhodesia's oil supplies and intensified South Africa's support with weaponry including pilots and helicopters.

Thus, the rivalries between the super-powers and the leaders of the Southern African states added to a dangerous mix which intensified the war to the extent that it escalated into the neighbouring countries. Rhodesian forces, in an attempt to staunch the flow of insurgents into the country, intensified raids into Zambia and Mozambique, attacking training camps and military bases but also destroying vital infrastructure such as roads and bridges.

In this story, I have painted a broad canvas, encompassing the intrigue within the senior Rhodesian military and intelligence organisations coupled with the continued influence of the British Government and MI6. Spies abounded in high places both in Rhodesia and within the leadership of ZIPRA/ZAPU and ZANLA/ZANU across the borders in Zambia and Mozambique. This manoeuvring and conspiracy is superimposed over the lives of fighting men in the Selous Scouts and Rhodesian Light Infantry (RLI), who were the instruments of external raids into Mozambique.

I have attempted to give the reader an impression of the day-to-day fighting that the men of these units were subjected to and how they coped with the enormous pressures brought to bear on them. The RLI was one of the units that bore the brunt of the famous Fireforce (reaction force) operations. Many of their number were recruited from the four corners of the world to fight alongside their Rhodesian brothers, under the same pay and conditions. They responded to callouts, come rain or shine, sometimes as many as three times a day, parachuting from low level and leaping from helicopters, into the unknown. They paid a terrible price.

On the Freedom Fighter side, the fighting men and women were subjected to unspeakable hardship and brutality. They faced the constant threat of Rhodesian airborne attack, ambushes and mines. Death stalked them from bomb, bullet, disease, hunger and their own leadership. Political trickery and rebellion within the ZANLA/ZANU leadership led to indiscriminate, violent purges, leaving many cadres dead or permanently disabled. Junior leaders were imprisoned and tortured, whether they were part of the conspiracies or not. The rank-and-file had little access to medical treatment where even the most minor wound or ailment was life threatening. Tropical diseases such as malaria, cholera, typhoid and dysentery were endemic.

I have tried, to the greatest degree possible (while still keeping the story exciting and interesting), to give an authentic impression of what it was like. I have used the military slang of the time (with explanations of course) and details of military tactics and weapons. I have also used the original radio voice-procedure, as this was the main source of communication. This can certainly be confusing for some readers, but I have left it in because it adds to the colour and authenticity. In a way, the feeling of confusion and uncertainty (even frustration) experienced by the reader is deliberate because … that is exactly what it was like, chaotic, confusing, frustrating … and terrifying.

The detail on military tactics and weapons is accurate and will appeal to a reader interested in military history and the subject of counter-insurgency.

In the end, this is a story that I have built up from a number of sources, some accurate, others embellished. For the purist, there are many histories and personal accounts written on the Rhodesian Bush War. My primary goal is to give the reader an impression of what it was like, what the characters were thinking ... while living and dying in those dark, uncertain days ...

P.S. Read the glossary first ... it will help.

'We are not fighting against the white man. We are fighting against a system...'
General Josiah Magama Tongogara, Military Commander, Zimbabwe African National Liberation Army (1979)

'The only white man you can trust is a dead white man.'
Robert Gabriel Mugabe, Political Leader, Zimbabwe African National Union (1978)

1

Fireforce Base, Buffalo Range Forward Airfield (FAF 7), Southeast Rhodesia (late 1970's)

A siren wailed across the swelteringly hot airfield, a mournful cry, reminiscent of an approaching air raid from a bygone era. The whining call reached a peak and then trailed off leaving an eerie silence in its wake. Heat haze shimmered off the tarmac as if a lake of cool, sparkling water surrounded the runway. It was hot, blisteringly hot, like only the Rhodesian Lowveld can get in mid-October.

Two men wearing grey/blue overalls came dashing out of a corrugated-iron hut. They ran across the hardstanding to where an ancient Dakota[1] stood, her nose pointing expectantly skyward. The men climbed up the stairs in front of the rear cargo door and disappeared inside. Parallel lines of parachute harnesses stretched out on either side of the cargo door, each capped with a scarred green motorcycle helmet.

Another man, also wearing overalls, stepped out from under the wing, a thin, green army-issue foam mattress draped over his shoulder. He yawned widely, shaking his head from an afternoon siesta in the shade of the aircraft. Making his way to the cargo door, he threw in the mattress and climbed the steps, shouting something to the pilots already inside. The firing of the starboard engine, which coughed loudly, drowned out the man's voice. The propeller rotated a few times and stopped. In the intense heat, the Avgas evaporated in the fuel lines. Again, the engine fired; it hesitated ... then caught, belching a cloud of black smoke over the wing.

As if angry bees disturbed at the hive, men suddenly appeared from all directions, some running towards the Dakota, others running to three Alouette III helicopters parked in oil-drum revetments covered by wire netting. The helicopters were already being pushed out onto the hardstanding. The K-car pilot swung into the right-hand seat, clipped on his harness, while gloved hands flicked skilfully across the instruments. Behind the pilot the choppertech fussed over the single 20mm cannon pointing menacingly out the left hand door. Another man, dressed in camouflage uniform, holding a clipboard and a fist full of maps walked purposefully towards the waiting K-car. He climbed into the left-hand, rear-facing seat next to the pilot, immediately placing the headset over his head. He began talking earnestly into the mic.

Turbines began their expectant whine, blades slowly turning.

Two lines of men, eight in each, formed up in front of the cargo door of the Dakota. The men feverishly hauled parachutes onto their backs, securing the harnesses, each methodically checking the man in front of them. All had kidney pouches and a rolled up sleeping bag attached to their webbing belts,

1 Douglas DC3 converted for delivery of parachute troops, also referred to as a Paradak. Military version called C-47. One Rhodesian "Dak" was rumoured to have taken part in the ill-fated Arnhem drop in World War II.

all wore an emergency chute over chest webbing and an FN rifle or MAG machine gun strapped inverted over the shoulder and secured to their sides. Most wore camouflage jump suits and streaks of greasy camouflage cream across their faces.

A man at the back of the line, Trooper Dudley 'Penga' Marais, slapped the man in front of him hard on the helmet.

'*Lekker* Le Beau, all ready to slot a few floppies[2] today, *Ek sê ... Ek sê*,' he shouted over the Dak engines, now both burping away loudly. The whole fuselage vibrated in tune with the engines. Marais, who was slightly built, was as short as Le Beau but at least ten years younger. His brown sandy hair, cut short, was tinged with black camouflage cream that covered his face in thick streaks, hurriedly applied.

'Fuck ooff Peenga, you preeek,' replied a smiling Trooper Jean-Paul D'aubigne, in his characteristic French accent, similar to the Frenchman in the TV series *Hogan's Heroes*, hence the nickname 'Le Beau'. D'aubigne had a 12kg MAG machinegun strapped to his side. The 500 rounds in his pouches and wound around his body added an additional 5kg.

Across the hardstanding, the helicopter blades were spinning in a wild blur, grit and dust swirling. Men, mostly in shorts and T-shirts under chest-webbing, rifles reversed, crouched over, dashed across, taking their positions inside the G-cars. The K-Car led the other two helicopters out onto the runway, the engines screaming their readiness to fly … then up and away … banking sharply to the east.

The prop-wash from the Dak threw back curls of stinging dust, forcing the men to stand with their backs to the engines, sheltering their eyes with their hands. The repartee between Le Beau and Marais was interrupted by the air force Dispatcher at the door waving for the men to load; they all shuffled forward, struggling up the stairs, hauled up by the Assistant Dispatcher, a giant of a man.

The last man through the door was Troop Sergeant[3] Jock McIntyre; he stood in the middle of the slanting fuselage, holding onto the grab handles attached to the roof with both hands.

'LISTEN UP …LADIEES …' McIntyre shouted on the top of his deep resonant voice. The volume overcame the competition from the Dak engines with ease. '… we have a scene in Ndowoyo TTL[4], Scouts[5] have called us in on a group of about thirty gooks … when you get on the ground, RV[6] with your Stop Commander … stay in your call-signs at all times.'

McIntyre studied the faces of the men sitting on the bench seats along

---

2 Rhodesian slang, what happens to a body when hit with a 7.62mm intermediate … it goes 'floppy'.
3 In the RLI, the Sergeant acting as the 2IC of the Troop was called Troop Sergeant. He could be a three-stripe Sergeant or a Colour Sergeant, three-stripes below the Rhodesian lion-rampant holding a tusk.
4 Tribal Trust Land.
5 Selous Scouts
6 Rendezvous

each side of the aircraft. It was the same every time, their faces returned blank, non-committal expressions, with the exception of Le Beau who always had a beaming smile on his face. Le Beau lifted his right hand and gave his Troop Sergeant a thumbs up.

'Pommie, did you make sure the spare radio is working?' called McIntyre to the third man in line on his side of the aircraft.

'Yes Colourr,' replied L.Cpl. Arthur 'Pommie[7]' Beamish in his characteristic Lancashire accent, a habitual, menacing scowl played across his face.

'Don't look so glum Pommie ... plenty of gooks for everyone,' laughed McIntyre, always ready to pull Beamish's leg. Arthur Beamish's scowl was part of his persona, whether he was happy or sad. It was designed to deflect officers and senior NCOs ... it generally worked.

'Not long to wait LADIES, maybe twenty minutes ... so switch on!' shouted McIntyre to the men.

McIntyre again cast his professional eye over the line of faces, making sure they were focused ... ready. When he was satisfied, he took his seat immediately next to the door.

Opposite McIntyre sat the 11 Troop Commander, 2nd Lieutenant Robert 'Dick', as in Dick Van Dyke in *Mary Poppins*, Van Deventer. Van Deventer was new to the troop, only two weeks, fresh out of the School of Infantry NS Officer's course. This was only Van Deventer's third operational jump. His face was bathed in sweat, his eyes wide, flicking left and right, expressing clearly how he was feeling ... petrified!

'Sir!' called McIntyre to get Van Deventer's attention.

Van Deventer was staring out the door as the Dak began to swing around to taxi down the runway. He looked up at McIntyre.

'Sir, I think when we get on the ground, try and get your Stop together as quickly as possible. Don't shout out in case the gooks are close by ... because your Stop will drop after mine, we may be a couple of hundred metres apart,' said McIntyre, his voice conversational. He did not want to sound like he was giving the new subbie instructions. Despite the vast difference in age, knowledge and experience, McIntyre was always mindful of the importance of showing his subbie respect. That was just the type of bloke he was.

Van Deventer nodded his head, grateful that McIntyre had said something to him. Studying McIntyre's smiling face, he could not believe his luck at having Jock McIntyre as his Troop Sergeant. McIntyre had only shown respect and support ... *what a good bloke!* Van Deventer knew that there was deep resentment within the Troop that a hopelessly inexperienced national service officer was posted to their Commando. These were mostly hardened regular soldiers, together for years, they had seen it all, unhappy with any national servicemen, let alone an 'appy[8]' officer.

---

7   Colonial slang, person from England (UK), can be both a term of endearment and derogatory, believed to derive from Prisoner of Mother England - convicts transported to Australia.
8   Apprentice.

The 'old girl' was gathering pace down the runway, her rudder and ailerons flapping side to side and up and down, like a dignified maiden aunt, checking her hat and dress were correctly in place. As the Dak accelerated down the runway, a Cessna 337G 'Lynx' turned in behind it. The Lynx mounted twin .303 guns above the overhead wing and two 16-gallon Frantan canisters and two Mini-Golf bombs mounted under-wing.

The sixteen men in the Dakota were divided into two stop groups, commanded by McIntyre and the Troop Commander Van Deventer. Each of the para-stops were, in turn, divided into two 'sticks' of four men in each commanded by a Stick Leader who carried an A-63 VHF radio. Two further stops were in the G-cars, which were already airborne on their way to the target. The attacking Fireforce[9], as it was called, was made up of one Alouette III K-car carrying the Fireforce Commander; two Alouette G-cars with four men in each; the Paradak and the Lynx.

Penga Marais, sitting next to McIntyre, leaned forward to talk to his Troop Sergeant.

'Hey Colour, how does it feel to be on your last scene?' he screamed above the droning engines and the howl of the wash from the open door.

'Just fine ... I am happy to see the last of you useless bastards,' replied McIntyre with a broad smile on his face, slapping the younger man hard on the helmet. McIntyre used the word 'bastard' to describe virtually everyone, including his closest friends. If he really liked the person, he would add the words 'bloody useless' to the description. The troopers all sat watching McIntyre in awe, a legend in his own time, fifty operational jumps, ten years of service, contract up, now time to retire to civy street.

The few moments before a jump always provided McIntyre pause to reflect. Today was more poignant, the last operational jump with his *ouens*, his boys. His mind was a jumble of emotions. He had fought alongside many of these men for years. They had shared everything together; pain, tragedy, sadness, triumph and joy. Their reliance on each other, their shared experience, was the glue that made an unbreakable bond, an intangible feeling of connection, difficult, if not impossible, to articulate. Looking from face to face McIntyre knew everything about these men, wives, girlfriends, their schools, the districts they came from, their likes and dislikes, their strengths and weaknesses. Most importantly, he knew that he would not replace any of them ... not for anything. Despite the fact that most were social misfits, dropouts and oddballs, he had moulded them into a body of men who were a reflection of his achievement as a soldier. This is what gave him his greatest source of pride and accomplishment. They were his 'Ladies' ... and proud of it! He knew he was going to miss them ... bullshit and all.

The Dak lurched violently to the left as the pilot altered course. They were flying at low level, no more than 1,000ft AGL, as the target was only

---

9   Quick reaction force usually manned by men of the regular Battalions of the Rhodesian Light Infantry (RLI) or the Rhodesian African Rifles (RAR). Fireforce was both heli-borne and Para-borne made up of helicopter gun-ships and troop carriers, plus a Lynx and a Paradak (Dakota)

twenty minutes flying time away. The hot midday thermals shook the aircraft, throwing the occupants viciously from side to side. The Dispatcher, holding on to the grab handles, walked up the fuselage checking each man in turn. The Assistant Dispatcher stayed at the door.

A young trooper, three weeks out of Training Troop, threw up, overcome by a combination of nerves, heat, the violent buffeting movement, plus too much lunch. The Dakota or 'Vomit Comet' was living up to its reputation.

'You little shit ... fucking up my aeroplane,' screamed the Dispatcher unsympathetically at the man, inches from his flushed face. He turned to McIntyre shouting at the top of his voice, 'Jock you make sure this little shit buys me a case of beers in the mess this evening,' a wink in his eye. McIntyre nodded his agreement, a smile still on his face. The 'old soldiers' in the troop sat stoically staring fixedly ahead, all making a mental note to nail the 'fresh poes[10]' for a round of drinks in the mess ... *aaasss well*.

'STAND UP' shouted the Dispatcher, wedged next to the door.

'HOOK UP.'

Each man stood up, clicking the clasp of the static-line onto the overhead cable running the length of the fuselage. All stood facing the door, tightly packed one behind the other. The violent movement of the aircraft threw the men up against the side of the fuselage, each man desperately trying to brace himself to keep his footing, all made more difficult by their unwieldy chutes, weapons and equipment.

'CHECK EQUIPMENT.' The Assistant Dispatcher moved down the aircraft, squeezing between the men, rechecking the equipment, quick-release box secure, reserve secure ... lift webs in place.

'ACTION STATIONS.'

Troop Sergeant McIntyre moved towards the door.

'STAND IN THE DOOR.'

The red light blinked on, everyone swallowed involuntarily. All stared at the light, the terrifying reality of jumping into a firefight etched on their faces. It didn't matter how often they jumped ... it was frightening and gut-wrenching, every time.

Green Light ... 'GO... GO ... GO.'

McIntyre was out the door in a split second, the Dispatcher hauled Marais bodily out of the door behind him, followed by Beamish and Le Beau.

'GO ... GO ... GO,' he screamed.

The men followed one after the other ... in nineteen seconds the aircraft was empty.

Arthur Beamish dived into space tucked up, waiting for the tug of the chute opening ... BANG ... *look up, check canopy, check lines, check men close by, grab for control lines ... which way is the fucking wind blowing? Did that Blue Job prick drop us at 500ft or less! ... Jesus are those Gooks down there? Ground coming up ... head tucked in, elbows in, legs together, bend knees ... Pull down hard on the lift webs ...* CRUNCH.

Beamish hit the ground hard, rolling to absorb the impact, staggering to

10 RLI slang, new soldier, *poes*, Afrikaans for female genitalia.

his feet. Penga Marais crashed to earth next to him, his canopy spread over an acacia thorn tree. Heavy gunfire could be heard from the east, the *'hondo'* was going hammer and tongs. As Beamish unclipped his harness, a CT appeared from around a tree, his AK at the ready. Beamish's FN was still strapped to his side, he grabbed for it, bracing himself for the bullets that must surely come. Penga was still struggling to get free of his parachute.

A rifle doubled-tapped, CRACK ... CRACK, the CT crumpled to the ground. Beamish looked across in the direction of the gunshots.

'You owe me a case of jimboolies[11] ... you useless Pommie bastard,' shouted McIntyre from twenty metres away, his characteristic smile on his face, his rifle cradled under his arm.

'Get your shit together Penga ... there's a war on,' demanded McIntyre, addressing Marais who had finally freed himself from the shroud. McIntyre's white teeth shone out from his pitch-black, camo-creamed face.

'Thanks ... Colourr,' said Beamish with the shocking realisation that Death had just passed him by.

'No problem Pommie, I hope that puts a smile on your face,' grinned McIntyre, shaking his head, amused at Beamish's facial expression that hadn't changed an iota. 'Pack that chute Penga ... lets move!'

The other members of the Stop were converging, no sign of injuries amongst them. The men threw their chutes into a pile together with their helmets to be retrieved later. Penga desperately tried to pull his parachute from the tree, tearing it to shreds in the process. The stop group had all landed within a short distance of one another; testimony to their experience from many operational jumps ... the fact that they were dropped from only 500ft AGL helped. The bush was very open, Beamish could see the other men approaching through the bush, McIntyre waving frantically for the men to RV.

Gunfire continued not far away to the east. Beamish looked up as a G-car flew low overhead, the gunner at the door. Green tracer lifted up out of the trees ... *Fook the Gooks are shooting at the helicopter.*

'Stop 3, Sunray, sweep to your east until you reach a large *donga*.' The K-car Commander, call-sign Sunray, was calling Jock McIntyre, Stop 3.

'Stop 3 copied,' McIntyre answered immediately, the handpiece clipped to his webbing next to his left ear.

'Okay *ouens*, spread out in a sweepline two metres apart, Le Beau, next to me on the left, Penga on my right, Pommie next to him.' McIntyre pointed to where he wanted his men to go.

The sweepline moved off at a fast pace in the direction instructed by the K-car Commander. Further to the east, no more than a kilometre away, the Lynx put in a fran[12] strike ... a loud thud, then the cloud of billowing flame and white smoke clearly visible. They reached the *donga* and McIntyre made the men spread out in cover along the edge. The *donga*, caused by erosion from years of overgrazing, was more than two metres deep and about five

---

11   Rhodesian slang, beers.
12   Frangible tank napalm bomb

metres wide.

The radio burst in McIntyre's ear.

'Roger ... Stop 3, I have Charlie Tangos to your front ... one hundred metres ... closing fast,' came the clipped message from the K-car Commander.

'Stop 3, copied,' McIntyre snapped his response, concentrating on the bush in front of him. Then, turning to his men he pointed in the direction that the CTs were expected, his arm out straight, with hand held vertical, then thumb pointing down ... *enemy approaching*!

Le Beau dropped the MAG onto its bipod and took aim at the other side of the *donga*. No sooner had he done so that the first CT appeared, running like the wind. The MAG barked into life, dust shot up around the running man, he went down spinning, the impact of the MAG rounds throwing him off his feet. More CTs appeared, running up to the edge of the *donga*, then realising that they were being fired at, ran back into the bush. Some returned fire, bullets flying high.

The K-car orbited above at 800ft, 'K-car firing!' The gunner dropped 20mm shells into the bush on the other side of the *donga*. Dust lifted high from the impact of the exploding shells.

'Stop 3, ... cross the *donga*, clear a village five hundred metres to your east,' called K-car to McIntyre.

'Roger, Stop 3 copied,' McIntyre got to his feet. He called to the stick commanded by L.Cpl. Eric Parnell, further to his right.

'Eric!' he shouted, '...cross the *donga* with your stick, we will cover you ... quickly man!'

'Okay Colour,' responded Parnell. Without hesitation, the four men dropped over the edge and scrambled up the other side. It was steep, so they had to make a few attempts, helping each other up over the edge.

As McIntyre watched his men struggling up the side of the *donga*, bullet strikes appeared in the dirt around them. The sound of a machinegun filled the air. McIntyre frantically twisted his head to see where the firing was coming from. In an instant, the ground in front of his face seemed to dissolve in dust as more machinegun bullets zipped towards him. His eyes filled with fine grit as the dust covered his face, sticking to the sweat and camo-cream. Realising that the CT had seen him, he rolled out of his cover, spinning his body as fast as he could, the sudden movement lifting the intensity of the bullet strikes.

Coming to rest against another thornbush, McIntyre screamed out, 'Can anybody see that fucking RPD?'

The RLI men were all firing now, trying to suppress the RPD machinegun.

Desperately trying to clear his eyes by wiping with his face-veil, McIntyre rolled onto his back. *Where is the hand-piece? ... Must get air support!* He felt for the radio handpiece that had dislodged from the clip next to his ear. Bullets whizzed angrily overhead, ripping through the bush above him, shredded leaves fluttered onto his face. A sudden feeling of panic coursed through his body as he realised that the CT was still shooting at him. Hands in the dirt by his side, McIntyre searched desperately for the handpiece ... *Shit ... I am going to die in my last contact!*

After what seemed an age, but really only a split second, he felt the cord trapped under his body. He rolled again, pulling hard to retrieve the handpiece.

'Sunray, Stop 3 we are taking heavy fire from somewhere to our east,' called McIntyre on the radio.

'Sunray copied, I have lost sight of you, mark your position,' came the instant response. The vicious banking, turning, bucking and jolting of the helicopter had temporarily disorientated the Fireforce Commander.

For fuck sakes, wake up! ... Bloody officers! McIntyre reached into his chest webbing to a pouch under his arm. He pulled out a smoke grenade. In one fluid motion, he pulled the pin and threw it out in front of him. It popped open, fizzing a cloud of bright red smoke.

'Sunray, Red Smoke.'

'Roger Stop 3 ... I have you visual ... stand by.' The machinegun fire continued ... *does that Gook never run out of ammo! ... There must be more than one RPD.*

'For goodness sake! ... Can anybody see that fucking RPD!' McIntyre screamed again.

'He's next to an anthill at two o'clock, about seventy metres,' responded Beamish almost conversationally.

'Well shoot the fucker Pommie ... for fuck sakes!'

The CT with the RPD saw the red smoke grenade pop open. Realising from bitter experience, that the helicopter was being called in, the CT stopped firing, got to his feet, and ran off to the south.

Silence fell over the battlefield, broken only by the rapidly approaching K-car.

McIntyre's eyes, reacting to the dust and grit, were glazed over with tears. He again wiped his eyes with the face-veil. Eyes still stinging, he crawled forward to the edge of the *donga*. Parnell and his stick were still taking cover in the bottom where they had been shielded from the RPD.

'Eric, get into the bush on the other side and cover us as we cross,' called McIntyre. Parnell looked up at him and gave a thumb's up. 'Is everybody okay?' The men all grunted a reply. 'Stay in cover until Parnell clears the bush on the other side.'

Slowly McIntyre's eyes began to clear as he watched Parnell and his men clamber up the other side of the *donga*. The soft soil and steep sides made it difficult. Two men got to the top and then leaned down to help their mates.

As if in slow motion, one of the men seemed to lift up, his chest exploding outwards. A look of shocked surprise crossed his face as he toppled forward over the edge, sliding into the bottom of the *donga*. The RPD gunner had reappeared to the south of the RLI position, seeing the exposed men crossing the *donga*, he took his opportunity.

Eric Parnell slipped down next to his stricken man, screaming, 'Man down ... Man Down ... Andy Nicolle's down ... MEDIC ... MEDIC!' He took out a blue smoke grenade and threw it to mark his position. The other man, alone on the edge of the *donga*, scrambled into cover, disappeared into the bush firing to the south.

Pommie Beamish heard the anguished cry from his friend Eric Parnell. He was the most experienced combat medic in the troop. Without hesitation, he leopard-crawled out of his cover. Slithering as fast as he could through the dust, he slipped over the edge of the *donga*.

This scene is turning to shit! ... 'Sunray, Stop 3 we have a man down in the *donga*, CTs to the south,' called McIntyre urgently.

'Stop 3, copied, we have the CTs visual, they are on the move to the south.' The K-car pulled in overhead and the gunner again threw 20mm shells at the ground below. In moments the CT gunfire stopped.

The radio crackled as the K-car pilot called in one of the G-cars for the casevac.

'Stop 3, Sunray, we will cover you as you cross the *donga*, go now!'

'Okay, everybody up ... get across the donga NOW! ... Go, Go, Go!' McIntyre bellowed. The men, needing no encouragement, leapt to their feet and dived over the edge.

McIntyre slid down next to Parnell, who was leaning over Andy Nicolle, shoving a first field dressing into the chest wound. Beamish was trying to support the man's head that was lolling loosely to one side. His whole uniform seemed to be covered in blood, mixed with dust and dirt. McIntyre glanced up at Beamish ... *is he going to be okay?* Beamish pursed his lips and shook his head fractionally ... *No*.

'Shit ... Arthur, help me with a drip ... we need to get a drip into him,' whispered Parnell, his voice racked with emotion.

McIntyre looked down at the stricken man, a bubbling chest wound, a bullet through his neck severing his spinal column ... he was dead. Andy Nicolle's expectant eyes were looking up into the sky, the deep blue Rhodesian sky, as if watching the white, puffy, cumulus cloud formations of early summer.

'Eric ... Andy's gone ... there's nothing we can do,' said McIntyre gently, taking Parnell's hands away from the saturated first field dressing. 'Come on Eric we need to clear that village up ahead. The choppers are coming for Andy.'

Together they gently lifted the lifeless body up to the waiting hands above. A G-car flared into an LZ nearby.

Trooper Andy Nicolle made his last chopper ride home.

'Stop 3 you must clear the village to the east ... move to the village,' the K-car Commander was calling.

McIntyre didn't answer; he led his men away from the *donga* as fast as they could. K-car could be heard giving Stop 4, Van Deventer, instructions to move to the north of the village.

Gunfire continued to the east, the heli-borne stops had been dropped on the far eastern side of the village where most of the CTs must have been hiding. The Lynx fran strike had lit a bushfire; thick black smoke was churning up into the sky. With no breeze, the black pall seemed to be suspended.

'Be careful guys … look under the bushes …' called out McIntyre as the sweepline reformed and moved forward at a fast walk.

They pushed forward to a cattle kraal on the edge of the village. Typical of kraals built for holding and protecting livestock at night, it was made of intertwined thorn acacia branches held in place with wooden stakes driven into the ground. There was no way through without dynamite. McIntyre's stop followed him in single file along the edge of the kraal, keeping themselves crouched over so as not to present an easy target.

Once McIntyre reached the end of the kraal, he knelt down and studied the village in front of him. There were no more than five or six huts; the ground neatly swept clean by the occupants. Scrawny chickens could be seen scraping in the dirt. Goats, standing on their hind-legs, were pulling on the leaves of a few sickly looking trees. The goats appeared to be oblivious to the sporadic gunfire going on around them.

'Sunray, Stop 3, I am on the edge of the village, are Charlie Tangos present? … Over.'

'Stop 3, … I am not sure … the main group of CTs was further to the east at the base of the *gomo* you can see in the distance.'

'Roger, … I am sweeping through the village now … Over.'

McIntyre felt uncomfortable, tempted to send Parnell through first. He looked across to where Parnell sat crouched with the remainder of his men. He thought about it for a second, making his decision.

'Eric, take your stick over to the left near that Msasa tree,' he said pointing in the direction indicated. 'I want you to cover us as we sweep through. If anything moves cull[13] it … do you hear?'

'Okay Colour.'

Parnell doubled off to the left with his MAG gunner behind him.

There was still no sign of life in the village.

McIntyre turned to his men, 'Okay … Penga with me, Pommie take Le Beau and clear the two huts to the right, we will clear the three on the left. Move out at the double … *Handei!*[14]'

The four men sprinted across the open ground to the huts. The doors all faced the centre courtyard where a communal cooking fire was still smouldering. Pots, pans and half-eaten meals lay about. A well-tended vegetable garden was situated at the centre of the courtyard. Tin plates lay upturned in the dirt; clearly, the locals had left in a hurry.

McIntyre crept up to the open door of the first hut, '*Kanjan, Gogogoyi!* … Hello … knock, knock! … We are Security Forces, anybody inside come out NOW,' he shouted in seShona.

Silence.

The familiar smell of burnt firewood and thatch entered the nostrils. The village seemed so peaceful … a goat bleated loudly.

McIntyre called out again; Penga crouched in close behind him. McIntyre

---

13 Rhodesian slang, killing, play on the word culling, the process of reducing numbers of big game such as elephants to reduce their impact on the environment.
14 seShona, Lets go! Run, or move as fast as you can.

contemplated throwing a grenade into the hut but the risk of terrified children hiding inside was too great. The faces of his own tiny children, Matthew and Amanda, flashed through his mind ... his wife Lily smiling at him ... *I will be home soon.*

He called out again, '... *Kanjan!*'

Everyone waited for a response. McIntyre looked over to the anthill where Parnell and his stick lay in wait, he pointed to show he was going to look inside, carefully edging his head around the door, his rifle at the ready.

McIntyre blinked to adjust his eyes from the bright sunlight to the pitch dark inside the hut ... he stepped into the doorway...

An AK burst out, CRACK ... CRACK.

As if in slow motion, McIntyre staggered back, he turned, his chest a mass of blood, he stood looking down at his chest, his face in utter disbelief, sinking to his knees. Penga leapt into the doorway firing his FN as he went, disappearing into the hut, his rifle fired round after round until the magazine emptied.

The shock of seeing McIntyre hit caused the men to open fire at the rest of the huts, the bullets easily penetrating the mud walls, chunks of mud cascaded onto the ground. Pommie and Le Beau threw grenades into each hut; the muffled thud could be heard as each one exploded. A paraffin tin in one of the huts ignited, instantly setting the hut ablaze, nobody was taking any more chances.

McIntyre lay on his back, still conscious.

'Sunray, Stop 3, CASEVAC ... CASEVAC, Colour McIntyre is down, I say again ... Colour McIntyre is down,' Parnell shouted urgently into his radio.

Arthur Beamish ran over to where McIntyre lay. He hastily examined the massive chest wound ... *Jock must have taken three rounds.*

'It's okay Colour, just a scratch. We will have you fixed in noo timmme,' said Beamish encouragingly.

'Put a fucking drip into me you useless Pommie bastard,' whispered McIntyre hoarsely, blood running from his mouth. He coughed up frothy, bubbly blood, spitting to clear his mouth. Beamish looked down at him, *shit he has been hit in the lungs!*

Tearing open a first field dressing, Beamish called out, 'Le Beau press down on this, hard ...' Then opening a drip kit, he inserted the catheter, squeezed the saline bag to remove the air and set about looking for a vein. He wrapped his face-veil around the top of the arm and pulled it as tight as he could. 'Hold this tight Eric,' he instructed, who knelt down to hold the tourniquet.

McIntyre was fading fast, his lips deathly blue, blood pressure dropping, arteries collapsing. He twisted his head to look at his men crowded around him.

A G-car closed in overhead looking for an LZ.

Penga came staggering out of the hut, his arms covered in blood to the elbows, dragging a dead CT behind him by the left boot.

'I got the bastard Colour,' Penga called out, 'I got him with a few rounds but he wouldn't die so I had to club him with my rifle …'

Penga dropped the lifeless boot and walked over to where Beamish was working. Looking down at his stricken sergeant, the sudden shock realisation was clear on his face.

'He is going to be okay … isn't he Pommie?'

Penga looked up at the faces of the men standing around. The men averted their eyes.

'Please Pommie? … He is tough … remember he took one at Inyanga!'

Beamish didn't answer, he looked up shaking his head, defeat etched on his face.

'NO, NOO,' Penga fell to his knees, 'Colour wake up, they are coming to fetch you … Please Colour …'

Shaking Beamish by the arm, Penga pleaded, 'Please help him Pommie. Please man, don't let him die!'

Tears welled in the young man's eyes; he lent forward to take his Troop Sergeant's hand, shaking it lightly as if to wake him up.

Jock McIntyre's deep blue eyes gently lost their shine … he died there, a pool of blood soaking into the soil around him; his men kneeling next to him, silently, as if in prayer.

Penga Marais was only nineteen; Colour Sergeant Jock McIntyre was the closest thing he ever had to a father.

> *Daylight again, following me to bed*
> *I think about a hundred years ago, how my fathers bled*
> *I think I see a valley, covered with bones in blue*
> *All the brave soldiers that cannot get older been askin' after you*
> *Hear the past a callin', from Ar-megeddon's side*
> *When everyone's talkin' and no one is listenin', how can we decide? …*
>
> *… Mother Earth will swallow you, lay your body down*
> *Find the cost of freedom, buried in the ground.*[15]

Nobody noticed a canvas bag of maps and documents, covered in blood, had slipped out of the combat jacket of the dead terrorist behind them.

---

15 *Find The Cost of Freedom*, Stephen Stills, Crosby Stills Nash & Young, released on the B-side of *Ohio*, 1970.

Contact – Ndowoyo TTL

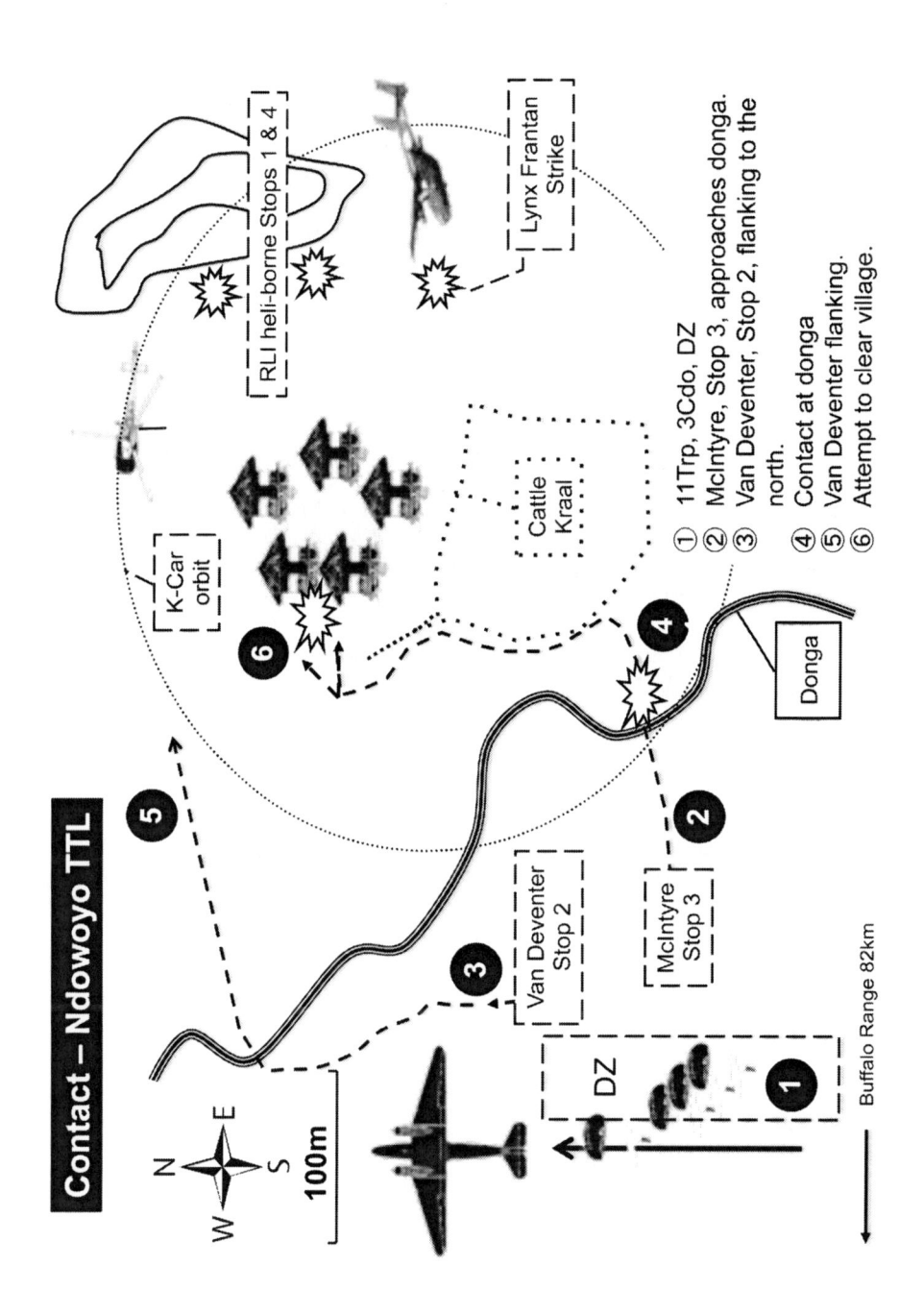

① 11Trp, 3Cdo, DZ
② McIntyre, Stop 3, approaches donga.
③ Van Deventer, Stop 2, flanking to the north.
④ Contact at donga
⑤ Van Deventer flanking.
⑥ Attempt to clear village.

- RLI heli-borne Stops 1 & 4
- Lynx Frantan Strike
- K-Car orbit
- Cattle Kraal
- Donga
- Van Deventer Stop 2
- McIntyre Stop 3
- DZ
- Buffalo Range 82km
- 100m

2

3 Commando RLI, Fireforce Base, Buffalo Range Forward Airfield (FAF 7), Southeast Rhodesia

11 Troop, 3 Commando, 1 Rhodesian Light Infantry (11Trp, 3Cdo, 1RLI) were drawn up outside of their barrack rooms on the edge of the Buffalo Range airstrip. This was no muster parade, a motley crew of twenty men dressed in various combinations of army camo-uniform, PT shorts and T-shirts. Some wore no shirts at all, while a few only had towels wrapped around their waists, testimony to the speed with which they had been summoned. The only man who was dressed in full uniform with beret and stable-belt was 2nd Lt. Van Deventer, who stood to the side of the men drawn up in three ranks.

The other Troops that made up 3 Commando, 12 and 13 were on Fireforce standby, 14 Troop was on R&R[16]. The Commando Sergeant-Major, CSM Cornelius Stephanus 'Butch' Strydom came marching across from the Orderly Room, his pace-stick wedged under his left arm, his right arm swinging shoulder high as if he was trooping-the-colour outside Buckingham Palace.

'Troop ... TROOP ATTEEEN ... SHUN,' shouted L/Cpl Beamish from behind the rear rank. The men shuffled into what approximated the correct position. Without McIntyre, Beamish was the most senior NCO.

Arriving briskly in front of the troop, Strydom came smartly to a halt, driving his boots into the dirt with a loud thud that could dislocate a knee.

'Okay, LISTEN UP,' he screamed, the veins in his neck bulging from the strain, his face almost puce. CSM Strydom was clearly not a happy man.

'Your activities last night have not gone unnoticed and heads are going to roll.' His voice was suddenly softer, more sinister. '... I want the men who participated in the fight at the Triangle Country Club last night to take one step forward,' he commanded.

The ranks remained rigidly still, nobody daring to blink.

'I would remind you of the respect you owe the memory of Colour McIntyre who loved this Commando and this Troop with a deep and abiding passion. He would not be happy to see that his men had turned into lily-livered wasters, with no sense of respect and responsibility ...'

Strydom glowered at the men who were clearly moved by his words. They had respected Jock McIntyre more than they had respected any other man in the Regiment. They would have followed him through the gates of hell and back ... they had! His loss was still an open wound.

There were a few furtive glances within the ranks, then, as if on some silent command, each man took one step forward.

'Nice one ... LADIEEES,' shouted Strydom indignantly, using the same description that McIntyre had always used to address his men. They were the 'Ladies' in a Commando that called itself 'The Lovers'.

---

16 Rest and Recreation (Recuperation), leave of absence.

Nobody in the troop minded being called 'Ladies' by McIntyre, but they resented anybody else calling them by that title. In fact, so much so, that a fight was guaranteed if someone from another troop called them that. Strydom clearly knew this and was now trying to 'needle' them.

'If you people don't come to the party with this information your troop will be assigned to camp duty for the foreseeable future. You will also have all privileges and passes revoked, denied access to the canteen, ... and I will even recommend to the Major that we cancel your next R&R!'

Strydom stood resolutely, unmovable in front of the men, waiting for a reaction.

'I have got all day to wait.... LADIEEES. We can stand in this glorious sunshine as long as it takes.'

Penga Marais, realising that he could not have his troop punished because of his actions, stepped forward.

'It was me Sir,' he said in a wavering voice. He was terrified of CSM Strydom.

'I should have known our little lunatic was at the bottom of another drama,' Strydom said condescendingly. '... Anybody else?'

'*Adjudant Chef,* I was pat of zee dispute,' said Jean-Paul 'Le Beau' D'aubigne stepping forward, addressing Strydom by the equivalent rank in the French Foreign Legion.

'I cannot believe that only two of you managed to fight the whole of 2RR[17] Mortar Platoon ... Who else was involved?' demanded Strydom pacing up and down in front of the ranks.

The men remained steady, no more recalcitrants stepped forward. The implication being that Penga and Le Beau had, in fact, taken on a platoon of territorial soldiers from 2RR.

'Okay, Marais ... Le Beau report for Commando Orders tomorrow at nine o'clock.' Strydom hesitated for a second, suddenly deep in thought, '... Oh, by the way, Colour-Sergeant Barker from 2 Commando will be joining this troop as 2IC next week, he has just finished the advanced drill and weapons course at Hooterville[18].'

Strydom made to turn when another thought struck him.

'BEAMISH'

'Sur.'

'They are giving you another stripe ... God save us all!'

'Troop ...TROOP ... DISMISSED.'

---

17 2nd Battalion The Rhodesia Regiment, part of the territorial army made up of conscripted national servicemen and men who had completed national service but who were now required to attend 'call-ups' – six weeks in six weeks out – continuous call-up.
18 The School of Infantry in Gwelo (Gweru).

*

Combined Operations HQ, Milton Buildings, Salisbury

While the 11 Troop RLI parade was taking place in the stifling heat of the Lowveld, a meeting was taking place in a small anteroom on the first floor of Milton Buildings in Salisbury, 380 kilometres north of Buffalo Range as the crow flies.

Milton Buildings, in Jameson Avenue in Salisbury, was an impressive colonial office block, complete with white plaster and clock tower. Milton Buildings housed the seat of the Cabinet Rooms, the Prime Minister's Office, the Treasury as well as the Ministry of Defence plus Air Force HQ amongst other government departments. More recently, it accommodated the offices of Combined Operations[19]; the unit designed for co-ordinating all Rhodesia's activities in prosecuting the war against the Patriotic Front.

The subject of the meeting in Milton Buildings concerned the package of documents that had been found on the ZANLA terrorist killed by 3 Commando in Ndowoyo TTL. As was the case after all contacts with the enemy, the Police Special Branch (SB), collected all the dead CTs, equipment, documents and prisoners. They then analysed the documents, 'debriefed' the captured terrorists and thereby built up a picture of what was going on in the area, and sometimes, what was going on across the border in Mozambique. In the present case, only the pile of documents had been recovered.

There were five men in the meeting, all dressed in various uniforms except the oldest man in the room, who wore a suit. A COMOPS secretary sat quietly in the corner of the room, ready to take shorthand notes.

A policeman, a Chief Inspector with SB, cleared his throat, 'Thank you gentlemen for attending this meeting, I have distributed a summary of the information which we have typed up and roneo'd.'

There was a shuffling of paper as the five men around the table looked at the documents presented to them.

'As you will gather, the documents show a set of detailed maps and satellite photographs of various key installations in our country, dams, power stations, fuel storage dumps, the steel plant at Redcliff, Sable Chemicals in Que Que, and the main railway sidings. From the documentation, it is clear that they are of Soviet origin, but you will also see hand written Chinese notations. You can also clearly see Chinese comments and descriptions on the photographs.'

The enormity of what they were looking at stunned the men into silence. Studying each document closely, the men around the table slowly and methodically paged through the file.

The policeman continued, '… you will also note that reference is made to groups of men located at bases near Chimoio in Mozambique. It appears that

19   The organisation set up to co-ordinate the activities of Air Force, Police and Army. COMOPS was also responsible for planning and executing External raids and also had direct control over special forces units, Special Air Service (SAS), Selous Scouts and RLI.

these are specialist saboteurs who are being trained to undertake attacks on our installations.'

'Do you think the CT killed by the RLI in Ndowoyo TTL is one of these men?' asked an air force Group Captain.

'No, we don't think so … we think he was a courier. We think he was trying to link up with groups that have already infiltrated the country … maybe some of these saboteurs.'

'What makes you think that?' pressed the Group Captain.

'Well, the man was very young, maybe twenty at most, plus the circumstances of his death, hiding in a hut during a contact, would indicate that he was very inexperienced. If he was a real player he would have been long gone during the Fireforce action … We couldn't find any ID on him.'

'Why would ZANLA trust an inexperienced cadre with such vital information? This could be a clever ruse, to lure us into a trap,' said a Major with SAS wings on his chest. He wore the distinctive pale blue stable-belt, his sandy/cream beret with the SAS winged-dagger, *Who Dares Wins*, on the table in front of him.

'It seems incredibly elaborate for a ruse, these are satellite photographs, the detail on the strategic installations is impressive. We have translated much of the Chinese notations and the descriptions are extremely accurate and what's more, they could have only been taken a few weeks ago,' added an Army Major wearing Rhodesian Intelligence Corps (RIC) insignia.

'To attack any of these targets, the enemy will need highly trained, almost special forces level, cadres. Plus they will need sophisticated demolition equipment and explosives. We have never come across any ZANLA Gooks[20] that come close to this calibre,' stated the SAS Major emphatically.

'That's true but I don't think we can ignore this threat completely,' replied the SB Chief Inspector.

The fifth man at the table had been quietly studying the faces of the other men in the room, listening carefully. He sat back in his chair, his elbows resting on the arms, his fingers interlocked in front of him. His age was difficult to estimate, although he had a mop of thick, unruly grey hair. Not a tall man, he was thick set with large strong looking hands. He was dressed in a crumpled blue suit, which had clearly seen better days, the sleeves frayed slightly at the edges. He wore a white shirt and a college tie, not any old college, Balliol at Oxford, *Azure, a lion rampant argent, the lion of Galloway, crowned or, impaling Gules, an orle argent*. The tie was clearly well used, showing the stains from many a raucous dinner, adding to his image of a 'nutty professor'. Nothing could have been further from the truth.

'George … what do think of all this?' asked the policeman, addressing the old man in the crumpled suit.

'I think we are in a spot of bother,' replied the man with an impeccable, upper class, English accent. The sort of accent heard while watching cricket at Eton or Harrow.

---

20 Vietnam slang for communist insurgent adopted by Rhodesian forces.

'I think our friend Bob[21] across the border is in receipt of help that goes way beyond that of a few second-hand AK47s and rudimentary platoon and section battle drills,' commented the man called George, still sitting back in his chair.

'What do you suggest we do George?' asked the policeman respectfully.

The grey-headed man sat forward, placing his elbows on the table, resting his chin on his hands. He seemed to be deep in thought, his eyes gazing at a spot on the wall above the head of the policeman sitting opposite him.

'I think we need a reconnaissance in depth to establish if such a training base exists ... and if so who is conducting that training,' replied George, stating his words precisely, almost in a whisper. The others sat forward, listening carefully to his slow ponderous speech. He continued in the same methodical fashion, 'We will need to capture one of these instructors, one of the ZANLA leaders, or ... at the very least, one of the trainees ... and then ask that person a few pointed questions to establish exactly where these saboteurs are in the country ... Then, gentlemen, we need to dispose of them ... A job for the Selous Scouts I would suspect.'

The SAS Major almost leapt out of his seat. 'This is clearly a job for us ... external ops are our turf,' he thundered.

The grey-headed man stared across at the SAS man. 'Major there are only three problems that I can think of with that proposition ... one, not enough of your men speak seShona fluently or more importantly, Portuguese for that matter ... two, none of your men are black ... and three, because of the previous two limitations you will have great difficulty infiltrating the camp, let alone capture and interrogate the people concerned.'

The SAS Major flushed with indignation was clearly about to launch an objection. The policeman interrupted to prevent any further escalation of the argument.

'George you know how jumpy the Government is about cross-border raids. They are trying to comply with South African pressure not to attack FRELIMO installations.'

'My dear fellow, this war is now at a critical juncture. The Government have been light on strategy since all of us can remember; as a result, we are losing the initiative rather precipitously. I am afraid we need to build a case to force this mission through ... there is nothing else for it.'

The SAS man interjected again, 'I agree, we need to hit them hard, ... where it hurts, in their Mozambique bases. We are the best trained and equipped to perform this task.'

The grey-headed man sighed, clearly disinterested in further debate. He gathered his papers and stood up.

'Despite the protestations from the lads of the 'winged-dagger', this needs to be a pseudo-op with Reid-Daly's boys, preferably with a few of his turned ZANLA and FRELIMO men. I think that is quite clear gentlemen.' Without any further debate, he left the room.

George, the grey-headed man, crossed the road outside Milton Buildings,

---

21   Robert Mugabe.

then walked a few blocks towards Livingston Avenue, then entered a large office block with the name Coghlan Buildings. The words 'Central Intelligence Organisation' marked the entrance to the offices; he took the lift to the sixth floor, then pushed open an office door marked, 'Deputy Director, George Stanbridge'. Sweating after his brief walk in the hot sun, he mopped his brow with a handkerchief. Moving to his desk, he picked up the phone.

'Iris, book me on the next plane to London please ... I'll stay at the East India Club ... also see if Ken is in ... I need to talk to him.' He was referring to the head of the CIO, Ken Rose.

Back at Milton Buildings, the meeting broke up with a general agreement on a plan. The SAS Major's nose was severely out of joint but the argument raised by George Stanbridge carried the day.

The petite and attractive COMOPS secretary, who had been seated silently at a table against the wall, slipped out of the room.

*

ZANLA Base Camp, 17km north of Chimoio Mozambique, 85km east of the Rhodesian Border

A remarkably similar meeting to the one being held in Salisbury was taking place near the small Mozambican town of Chimoio. While the subject matter was similar, the surroundings could not have been more different. Two men sat at an old kitchen table, that at one time would have been painted white. The top of the table, scraped clean of paint, showed signs of extensive usage, engraved with countless names, a few burn marks caused by hot cooking pots and a tight grouping of bullet holes. The room, in the distant past, would have been painted a light green. It was still being used for its original purpose, a school staff room.

The school was called *Chindunduma* by ZANLA, named after the battle of the same name near Mt Darwin during the Shona rebellion of 1896. The difference was that the education was no longer Portuguese. The students, however, were still essentially, children. This was now a school of war, where children as young as fourteen were being taught the art of guerrilla warfare. The state of the room and the surrounding buildings bore the marks of a recent attack by Rhodesian security forces. Signs of this attack were everywhere, a neat line of bullet holes stretched across the back wall, as if the shooter had lined them up with a ruler. The windows were steel cottage-pane, devoid of glass, with chunks of plaster missing from the walls in places. Bullet holes in the corrugated iron roof allowed streams of sunlight to penetrate. The thin shafts of sunlight illuminated the occupants of the room like spotlights in an intimate theatre. A faded, black-framed picture of the Mozambican FRELIMO leader, Samora Machel, was the only form of decoration on the walls.

The two men sat in silence waiting for the meeting to start. The noise of distant gunfire from a rifle range, and the shouted drill instructions to marching recruits drifted into the room. Outside, the school was a hive of activity; weapons instruction and political lectures were taking place with the use of blackboards under large shady trees. The dusty school grounds showed clear signs of war damage. A large crater from an aerial bomb dominated the parade ground. All the buildings were damaged in some way, pockmarked with shrapnel and bullet holes. Many buildings were abandoned shells with torn-off roofs and tumbled down walls.

Another two men entered the room, silhouetted against the bright sunlight outside. The taller of the two men was General Josiah Magama Tongogara, the Chairman of ZANLA's High Command and Secretary of Defence of the ZANU War Council, the *Dare re Chimurenga*. The other man wore the khaki military uniform with the insignia of a Shang Wei (上尉), Captain, in the People's Liberation Army of China.

General Tongogara welcomed the two seated men in a polite and business-like, but slightly distant fashion. Felix Mhanda, Commander of the ZANLA Manica Province Operational Area, acknowledged his leader with a slight nod of the head while, Peter Hamadziripi, Commander of the ZANLA Gaza Province Operational Area, made no acknowledgment at all. Both men shuffled to their feet out of respect to the General.

The Manica Operational area was south of the Rhodesian town of Umtali, while Gaza was in the southeast, centred on the town of Chiredzi. While these men were commanders of these regions, they were not active on the ground, instead basing themselves at the ZANLA HQ near Chimoio.

Without any further ceremony, Josiah Tongogara opened the meeting.

'Please be seated. I would like to bring this meeting to order gentlemen,' said Tongogara in strongly accented English. '… I would also like to welcome Comrade Zhang Youxia who has just returned from China with great news … we will conduct the meeting in English and not in seShona so that Comrade Youxia can contribute.'

Tongogara was a man who stuck to formality and protocol, as is most common amongst people with poor education who have learned by observation and rote.

'Thank you Comrade Tongogara, it is good to be back,' replied Zhang Youxia in excellent English, as he took a seat at the table. He bowed his head as a sign of respect to the senior officer. He gently placed his combat cap, with the red communist Chinese star, onto the table in front of him.

Josiah Tongogara did not sit down; he stood to his full height of over six foot, ramrod straight and erect. While he was not heavily built, he exuded fitness and strength, testimony to the rigours of war and the prolonged periods of living rough in the bush. Despite his fearsome reputation, Tongogara had a compassionate face, although pockmarked from teenage acne, with greeny-brown eyes, short-cropped hair, and the straggly beard and moustache so popular in the 1970s. His face displayed an expression of seriousness and determination, he was not a man given to frivolity. The General, nicknamed *Nyenganyenga*, or Swallow by his followers, commanded by both fear and love. His many enemies feared him as a ruthless, ambitious and implacable fighter, while his supporters loved him as a faithful and caring leader, always putting the needs of his soldiers above his own. He was a leader that deserved to be followed, who people trusted with their lives and the lives of their children.

Tongogara was known as an attentive listener, he would concentrate intently on conversations and seldom spoke himself. When he did speak, he was animated and articulate. The freedom struggle was his fanatical obsession; he felt the suffering and oppression of his people deeply and passionately.

By a strange coincidence, Tongogara had been born on the farm owned by the parents of Ian Smith, the Rhodesian Prime Minister, near the town of Selukwe. He was from a poor farm-labourer family, not well educated, with an abiding distrust of politicians and intellectuals. This endeared him to his followers, who were mostly drawn from the peasant class. Tongogara also understood the importance of traditional religion and superstition and used this effectively to entrench his leadership. He believed without question that he would die in battle, at the barrel of the gun. In fact, he was very preoccupied with his own death. He spoke about it often to his followers. Entirely prepared to die for the people of 'Zimbabwe', he expected that others should equally, unquestionably, be prepared to die for the cause.

Felix Mhanda and Peter Hamadziripi shared a distrust of their leader. They were both well educated and shared great political ambition. While they shared ambition, they also projected arrogance and an air of superiority. This did not endear them to their leader who was a man of the people, a peasant revolutionary. Both men were very much opposed to Tongogara's draconian, dictatorial style and resented the unswerving support he received from amongst the rank and file. Both Mhanda and Hamadziripi were wary of Tongogara because of the brutal and uncompromising way he had put down the 1974 Nhari Rebellion of young ZANLA officers. He had executed the perpetrators in cold blood. He was also suspected of the murder of his rival, Herbert Chitepo, in Zambia in March 1975. Despite being arrested and briefly imprisoned by the Zambians for the crime, his guilt was never proven.

Josiah Tongogara was not a man to trifle with.

Mhanda and Hamadziripi sat silently, making no comment, ignoring the Chinese captain completely, as if he was invisible.

'Comrade Zhang, would you tell us your news first,' asked Tongogara in a soft respectful voice.

'Thank you Comrade General ... as you know I left Mozambique two months ago with twenty men who came with me to China on an advanced demolition course,' explained the Captain earnestly, leaning forward as he spoke. He watched the faces of the other men in the room who were now all studying him intently. 'I am happy to say that the men have completed their training and are ready for their first mission. They are presently based near a small village about twenty kilometres to the south of Chimoio to make sure that they are safe from attack by the Colonists.'

Captain Youxia was a student of the Maoist Doctrine that focused on the 'people's war', that emphasised political indoctrination above weapons technology. He was careful; therefore, to always refer to the Rhodesian enemy, as 'colonists', 'white invaders' or 'the racist regime', depending on his audience.

'Can you tell us of this mission Comrade?' asked Hamadziripi.

'I cannot at this time Comrade … because our reconnaissance of the targets is not yet complete … we have still to set priorities. I am also waiting for more satellite photographs, but as you know these take time to get to us because they come from our friends the Soviets.'

'When will this be ready?' enquired Mhanda.

'I am hoping in a few days Comrade. We have infiltrated two groups of reconnaissance scouts to look at the softer of the targets. I am expecting them to report back soon.'

'Why were we not told of these scouts?' snapped back Mhanda, his irritation starting to show. He was known to have a short temper.

Youxia hesitated at the sudden change of mood.

Seeing the potential for an argument, Tongogara interjected, 'You were not told in the interests of security Comrade Mhanda.'

'We are members of the ZANLA High Command, how can we be a security risk?' asked Hamadziripi indignantly, raising his voice, his agitation also starting to show.

' … Because we have had leaks in the past and I wanted to protect you both from any allegation that the leaks could have come from you,' answered Tongogara forthrightly, but still in a quiet respectful voice. He fixed the two men with a stare that would melt steel.

Tongogara's comment had an instant effect on the two men. It was well known that the ZANU/ZANLA leadership had difficulty keeping secrets. Many were suspected of being double agents, particularly in light of recent, very accurate, airstrikes and ground attacks on military installations in Mozambique. These concerns were growing. The Mozambican leader, Samora Machel, had summoned the ZANU Supreme Leader, Robert Mugabe, to Maputo to discuss the problem of high level leaks.

Not waiting for any further comment, Tongogara continued the meeting, 'The reason I have asked you to attend this meeting is that the first two targets are most likely within your operational regions. We need your help to infiltrate our demolition teams, to protect them, and to conduct diversionary raids to ensure they have the best chance of success.'

Tongogara now had the men's undivided attention.

'I need you to choose thirty of your very best men in each region and hand them to Comrade Youxia for specialist training. This must be done in the next few days … is that clear?'

'Yes Comrade,' the two commanders answered in unison, now completely submissive.

'Once the men are trained and the targets are set – you will be informed,' said Tongogara.

'Yes Comrade.'

'Well that will be all – *Pamberi ne Jongwe, Pamberi ne Hondo*[22]' he shouted. '*Pamberi ZANLA, Pasi ne Smeeth*[23] ... Viva China, Viva Mozambique, VIVA, VIVA, VIVA !!'

They all stood up to join in, chanting loudly, thrusting clenched fists to the sky. Both Hamadziripi and Mhanda noted that their General did not hail the leader of ZANU, Robert Mugabe. He never did.

Outside of the door to the 'staff room' at *Chindunduma* School, a soldier dressed neatly in Chinese khaki fatigues stood back. He had been able to hear virtually all that had been said inside. The man was deep in thought, his mind racing with what he had heard.

'Comrade Nyathi!' called General Tongogara as he stepped out into the bright sunlight.

The soldier jumped at the call, snapped out of his reverie.

'*Yaa Nyenganyenga*[24], *Zviri kunakaka*? Yes Swallow. Is everything all right?' asked Godfrey Nyathi, Detachment Commander, leader of the General's bodyguard.

'All is well Nyathi, call for the vehicles. We must be on our way,' said Tongogara gently, a look of deep satisfaction on his face.

*

Stanley Avenue, Salisbury City Centre

A young woman, wearing a trendy navy-blue pantsuit with wide bell-bottoms, was walking confidently east down Stanley Avenue. She stopped at the intersection with 1st Street and carefully scanned the road north and south, as if checking on traffic before she crossed. The woman was medium height with a petite, slim build, and large tortoise-shell sunglasses that covered most of her face. Her hair was long and dark, almost black, hanging over her shoulders with soft curls, remarkably similar to Jaclyn Smith in *Charlie's Angels*. She turned to look back down Stanley Avenue, confirming that she was not being followed.

It was late afternoon, with about half an hour before the shops were due to close. The woman was carrying, what looked like, a round hatbox, tied with a wide green ribbon giving the impression that it was to be given as a present. She crossed 1st Street, hesitating again on the other side. She looked into the Edgars display window studying the latest trends. The display window reflected quite clearly the scene behind her across the street. She seemed satisfied, turned the corner and entered the first door on the right into Edgars clothing store.

---

22 Forward with the Rooster, the symbol of ZANU/ZANLA, forward with the war.
23 Down with Smith, Ian Smith the Prime Minister of Rhodesia, the architect of UDI.
24 seShona, Tongogara, like many respected leaders of the Liberation Struggle, had a nickname, his was 'Swallow'.

Nobody gave her a second glance, a thoroughly modern young woman shopping for clothing. She glanced left and right as she entered the store, then made her way directly to the Women's Department. Browsing amongst the racks of clothing, she picked out a set of short floral skirts and made her way to the fitting rooms. An elderly shop assistant watched her choosing outfits and walked across.

'Is there anything I can help you with?' asked the shop assistant; her nametag read 'Elizabeth Shaw'.

'No thank you,' the young woman replied, 'I have a few things to try on.'

'We have some more skirts on the racks over there,' said the shop assistant pointing to her left.

'I might have a look at those a bit later,' was the reply, 'may I try these on please?'

'Certainly you may, just let me know if you need anything. Is that hat a present for someone?' asked Mrs Shaw politely, pointing to the hatbox.

'Yes it is, a friend of mine is getting married and I thought I would buy her a hat for her honeymoon Down South[25]. It will be just what she needs for the beach.'

'Wonderful, do you know where she is going?'

'Umhlanga Rocks[26], I think.' The young woman flicked her head slightly in the direction of the fitting rooms as a sign of impatience.

'Well it is a bit big for the fitting room, can I hold it for you?' asked Mrs Shaw.

The young woman hesitated as if trying to assess the situation. If she had not been wearing sunglasses, the flashing of her eyes left and right would have set off alarm bells in Mrs Shaw's head. Mrs Shaw had been around the block a few times; she knew a shoplifter when she saw one.

It was a bit strange that the young woman had not removed her sunglasses to look at the clothing ... *ah well the youth of today!*

'Not to worry, let me leave it by the door,' replied the young woman, placing the hatbox next to the entry to the fitting rooms. She then entered one of the cubicles, pulling the curtain across behind her. Working hastily, she slipped off the pantsuit, and put on the first of the skirts. She knew Mrs Shaw was still hanging about outside.

'What do you think?' the young woman asked as she pulled aside the curtain.

'It looks absolutely stunning ... you have a beautiful figure,' replied Mrs Shaw who knew her business well. Another customer arrived at the entrance to the fitting rooms carrying an armful of clothing. Mrs Shaw was immediately distracted as she welcomed the new customer. The young woman grabbed the hatbox and slipped it into the cubicle. She unclipped the lid and reached inside. She then closed the lid again and tightened the bow around the box.

'I have just remembered, I need to get to the bank before they close, please

---

25 Rhodesian colloquialism, 'Down South' referred to South Africa.
26 North Coast of Natal, South Africa, a popular holiday destination for Rhodesians.

put these to one side ... I will come back tomorrow,' said the young woman, smiling as she handed Mrs Shaw the clothing.

'Not to worry dear, just ask for me when you come in. My name is Elizabeth.'

'Thank you Elizabeth, have a good evening ... see you tomorrow,' replied the young woman as she walked purposefully towards the door ...

Mrs Shaw watched her go, marvelling at her figure ... *Ah those were the days.* Suddenly realising that the woman had left her hatbox behind, the older woman looked back to where the hatbox had been left but it wasn't there. She rushed to the cubicle, swung the curtain open ... there was the hatbox. She grabbed it, instantly surprised at the weight ... *my, my ... this must be a very heavy hat!*

Not to be deterred, Mrs Shaw dashed for the door ... she didn't make it.

A kilogram of Soviet PVV-5A explosive surrounded by nails and scrap metal exploded in Mrs Shaw's hand as she approached the front door of Edgars. Her body was shredded to pieces ... all that was recovered three days later was her left hand and wedding ring. The thudding blast shook the building to its foundations, bursting sheet glass outwards over the pavement, killing two passers by. Concrete dust billowed out the building, windows across the street were shattered, and glass cascaded onto the pavement.

As the dust hung in the late afternoon breeze, the City stood still.

The news of the Salisbury bombing was lost on the outside World. At precisely 9pm on that very same day, the IRA detonated a firebomb outside the window of the Peacock Room in the restaurant of the La Mon House Hotel, about 23km southeast of Belfast, killing twelve people and injuring thirty others. The international press never quite got around to drawing a comparison.

3

Suburb of Ridgeview, 3km Southwest of the Salisbury CBD

Faye Ann Chan, Secretary COMOPS, rushed from the bus stop on the corner of Ganges and Boeing Roads in the suburb of Ridgeview.

Ridgeview was a suburb allocated almost exclusively to the Asian, Indian and Chinese communities. Faye was a first generation Chinese-Rhodesian, twenty-two, 5ft 4', with long straight black hair that hung to the middle of her back. She was dressed neatly in a knee-length grey skirt and white blouse with a large bag over her shoulder. She would be described by anyone who met her as stunningly beautiful. Most often, she wore her hair loose, but on hot days, she would tie it up in a high ponytail or a tight bun at the nape of her neck. Her height and petite figure - her mother felt she was too thin - and her upright deportment, made Faye a striking picture. Her skin was like highly polished porcelain, free of any blemish save for a tiny black mole on her lower cheek, serving only to exemplify her perfect complexion. She was the sort of woman that turned heads.

As was the custom of her culture and her upbringing, Faye was profoundly respectful to her elders and she spoke in soft gentle tones. She was fluent in Mandarin, her parent's home language, and her English was spoken with an accent that could be easily confused with someone born and brought up in England. This was testimony to the excellent English tutor that her father had insisted upon as part of her education.

While Faye was an extremely attractive girl, she suffered terribly from shyness. She was the sort of person that found making friends very difficult as she could not bear superficial, shallow, relationships. The few friends she had made at school she cherished, being loyal, attentive and generous. She had attended The Dominican Convent High School, as most Asian girls did, and then studied a secretarial course at Speciss College in Salisbury. Her friends included two white girls, Helen Parkinson and Mary Lloyd, and an Indian girl, Adrika Ramji.

Part of the problem in making friends was that Faye was acutely aware of her race, her 'Chineseness'. While her friends loved her as much as she loved them, the feeling of being an outsider had upset her from a very young age. She was one of the 'different' people in her class at school. She was never bullied or discriminated against by her teachers, quite the contrary; she enjoyed her school and her teachers. Despite all of this, Faye begrudged the fact that she could only attend the Convent School because she was Chinese. While her school had provided an excellent education, probably far better than at the 'white' government schools, that did not diminish her feelings of alienation, of disconnection.

The Chan family had arrived from Kenya in late 1955, seeking a new life after the ravages of the Mau Mau Rebellion. Faye's father had a successful trading store near Eldoret in the highlands of the Rift Valley Province. The store had been attacked and ransacked by a mob, and her parents, fearing for their lives, decided to leave Kenya. The choice of Rhodesia as a place to settle was because Faye's parents both carried British passports and Rhodesia was encouraging immigration at the time. The thought of moving to England with the rain and cold was out of the question. Rhodesia seemed a safe option in 1955. Her parents were also of the view that Rhodesia would be able to avoid a civil war like the Mau Mau Rebellion, as it had been incorporated into the Federation of Rhodesia and Nyasaland. This was the British Government's attempt to create a more economically viable political grouping of Northern Rhodesia (Zambia), Southern Rhodesia (Rhodesia) and Nyasaland (Malawi). The Federation was doomed to failure because of worldwide decolonisation pressure, while the political leaders in the three countries pushed hard for their respective independence[27].

Faye was born soon after the arrival of the family in Southern Rhodesia, as it was called then, and she was brought up in a privileged environment. Her father had efficiently rebuilt a business around distribution of basic products, such as buckets, brooms and tableware to rural trading stores and was very successful. When arriving in Rhodesia, the Chan family soon discovered the complexity of not being either white, on the one hand, nor black on the other. Asians and people of mixed race were left in a vacuum that restricted their property rights and prevented their children from attending 'white' schools.

Mr Chan had hoped to be able to buy a farm, but the law prevented the sale of agricultural land to non-whites. He discovered, to his great distress, that being Chinese made his official classification 'non-white'. Faye's father complained bitterly at being discriminated against in business, in particular the fact that he was prevented from purchasing land. Her father's anguish greatly influenced Faye's view of the world, building a nagging acrimony and resentment.

As the years passed, and emigration from the country increased, the stigma against employing Asians fell away and Faye was recruited out of secretarial college into the government Treasury Department. Her obvious intelligence and work ethic assisted her subsequent application for a job in the Prime Minister's Office. The Prime Minister's Office also acted as a front for recruitment to COMOPS. As she was polite and respectful, highly intelligent, and like greased-lightning at typing and shorthand, the staff around her quickly accepted her. A quiet girl, she kept to herself, not seeking to socialise with her colleagues at work, despite the attentions of a few enthusiastic army officers.

After getting off the bus, Faye Chan walked purposefully the three blocks home to Anson Road. She was excited beyond measure. Her hands were

---

27 The Federation of Rhodesia and Nyasaland lasted from 1953 to 1963. Decolonizing pressure from the United Nations, the Organisation of African Unity and black African nationalist organisations doomed the Federation to failure. Northern Rhodesia gained independence from the UK as the new nation of Zambia and Nyasaland gained independence as the new nation of Malawi. Southern Rhodesia became known as Rhodesia and remained in political limbo.

shaking, as she pushed open the front door to the house, almost running to the kitchen to turn on the transistor radio. As the voice of the RBC announcer began, the distinctive beeps of a Police Message rang out.

This is a Police Message ... at approximately four forty-five pm this afternoon an explosion took place in Stanley Avenue in Salisbury. The Police are anxious to speak to anyone who may have information regarding this explosion and they are urged to contact their nearest Police Station as soon as possible ... the announcer then repeated the message finishing with ... *This is a Police Message ...*

Faye sat down on one of the kitchen chairs; she was shivering uncontrollably from the release of stress and tension. Tears of relief and joy ran down her cheeks, she felt like she wanted to scream out her victory. She opened her bag and pulled out a dark-haired wig and a navy-blue pantsuit. Her first mission as a saboteur for the freedom struggle had been completed. The excitement of making such a valuable contribution coursed through her, her whole body was trembling from the adrenalin rush. She stuffed the wig, sunglasses and pantsuit into a rubbish bag and threw it in the bin. Then she made herself a cup of tea and went straight to her bedroom, relieved that her parents had not yet returned home from work.

Sitting down in front of her ancient Underwood 5 typewriter, Faye took a deep breath as she began to distil the information she had recorded in the COMOPS meeting that morning. When satisfied with her recall, she began banging away enthusiastically, concentrating hard on getting all the information down in the right sequence.

Faye Chan kept a secret, a very dark secret with great consequences.

Not only was she a trained saboteur, she was an agent for the ZANLA High Command, a mole deep in the recesses of COMOPS, with access to the most sensitive information. She typed up a large proportion of documents marked 'Classified', 'Secret' and 'Top Secret'. Her accuracy at shorthand and her typing speed and efficiency meant that she was always first choice for typing up important documents. She would duplicate copies on the Roneo machine and manage the 'Top Secret' distribution; often an extra copy would be slipped into a nondescript envelope to be posted to her home address under the title 'payslip'. She was a gifted and resourceful girl with an almost photographic memory, often returning home at night to type up a copy of a document from memory, almost word perfect.

The COMOPS plan to investigate the secret training base for saboteurs in Mozambique was a particularly vital piece of intelligence that Faye committed to memory. The fact that a freedom fighter had been killed while carrying the ZANLA planning documents needed to be filtered back to the leadership at their HQ in Chimoio, Mozambique as soon as possible.

*

ZANLA Training Camp, 17km north of Chimoio Mozambique, 85km east of the Rhodesian Border

Comrades Felix Mhanda and Peter Hamadziripi had not returned to the town of Chimoio with their great leader, Josiah Tongogara. They had made the excuse that they wished to inspect some of the training methods that the Chinese were employing with the recruits in Chindunduma School. Both men were well educated; they had attended University in Zambia and had been trained in the Soviet Union in the late 1960s.

Both men carried a pedigree in the freedom struggle. Peter Hamadziripi was the nephew of Henry Hamadziripi, who was one of the founding members of ZANU under the leadership of Ndabaningi Sithole. Henry Hamadziripi and Sithole had met to form ZANU in August 1963 together with Mukudzei Midzi, Herbert Chitepo, Edgar Tekere and Leopold Takawira. That famous meeting took place at Enos Nkala's house in Highfield, Salisbury. Henry Hamadziripi still had a seat on the *Dare re Chimurenga* with significant influence, but he was a marked man for his open criticism and hostility to Mugabe and his Marxist agenda. He had the same hostile attitude towards Josiah Tongogara for his violence and intimidation, despite the fact that the Hamadziripi clan were also Karanga.

Henry Hamadziripi's attitude and philosophy had been passed on to his nephew Peter, who now held them as his own. Tongogara was aware of the attitude of the Hamadziripi clan towards him, but the clan's Karanga heritage counted a great deal. The clan's opposition to Marxism meant he saw them as potential allies in a leadership challenge.

Felix Mhanda was the youngest brother of Wilfred Mhanda[28] a senior ZANLA commander and radical pro-Marxist. Wilfred now languished in jail in Mozambique after one of Robert Mugabe's leadership purges. Wilfred had openly stated his opposition to any thought that Mugabe should be the leader of ZANU and certainly never President of the new Zimbabwe. Tongogara shared Mhanda's opposition to Mugabe but that was all. He had arrested Mhanda because of his extreme Marxist-Leninist agenda. Tongogara's principal motivation was to stamp out any idea of a Marxist-Leninist state in Zimbabwe.

The much younger Felix Mhanda now thirsted for revenge and the freedom of his brother languishing in jail. His saving grace was that he did not share his elder brother's extreme Marxist-Leninist philosophy. That was why Tongogara tolerated him, coupled with the fact that he was an excellent leader and soldier.

Felix Mhanda and Peter Hamadziripi had been together since the beginning of the armed struggle. In 1973, they were amongst the first batch of freedom fighters to be trained at the international terrorist training camp

---

28 Mhanda took the Chimurenga or war name of Dzinashe Machingura. His rebellious movement of young officers was called the *Vashandi* (Workers).

set up at the Libyan Sabha Air Force base. The base had been set up in the desert, just south of the City of Sabha, 650km south of Tripoli. The base was also being used to train Zimbabwean and MPLA[29] pilots for the Soviet Mig-21s that had been promised.

Mhanda and Hamadziripi had met Brian Keenan in Sabha, the man sent by the IRA to negotiate arms shipments from Libya. He had been a great source of inspiration and his knowledge of logistics and the operation of small, independent, terrorist cells was to be the foundation of the model implemented by ZANLA in the early part of the war.

Of course, the greatest inspiration of all for the impressionable young men was the revolutionary leader Muammar Gaddafi. It was his Third International Theory that provided the vision they thirsted for. Gaddafi's theory rejected traditional instruments of government - parliaments, parties and referendums - and contrasted them to the concept of direct popular democracy based on people's congresses and people's committees. This was precisely the philosophy that the young Mhanda and Hamadziripi believed in. They agreed that democracy and other freedoms were in fact nothing but a kind of dictatorship. Democracy could be easily perverted by ethnic and tribal differences, by corrupt representatives and unscrupulous party leaders. The Third International Theory offered to create a special hierarchical structure of people's congresses and committees, resulting in a system where management became popular, control became popular, and the old definition of democracy as 'control by people over the government' was replaced by its new definition, as 'the people's control over itself'.

It was clear to both Mhanda and Hamadziripi, and to many of the other well educated officers in ZANLA, that there was a risk that if either Tongogara or Mugabe became President of the new Zimbabwe, that they would seek absolute personal power above all else. The people would suffer terribly as a result. The political party ZANU would be the instrument of a dictatorship, hiding in the shadow of western democracy, distorting the parliamentary system and the processes of government.

The two men were also devoutly anti-communist, being victims of the naked Soviet racism in the city of Tbilisi in the Soviet Socialist Republic of Georgia. That was where the freedom fighters had been sent for their military and political training. Mhanda had been violently beaten by a mob of white university students, who were bitterly opposed to the many privileges the freedom fighters had been granted by the CPSU[30] African Section.

Peter Hamadziripi was the more politically focussed of the two men, while Mhanda's interests lay more in the military, with hope of a leadership role in the future Zimbabwe People's Army. Hamadziripi, like his uncle, disliked both Mugabe and Tongogara and despaired at what either of their

---

29 *Movimento Popular de Libertação de Angola,* Popular Movement for the Liberation of Angola.
30 Communist Party of the Soviet Union. The CPSU had created the so-called Soviet Solidarity Committee who's job it was to co-ordinate training, weapons and logistics for the freedom struggle.

presidencies would do to the new country. He had a vision for a regime sympathetic to the Third International Theory that flew in the face of Mugabe's slanted version of Marxism. Tongogara's ruthless suppression of the Nhari rebels, and any other opposition, showed how dangerous he could be if he became President. His violence, together with his poor education, reliance on traditional religion and tribal alliances, made him totally unsuited to political leadership.

'What do you think about this saboteur strategy, Comrade?' asked Hamadziripi of his friend and ally Mhanda. The two men were walking between classrooms in the sprawling training base that covered many hectares.

'We need to apply more pressure to the Colonists. In that sense it is good, but things we break, in the future we will have to fix,' replied Mhanda. Hamadziripi nodded his agreement, swatting a nagging fly from his face. It was a hot, humid day.

'Comrade Tongogara seems to be consolidating his power to an even greater degree. I am convinced that he believes that he will be the future leader of the struggle,' continued Hamadziripi, dropping his voice to a whisper, despite the fact that there was nobody else within a hundred metres. The fear of the consequences of Tongogara's wrath was deep seated, there were spies everywhere.

'What can we do, Comrade? We have no power of our own other than the few officers in our own units. The leadership of the *Dare re Chimurenga* is fearful, they will not challenge each other until the *murungu*[31] are chased from our land,' replied Mhanda softly, also looking about him furtively.

'Maybe the Colonists will kill him ... or maybe he might have an accident Comrade!' stated Hamadziripi decisively, as he stopped walking to look at his friend. Mhanda studied Hamadziripi's face as if he could not believe what he had heard. 'Maybe we can arrange such an accident Comrade, nobody would ever be able to blame us. We could then step up into the leadership, our men would support us. We can deal with Mugabe later.'

The mere mention of such a conspiracy was enough for both men to look around them once again. Mhanda nodded his agreement at the sentiments expressed by his friend.

'I will make a plan Comrade,' said Hamadziripi, 'don't be concerned, all will be well. A great responsibility sits upon our shoulders. We must act to protect our revolution and our people!'

---

31 seShona, derogatory term for white people.

4

3 Commando RLI, Fireforce base, Buffalo Range Forward Airfield (FAF 7), South-east Rhodesia

'Double in, DOUBLE In ...LEEEEFT, RIGHT, LEFT, RIGHT ... LEFT' screamed CSM Strydom in the ears of the two recalcitrants. These were the alleged perpetrators of the attack on 2RR Mortar Platoon at the Triangle Country Club. Both men doubled across the open area between the Orderly Room and the office of the OC[32] of 3 Commando.

'HALT.'

The men came smartly to a halt outside of the office door. Two flagpoles stood outside the OC's office. One flew the Rhodesian flag, the 'Green and White', the other the 3 Commando Flag, a large yellow banana with a grey '3' superimposed on a green background, the words 'The Lovers[33]' embroidered above the banana. The banana, in this case, did not signify nourishment, but, instead, the fruits of the flesh.

The CSM knocked loudly on the door and opened it, 'Commando Orders whenever you are ready ... Sir,' he said in his authoritative, 'CSM' voice.

'Carry on please CSM,' came the call from inside the office.

'Troopers Marais and Au ... Aubergine present for Commando Orders ... Leeeft, right, left, right, left.'

The two accused marched smartly into the Major's office, driving their boots into the concrete floor, coming smartly to attention. Both stood ramrod straight staring unblinkingly at the map on the wall behind the Major's desk. It was hot and stuffy, the men could feel sweat running down their backs.

Major Harold Tomlinson ignored the two soldiers standing in front of him, concentrating instead on earnestly shuffling the papers on his desk, as if in the middle of the plan for the D-Day landings. The Major was interrupted by the mournful cry of the callout siren as it rolled through the fireforce base. The sound never failed to strike at the chest, like a heavy compressing weight, shortening breath ... *is it my turn?*

'Confirm 13 Troop are on callout CSM?' asked Tomlinson.

'Affirmative, Sir!' cracked the CSM, his voice like a whip.

Nodding his head, Tomlinson went back to the papers on his desk. This was the second callout of the day; the first had been at first light. The sound of engines winding up carried through the open window. The siren stopped, the Major sat back in his chair and looked up at the two 'horrible little men', as the CSM had called them.

The two men were incongruously similar in size and stature, despite the ten years that separated them. That was where the similarity ended. Jean-Paul D'aubigne's face showed the signs of hard times, of battles long since

---
32 Officer Commanding.
33 From all accounts, the nickname 'Lovers' came from the fact that in the early days of the unit the 3 Commando troopers produced the highest number of illegitimate births.

forgotten. He had been a legionnaire with 2*ᵉ Régiment Étranger d'Infanterie, (2ᵉ REI)* (2ⁿᵈ REP)[34]. A jagged white scar cut across his right cheek, from just below his ear halfway to the corner of his mouth. When he did smile, which was often, the scar made him look literally like he was smiling from ear to ear. His skin showed the effects of an inordinately long time spent in the hot sun, a dark tan on an already swarthy complexion. D'aubigne's was the type of face that always showed the shadow of a beard despite the fact that he had shaved only hours before. Deep furrowed lines cut across his forehead, as if in a perpetual frown, making him appear much older than his twenty-nine years. A large, broken Roman nose, so typical of French noses from the ancient Riez region of Provence, sat above a strong protruding jaw. This was a face describing any number of emotions and contradictions, hardness, toughness, pain, humour and a deep and abiding sadness. D'aubigne had strikingly deep blue, cheeky eyes that softened an otherwise forbidding face, confirming a disposition given to levity and mischief.

Penga Marais, on the other hand, had a face that showed the openness and innocence of his youth. While his skin was also tanned, it was smooth and unblemished. At nineteen years old, Marais was hard pressed to grow any facial hair at all, only shaving every other day. His face always held the expression of being deep in thought, but also of uncertainty and lack of confidence. Marais' most distinctive feature was his large, deep brown, haunted eyes, disturbingly similar to those of Linda Blair in *The Exorcist*. His face showed the internal battles of a difficult upbringing, coupled with the petulant confusion, ambiguity and defiance of adolescence. Dudley 'Penga' Marais had the sort of face that looked like he had either just stopped crying, or was about to burst into tears.

'You are aware of the charges placed against you, to wit ... *Fighting-with-and-beating-up-on-fellow-soldiers-for-no-rhyme-or-reason-and-causing-severe-damage-thereto'*, stated Major Tomlinson formally, scrutinising the two felons as he did so, a flicker of a smile on his face. 'Put simply, the charge is damage to Government Property,' said the Major, placing his pencil neatly on the desk in front of him.

The two men made no comment, resigned to their fate. This was the army, *presumed guilty unless innocence could be discounted*!

'Have you anything to say in mitigation of sentence ... firstly you Trooper D'aubigne?'

'*Majeur*, we were drinking beeer in zee bar when the people from 2RR came in. They called us names and we zen attacked them with our feests. We deed not use any weapurns otherr than our feests.'

'How many 2RR men were there?'

'I thinnk zer were *dix*, ten, Serr.'

'Thank you D'aubigne ... now you Marais, what do you have to say?'

'Sir ... Le Beau, I mean ...Trooper Aubergine and I were drinking a few jimboolies in the bar and tuning the chick behind the bar, she was *mush* and I schemed that I had a chance for a *nigh*, then the 2RR jam-stealers rocked up.

34 2nd Foreign Infantry Regiment, French Foreign Legion.

The one asked me why I was chatting up his crow, so I told him to get fucked. He then *chovaed* me, and called me a RLI *skate* and checked me *skeef*. I *chovaed* him back and gave him a *flatty*. Then we had a *mushe* rort ... me and Le Beau, we fucked them up ... all ten ... Sir![35]'

Major Tomlinson, struggling to keep a straight face, tried to interpret, 'So, would you say that you were provoked, Trooper Marais?'

'Sir ... I scheme that jam-stealers should not call us skates when we are the ones culling all the Gooks, ... plus we had only just lost Colour McIntyre and Le Beau and me were drinking to him ... Sir!'

Tomlinson sat back surveying the two hapless perpetrators, now convinced that neither of them understood the word 'provoked'.

'Thank you gentlemen ... any other comments you wish to add?'

There was no reply, just concentrated focus on the map behind him.

Major Tomlinson sat forward again and shuffled a few more papers around his desk, obviously deep in contemplation. His most abiding concern was that 11 Troop at present had only five operational sticks, twenty men. Removing two men meant the loss of another stick, unacceptable in the present circumstances. He decided on a course of action.

'Your behaviour has severely undermined the reputation of the RLI and 3 Commando. It has also damaged our relationship with 2RR. Not to mention the damage to the bar at Triangle Country Club. These are serious matters. One week confined to base ... one week suspension of canteen privileges ... one week latrine duty ... That will be all.'

'SIR!' shouted CSM Strydom, preparing to remove these two pieces of filth from the Major's office.

Tomlinson interrupted, 'by the way CSM, 2RR Mortar Platoon have deployed to Vila Salazar. They have a broken TR48 and need a replacement. I think Marais and D'aubigne should help to provide the escort ... to help mend relations.'

'SIR!' shouted CSM Strydom again, called about turn and the two men were marched smartly out of the office into the bright sunshine.

---

35 The RLI had unique slang, which was largely unintelligible to anyone outside of the unit. The slang included English, Afrikaans, Chilapalapa, seShona and siNdebele. What Marais actually said was 'Trooper D'aubigne and I were drinking beer and talking suggestively to the lady bartender, she was very nice and I thought that I had an opportunity for a sexual liaison when the 2RR rear echelon men arrived. One of the men enquired as to whether I was making sexual advances to his girlfriend so I swore at him. The man then pushed me and called me an RLI show-off, and looked at me in a threatening manner. I then pushed him back and gave him a hard slap with the flat of my hand, and a fight broke out where D'aubigne and I succeeded in defeating all ten of our assailants.'

*

Selous Scout HQ, Andre Rabie Barracks, Inkomo 40km northwest of Salisbury

Sgt Cephas Ngwenya BCR[36], 3 Group, Selous Scouts[37] was called to the central briefing room at Andre Rabie Barracks, tucked away in a corner of the sprawling military base called Inkomo Barracks. Ngwenya was twenty-nine, an ex-policeman, trained by Special Branch in intelligence gathering and counter-insurgency. He was not a physically imposing man despite his family name, *Ngwenya*, meaning 'crocodile' in siNdebele. While he was slightly built, he had the hunting instincts of a crocodile, silence, patience, and speed, with the attack vicious and deadly. He was a Matabele by birth being brought up in a region called Tjolotjo about 100km northwest of Bulawayo in Matabeleland. He had been part of the original 'pilot' pseudo scheme set up by the police Special Branch.[38] Sgt Ngwenya had achieved much success from the Selous Scout base in Bulawayo against ZIPRA, including a very successful 'snatch' of senior ZIPRA officers on the road between Gaborone and Francistown in Botswana. That mission had earned him the BCR. His group, called 3 Group, specialised in operations against the Matabele-dominated ZIPRA. As with most black people in Rhodesia, he was also fluent in seShona, the language of the majority of the population.

When the Selous Scouts were formed in late 1973, Ngwenya volunteered for selection primarily because he had heard that the pay would be more than double what he had been earning in the police. That had proved not to be completely correct, but the danger and excitement provided by the Scouts had compensated to some degree. More importantly, he enjoyed the informality of the unit and the freedom of movement it offered during operations. The black soldiers in the Selous Scouts were recruited from all branches of the police and army; many came from the Rhodesian African Rifles. The Selous Scouts were trained in so-called 'pseudo' operations. They were taught to pose as terrorists, to infiltrate the terrorist organisation. They were taught how to approach a village, how to approach a band of terrorists in the field, passwords, pass signs, liberation songs and how to collect food from the local population. The skills the Scouts were taught included 'turning' captured terrorists; the unit had already recruited a good many 'converts', who now enthusiastically fought with the Rhodesian forces against their previous

---

36 Bronze Cross of Rhodesia, awarded for valour in the face of the enemy.
37 The Selous Scouts were an elite unit trained in long-term infiltration of enemy held areas, internally and outside of the country, coupled with highly skilled observation skills. They were the supreme masters of intelligence gathering through observation. The unit included both white and black soldiers; the black soldiers were mostly drawn from the Rhodesian African Rifles but included policemen drawn from BSAP Special Branch and Ground Coverage.
38 Set up by Superintendent Peterson of Special Branch in Salisbury in January 1973. The first few, largely unsuccessful, deployments with the team were in Bushu and Madziwa Tribal Trust Lands.

comrades.

What impressed Ngwenya was being summoned to a meeting to be conducted by the OC of Selous Scouts, Colonel Ron Reid-Daly. This had not happened to him before, although he had met the Colonel many times informally. He knocked on the door of the briefing room and was ushered in.

'Welcome Cephas,' said the Colonel walking towards the new arrival, a broad smile on his face. He shook Ngwenya's hand firmly. The Colonel had a personal relationship with all his men, particularly those who had excelled as Ngwenya had done. 'Let me introduce you to Sergeants Dave Seals, Dennis Kumpher and Captain Chris Schultz. I am seconding you to Recce Troop for this mission.'

Reid-Daly spoke in a slow clipped fashion, making each word sound more important than the preceding one. This was a hangover from his days as RSM of the RLI, where he had to constantly 're-educate' unruly and inexperienced young men.

'Yes Boss,' answered Ngwenya respectfully, he was in auspicious company.

The men shook hands. Ngwenya was immediately struck by the relaxed informality between the men. Seals, Kumpher and Schultz smiled their welcome.

The Scouts were not hot on military protocol, most troopers and NCOs called each other by their first names. Reid-Daly was called 'Boss', 'Uncle Ron' or 'Colonel'. He was tough on his men and he was tough on himself. His devotion and dedication to the Selous Scouts and his deep concern for the welfare of his men earned him loyalty and respect. These men would follow him unquestioningly into the 'valleys of death' the Honde, the Save, the Pungwe, the Buzi, the Limpopo and the Zambezi.

Schultz, Kumpher and Seals were legends in the unit. Captain Schultz SCR[39], a South African, had been one of the first officers recruited into the Selous Scouts. Like so many others, he had begun his career in the RLI. His exploits into Mozambique, Zambia and Tanzania were already part of military folklore.

The black members of the Selous Scouts had given Schultz the nickname *Tsere* or Honey Badger. The similarities between Schultz and his namesake, the Honey Badger, were stark ... *short with stocky limbs, enormous upper body strength, mainly nocturnal, most active during the early morning and late afternoons, generally solitary, but often two or more moving and hunting together. Normally shy and retiring ... often, with only the slightest provocation become extremely aggressive.*

Schultz was a highly skilled reconnaissance operator, often working alone and always deep within enemy territory. He preferred working alone or with his trusted number two, Sgt. Roger Muhondo. Sgt. Muhondo was recovering from wounds sustained in a recent external raid, hence the recruitment of Ngwenya for this job.

39 Silver Cross of Rhodesia, the second highest award for valour issued during the bush war.

Dennis Kumpher BCR and Dave Seals had years of operational experience, both as pseudo operators and intelligence gatherers on long-range reconnaissance. Both had recently returned from a trip to Mozambique that included blowing up railway lines and bridges. Dennis Kumpher was famous for a two-week escape and evasion from enemy troops after being separated from his call-sign. He had walked over 100km back to the Rhodesian border, without food or water, constantly hunted by the enemy. Yes, the Selous Scout Reconnaissance Troop were men not to be trifled with.

Reid-Daly turned to the other man in the room. 'This is Major Smyth from COMOPS who will give you your detailed operational briefing later.'

A large-scale map was spread over the chart table that was at least two metres square. The Boss held a snooker queue as he indicated major landmarks. The map was familiar to Ngwenya; it was the ZANLA Manica Operational Area in Mozambique.

'Captain Schultz will lead the team on a reconnaissance, including a snatch operation to Chimoio. The other members of your team will include Trooper George Kachimanga, who, as you know, is ex-FRELIMO, speaks both seShona and Portuguese, and Trooper Simon Nyandoro who is ex-ZANLA, only recently turned. I have not included them in this briefing for obvious reasons.' The Colonel took a breath. It was always a risk to include the turned terrorists on sensitive briefings, as there was always a niggling doubt about their allegiance. This was despite the good work both these two men had already done on operations.

Reid-Daly continued in the same ponderous fashion, not changing the tone of his voice, 'You will HALO[40] jump into Mozambique to the south of Chimoio. The Air Force have picked up what looks like a training base in this area.' He was pointing to the map, waving at a wide area to the south of the town. The problem Ngwenya observed was that Reid-Daly was waving the pointer around an area at least 50km square. 'COMOPS have int that ZANLA have got themselves some high powered demolition experts training at a camp somewhere here, probably supported by Chinese or North Korean advisors.'

'Is the camp identified in aerial photographs, Boss?' asked Captain Schultz, in his matter-of-fact way.

'Not yet, we have asked the Blue Jobs to send over a Canberra to get some photos. We should get them from JSPIS[41] tomorrow.'

'Do you want us to kill these bastards, Boss?' enquired Captain Schultz, a broad smile now on his face. The other men watched the interplay between Schultz and the Colonel; the mutual respect between them was obvious.

'Not initially, we need to snatch one of these people, preferably one of the leaders of the group … a Chinese advisor would be nice.'

'Do you want us to interrogate him on the spot, Sir?' Schultz was known for his enthusiastic interrogation.

'Only as an operational expedient …We don't want the goods damaged

---
40   High-Altitude-Low-Opening parachute jump.
41   Joint Services Photographic Interpretation Service.

in any way, this is too important ... we will send a helicopter to fetch the merchandise once you have got him. Anyway Schultzie, your Chinese is somewhat lacking.'

The men laughed, the Boss wasn't strong on jokes, when he did crack one, it was worth laughing.

'What do we do then, Sir?'

'You will be extracted once you have mapped the base, assuming it exists, for a later air strike. You will set up those new-fangled target indication flares for the Blue Jobs.[42]' Reid-Daly then got to his feet, 'Major Smyth will finish the briefing and then it will be up to you to work out the finer points of the plan.'

The Colonel studied his men. These were the best he had, probably the best the Country had. The danger that he was sending them into was extraordinary; the possibility of them not coming back from Mozambique was always high. Yet, this is what they were trained to do, frankly, this is what they loved doing.

Reid-Daly stopped at the door and turned to his men, 'Boys this is a tough job, but it is probably the most vital assignment this unit has been given in its short history ... good luck.'

Not waiting for any response, he left the room.

*

Library, University of Rhodesia, Salisbury

It was 5:30 in the late afternoon when Faye Chan entered the university library through the main entrance. She immediately moved towards the history section. Faye had not had the opportunity to go to university straight out of school as she had only completed the Cambridge Senior Certificate. Her father had been very anxious for her to join him in the family business, and while he valued education, he did not view a university education as necessary ... for a girl anyway.

As she was now a few years older, and had produced excellent exam results for her secretarial course at Speciss College, the University of Rhodesia had accepted her into a Bachelor of Arts. The fact that she had a job at the Prime Minister's Office helped a great deal, her boss had written to the Dean of Admissions on her behalf.

While the high school education system in the country was racially segregated, the University of Rhodesia was completely open to all, regardless of background. Many of the black leaders of the freedom struggle had studied at the university before fleeing into the neighbouring countries. Faye had not known what to expect when she started her course. She had been very nervous, but she had since immersed herself in her subjects, loving every

---

42 The Rhodesians had devised a system of target indication flares that could be ignited by a radio signal from the Canberra navigator/bomb-aimer while on the bomb-run. If the flares were positioned correctly, at a precise distance from the target, the bombsight could be offset accurately allowing for very accurate bombing at night.

minute of it.

As is almost inevitable at university, Faye had met a boy. She had never had a boyfriend before, having attended convent school and with strict Chinese parents. Her father had insisted that she would be matched with a Chinese boy when a suitable family could be found. Faye, being painfully shy, and acutely aware of her Asian heritage did not go out at all, other than with her parents and their friends. That was until she met Rugare Mangwende.

To say that Rugare had swept Faye off her feet was an understatement. He was tall, good looking, well educated and smart. He had a great sense of humour and made her laugh. Faye was completely infatuated. They would sit together in evening lectures, as Faye was a part-time student. He chatted to her about all subjects under the sun and kept her amused with many stories of his home life near the town of Mrewa in Madwende Tribal Trust Land, northeast of Salisbury.

Rugare was descended from the great Mangwende Chiefs of the Nhowe clan of the Zezuru who had fought the white settlers during the Shona Rebellion of 1896. The family had resisted the white man at every step since that time. The present chief, Rugare's uncle Johannes Munhunepai, was currently incarcerated in the regime's jail at Gonakudzingwa Detention Centre for seditious activities. Rugare Mangwende followed in the footsteps of his ancestors, focused completely on the expulsion of the white man from his land.

When they had first met, it was entirely predictable that the conversation would turn to Faye's job, which she had freely discussed with him. The fact that she had begun work in the Treasury Department and had recently been transferred to Combined Operations was a subject that Rugare found fascinating.

The relationship had blossomed and progressed briskly to a deeply passionate affair. Faye Chan had fallen in love, both with a man, and with an ideal. She was ripe and ready to be seduced by both, infatuated with the ideal of a new socialist Zimbabwe, where all men and women were free. All means were necessary to achieve their goal, no matter how many people must be sacrificed.

Rugare Mangwende had very effectively recruited and trained her as a spy for the revolutionary forces.

'Faye ... I am over here,' called Rugare Mangwende softly when he saw Faye enter the history section.

'Rugare, did you see the news?' she stammered, so excited she felt she would burst.

'Not here Faye, come, let's speak outside,' replied Rugare calmly, scanning the empty aisles in the library.

The two lovers casually left the library, looking no different to any other student friends on the campus. They never showed overt affection in public, a black man with a beautiful Chinese woman, would have attracted undue attention.

'You have struck a great victory Faye. I cannot tell you how proud I am of you,' whispered Rugare intensely, squeezing her hand, looking into her bright brown eyes.

Tears filled Faye's eyes, running down her cheeks. She lifted her hand to brush them away ... *he is proud of me ... of my achievement!* The tension in her body made her feel that she could scream.

'I cannot believe that I actually did it. I was terrified, but I did everything you said. It worked perfectly. I was shaking ... look I am still shaking!' said Faye, stumbling over her words, trying to get all the information out at once. 'We have shown these pigs that there is no hope for them ... this is just the beginning ...'

Her voice held a steely resolve, a power that Rugare could hardly believe was possible.

'You will be a hero of the revolution Faye; people will speak of your exploits forever. I cannot wait for the day when we can be married,' murmured Rugare into her ear, smelling her subtle perfume.

Rugare made sure to speak of marriage with Faye at every opportunity. Just the mention of the word brought tears to her eyes.

'Yes ... Yes Rugare, I so want to be married, it is all I can think about,' whispered Faye, her voice racked with emotion. She imagined in her mind that wonderful day when she would become a wife and live in happiness in this beautiful land where all men and women were equal.

'Our struggle is almost over, the Colonists cannot hold out much longer, soon we will be free to be together Faye. We can be together forever,' urged Rugare placing his hands on her shoulders squeezing his encouragement. He could feel her body shiver, taut like a violin string.

Tears began to run down Faye's cheeks again as she contemplated her future with this great man, the man who had introduced her to love and to this great calling, the struggle for freedom ... *what could be more important than giving this man everything I have ... my life if I have to ...*

'Don't cry my dearest. People must not see our love,' said Rugare, wiping her tears away with his hand. 'Come, we must get to our lecture. Afterwards, I have another assignment for you, even more important and exciting than the last!'

The touch of his hand on her cheek was like an electrical charge, Faye could feel the energy course through her body ... now an instrument of death ... his instrument to do with as he wished.

The two young lovers walked side by side to the lecture theatre, the subject ... ironically, The 1848 Revolts in Europe.

5

3 Commando RLI, Fireforce base, Buffalo Range Forward Airfield (FAF 7), Southeast Rhodesia

The outpost of Vila Salazar was about 110km due south of Buffalo Range, as the crow flies. Unfortunately, the distance was a lot longer by truck on poor dirt roads that were often ambushed and strewn with landmines. Vila Salazar was built as a customs post on the railway line travelling between the port of Maputo[43] in Mozambique and Rhodesia. This railway line had been a major artery for Rhodesian mineral exports and product imports which, since the collapse of the Portuguese colony, had been cut. The outpost was now an isolated vestige of the past, surrounded by the wild and forbidding Gona-re-zhou National Park on the one side, and the hostile and aggressive FRELIMO regime on the other.

Two Mercedes Benz Four-Five armoured vehicles were parked outside the Ops[44] Room at Buffalo Range. These were the vehicles designated to run the gauntlet to Vila Salazar from Buffalo Range, via Triangle and Mbizi Siding. The commander of this mission, the newly promoted Corporal Arthur 'Pommie' Beamish, was not a happy camper.

Arthur Beamish seldom projected an aura of happiness, unless drinking a skin full in the pub, or enjoying the favours of a compliant, preferably black, prostitute. Having said that, Beamish still had the inherited, dry Pom sense of humour plus he enjoyed a prank and a song or two. He was not a tall man, possibly only an inch or two taller than Le Beau D'aubigne, who would have been classified as short. He blamed his lack of height on poor air quality and the fact that he had spent most of his youth hungry. He had light brown hair, which he kept closely cropped, dark green eyes, and a nose that once would have been described as pointy, but now deviated alarmingly to the left. The broken nose was the result of being hit with a pint mug in a bar fight with an off-duty copper at The Crescent Pub in Salford. His nose made Beamish's face look lopsided, and the fact that his mouth was drawn back in a perpetual sneer, gave Beamish an intimidating aspect. His was the sort of face that reflected the receipt of continuous, unrelenting, bad news.

Beamish, born Arthur Tweed Beamish, the youngest of three boys, was brought up in the tough working-class neighbourhood of Salford to the west of the great industrial City of Manchester. He shared his first name with his great-grandfather, Arthur, who had fought with the 2nd Battalion, Lancashire Fusiliers at the Battle of Spion Kop during the Boer War. Great-grandfather Arthur was lucky to survive on that fateful day when 243 of his comrades died in the heat and stench, under merciless Boer artillery fire. Arthur Beamish Snr. was never the same again, drowning in February 1906 at age twenty-five, in a drunken haze in a gutter filled with only two inches of water.

Beamish's second name came from Captain Thomas Tweed who was

---
43 Lorenzo Marques under Portuguese Colonial rule.
44 Operations Room.

the Commander of B Company of the 2nd Salford Pals, 16th Battalion, Lancashire Fusiliers in World War I. William, Beamish's grandfather, served under Captain Tweed at the battle of Thiepval Ridge, part of the Battle of the Somme in July 1916. Captain Tweed saved old man William Beamish's life by carrying him a mile through exploding shells, rain and mud to an aid station after he was struck in the chest by a sniper bullet.

Beamish's father, George, served with the 11th Battalion Lancashire Fusiliers in the defence of Malta, and then in Italy, during World War II.

The Beamish family had certainly made their contribution to the Empire, but their rewards were few. The family had lived in the same house in Goulden Street for three generations, desperately poor, living just above the breadline. While they were poor, none of the Beamish family had ever made a claim for unemployment benefits. Old man William Beamish received a tiny medical pension from the army, everyone else worked long and hard to make ends meet.

George Beamish was a proud man, a leader in the post-war movement to protect workers rights, himself a labourer most of his life. He drank heavily, ruling his family with a rod of iron, literally and figuratively. Young Arthur Beamish cringed with the memory of some of the beatings that he and his brothers endured. Beamish's mother worked as a maid in one of the wealthy suburbs of Manchester where she became deeply embittered by the attitude and behaviour of the privileged class. The fact that they were so poor, while 'the rich' lived off the backs of the working class, was a constant point of resentful conversation in the house. Both parents would rant and rave about 'the rich' at every opportunity, particularly after a few pints at the local.

What Arthur Tweed Beamish was good at was singing. He sang in the choir at St Paul with Christ in Broadwalk, Salford. Singing provided Beamish with an outlet, a release from the depression of the family home. His voice, a lyric baritone, lent itself to singing army songs and it had stood him in good stead.

Arthur Beamish arrived at the gates of St George's Barracks, Sutton Coldfield, on a cold November morning in 1966, having walked all the way from Wilde Green Station. Serving in the army was a natural progression for the young Arthur Beamish; he was a poor scholar and had few prospects. The army presented the opportunity for an early escape from the depression of the family home. After his basic training, the Beamish family's past service to the Lancashire Regiment, ensured his posting to B Coy, 1st Battalion Lancashire Fusiliers at Weeton. In 1969, he was posted to 2nd Battalion Royal Regiment of Fusiliers[45] at Watchet, Somerset, and moved to Berlin were he did border patrols and guard duty, including Spandau Prison with its only inmate, Rudolf Hess.

Both of Arthur's brothers left home at sixteen to join the army. His eldest brother, Edward, lost his life to a bomb in Belfast in 1971 while serving with

---

45   The regiment was formed on April 23, 1968, made up of the Royal Northumberland Fusiliers, the Royal Warwickshire Fusiliers, the Royal Fusiliers and the Lancashire Fusiliers.

3 Para. Edward had been the hero in the young Arthur's life, the protector, the confidant, the friend and the supporter. When Edward died, Arthur felt his life fall apart. The memory of attending his brother's funeral, with all the pomp and ceremony of the Parachute Battalion, still haunted him.

In September 1971, only months after his brother's death, Beamish was sent to Belfast, Northern Ireland. That was the worst experience of his life. Initially, he had visions of avenging his brother's death, but those thoughts were soon dispelled. One tour of fighting Irishmen in their home country, and seeing close friends killed by snipers was enough for Beamish. After he saw a recruitment advert in the London Times for the RLI, he resigned from the British army and left for Rhodesia and a new life. The fact that he had no skills beyond soldiering, meant that the Rhodesian Light Infantry provided the escape and the fresh start he so desperately craved.

What Beamish had found so endearing about his adoptive country was that nobody cared about the fact that he spoke with a Lancashire accent, or was from a poor working class family on the 'wrong side of the railway tracks', or was poorly educated. He was treated as an equal despite the fact that he had to endure some merciless 'leg-pulling' because he was a Pom. This, he felt, was a bit rich, as close to 80% of the white population of Rhodesia carried British Passports. This unreserved acceptance, for the first time in his life, meant that Beamish built an abiding love and loyalty to his new country. He had something fresh and exciting to be part of, to live for.

This newfound confidence did not mean Beamish had to show any enthusiasm, co-operation, or initiative, in front of senior NCOs and officers. He was still a soldier after all!

*

The Troop had not been released for Jock McIntyre's funeral. The number of RLI casualties had grown to the point that attendance at funerals would have severely disrupted operations. Instead they were left to mourn on their own, to create their own individual way of coping with his loss. There was no such thing as 'counselling' in those days, and while the RLI had a chaplain, he was too busy to get out to the Commandos when someone died ... he had a fulltime job presiding over funeral arrangements.

Beamish had got the men together for a wake in the canteen. Support staff in the camp joined them, but all the other 3 Commando Troops were out on operations. Beamish felt it was up to him to say a few words for Jock and Andy Nicolle.

'First, we should drink to Andy Nicolle, he was a good bloke ... for a Nasho ...'

The men murmured their agreement, a few laughed. Andy had only been with them a short time and was not well known to Beamish.

'Do you want to say something for Andy ... Eric?' asked Beamish of Eric Parnell, Nicolle's stick leader.

Parnell stepped forward. He coughed to clear his throat and drew himself up to his full height to deliver his personal eulogy.

'Andy was a good bloke. I liked him and I think you all liked him too ...' the men grunted their agreement. 'Andy was a good soldier and a credit to the RLI ...' Parnell lifting his beer glass, '... to Andy.'

'To Andy,' the men replied. Parnell took a long drink, a man of very few words.

There was a moment of silence, ... Beamish stood forward again.

'I just want to say that Jock McIntyre was a good man and a good soldier. I have seen many men, and I have seen many soldiers, and he was among the best ... I was proud to know him and proud to be in his Troop ... God rest his soul,' said Beamish, his voice washed with emotion, hardened soldier that he was, croaking out the last few words. Then, taking another deep drink of beer to steady himself, he added, 'We should think of Lily and the kids at this time.'

The men grunted their agreement. Beer glasses were raised and most were drained as they all collectively tried to manage their emotions. The duty barman had fresh beers lined up on the bar.

Gathering himself again, Beamish lifted the old battered Bible he had been given by his father for his Confirmation. He then began to read a passage from the Bible that he remembered from his brother's funeral, Ecclesiastes 3: 1-11.

> *There is a time for everything, and a season for every activity under heaven:*
> *a time to be born and a time to die ...*

Beamish hesitated, his emotions suddenly in turmoil.

> *a time to plant and a time to uproot,*
> *a time to kill and a time to heal ...*

The memories of his brother's funeral inexplicably rushed back, like an unexpected tide. It was as if a wave had bowled him over, he was tumbling, panicking, holding his breath, swimming for the light ... to breathe. An involuntary tear ran down his cheek. He sucked for air ... his voice shuddering ...

> *... a time to tear down and a time to build,*

The men stood solemnly together, bowing their heads in absolute silence. All were intimately aware that Beamish was fighting his own internal demons. Beamish lifted his voice, broken as it was, trying for all he was worth, to keep it together ...

> *a time to love and a time to hate,*
> *a time for war and a time for peace ...*

Dudley 'Penga' Marais stood transfixed in front of Beamish, tears running freely down his cheeks, his hands shaking uncontrollably. Le Beau stepped forward and threw his arm around the young man's shoulders, holding him tightly.

> *I have seen the burden God has laid on men.*
> *He has made everything beautiful in its time ...*
>
> Amen

'Amen,' the men repeated in unison.
'To Jock,' rasped Beamish, clearing his throat, lifting his glass.
'To Jock,' came the reply.
The men clearly appreciated Beamish's stilted effort ... this was all the mourning they would get. There were no words said, just a silent understanding ... an understanding only shared by soldiers who have lost a leader, a friend, a companion. They had lost a person who had shared their pain, their fears, their hardship, their laughter and their sorrow.

After a brief pause, Beamish wiped his face with his sleeve, finishing his beer in one relieving gulp. The cold liquid rushing down his throat provided a form of solace, a momentary escape. He took another beer off the bar and filled his glass, sipping the white frothy head.

Beamish raised his glass again and stood up on one of the chairs.
'Sing with me boys,' he said.
His voice rang out through the canteen and out into the quad outside.

> *Bread of Heaven, Bread of Heaven feed me till I want no more.*
> *Bread of Heaven, Bread of Heaven feed me till I want no more.*

The men stood respectfully to attention while Arthur Beamish sang ...

> *Guide me oh thou Great Jehovah,*
> *Pilgrim through this barren land.*
> *I am weak but thou art Mighty.*

Spontaneously, the gathered soldiers sang out the chorus ...

> *Bread of Heaven, Bread of Heaven feed me till I want no more.*
> *Bread of Heaven, Bread of Heaven feed me till I want no more.*

The clear rousing voice carried to the Officer's Mess where they stopped their evening meal to listen.

> *Guide me, O thou great redeemer,*
> *Pilgrim through this barren land;*

I am weak, but thou art mighty,

Bread of Heaven, Bread of Heaven feed me till I want no more.
Bread of Heaven, Bread of Heaven feed me till I want no more.

CSM Strydom stood silently to attention outside of the Orderly Room.

Hold me with thy powerful hand;
Bread of heaven, bread of heaven
Feed me till I want no more; Feed me till I want no more.

Bread of heaven, bread of heaven
Feed me till I want no more; Feed me till I want no more.

Beamish held on to the last note. The song finished. It was done.

The Troop missed Jock McIntyre desperately; he was one of so many that had been killed. While the other members of the troop managed, in their own way, to move on, Penga Marais couldn't, he was disconsolate, a ticking emotional time-bomb.

*

The behaviour of two members of his stick, Marais and D'aubigne, had put Corporal Beamish into the invidious position of having to travel to Vila Salazar. Their punishment was now his punishment! The small detachment stood in a group in front of a senior officer who was briefing them.

They were all dressed in green T-shirts and shorts with leather 'lightweight' combat boots, combat caps and chest webbing for eight, twenty round, FN magazines. A webbing harness attached to their web-belts supported kidney pouches and water bottles, a sleeping bag tied to the harness in the small of the back. The chest webbing and harness also carried an assortment of coloured smoke, white-phos and fragmentation grenades. All carried first field dressings, tape, a saline drip and drip-kit, plus an ampoule of morphine on a cord around their necks with their dog-tags. This was standard Fireforce attire for most RLI troopers; there was no need for heavy backpacks … home in time for dinner in most cases. Le Beau D'aubigne, the MAG gunner was draped in belts for five hundred rounds, plus each trooper carried a spare hundred round belt in their pouches.

'Corporal Beamish, you need to travel to Vila Salazar via the National Park camp at Mbalauta,' instructed Captain Ian Liversedge the 2IC of 3 Commando. Beamish, who was a good deal shorter than the Captain, had a look on his face that could sink a battleship.

'Why do I need to go to Mabalauuuta … Sur?' Beamish asked, trying to demonstrate as much discontent as possible. Beamish's accent was pure Lancashire where the last word in each sentence was drawn out until he was forced to start a new one.

'... Because you need to collect a trailer of mortar rounds for the mortar platoon at Vila Salazar.'

'Why can't 2RR resupply their own mortar platoooon, Sur?'

'... Because they heard you were coming and are taking the opportunity for a resupply that Marais and D'aubigne have kindly provided,' replied Liversedge, careful to make sure he implicated the two guilty parties.

'It's too far to get into Vila Salazar and out in the same day, Sur. We will not be available for our Fireforce dutieeees, Sur,' explained Beamish, demonstrating his deep understanding of the tactical situation in the operational area. This was a last-ditch stand to avoid this mission.

'Not to worry Corporal, we will manage without you for a day or two ... by the way a few words of advice. Make sure that the rear vehicle tows the trailer carrying the mortar rounds ... you don't want it hitting a landmine, as it will likely vapourise both vehicles and their occupants. Second, don't even think of driving back here after dark, the risk of an ambush is too great. Third, when you get to Vila Salazar make sure to bunk down in one of their trenches as they have reported being mortared every night this week.'

Liversedge finished his briefing with a broad smile on his face, amused at the obvious discomfort of the corporal from Lancashire.

'Thank you Suuur,' Beamish replied in as surly a manner as possible, 'You said a day or TWOOO Sur ... we will be back tomorrow, Suurr?'

'Stranger things have happened Beamish, you may like it and want to stay.'

Liversedge threw his head back and laughed, a hearty deep-throated laugh that was infectious. Beamish's pommie sense of humour obliged him to break into a smile, he had been outmanoeuvred ... he was going to Vila Salazar and that was that. Any hope of a reprieve was dashed.

'Also, Beamish, you can take our new man with you, show him the ropes,' instructed the Captain, turning to a man standing in the shade of the veranda in full combat kit including MAG. '... meet Trooper Jim Kratzman III, late of the 1st Cavalry Division, Airmobile, recently joined us from Fort Bliss, Texas, via Cambodia.'

The new man stood at 6ft 4" if he was an inch, a truly enormous man, a barrel shaped chest, his posture perfectly upright, shoulders held back. While he was tall, he was also slim, like an athlete, exuding a quiet strength. His hair was a browny-reddish colour, that curled out from under his combat cap. He had a deep tanned face that was lit up in a broad friendly smile. He could be described as good looking in a Steve McQueen sort of way. He shared the same striking blue eyes as Steve McQueen and the same rugged complexion. His eyes were flanked by furrowed laugh-lines that crinkled up whenever he laughed, which he did often.

Beamish pretty much ignored the new man who stepped forward proffering his hand, pointing instead for him to climb onto the vehicle ... *fookin yanks!*

'Oh Yes, Corporal Beamish, you and your men are not to touch a hair on the head of any of the 2RR men, no matter how you may feel like doing so ... is that clear?'

'Yess Surrr!'

Beamish turned and marched off to the toilet to take a piss, shaking his head and muttering under his breath, *what did I do to deserve this! Fookin Maniac, fookin Frog ... now a fookin Yank! Goi'n to fookin Vila Salazar ... fookin army!*

The forlorn detachment drove out of the camp gates and turned right towards the town of Triangle, only 12km down the road. From Triangle, they were to follow the dirt road to Mbizi Siding on the railway line between Malvernia in Mozambique and Rutenga in Rhodesia, then onwards to Mbalauta. Penga Marais and Le Beau D'aubigne were placed in the rear vehicle, Beamish quite clearly struck by the warning of potential 'vapourisation'. The Four-Five was built on a Mercedes chassis that had an armour-plated body, with heavy double doors at the rear. The body was built with a deep-V shaped hull to deflect gunfire, RPG-7s and most importantly, landmine blasts. The vehicle cab had a roof over it with a hatch to allow for the mounting of a MAG. The back of the vehicle was open to the elements, with two rows of side-facing seats with small metal hatches, to allow rifles to be pushed through. It was standard procedure for the occupants to strap themselves in when driving on dirt roads, to prevent becoming a human missile in the event of hitting a landmine.

The vehicles passed over the wide Lundi River, travelling to the south through field after field of irrigated sugar cane and citrus fruit trees. The area was developed as an intensive agricultural area fed by large dams for irrigation purposes, all part of the small landlocked, sanctioned country becoming independent of imported commodities.

Clouds of fine white dust were thrown up; hanging in the air long after the vehicles had passed. The result was that those in the rear vehicle were soon covered in a film of dust, despite the driver's attempt to sit back some distance from the lead vehicle. It was hot and uncomfortable, doubly difficult for Le Beau who had mounted his MAG on the roof of the cab, exposed to the dust and heat. He eventually gave up, sat down on the bench seat behind the driver and strapped himself in. The road got increasingly corrugated, adding to the discomfort.

Penga Marais sat in his seat back-to-back with Le Beau. The noise of the truck, the rumble of the tyres and the constant, vicious bouncing made conversation impossible. He was deep in thought, two years into a five-year contract with the army. He had relied heavily on Jock McIntyre for emotional support ever since joining 11 Troop from Training Troop at Cranborne Barracks.

Marais had never known his biological parents; his mother must have been desperate to ensure that he got a decent chance, as he had been abandoned as a baby on the steps of the Andrew Fleming Hospital in Salisbury. He had been named 'Dudley' by the Hospital Matron after her own eldest son. He was fostered from the age of six with a family that brought up two older boys and a younger girl. If the truth were known, the family had taken Dudley in for the money provided by Social Welfare. The family were poor by Rhodesian standards; the mother was a secretary for an estate agency and the father worked on the railways. He was often away from home as a result. Dudley and the rest of the kids wore second-hand clothes from the Salvation Army and relied on the Church for at least one square meal a week. The family eventually adopted him and the surname 'Marais' was added to his 'Dudley'. His adoptive mother enjoyed a drink and spent a fair amount of time visiting 'friends' while the father was away. The young Dudley slept on a stretcher camp bed in the kitchen until his elder brother left home to do his national service. After that, he was promoted to share the bedroom with his other brother. It was a loving family after a fashion. He wasn't abused or beaten, or in any way mistreated, but he still couldn't wait to leave, he just never felt part of it.

Dudley Marais was not stupid, in fact, he was quite bright, but he suffered from undiagnosed acute dyslexia. Dyslexia was virtually unheard of in the 1970s. The disadvantaged child became the severely disadvantaged student. His teachers consigned him to the scrapheap ... many described him as retarded. His learning difficulty drove a profound frustration that manifested itself in disruptive behaviour and many beatings from the headmaster.

He often thought about what had happened to his real mother. What she was like, why she had abandoned him ... *where did she go?* It played on his mind, so much so, that he became an intensely unhappy teenager. Most teenage boys are morose and non-communicative, but Marais took this to an entirely different level. He effectively cut himself off from the family and those around him; he had few friends and was hopeless at conversation on any level. He spent his spare time walking in the bush that surrounded his suburb, shooting birds with his home-made catty[46].

The gardener at their home in Dunmore Avenue had introduced Dudley to marijuana, *mbanji*[47], as Midnight called it. Midnight had also taught Dudley to speak Chilapalapa, with the result that most of his sentences were a mixture of English and Chilapalapa. They built up a successful cottage industry cultivating a crop in the bush in the Mukuvisi Woodland, a few blocks to the north of the suburb. Midnight came from Malawi; his job in the partnership was distribution into the black townships, the 'locations'. The two of them collected old petrol cans to help with irrigating their crop. It was a backbreaking task hauling water into the bush. The crop thrived, and Dudley learned to love the bush. He would disappear for days on end, sleeping in the bush next to his 'crop', roasting Redeyed Doves, that Midnight called *Bvukutiva*, over the fire.

Marais exuded a chilling sadness, a coldness, that put people off. The fact that he was 'high' most of the time, together with his frustrated, anti-

---

46 Catapult, forked stick with thick twisted rubber bands attached to a leather pouch for holding stones.
47 seShona, cannabis, dagga, dope. Also zoll, grass, weed, gunja.

social behaviour, had given rise to the nickname *Penga*, meaning madness in seShona. He had not been called by his first name 'Dudley' since his thirteenth birthday.

The troubled orphan had attended Cranborne High School in Salisbury, situated across a stretch of bush from the home of the RLI at Cranborne Barracks. It was a tough school with tough kids. Penga and his brothers fought both each other and all-comers. While he was younger than his brothers and slightly built, his brothers would protect him from bullies, which abounded. The young Marais had to learn to fight to survive, he honed his skills at every opportunity. When he was in a fight, he literally went mad, not stopping unless rendered unconscious himself, or reducing his opponent to a gibbering wreck.

The unhappy boy was placed in the RLI at the tender age of seventeen on the insistence of his high school headmaster. It was clear that Marais was never going to finish school; his reading and writing skills never exceeded that of an eight year old. The family and the headmaster believed that there was a real possibility that he may end up in jail, or worse, kill someone. Capital punishment was still the norm in Colonial Africa.

Even after joining the army, Marais was constantly in trouble. During his basic training, he spent one 28-day stint in Detention Barracks in Bulawayo for assaulting a fellow recruit. If it had not been for the serious shortage of men, the RLI would almost certainly have discharged him.

Penga Marais' troubled life showed its first glimmer of hope after he was posted to 11 Troop under Jock McIntyre. Jock was the first person to see something positive hidden within the messed up kid's soul. His greatest challenge was to get the kid off the 'weed'. They reached an understanding after he took the young miscreant under his wing and began the process of turning him into a good soldier, focussing his anger on the enemy, not on his fellow soldiers. Jock figured that if he could train Marais to be the best soldier he could be, then, hopefully, that would get his life on track; give him something to believe in, to live for. Jock's nurturing did not prevent another 28-day trip to DB for Penga, after assaulting a corporal from 1 Commando in a bar in Salisbury.

Penga had no tolerance for alcohol, out of control after three beers, which made him high risk at a party. Alcohol coupled with 'weed', added to his aggressive behaviour. His fellow troopers always took turns to keep an eye on him when he was out on the 'piss'. The situation at the Triangle Country Club was a typical example, out of hand before Le Beau could calm it down, leaving him no option but to support his mate in the fight.

Since the death of Jock McIntyre, Penga felt numb, completely lost and isolated. He was deeply hurt, listless; the direction he had been given under McIntyre was lost. He didn't know what to do or what to say. Jock had been a central part of his life for the past two years, inviting the 'orphan' home for R&R as he simply had no place else to go. McIntyre's wife Lily, together with her two young children, took in the young soldier and treated him like one of the family. Jock's strict rule was 'no weed' or 'no R&R'. This finally got the young man off the stuff. It was the happiest time of Penga Marais' young life; he loved Lily as if she was his own sister. Lily refused to call him Penga, insisting instead, on calling him Dudley. He appreciated her calling him by his proper name, it gave him a strong feeling of belonging.

Dudley had yearned to see Lily since Jock's death, to speak to her. He had written to her but his poor command of English and the lack of writing skills, made his letters read more like *Janet & John* children's books. Beamish, who frankly also had a poor command of English, had helped write a few letters for Marais and he took the time to read Lily's replies when they arrived.

*

The small convoy eventually arrived at the Gona-re-Zhou National Park camp at Mbalauta. The camp had an airstrip that had been used previously as a Fireforce base and as a launch pad for external raids. B Company 2RR were presently based next to the airstrip from where they patrolled the neighbouring TTLs and the national park itself. 2RR was one of nine territorial force battalions made up of civilian conscripts. The companies in the battalion rotated on a 'six-weeks-in, six-weeks out' basis, referred to as 'continuous call-up', the men trying to juggle the army, family and a job all at the same time. Few succeeded.

Mbalauta and the surrounding Gona-re-zhou National Park was a dry desolate place, hot as Hades. At the height of the dry-season, the only permanent water was in the Nuanetsi River that meandered through the park. The water was not easy to get to in most places as the river had cut a deep gorge through the flat surrounding countryside.

The RLI men stopped their vehicles next to the largest of the tents and Beamish got out of the truck to look for the trailer of mortar rounds. The drivers and the other men got off the trucks to get out of the heat. They found a large shady tree and sat down to drink some water. There was no sign of life.

'Bloody TF wankers are in their fart-sacks, I bet you,' commented Penga, using the army description for sleeping bags.

Nobody disagreed. The new man, carrying his MAG by the grab handle, walked across from the lead vehicle.

Watching him approach, Penga spat, 'Fresh Poes!'

Le Beau merely grunted his assent, too hot and tired to get into a conversation with Penga.

Jean-Paul 'Le Beau' D'aubigne sat silently in contemplation, studying the surrounding bush. He was a complex character. He shared some of the same tragic history as Penga Marais in the sense that he had been abandoned at birth on the steps of the chapel *Notre Dame de Beauvoir*, perched on the 830-metre rock above the town of Moustiers-Sainte-Marie in Provence. The priest of the church deducted that the child must be from a Catholic mother, and therefore, was baptised with the name of his favourite Pope, John XXII[48].

---

48 Pope John XXII, French born Pope, 1316 to 1334

This Pope had been born in the priest's hometown of Cahors. When he was old enough, orphan John was sent to the Catholic orphanage in nearby Riez.

There followed a life of childhood hell. John and the other children were subjected to the most brutal abuse at the hands of the priests that would have sent most people to a mental institution, never to recover. John was made of stern stuff, escaping at the age of fifteen to hide in the wooded hills above the town of Riez. He survived by stealing food from houses in the village and trapping rabbits in the surrounding fields. The pain and resentment he felt towards the Church, and what it had done to him, was relieved in a small way, one dark night. He ambushed the priest in charge of the orphanage as he made his way home from a local tavern. The priest's death came slowly at the hands of the boy. Using a large kitchen knife, he slit the throat just enough so that the man lasted an hour before he died. In that hour John purged his hate on the man, who he was convinced went straight to hell.

On the run from the police, he made his way to the city of Marseille where he decided to get a job on board a ship. On the way to the harbour he passed *69 Corniche du President John F Kennedy*, the French Foreign Legion recruitment office. He walked in, lied about his age and lied that he came from Switzerland. The recruitment officer issued him a new name on the spot, Jean-Paul D'aubigne, and he started a new life. Jean-Paul always told the amusing story about how his surname came from the butchery four doors down from the recruiting office, *Boucherie D'aubigne*.

The intense heat and dust took Jean-Paul's mind back to his first experience of Africa. His introduction to Africa was a posting to the extremely severe topography and brutally hot climate of Chad. 2nd REP was sent to Fort Lamy in Chad in March 1969 as part of the French support for President François Tombalbaye. Tombalbaye was under siege by an insurgency from the Muslim, *Front de Libération Nationale du Tchad* (FROLINAT) that enjoyed support from Libya, the Sudan, and the Soviet Union. Jean-Paul was blooded in battle near the village of Malgalmé when 300 rebels ambushed the convoy he was travelling in. 2nd REP was full of battle-hardened veterans from Vietnam and Algeria and they decimated the rebel attack.

The horrible scar across Jean-Paul's face came from a Soviet SKS bullet. His patrol was ambushed in the mountains of the Tibesti region of northwest Chad. The rebel threat in this area was considerably stronger than further south; here they faced a fierce tribe of Muslim warriors known as the Toubou. In the opening salvo the bullet skidded across Jean-Paul's face, narrowly missing his eye, peeling the skin back, exposing his skull. He was casevaced back to Fort Lamy near N'Djamena. The doctors fixed him up, but a severe infection forced his evacuation back to France where his lengthy recuperation used up the balance of his five-year contract. Not wanting to stay in France or sign up for another contract, the draw of Africa brought Jean-Paul to Rhodesia and the RLI.

When deep in thought, Jean-Paul ran his finger down the scar on his face, tracing the hard crevice left by the SKS bullet. The scar marked him as a soldier, he was proud of it, and strangely enough, it had a positive effect on the ladies.

The horrific ordeal of his childhood made Jean-Paul a deeply compassionate man, very sensitive to the feelings of others. As a result, he understood intimately the pain and anguish felt by Penga at the loss of Colour McIntyre. More importantly, he understood Penga's behaviour and his frustration. For this reason he had appointed himself as Penga's support and protector, this despite the fact that no words were said by either man on the subject.

'Waal Good Day to y'all,' smiled the new man Kratzman.

Nobody answered him. Le Beau and Penga looked up disinterestedly, too hot to bother. The constant stream of new faces had hardened the veterans against newcomers. The emotional energy invested in friendships, when so many men were being killed, was a wasted effort.

Not being put off by the poor reception, Kratzman carried on in the same friendly manner.

'My name is Jim Kratzman from Maces Spring, Scott County, Virginia, in the good ol' US of A.' There was still no response, nobody even looked up at him. Jim gazed up into the branches of the tree as if looking for inspiration.

'Now y'all probably don't know Maces Springs, but it is a quiet little town, just off Route 614, at the foot of Clinch Mountain in the Appalachian chain ... in southwest Virginia. I guess there couldn't be more an' six hundred people in our town, but we are the home of the Carter Family. You must have heard of June Carter, she done run off with Johnny Cash. Caused a right stir I can tell you!'

At this point Penga Marais glanced up at the giant American, Le Beau made like he was asleep.

'Waal we have a good an' hot day today ... hotter than a pepper sprout,' said Kratzman with a laugh, amused by his reference to the song *Jackson* by Johnny Cash and June Carter. His comment was completely lost on the other men.

Still unfazed by the fact that the others were doing their best to ignore him, Kratzman continued, 'Y'all reckon we will get into a few Gooks today?'

'Do you people still ride horses ... you were in the Cavalry?' enquired Penga, '... I used to watch *F Troop* on TV.'

Before Kratzman could compose an answer, Beamish came walking back from the tent accompanied by another man who was dressed only in a pair of shorts.

'The trailer is in the MT[49] yard in the Ranger's compound. This man will show us,' he grunted to no one in particular, walking purposefully back to the trucks.

They all climbed back onto the vehicles and drove around the airstrip to the permanent brick buildings that housed the National Parks Rangers and their scouts. The trailer with the mortar ammunition was identified and hitched on to the rear vehicle. The man from 2RR, who turned out to

---
49 Motor Transport.

be the CQMS, asked whether they wouldn't mind taking down a trailer full of rations as well. Beamish merely grumbled a begrudging consent and the other trailer was hitched on to the lead vehicle. The only thing he asked was whether it had anything in it that could go ... Bang!

Once the trailers were hitched securely the CQMS, a Colour Sergeant, volunteered some advice, 'I don't want to tell you people how to suck eggs, but my advice is drive as fast as you can ... if you get 'bushed don't stop ... there are *maningi*[50] Gooks out there. Also about twenty clicks out, you will see a police Land Rover that hit a tin[51] last week ... be careful because it's partly obstructing the road.'

Beamish looked down from the truck, his mind racing. His total force included two drivers, Le Beau, the new Yank, Penga and himself.

'Does anybody need a lift to Vila Salazar?' asked Beamish, hoping for re-enforcements, trying to hide his concern.

'You have got to be joking ... that place is hell on earth,' replied the CQMS, shaking his head in amusement. 'The mortar platoon are the only people that can handle it ... you'll see.' This last comment seemed to amuse the man even more, he laughed out loud as he turned to resume his afternoon sleep ... *a lift to Vila Salazar ... for fuck sakes!*

In addition to the replacement TR48 HF radio, Beamish had brought his own 'big-means'. He turned it on to call the Ops Room at Buffalo Range to confirm his departure and to make sure it was working. Each vehicle also carried an A63 VHF radio so they could talk to each other.

The vehicles moved out onto the road, back the way they had come, until they reached a T-junction where a broken sign full of bullet holes read, 'Vila Salazar – 32km'. A cardboard sign was propped up next to it with the hand written message ... 'Road to No-Where'. Another handmade sign read, 'Abandon hope all ye that enter here!'[52]

The road to the south was dead straight. Soft red sand forced the 4×4 vehicles into low-range, maximum speed no more than 30km/hr. The terrain was perfectly flat no physical features were visible in any direction. All the men were tense; this place had a fearsome reputation.

Sure enough, at 20km from Vila Salazar Beamish could see the damaged police vehicle in the distance. As the small convoy approached, the drivers changed down to keep up the revs, the rear vehicle, towing the mortar trailer closed up the following distance. As the driver in the front vehicle reached the obstruction, he engaged first gear, revving the engine hard to keep forward momentum. They would have to drive their vehicles around the destroyed Land Rover that was missing most of its front end.

Suddenly, the outside of the truck sounded as if it was being pelted by hailstones. The crack and thump over the top of the open vehicle told a different story.

---

50 Chilapalapa, plenty, a great many.
51 Rhodesian slang, landmine, most likely a TM46 Soviet anti-tank mine.
52 The supposed inscription at the entrance to Hell, from Dante's *Divine Comedy*, 1321.

'Ambush right, AMBUSH RIGHT' screamed Beamish. 'Keep Driving ... Keep Driving,' he yelled at the driver.

Kratzman clicked off his seatbelt, and in one fluid motion, cocked the MAG and brought it up over the edge of the vehicle. With his finger on the trigger, 7.62mm rounds clattering in reply, the belt jumping in the breach of the MAG. Spent shell casings bouncing on the floor of the vehicle. Beamish dropped the metal flap of one of the rifle slits, thrust his rifle through, clipped the FN onto automatic, and put his finger on the trigger. The noise inside the vehicle was deafening as the weapons emptied. Kratzman's first 100-round belt finished, he dropped back down to fit a new belt, then up again, spraying bullets into the bush.

'DRIVE!' Beamish yelled at the driver, bullets still pelted the vehicle which was struggling to gather speed in the thick sand, the heavy trailer full of rations acting like a drag-anchor.

Beamish grabbed for the A63, 'Contact ... Contact ... Contact,' he called into the handpiece, 'This is 31Charlie ... Contact.'

A response was almost instant.

'31Charlie this is 74, reading you fives, confirm your loc ... Over,' a very calm voice replied. 74 was the call-sign for 2RR Mortar Platoon at Vila Salazar.

'Roger 74 we are twelve clicks north of your loc, over.'

'31Charlie, drive through the ambush, confirm, drive through the ambush ... Over.'

'We ARE driving through the fooking ambush,' Beamish howled into the radio. Clearly, no form of assistance was going to be forthcoming.

In the rear vehicle, carrying Penga and Le Beau, the driver saw Beamish's vehicle taking incoming fire. An RPG-7 round screeched past, disappearing into the bush to explode against a tree. The man panicked and stalled the vehicle. Penga saw the danger, grabbed the man by the shirt and hauled him out of the driver's seat. He then engaged the clutch and pressed the start button. The engine fired immediately.

'Le Beau I am going to chase these Gooks,' he shouted. He then flattened the accelerator, the truck leapt forward; Penga fought the vehicle out of the sandy ruts and into the bush on the right. The trees were largely scrub acacia, the ground virtually devoid of grass cover; this was the height of the dry season. The vehicle bashed through the trees, Le Beau lifted his MAG onto the roof of the cab, cocked the weapon waiting for a target.

They did not have to wait long. The CTs, comfortable with attacking policemen and TF units, were chasing after Beamish's vehicle, the RPG man fitting another projectile. They did not expect to see another Four-Five coming out of the bush at them.

Penga's vehicle bounced over a tree that had been pushed over by elephants, and there in front of him was a band of six CTs. They turned in horror to see the growling vehicle revving in the red line. Le Beau let go with the MAG, a hail of bullets and red tracer kicked up dust at the feet of the men who took off into the bush.

A man fell with two rounds in the back; Penga drove straight over the top of him.

Looking to his left, Penga could see Beamish's vehicle still on the road, muzzle flashes blinked as Kratzman played the MAG rounds left and right into the bush. Penga chose another CT to chase, the man sprinting out in front of the vehicle, Le Beau walking MAG rounds in behind him until he too fell into the dust. The other men disappeared into the bush; it was impossible to follow any further.

Penga turned the vehicle back onto the road behind Beamish and the small convoy carried on to Vila Salazar as fast as they could. This was clearly 'Injun Territory' as Kratzman called it. Le Beau spoke to Beamish on the radio to confirm that they were uninjured.

As they approached the isolated outpost, scorched craters appeared on either side of the road. The first thing they saw in the distance was a tall radio mast and a water tower on a steel scaffold. They then passed through a fenced-in corridor of high barbed wire. A large sign, covered in bullet holes read, 'BSAP Vila Salazar'. They drove through the gateway enclosed with thick rolls of barbed wire. A double fence flanked the road with signs every ten metres that read, 'Danger Minefield'. Some wit had created his own sign, 'Kilroy was Here!' copying the famous World War II graffiti artist. Another gate barred the way; this one read, 'No Through Road – Customs Ahead'. As they approached, the gate swung open and the convoy drove through the protected perimeter.

The driver of Beamish's truck, unsure of where to park, drove into the middle of the compound and stopped. Before he could turn off the engine the vehicle was surrounded by tanned bodies, clad only in metal helmets with green army issue shorts or underpants. There was no hello or welcome of any kind just … 'have you brought mail?' and 'have you brought beers?'

A tall radio mast dominated the centre of the compound. Giant, conical speakers were attached to the mast about halfway up. The courtyard was surrounded on three sides by buildings and outhouses that were protected by sandbags. The buildings were all covered in bullet holes; one building had collapsed from a 'direct hit'. A network of slit trenches had been dug between the buildings, with underground bunkers at intervals, covered with reinforced concrete roofs and sandbags. A swimming pool, with crystal-clear water, sat shimmering in front of an old colonial-style farmhouse with wrap around verandas. A soldier, stark naked except for the helmet covering his face, lay on a towel next to the pool. The arrival of the trucks did not disturb him in the slightest. A group of soldiers were playing volleyball on the small lawn in front of the farmhouse. It was lush and neatly trimmed. Two flagpoles stood in front of the house; one flew the Rhodesian flag, the other, light blue background, emblazoned with a red skull above a cross of two mortar bombs, the words '2RR Mortar Platoon' in large black embroidered letters across the bottom.

Without any instruction, the 2RR men began unloading the trailers, the contents disappearing rapidly into the underground shelters.

'Hot dog, now this is some firebase!' exclaimed Kratzman. Still nobody paid any attention to him.

Out in front of the pool, in the direction of Mozambique, were six deep mortar pits, each contained a 81mm mortar. Another two mortar pits were situated to the east and west of the compound.

The RLI men climbed out of their vehicles. Nobody approached them or showed any interest in them at all ... nobody enquired about their 'contact'. Beamish self-consciously led his men across to the old farmhouse, or whatever it was, and climbed the steps onto the veranda.

'Nice vegetable patch!' commented Kratzman pointing at the neat rows of vegetables in a cultivated area next to the swimming pool. The 'vegetables' were not all for eating. 'Y'all got a nice crop of 'grass' growin,' he said to no one in particular.

'So, here we have the steely-eyed-killers-from-the-sky?' a man was heard to say. Thick curtains covered the doors and windows so it was impossible to see inside. On the eastern-facing veranda, a bar had been set up; stools, fridge and liquor cabinet.

'Do you *ouens* want a *jimboolie, Ek sê*,' laughed someone from inside the house, mimicking the RLI slang. Still nobody was visible.

'*Yebo* that would be *mushe*,' Penga answered for everyone. He looked attentively at the 2RR men playing volleyball to see if he recognised any from the fight at Triangle Country Club.

A thin man with pointed features, wearing what appeared to be the standard Vila Salazar uniform of helmet and shorts, pushed open the curtain across the front door.

He offered no introduction, 'So, you *ouens* got 'bushed by terrs on the way in?' It was a rhetorical question. '... You were lucky that you didn't hit a tin, they normally lay a tin for the resupply trucks ... they probably didn't expect you so soon.'

He opened the fridge and handed an ice-cold Castle beer to each of the RLI men.

'You don't have a *Shumba*,' asked Penga, he preferred Lion Lager.

The thin man ignored him.

'Just as well you *ouens* arrived with the beer, or I wouldn't be so generous,' he laughed, opening one for himself, lifting it to his lips and sucking half of it out in one gulp. '*Mushe sterek*[53]' he burped. The way the thin man said '*ouens*' left no doubt that he was having a go at the boys from the RLI.

Another man, of indeterminate age, came out through the curtain, sporting sandals and a khaki slouch hat with a Leopard skin band and a small beer paunch. He looked at the RLI men disinterestedly.

'So you people got revved by the 'Pora Gang' on the way in?' he stated, also a rhetorical question.

Beamish, taking his role as leader seriously, asked 'So who are the Pora Gang?' sucking on his beer.

---

53 Rhodesian slang, the word 'mush' was used to describe anything good or nice. *Sterek* was derived from seShona meaning 'great'.

'Just some FRELIMO gooks who use us for training their people on ambushes and platoon and section battle drills … they come across from time to time. They have cut a hole through the *Cordon Sanitaire* that the Engineers just can't find. Clever bastards!'

'Well there are at least two less than there were yesterday,' Penga chimed in.

Ignoring Penga's comment, the man with the slouch hat spoke to the man behind the bar, 'The Boeing has gone over Frik … give me a beer man … its time.'[54]

'Sure Sarge,' the thin man Frik replied, having already finished his first beer and opening another. 'Where's the Boss?'

'Ag, he's just checking out the radio scheds and finishing the sitrep,' replied the Sarge with the slouch hat.

The RLI men, taken aback by the extreme informality, just stood and watched, not even Penga could think of anything to say.

The speakers on the mast overhead burst into life. Cliff Richard boomed out across the swimming pool, volleyball court and out into Mozambique, less than a thousand metres away.

> *We're all going on a summer holiday*
> *no more working for a week or two.*

On cue, the men in the courtyard stopped what they were doing and joined in with the song. Some were saluting the 2RR mortar platoon flag.

> *Fun and laughter on our summer holiday,*
> *no more worries for me or you,*
> *for a week or two.*

Now all the 2RR men were in full voice.

> *We're going where the sun shines brightly*
> *we're going where the sea is blue.*
> *we've all seen it on the movies,*
> *now let's see if it's true.*

The chorus was repeated enthusiastically, some men dancing a little jig on the spot. Rifle shots broke out in the direction of Mozambique, adding to the cacophony. In one of the mortar pits, someone dropped a bomb down a tube. THUD … the missile flew up and out into the neighbouring country. The impact of its explosion was clearly audible above the joyful Cliff Richard.

---

54 Rhodesian slang, the Boeing referred to scheduled airline flights that flew over at exactly the same time every day. The afternoon flight clearly signalled time for a beer.

> *Everybody has a summer holiday*
> *doin' things they always wanted to*
> *So we're going on a summer holiday,*
> *to make our dreams come true*
> *for me and you.*
> *for me and you[55].*

The song finished with the scratching of the record player over the speakers. There was a momentary period of reflection, then the 2RR men went back to what they were doing, swimming, volleyball and sunbathing.

'Welcome to Vila Salazar gentlemen,' a third man had pushed through the curtain.

He was the only man they had seen thus far who had a shirt on, a torn green T-shirt with a skull and skeletal arms holding a frothing beer tankard screen-printed on the front, the words 'Cheers Gook!' printed underneath. The other part of the dress code, the metal helmet, was present, on top of a large head. Thick curly, greasy, black hair stuck out from under the helmet that merged with an equally black beard. The beard seemed to cover the whole face except for the forehead, nose, lips and eye sockets. Eyebrows joined in a thick forest above a large bulbous nose. Deep green eyes peaked out through the hair. The beard and moustache were so dense that it was impossible to see the man's lips moving when he spoke.

'Captain John, these are the glory boys from the RLI come to pay us a visit,' stated the Sarge with the slouch hat.

'Good eveningg, Surr, Corporal Beamish, Sur, eleven troop, three commando, RLI ... Surr!' Beamish formally paid his respects in typical Royal Regiment of Fusiliers fashion. Beamish made a point of being careful around officers he did not know ... *they can't be trusted.*

'That is more 'Sirs' than I have heard in a month Beamish, my good man,' said the Captain. The only sign that he may have been smiling was the glint in his eyes. 'No need Beamish, please call me John, that's my first name ... only first name basis needed here in 2RR Mortar Platoon from the teeming metropolis of Bulawayo.'

The RLI men looked at each other in shock, they had heard of the informality in the territorial outfits but this was truly amazing. Their lives in the RLI were so regimented by comparison; harsh discipline was rigidly enforced, while their officers were generally distant and aloof.

'I will show you around before it gets dark,' said Captain John in his friendly fashion, indicating for them to follow him.

He led them across the courtyard past the pool, which was now crowded with men playing a violent game of waterpolo. Boisterous beer-drinking spectators urged on the participants.

'You boys enjoy our song?' the Captain commented as they walked past. '... That is our platoon anthem and we play it everyday at five pm for our

---

55 Sung by Cliff Richard, © EMI Music Publishing, lyrics by Bruce, Bennett and Welsh.

friends across the border. It usually pisses them off. They try and shoot the speakers but they can't … we drop a bomb on them when they try … that normally shuts them up.'

John the Captain rambled on, 'We are three weeks into our six-week summer holiday … beautiful weather we are having … hot one day … fucking hot the next!'

As if in his own world, Captain John sang a few lines to Terry Jacks' *Seasons in the Sun*.

> *We had joy, we had fun, slotting[56] floppies in the sun.*
> *But the hills that we climbed*
> *for no reason out of time.*

The visitors were led down a set of wooden railway-sleeper steps into the main control bunker. A string of red Christmas tree lights lit the room while a bank of radios and other equipment lined one wall. Red, green and orange lights from the equipment blinked brightly. A black and white television screen sat in the middle of the bank of radios. The screen showed a few people walking about, some distance away. A single operator sat on a swivel secretarial chair. As the visitors entered, he swung the chair around to face them. He was clad in what looked like a caftan made out of Rhodesian camouflage material, with strings of beads around his neck and a colourful bandana wrapped around his head, holding back long, thick curly hair.

A Supersonic record player sat on the desk next to a small collection of LP records, their covers showing signs of wear. Cat Stevens' *The Wind* was playing softly in the background. The soiled album cover of *Teaser and the Firecat* was propped up against the side of the TV screen.

> *… I listen to my words but they fall far below*
> *I let my music take me where my heart wants to go*
> *I swam upon the Devil's lake...*
> *But never, never, never, never*
> *I'll never make the same mistake*
> *No - never, never, never …*[57]

The man was the splitting image of John Lennon as he appeared in the David Frost interview in 1969, long hair, beard and round glasses[58]. Beamish was shocked to see he was wearing sandals. Poor light and a thick smoky haze made it difficult to pick up detail. Judging by the distinctive smell and the vacant state of his eyes, the man hadn't been smoking Kingsgate[59].

---

56 Rhodesian slang, to shoot or to kill by shooting.
57 *The Wind* as written by Lenny Wolf, Danny Stag, Martin Wolff, John Burt Frank, Lyrics © Universal Music Publishing.
58 See YouTube video.
59 One of very few brands of cigarette in the country, made by British American Tobacco.

'Afonso, meet our brothers from the RLI,' said Captain John enthusiastically.

'Whoa! Big John ... always a pleasure to meet the Saints[60] ... Outta sight!' Alfonso spoke in the same smooth tones as Donald Sutherland in the movie *Kelly's Heroes*, helped by the fact that his brain was mostly pea soup.

'Show our visitors your kit Afonso,' said Captain John, pointing expansively at the bank of radios.

'Coool Big John ... just dig my TV set man!'

The operator Afonso seemed to move in slow motion, in time with his speech. He began a demonstration of the camera that was mounted on the top of the mast outside, each aspect of the explanation punctuated with 'Groovy', 'Coool' or 'Man' or 'do you dig it?' The camera had a telephoto lens that could zoom into the various buildings across the border. Afonso, leaning back in the chair, smoothly panned the camera across the town on the other side of the border.

'What you are looking at is Malvernia man, the railway siding, a church, a few shops, houses ... Coool!' Afonso gave a slow running commentary of what the camera was picking up. The picture was in black and white but crystal clear.

'Afonso, show these people how you talk to our neighbours,' instructed the Captain excitedly.

Afonso pressed the transmit button on the radio mic, and out burst rich Portuguese tones, '*Olá amigos da bela Moçambique, desejamos-lhe paz e prosperidade, das pessoas cool de 2RR.*'[61]

Afonso sat back and smiled at his handiwork. He zoomed in the camera on the main street, a man could clearly be seen raising two fingers in the direction of the Rhodesian border.

'Check out the negative vibe man! Peace to you too brother,' said Afonso holding up two fingers to the man on the television screen, 'Mellow out man!'

'Are these bunkers strong enough Su ... John?' enquired Beamish asking the question on the lips of all of his men.

'Absolutely Beamish,' Captain John replied, '... our friends have not mastered the use of eighty-two millimetre mortars and Katyusha rockets. In all the time we have been here, we have only had one direct hit. All the rest have flown well over, sometimes five kilometres behind us.'

'What damage did that do ... John?' asked Penga, enjoying the novelty of calling an officer by his first name.

'Oh ... the bunker collapsed but fortunately nobody was inside at the time.'

---

60   The RLI were called the Saints, it was a nickname that arose out of the Regimental March, *When the Saints go marching in* ... that had been adopted by the men soon after the Regiment was formed in 1960. A bagpiper, L.Cpl. 'Mac' Martin, had played the tune on his pipes during early route marches. New words were added to the tune in later years.
61   'Hello friends from beautiful Mozambique, we wish you peace and prosperity, from the cool people of 2RR.'

Captain John paused in contemplation, his hand in his beard where his chin must have been, ' ... could have hit a weak spot,' he said quietly. Then continuing in the same enthusiastic vain, ' ... anyway ... we look for their mortars and rockets all the time so when they position them ... we drop our bombs neatly on top. That means they have a fair amount of ... staff turnover ... so to speak.'

The RLI men looked at each other, completely unconvinced.

'... Come on lads I will show you your accommodation for tonight ... you will have the honeymoon suite.'

Captain John threw his head back and laughed on the top of his voice, a manic sort of laugh. Alfonso joined in, laughing loudly, shaking his head and holding his arms across his chest.

'Coool Big John ... let the Saints have the honeymoon suite.' Afonso had tears running down his cheeks, his body shaking with laughter.

The lads from 11 Troop looked on, uncertain of the joke, sceptical of Captain John's explanation, convinced they had entered some strange new world populated by aliens.

Someone started banging vigorously on a strung-up piece of railway line with an iron bar.

'Great! ... *Skaaf*[62] time lads,' exclaimed Captain John excitedly.

---

62 Chilapalapa, food.

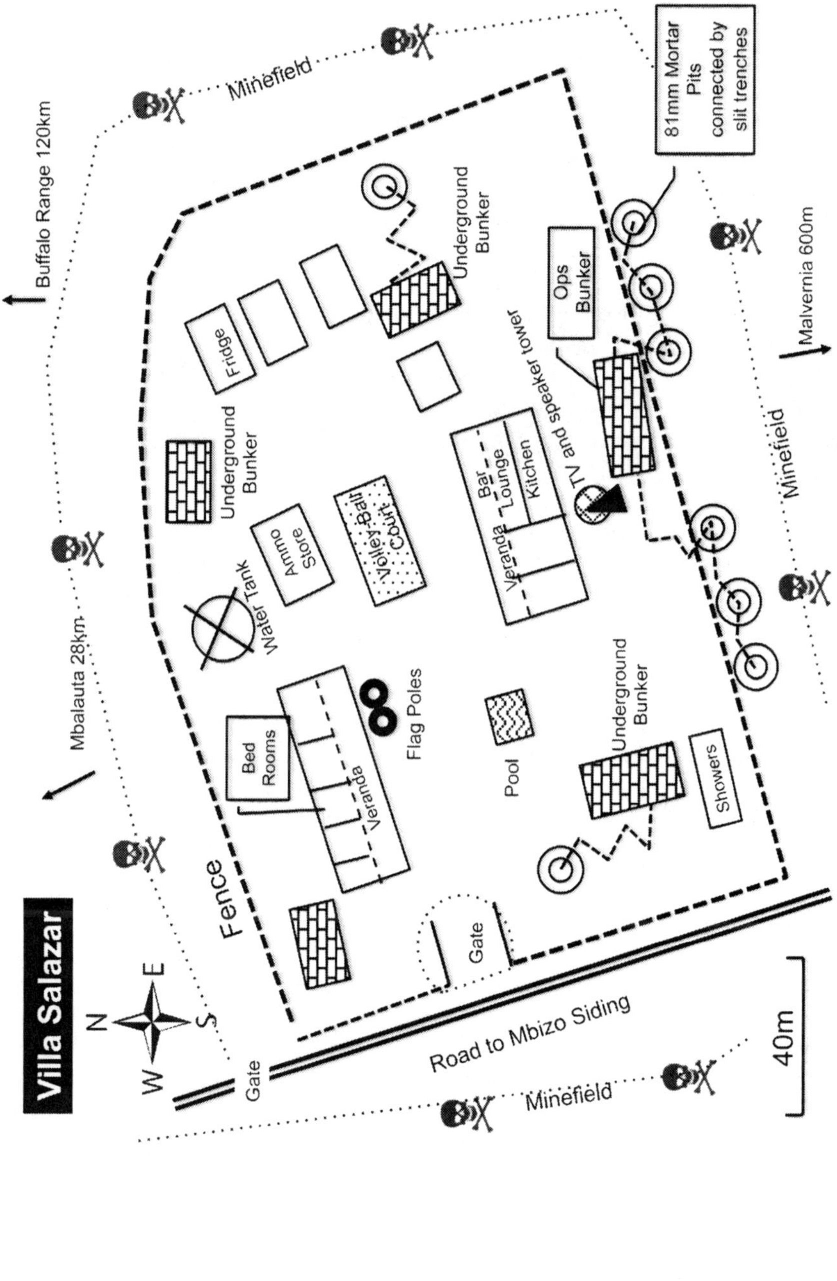
Villa Salazar
N
E
S
W
Buffalo Range 120km
Mbalauta 28km
Malvernia 600m
Minefield
Minefield
Minefield
81mm Mortar Pits connected by slit trenches
Fence
Gate
Gate
Road to Mbizo Siding
40m
Underground Bunker
Underground Bunker
Underground Bunker
Fridge
Ops Bunker
TV and speaker tower
Bar
Lounge
Kitchen
Veranda
Volley Ball Court
Ammo Store
Water Tank
Flag Poles
Bed Rooms
Veranda
Pool
Showers

*

São Jorge do Limpopo, southwest Mozambique

As the dinner gong was calling the men at Vila Salazar to their evening meal, so 84km to the southeast, another meal started. A woman, dressed in khaki combat fatigues placed a large pot of *sadza*, cooked maize meal, on the table together with another pot of stewed chicken, mixed with chunks of tinned vegetables. A next-door room was piled high with bags of ground maize meal marked, 'UNHCR - Not for Resale'. Boxes of tinned food were marked, 'Donated by the World Council of Churches'. In attendance at dinner were, Comrades Felix Mhanda and Peter Hamadziripi (ZANLA), together with Comrade Captain Zhang Youxia (PLA) and Comrade Edward Sibanda (ZANLA - saboteur).

ZANLA had taken over an abandoned colonial farmhouse on the southern outskirts of the village of São Jorge do Limpopo. This was the HQ for the ZANLA Gaza Operational Area. São Jorge do Limpopo was originally built as a railway siding on the line between Rhodesia and Maputo. It now serviced a fledgling agricultural extension scheme, heavily impacted by the war to the north and the constant attacks on the railway line by Rhodesian Selous Scouts.

'Comrade Sibanda, how do you feel about your pending mission?' enquired Hamadziripi in English.

'I am confident Comrade Hamadziripi,' replied Sibanda. He was in his mid-twenties, a short wiry man, already a veteran of the struggle with two long-term deployments into Rhodesia under his belt. He had been selected for this mission because of his special training but also because he came from the small village of Mkwaseni to the east of Chiredzi. He knew the area and his target very well. Sibanda's father still worked on Hippo Valley Estates, the massive fruit and vegetable irrigation project just south of Chiredzi. Sibanda had himself worked on this estate before he had been recruited to the struggle and exfiltrated to Mozambique.

The Rhodesian Lowveld was the heart of the confluence of six major rivers all flowing south. The Nuanetsi, drained into the Limpopo; the Lundi, Tokwe, Mtilikwe and Chiredzi, drained into the Sabi River, then on to the Indian Ocean under the name 'Save' in Mozambique. An extensive irrigated agricultural project had been developed using the water generated by these rivers, supporting sugar, fresh fruit and vegetables, canned fruit and forestry industries. The heart of this project was the target designated by Group Chitepo, the code name for Sibanda's mission.

'Do you believe that we are properly prepared for this mission Comrade Zhang?' asked Mhanda as he dipped a ball of *sadza* into the pot of chicken with his left hand.

'Our agents have infiltrated the target, Comrade. They have sent us radio messages to confirm they are ready. Comrade Sibanda will need to co-ordinate his attack with them when he gets into position. There should be no problem, these men are well trained and are our most experienced,' stated Youxia; cutting a piece of chicken, preferring to eat with chop-sticks he carried with him.

'We leave tonight Comrade Mhanda,' said Sibanda, 'we are being driven by truck to the border, our Frelimo brothers have cut a path through the minefield, once we are through it is no more than three days walk to our transit camp near Mbizi Siding. From there, our agents will pick us up to take us to the target.'

'God speed Comrade Sibanda,' said Hamadziripi piously. Sibanda's father was a lay preacher in the Church of England ... he nodded his head in appreciation.

The men finished the meal in quiet contemplation. A few whispered words of reassurance and support were given before the men left the room. An aged Izuzu tip truck was parked on the street; this was Sibanda's transport for the two hour drive north to the border.

As the trucks disappeared into the distance, the two friends watched from the veranda.

'Do you think we can trust the Chinese, Comrade?' asked Mhanda.

'We can trust them as long as the struggle continues,' replied Hamadziripi. 'Once victory is secured they will, however, seek reparations in mines and land. While they speak of supporting the struggle for ideological reasons, it is really our natural resources they are after. For them we are just another opportunity to project their influence and to get their hands on resources they don't have.'

'If we kill Tongogara, who will resist them? Mugabe and the others are weak,' said Mhanda.

'Ah yes, but we are strong my brother. The people will triumph, we will ensure the people keep the riches of their country. That is why we must prevail,' stated Hamadziripi, his face reflecting the power of his conviction.

*

Rua 3 de Fevereiro, central Chimoio north Mozambique

Comrade Godfrey Nyathi, Detachment Commander-in-Charge of General Josiah Tongogara's bodyguard, stood on the veranda of his leader's house. The house was of the Portuguese colonial style, in Rua 3 de Fevereiro in central Chimoio, just across the road from the *Escola Secundaria de Vila Pery* (Vila Pery Secondary School). It was early evening, he had lit himself a cigarette to relax.

Nyathi, in his later twenties, was not as tall as his General, maybe three inches shorter at 5ft 9', with the thin wiry build of a long-distance runner. He was a man with enormous natural strength and agility who seemed always to be able to move in absolute silence. He had the knack of appearing, almost by magic, without anyone being aware of his presence. He had long wiry hair that curled out from underneath his combat cap that he wore almost every minute of the day. His eyes were a rich brown, bright and alert, giving his face an openness that left the impression of animated interest in his surroundings. This was indeed true; Nyathi took a deep awareness of his surroundings, constantly attentive to things going on around him. He was a man of few words, who spent most of his time listening. When he did speak, he was direct and insightful, always delivering his thoughts in a soft but commanding voice. His orders to his men were issued in a clipped, precise fashion, leaving no doubt that they should be followed to the letter. Punishment for making mistakes or improper conduct was quick and brutal.

Universally feared by his men and by the whole ZANLA leadership, Godfrey Nyathi was the instrument of his General's wrath. He had earned his position through loyalty and dedication and most importantly, through disposing of the General's enemies. When the group of rebel ZANLA army officers led by Thomas Nhari took over the Chifombo training camp in Zambia in 1974, Nyathi had been part of the force of 300 men brought in from the Mgagao in Tanzania, mustered by Tongogara to take back the camp. His leader noted Nyathi's bravery and ruthlessness in that violent action. Tongogara had asked him to execute the leaders of the Nhari Rebellion, as he was unhappy with their lenient treatment after the military trials. Nyathi did so without question. Since that time, Nyathi had been ordered by his General to assassinate other potential rivals and people suspected of treachery. He followed his orders quietly and efficiently without any fuss or bother. In this sense, he was a born soldier, the sort of very special soldier that took on the most difficult and dangerous of tasks. Protecting General Tongogara was such a task.

Working for the General was stressful and demanding. Since the Rhodesians had all but wiped out the ZANLA base at Chimoio, most of the senior leadership had taken houses in the town of Chimoio itself. The Mozambicans were not massively enthusiastic about this, as they felt it was only a matter of time before the Rhodesians discovered where the ZANLA leaders were living and put in a strike. Many innocent people could be killed. Still, for the time being, Comrade Nyathi was making the most of the comfortable accommodation and the benefits of living in town.

The bodyguard detachment included forty men who travelled with the General, day and night, rain or shine. The detachment worked in four six-hour shifts if they were not on the move, ten men on every shift. The General had two men outside his bedroom all night and the balance of the men patrolled the grounds and the street outside. All of Nyathi's men were handpicked and Chinese trained, except for Nyathi himself; his training had been performed by others.

Nyathi was part of an elite group of recruits sent to the Soviet Union for training. The story was that Nyathi had been recruited fresh out of school by ZANLA. He had been identified for his deep and abiding hatred of the white 'Invaders' of his country. Born and brought up in a village in Selukwe Tribal Trust Land, east of the town of Selukwe in the Midlands, he was educated at the local St Francis Catholic Mission School. He had escaped from the country at his first opportunity.

In the Soviet Union, he had been taught guerrilla warfare at the liberation movement training camp set up by the Soviets in Perevalnoye in the Crimea, near the city of Simferopol. This camp was also used for training freedom fighters from Angola, *Umkomto-we-Sizwe* from South Africa and SWAPO from South West Africa. In Perevalnoye, Nyathi was trained by World War II Crimean guerrillas, who had operated in the mountains, forest and bush, in terrain not very different from Southern Africa. The military training course covered many subjects including communications, insurgency, surveillance, secret writing, secret meetings, photography, military management, ambush, attack and small arms. His Soviet instructors had identified Nyathi as a man with great potential, not so much as a leader, but instead as a special-forces soldier.

Godfrey Nyathi's family was descended from the great Karanga chief Changamire Dombo[63], *Mwenemutapathe*[64], the leader who united the many Shona clans into the Rozwi Empire, centred at Great Zimbabwe[65]. Changamire had destroyed the Portuguese attempt to annex the great gold mines of the central plateau, and chased them from the country. Rozwi supremacy was established over all of Rhodesia including parts of Malawi. The area around Great Zimbabwe became the trading capital of the wealthiest and most powerful society in south-eastern Africa.

General Tongogara was a traditionalist who understood the importance of tribal and clan allegiance. It was for this reason, he selected a bodyguard from his own Karanga clan, with the same totem. People of the same clan use a common set of totems. Totems are usually animals and body parts. Both Tongogara and Nyathi were Karanga from the central districts of Rhodesia, descended from the Moyo or 'heart' totem. People of the same totem are the descendants of one common ancestor, the founder of that totem. This identification by totem has very important ramifications at traditional ceremonies such as the burial ceremony. In Shona tradition, a person with a different totem cannot perform the ritual functions required to initiate burial of the deceased. Tongogara was very preoccupied with his own death and, therefore, having a member of his own clan and totem with him at all times gave him much comfort. This clan and totem connection was the most important reason for Nyathi being selected by Tongogara as the leader of his bodyguard.

Although he had not said so in as many words, Nyathi believed that Tongogara was deeply concerned about the loyalty of his 2IC Rex Nhongo, and his political opposite number, Robert Mugabe. The main reason for his suspicion stemmed from clan history and loyalties. The Shona people are a fragmented horde of tribes with very tenuous bonds of unity between them. Most Shona people identify with a particular clan rather than with the Shona group as a whole. The Shona clans also have language differences, the

---

63   Ruled from 1660 to 1695.
64   seShona, Lord of the Conquered Land
65   Great Zimbabwe refers to the rock-built acropolis that was at the centre of the Munhumatapa and subsequent Rozwi Kingdoms.

Korekore, Zezuru, Manyika, Ndau, and Karanga.

Both Mugabe and Nhongo belonged to the Zezuru clan from the region north of Salisbury. The crocodile, in the Zezuru dialect, *Garwe*, is the clan totem of Mugabe's Zezuru clan that adopted the old Munhumatapa Kingdom name of 'master pillager'. In Tongogara's mind, the Zezuru could not be trusted with leadership. He was determined that the future leaders of Zimbabwe would be Karanga. Nyathi was convinced Tongogara believed that the spirit of the 'master pillager' lived on in Mugabe.

One of the tools that Godfrey Nyathi needed most of all was an HF radio. The ZANLA forces had very few HF radios. Those they did have had been provided by the Chinese. Each training camp and each Provincial Commander had access to one. The General's staff had two HF radios; one was kept in the radio room in his house while the other was in the back of one of the white Toyota Landcruisers that he and his bodyguard used to travel around Mozambique. Nyathi only had two trained signallers and himself to operate the radios; the General was not interested in learning how they worked. All the instructions and labelling on the radios was in Chinese which made it doubly difficult to learn how to use them. The radios were notoriously unreliable, most were unserviceable at any given time, but Nyathi made it his business to ensure that the radio in the Landcruiser was always working.

The General and his bodyguard had the use of two armoured personnel carriers, BTR-152s, both mounting DShKM 12.7mm anti-aircraft machineguns and a fleet of four Toyota Landcruiser FJ55s. The General loved driving and took the opportunity to drive one of the Landcruisers at every opportunity. They had the uprated 4.2L 2F straight-six petrol engine that had plenty of power but were downright dangerous in the wrong hands. Nyathi was terrified of his General's driving, which was always way too fast on the poor dirt roads of Mozambique. As the BTRs were slow by comparison to the Landcruisers, Nyathi always had to send them on ahead. The Landcruisers, despite their relative comfort, were impractical because they had petrol engines and ridiculously high fuel consumption. Nyathi was constantly on the hunt for supplies of petrol, which were hopelessly erratic with the Rhodesians blowing up all the roads and bridges.

Finishing his cigarette, Nyathi walked down the steps onto the dirt driveway. His AKM was strapped over his shoulder and he always wore his full combat webbing. He took his job very seriously. The Landcruisers were parked in a neat row in front of the house, while the two BTRs were parked back to back in the street with both 12.7s manned at all times.

'I am going to have a look around the suburb,' shouted Nyathi to the men patrolling the perimeter. It was standard procedure to patrol the surrounding streets when the General was in residence, just in case the Rhodesian SAS had the house under surveillance. They could be anywhere, anytime, ready to attack.

'Can you bring back some Coca-Cola?' one asked.

'Sure, give me some money,' replied Nyathi as he opened the door to one of the Landcruisers. He started the engine and drove carefully out into the street, turning left onto Rua 3 de Fevereiro.

The eastern skyline of Chimoio is dominated by a giant granite massif called *Cabe a do Velho*. Nyathi drove towards the massif that loomed up in the darkness, reflecting the moonlight off its sheer, smooth face. He pulled off the road and parked under a large tree, well away from the nearest houses. He opened the door, walked around to the back of the vehicle and opened the doors. The radio was mounted against the left side next to the wheel-well. He picked up the handpiece, at the same time setting the manual tuning-knob to a frequency that he had memorised.

He spoke softly into the handpiece in seShona, *'Chiremba ... Chiremba, Zizi*[66] *... Ngombe dzenyu dzinopa mukaka?* Doctor ... Doctor this is Owl, Do your cows give milk?'

'Ehe, Yes,' came the instant answer.

'Mine are not giving milk, I may have to sell them.'

Comrade Godfrey Nyathi, codenamed 'Owl', then sent a short message in code, including map references and times.

---

66   seShona, Owl.

6

East India Club, London, England

The East India Club at 16 St. James's Square, Westminster, is an impressive three-story building built in the best tradition of Georgian architecture. It was built as a convenience for the 'servants of the East India Company' that included administrative, military and naval personnel. Membership is strictly by invitation with a substantial overseas membership as befitting its history. The Smoking Room is located on the first floor above the Dining Room. On this particular morning, in early autumn, the room was almost empty. Two elderly gentlemen sat reading newspapers near the door, while another sat next to the front windows, looking out onto St James's Square, with the magnificent Chatham House to the left.

'Stanbridge, my good fellow!' called a well-dressed man entering the room. The two old gentlemen at the door ignored the new arrival, deeply engrossed in the news of the day.

George Stanbridge, Deputy Director, Rhodesian CIO, stood up to shake hands.

'Jeremy, so good to see you ... my, my, you are looking well, the Foreign Office clearly agrees with you,' replied Stanbridge with a beaming smile.

Jeremy Hughes-Hall, who was tall with sharp chiselled features, bordered on being too thin, testimony to a stressful job with very long hours. His face was slightly flushed after the short, but brisk walk across from the Foreign Office in Whitehall.

'Why, thank you George, always good to see friends from the Colonies,' replied Hughes-Hall with a wink, quite prepared to have a dig at his Rhodesian colleagues for their illegal Unilateral Declaration of Independence, UDI.

'Looks like we have a good team this year,' Stanbridge commented as the two men sat down. He was referring to the 1st Rugby Team at the Tonbridge School in Kent that the two men had attended. It being Friday both men sported their Tonbridge Old Boy's tie.

'Yes I like the look of that boy Reynolds on the flank, shows great promise ... knew his father you know ... from The Rifles,' said Hughes-Hall, casting his eye around the room.

While Jeremy Hughes-Hall had served as a Captain in the 2nd Green Jackets, The King's Royal Rifle Corps, his career included a stint in British Intelligence, MI6, more recently seconded to the Africa Desk in the Foreign Office.

'Tea?' Stanbridge enquired ... Hughes-Hall nodded; all that was needed was a gesture to the steward who had silently entered the room, hovering to take an order.

'Well what brings you to London with such alacrity George?' Hughes-Hall was anxious to get down to business; he had to prepare for a meeting with the Foreign Secretary that evening.

'I am afraid we have come across some disturbing intelligence Jeremy. It seems our friends Mugabe and Tongogara have recruited and trained some rather dangerous fellows who appear to be preparing to have a crack at some of our key installations. As you know, we are a bit short on resources and we just cannot protect them all sufficiently.'

'Do you know where these people are?'

'Not exactly but I am convinced that this is the work of Comrade Tongogara and his chums the Chinese,' stated Stanbridge satirically. 'They have satellite images and really detailed schematic diagrams, very professional stuff, the sort of thing your SAS boys are good at.'

Stanbridge paused, studying the face of his school friend, looking for signs of recognition.

Hughes-Hall, an old campaigner, was too professional to give anything away. 'So are you intending to neutralise this threat?' he said, choosing his words carefully.

'It's a bit like finding a needle in a haystack I'm afraid. I have a mind to have another go at Tongogara himself,' ventured Stanbridge, now very keen to gauge the reaction.

'I see,' replied Hughes-Hall, clearly deep in thought, his mind skilfully processing a suitable response. This was dangerous ground. 'Now George you know that the PM and the Foreign Secretary are both Nkomo men even though they hold deep reservations about his true convictions. We are also very concerned about the Soviet influence and support for Nkomo; they clearly have a broader agenda afoot. Then we have Mugabe and his Chinese, it is difficult to choose the lessor of two evils.'

'If the PM is well disposed towards Nkomo, why won't you help us against Mugabe and Tongogara then Jeremy?'

'The problem we see is the Fraser Government in Australia. Fraser is openly promoting Mugabe in the Commonwealth. He has set himself up as some sort of 'Saviour of Africa'. If it wasn't so tragic it could almost be amusing, he doesn't seem to have a problem seeking the support of one-party state dictators. Obasanjo in Nigeria and Nyerere in Tanzania are supporting Fraser's active promotion of Mugabe. With Frazer and the Africa lobby, together with Trudeau in Canada, they are putting enormous pressure on the PM to support Mugabe's claims.'

Stanbridge lent forward earnestly, 'Surely you should be concerned about the Chinese ambitions in the region Jeremy?'

The steward came back into the room carrying a silver tray with a large silver pot of English Breakfast tea, a plate of cucumber sandwiches and two china teacups sporting the club crest. He approached at a steady pace to allow the guests time to cease their confidential conversation. The tray was placed on the table between them and the man disappeared as quietly as he had arrived.

Stanbridge poured the tea. Hughes-Hall waited politely for him to finish, then leant forward to address his friend.

'Of course we are concerned by the Chinese and North Korean influence

– but what can we do about it? Politics exceeds common sense in this case.'

'So what are you telling me? Are you suggesting that you would not support us in a strike against Tongogara?' enquired Stanbridge forthrightly.

'Come on George, don't be naive, while we don't support Mugabe, he is the front-runner at the moment. We see Tongogara as a moderating influence on Mugabe. We are also not too impressed with the alternative ... Rex Nhongo[67].'

'I hear what you say Jeremy, but we have a serious situation here, these saboteurs may already be in the country, we have no way of knowing for sure. If I can strike at the head maybe I can kill the snake.'

'Well George, I will be honest with you, we cannot support an attempt by you on Tongogara's life. We believe that we are going to need him later on, one way or the other. In any event, by killing Tongogara you would just be paving the way for the passage to the leadership of a more militant alternative ... there are some pretty unpleasant fellows in Mugabe's leadership group ... Now if you will excuse me, I must get back.'

The two men got to their feet and shook hands; despite their differences, it was clear that they had a high degree of mutual respect. Hughes-Hall hesitated for a moment.

'By the way George ... I think you should know, we think you have a mole in your COMOPS. We have picked up some strange radio traffic recently ... might have something to do with your present predicament.'

Stanbridge tried his best not to show it, but he felt like he had been hit by a brick. His worst fears had been confirmed.

'Thank you very much Jeremy, I appreciate your thoughts. I will let you know what I can find out.'

'One other thing George, those rugby balls you enquired about are ready to be collected. I hope that they improve your season,' said Hughes-Hall with a smile. Seeing the obvious distress on his friend's face he added, '... come on George buck up ... all is not lost old boy.'

The men parted, Stanbridge sank back into his chair, and the enormity of what he had just been told struck him like a body blow. His stomach turned ... *damn and blast! I knew we had a problem!*

The 'rugby balls', really second hand GQ Dominator parachutes designed for High Altitude Low Opening, HALO, would be well received.

*

New Sarum Air Force Base – Parachute Training School, Salisbury

A small group of six men clustered around a large wooden crate in the middle of a cavernous aircraft hanger. Two parachute instructors, dressed in camouflage uniform but with Air Force berets, were talking earnestly to the men, emphasising the points they were making with their hands. The six men were from the Selous Scouts designated as 'Operation Wedza' after

---

[67] Tongogara's 2IC, Rex Nhongo was his Chimurenga or 'war' name. His real name was Solomon Mujuru.

the farming district where Sergeant Dave Seals came from. Three of the men looked comfortable with the briefing while the other three looked on with big round eyes, their faces covered in sweat. Trooper Kachimanga ex-FRELIMO and Trooper Nyandoro ex-ZANLA, had only six operational static line jumps, with only two night jumps. Sergeant Ngwenya had been on a free-fall course but had never had a night HALO operational jump.

In the previous few days, the three black soldiers had jumped free-fall twice a day with average results. Their ability to 'fly' in close formation in free-fall had been somewhat lacking. Nyandoro pulled the ripcord too early on one occasion, resulting in a twenty-kilometre flight and a long hike back to civilization carrying his parachute.

The three white Selous Scouts were all very experienced HALO jumpers. Kumpher and Seals were national free-fall parachute champions. They had practiced jumping alongside their black colleagues, holding onto them from the time of leaving the aircraft to the opening of the chutes. This had reduced the 'spread' at the landing site and in so doing, built up the confidence within the team.

'Listen up people ...' said the senior parachute instructor, '... you now understand the basics of jumping with this box, now we will have a practice jump so that you can learn how to jump in formation with it.'

The 'box', was a simple pinewood crate that contained extra water and rations for what was to be a potentially very long deployment into Mozambique. The crate had been reinforced with nylon strapping. Three types of parachute were attached to the crate; spring-loaded pilot chutes, then a normal reserve chute would, in turn, drag out the main chute. The box had been invented by the Air Force and the SAS and used extensively by them, but this was the first time that Selous Scouts were to use it. The system for opening was as simple as it was ingenious. Nylon string was sewn through safety fuse that was cut to the correct length for the period of free-fall. At the time of launch the safety fuse was lit with an electric igniter, once the safety fuse burnt through the nylon string the reserve chute was released to burst open. The spring-loaded pilot chutes would then pop open and drag out the main chute. A flashing red strobe light was attached to the top of the box so that it could be seen as it fell and to help find it after landing. All was very straight forward, as the senior instructor had said.

The heavy box was lifted by the men and carried to the waiting Paradak parked on the hardstanding outside the hanger. A group of twenty RLI troopers jogged past the aircraft, part of another static-line jump course. Seals and Kumpher were both ex-RLI, they swore loudly at the young troopers as they passed.

The Dak lifted off into hot morning thermals on its long, laborious climb to the designated altitude. The men sat quietly waiting for the aircraft to reach the jump height. They did not have their rifles and operational kit, just their jumpsuits, helmets and parachutes. Both air force free-fall instructors were suited up with them. Ngwenya sat rigidly in his seat, the other two black soldiers looked like death, their eyes flicking left and right as if looking for a way of escape. This was definitely not their natural element. At 6,000ft, the temperature dropped markedly. At 12,000ft, the instructors attached oxygen masks to each man. The flexible plastic tubes were attached to a line running the length of the aircraft, to the oxygen bottles in a rack next to the cockpit door[68].

Eventually the aircraft reached the correct altitude of 15,000ft, the co-pilot looked back at the Dispatchers who pushed the wooden box into the door. The red light glowed at the door and the Selous Scouts stood up to begin the final equipment check. Seals held Kachimanga. Kumpher held Nyandoro, while Captain Schultz held Ngwenya. Without thinking, Nyandoro removed his oxygen mask ready for the jump. It was only a few minutes before he felt the beginnings of hypoxia, a tingling sensation in his lips and his fingers got pins-and-needles, he felt dizzy and his legs sagged against Kumpher[69]. He then collapsed to the floor almost unconscious. Kumpher ripped off his own mask and placed it over Nyandoro's face, then grabbed a spare one for himself. The other men stood in shocked silence as Nyandoro slowly recovered, sucking in oxygen in huge gulps. A valuable lesson learnt. The Dispatcher signalled for the pilot to go round again as Nyandoro regained his senses.

'Okay, let's go through this again,' called the Dispatcher. 'Stand in the door, take three big breaths of oxygen, then when we shout GO, take a deep breath then jump. Hold your breath as long as possible, you should be able to breathe normally after about ten seconds … You got it now?'

The men all nodded their understanding. Ngwenya played his instructions over in his mind … *take a big gulp of oxygen and hold your breath …*

The green light flashed and the Dispatchers kicked the box out the door, followed by the Selous Scouts. Nyandoro, still groggy, was not in complete control, trying desperately to assume the standard 'frog' position, knees bent at ninety degrees, arms outstretched level with the shoulders. Kumpher held Nyandoro's arm so tightly his fingers felt numb from lack of circulation.

Ngwenya caught sight of the box spinning below him, it seemed to stabilise, with one end lower than the other, then a sudden spin into a new position, stabilise, then spin again, at the same time tracking across the sky. The men tried to follow it, now joined by the two instructors who flew between the falling men, giving hand signals.

Kumpher and Nyandoro flew past beneath Ngwenya, no more than 30ft. The split-second fear of mid-air collision caused Ngwenya to lose concentration. He broke loose from Schultz's grip, tumbling away out of control. Panicked, Ngwenya desperately tried to get back into the stable position, his arms flailing about, his head up, then down, upside down, right way up, spinning left and right. The harder he tried to apply his training, the

---

68 The Rhodesians did not have the HALO jumping equipment which would have included oxygen masks attached to an independent oxygen supply to support the soldier while waiting to exit and on the long way down.
69 Altitude Sickness or hypoxia occurs above 8,000ft. The onset at 15,000ft can be rapid when a person is physically active or stressed.

worse it became. He spun further away from the rest of the group, flicking wildly from his stomach to his back, flashing sky, then the ground racing towards him ... closer with each spin. He fought the urge to scream out in terror ... he felt a strong set of hands clamp onto him, as if to pluck him out of the sky.

An instructor appeared in Ngwenya's face only inches away, resembling an old man with loose skin and flapping jowls. Grabbing at Ngwenya's arms, the man pulled them into the correct position ... as if by magic, Ngwenya stabilised. Still firmly in the grip of the instructor, Ngwenya slowly tracked back towards the others now a good 200ft below. As they passed through 4,000ft, Ngwenya checked his altimeter. Still feeling hopelessly disorientated, his mind had gone completely blank. The instructor, only inches away, held up two fingers to remind him that opening was at 2,500ft.

Seventy-four seconds after leaving the aircraft all six chutes opened, the box flew on to open at 2,000ft. Ngwenya checked his canopy was correctly developed. The feeling of relief was overwhelming. He looked around to see his teammates spread over the sky. Grabbing the control lines, he tracked in above and behind the other men who all seemed to be in control. The ground came up and he braced for the landing ... pulling on the control lines his speed stalled, then gentle and in control, he landed. He didn't even need to roll. Pulling in the parachute lines, Ngwenya looked around the open field for the others, the box was only a hundred metres away. Schultz, Seals and Kumpher were standing next to it, their black colleagues happy to be within two hundred metres of each other, broad smiles on their faces, the look of relief palpable.

When the men had gathered next to the box, Schultz smiled, 'Night-jump with the box and full kit tonight boys ... we go for a visit to sunny Mozambique tomorrow night.'

*

Vila Salazar, south-east border with Mozambique

'*Kanjani Mafuta*, Hello Fat Man,' called out Captain John, OC of 2RR Mortar Platoon.

'*Ndebvu, Manheru Litshone njani*, Mister Beard, good evening,' replied Peter Mnangagwa, civilian chef, Vila Salazar.

'*Mafuta, kangela! Teena shamwari ka'lo RLI. Ena funa lo nyama*[70],' said Captain John in Chilapalapa, introducing his guests from the RLI.

Peter the chef was an enormous smiling man, tall, with arms like bound rope. He wore a crisp white uniform; a starched apron accentuated his protruding stomach. The standard Vila Salazar headdress of steel helmet was clamped on his head. The helmet seemed to be wedged onto Peter's massive head as if two sizes too small. He was standing over a *braai*, made from a forty-four gallon drum cut in half length-ways with holes bashed through

---

70 Fat man, look! We have friends from the RLI. They would like a really good steak.

it to allow the fire to draw. A thick steel mesh sat over the drum, every inch of which was covered in sizzling steak, strings of *boerewors* marked the perimeter.

'This must be a special occasion ... steak for dinner,' announced Captain John, turning to his guests. His bushy mouth was open, which could be assumed must be a smile, '... nothing but the best for the *ouens* from the RLI, *ek se, ek se!*'

Frik and Sarge laughed loudly at Captain John's use of RLI slang. Beamish and his boys smiled back, thinking more about flame-cooked steak than their leg getting pulled.

The braai was set up on the lawn between the swimming pool and the pub on the veranda. The 2RR men had collected in a semi-circle, each with a tin plate and *grazing-irons,* knife and fork. Some had dressed for dinner; a few wore bright floral shirts that would not have been out of place in the TV series *Hawaii Five-O.* Swarms of biting mosquitoes replaced the heat of the day. The 2RR men had collected piles of elephant dung from the national park which now smouldered away gently beneath their camp chairs. Burning elephant dung made an excellent mosquito repellent. The smouldering dung added a sweet aroma to that of fire-roasted meat. The scene looked, for all the world, like the set from the rock opera *Jesus Christ Superstar* ... but with steel helmets and Castle Pilsner. The contrast between the men from the RLI, with their short-cropped hair, camo-cream and webbing and the longhaired, laidback and irreverent 2RR men from Bulawayo, could not have been more striking.

The RLI men were issued with plates and utensils and were given first choice of the steaks. The slightly self-conscious detachment queued in front of Peter who placed a giant steak on each plate; they helped themselves to salad and baked-potato with a spoon full of onion gravy. The 2RR men, all holding beers in their hands, patiently waited their turn, laughing and joking with each other, as if waiting to watch a rugby match. Nobody, other than Captain John, made any attempt to welcome or talk to the RLI men. They were completely ignored. Both Penga and Le Beau scanned the faces of the 2RR men to see if they recognised any of them from the fight at the Triangle Club but it was impossible to tell.

'Alfonso put some music on, I feel like a party tonight with our special guests,' called Captain John to his radioman.

'Cool Big John.'

Alfonso, still dressed in his camo-caftan, scurried down into the control bunker. Sweet's *Fox on the Run* blared out of the overhead speakers. The people of Malvernia would now also be included in the party.

> *I don't wanna know your name*
> *Cause you don't look the same*
> *The way you did before*
> *OK you think you got a pretty face*
> *But the rest of you is out of place*
> *You looked all right before*

Fox on the run
You screamed and everybody comes a-running
Take a run and hide yourself away
Fox on the run
F-foxy, foxy on the run and hideaway ...[71]

The Soviet Katyusha multiple rocket launchers are a type of rocket artillery first built and fielded by the Soviet Union in World War II. The Germans gave them the name 'Stalin Organ' during the battle of Stalingrad after the Soviet leader Josef Stalin. The launch tubes resembled organ pipes and made a distinctive screaming whooshing sound when fired. On this particular barmy night, a Soviet Ural-375D truck mounting a rack of forty BM-21 *Grad*[72] 122mm rockets was parked on the southern approach to Malvernia, not far from the railway line. This truck was part of a diversion to ensure the safe infiltration of a team of highly trained saboteurs into Rhodesia. The rockets were elevated over the unprotected truck-cab in the general direction of Vila Salazar. The inexperienced FRELIMO operator estimated that he was about 5,000m from his target, the minimum effective range, when in actual fact, he was probably closer to 3,000m. He could hear the song *Fox on the Run* quite distinctly in the perfectly still early evening.

The BM-21 has a range of over 20km and is designed as a saturation bombardment weapon, which meant that it was unsuitable for precision or accurate shelling. It is unclear whether the operator had any intention of hitting the Rhodesian base at Vila Salazar, as the full rack would cover an area of about 4 hectares[73].

The operator consulted his watch, deciding he had time for one more cigarette before his attack. He entered into an animated conversation with his assistant in his native Portuguese.

On the other side of the border the 2RR Mortar Platoon and their special guests were finishing the evening meal. Peter Mnangagwa and his kitchen staff collected all the empty plates and carried them back to the kitchen, everyone delighted with the quality of the meal. Peter prided himself on his cooking skills which he had learned at the Lion and Elephant Hotel on the banks of the dry, sandy Bubi River, 130km to the northeast ...

... The sound of the first rocket igniting carried across the bush to Vila Salazar.

---

71 Sweet, RCA Records, written by Andy Scott, Brian Connolly, Steve Priest and Mick Tucker.
72 Hail
73 10 acres.

7

Suburb of Ridgeview, 3km Southwest of the Salisbury City Centre

Faye Chan was excited. She had already made one dead-drop with all the information concerning the infiltration into Mozambique by the Selous Scouts. Now, after her morning spent taking notes in another meeting, she had the date and time for the commencement of the operation, Operation Wedza. The message did not take long to type, a few paragraphs at the speed of ninety words per minute without errors.

The message was completed and placed in a brown envelope. Faye placed the envelope in her sports bag, grabbed the dog-chain hanging behind the back door and went outside. Trudy the Labrador needed no second invitation; the sound of the chain being taken from the door was all she needed. She was around the house and in front of Faye in a second, jumping and squealing her excitement. This was their evening routine, a good walk before dinner.

Faye opened the front gate and turned left down Anson Road, walked a few hundred metres, then left again into Avro Road. She let Trudy off the leash and the dog disappeared into the bush on the opposite side of the road. This was Trudy's element as she dashed left and right, searching for signs of field mice. Finding a hole, she would dig the hard ground excitedly. She had yet to catch one.

To any passer-by, this was a typical evening scene, a young woman walking her dog after a day at the office. Faye walked to the end of Avro Road and then left again into Hurstview Road with Sunrise Sports Club now on her right. Sunrise Club had mostly Asian and Indian members who were excluded from the white-only sports clubs in the city. Faye slowed her pace as she passed a large umbrella thorn acacia, *Umshishene*, next to the road. She glanced left and right to see if anyone was about. The quiet suburban road was deserted. At the base of the tree was a short piece of stick, the sort of stick that a Labrador would love to fetch. She placed the stick in the fork of the tree, pushing it down firmly to wedge it in place. Calling for Trudy, she continued down Hurstview Road.

While Rugare Mangwende had trained Faye as a spy, they did not meet off the University campus. Their lovemaking was confined to a room that belonged to one of Rugare's friends in the University residence, Manfred Hodson Hall. Faye had been taught the art of dead-drops. A set of six dead-drop sites were located around the city. The one in Hurstview Road was chosen because it was so close to her home.

The main cricket oval of Sunshine Sports Club was a great place for Trudy to run safely. Faye took out an old tennis ball and threw it as hard as she could; the dog took off after it. Beginning her walk clockwise around the oval, Faye stepped behind the old, dilapidated sightscreen, removed the envelope from her bag and pushed it into a gap between the timbers. She then finished her circuit of the oval and wondered off home, followed by Trudy at her heal, too tired for any more running.

One of the workers in the compound in the club grounds came out of his small room; he was dressed in dark blue overalls, as was the case for most workers. He picked up his bicycle leaning against the wall and rode off down the service road towards Hurstview Road, turning left to ride past the acacia tree. He noted the stick wedged in the fork of the tree, then, checking that there was nobody about, rode up, pulled the stick free and dropped it back into the grass. He then continued up the road, blending in with the hundreds of other workers in Salisbury, riding home to the location[74] for the evening. He stopped at a café to buy cigarettes in Coventry Road and then returned, by way of a different route, to Sunshine Sports Club. He diverted past the sightscreen, retrieved the envelope and returned to his room.

John Mawere, an excellent gardener and groundskeeper, was an even more excellent agent for the freedom struggle. Concealed in a disused water tank, he had the latest in Chinese radio communications. Mawere sent a daily flash radio message to a ZANLA base deep in Tete Province in Mozambique. This was a coded message using a one-time message pad system. Both sender and recipient use copies of the same code-key pad system to encode/decode a single message. The code sheet is then destroyed and a different code sheet used for the next message. These messages were made more difficult to monitor because the flash messages were transmitted at different times of the day. The Rhodesians could not break the code without the message pad which they did not have. By way of contrast, the daily 'Shackle' and 'Button' codes used by the Rhodesians were in the hands of ZANLA within hours of issue through a network of spies and informants.

Mawere coded up the few paragraphs typed by Faye Chan and waited for the appointed time for the flash message. The radio blinked a green light and Mawere pressed the send button … the game was on!

*

Border Fence *Cordon Sanitaire* approximately 8.7km northeast of Vila Salazar

Comrade Edward Sibanda and his eight Group Chitepo cadres crouched next to the dirt track on the Mozambique side of the border. They were heavily loaded with equipment including large packs of plastic explosive, TM 46 landmines and an array of anti-personnel mines. Each man carried an AK47 plus chest webbing with eight 30-round magazines plus four Chinese copies of the Soviet RGD-33 stick grenades. Adding to the load, three cadres had RPG-7 rocket launchers strapped across their backs plus four projectiles while each of the other men carried two extra projectiles in their packs. They all wore the ubiquitous blue worker's overalls; the only distinguishing

---

[74] The black townships around cities and towns in Rhodesia were referred to as 'locations'. These were the places that black people were allocated to live in. Black people were not allowed to live in white designated suburbs unless they were domestic servants. All black people had to carry a 'pass' or identity card.

features were the words 'Hippo Valley Estates' embroidered across the shoulders. They sported a variety of hats including canvas floppy hats and wide brimmed hats weaved from elephant grass or reeds. If they were forced to ditch their weapons and kit, these men would pass for agricultural workers without any difficulty.

The plan was to wait for the rocket bombardment to commence and then pass through the border fence and minefield.

Comrade Captain Zhang Youxia whispered into Sibanda's ear that the time for the diversion was only a few seconds away. Two FRELIMO cadres had already cut the fence and had marked the route to the edge of the minefield. They had spent a great deal of time over the past two months slowly clearing a path through the minefield. The Rhodesian Engineers had found the breach in the fence and repaired it but they had not checked the minefield itself. In addition to cutting the fence, the FRELIMO men planted TM46 landmines in the border track fifty metres north and south of the breach.

To the southwest, the sound of exploding missiles carried across the silent bushland.

'Go Comrade' Zhang tapped Sibanda lightly on the shoulder and the men rapidly crossed the open ground, crawled under the fence, disappearing into the thick bush beyond. The two FRELIMO men came back through the fence sweeping their path with cut branches. Zhang waited for a few minutes and then signalled for the guides to return to the vehicle.

Group Chitepo's immediate RV point was a man-made water hole with wind pump, some 29km to the northwest inside the Gona-re-zhou National Park. There they were to wait for a guide who would take them to the village of Tswiza another 5km further on. The heavy load and thick uncompromising sand meant that it would take all night to reach the RV point.

*

Airspace over Mozambique Border

The men of Operation Wedza led by Captain Chris Schultz sat silently in the bucking Dakota as it crossed the Mozambique border at 10,000 feet near Cashel, a farming village approximately 60km south of the city of Umtali. The bulk of their equipment was in the wooden crate next to the open cargo door. Each man carried an AK47 strapped to his side, Chinese webbing over FRELIMO greens, over that an assortment of jerseys and overalls to keep out the freezing temperature. The Air Force Despatcher crossed over to the men to help fit oxygen masks as the aircraft continued to climb through 15,000 feet, showing the thumbs up to make sure each man was breathing normally.

> *I like to spend some time in Mozambique.*
> *The sunny sky is aqua blue.*
> *And all the couples dancing cheek to cheek.*
> *It's very nice to stay a week or two*[75].

75 Bob Dylan and Jacques Levy, song *Mozambique* on the album *Desire* (1975) by

Schultz checked his watch and altimeter and signalled to the men ... fifteen minutes to the drop zone. Tense nervousness ... furtive glances left and right. The plan was to exit the aircraft at twilight, the theory being that it would be light enough to see and manoeuvre in the air but dark enough when on the ground to hide their arrival.

Sgt. Ngwenya checked his altimeter, set to a negative height equivalent to the difference between the altitude of New Sarum and the lower altitude of the drop zone. He had heard the more experienced jumpers discussing this bit of physics but it was lost on him. He fixed his eyes on the altitude that Schultz told him he needed to open the parachute, trying to picture it in his mind.

Ngwenya always worried about deploying with his white colleagues on this sort of job, their inherent 'whiteness' created huge risks. The white troopers struggled to keep 'black'. They had to be constantly aware of the camo-cream wearing off, needing to touch-up all the time. Some white soldiers even resorted to bathing in Condy's Crystals, potassium permanganate, to literally die their skin black. While the Condy's Crystals worked, the nose and ears still needed touching up from time to time. Ngwenya had a close shave when a CT in a group they were infiltrating had recognised one of their would-be comrades as a *mukiwa!* The ensuing firefight had resulted in the deaths of all the CTs in the band which had defeated months of painstaking preparation and loss of vital intelligence.

The briefing he and others had received had emphasised the need for pinpoint accuracy on the drop zone. This was mainly because of the flat terrain, the many villages and the extremely poor map coverage of the area. The most prominent navigational aids were two road intersections, one on the road south of Chimoio to Sussundenga, the other on the other road south of Chimoio at the road intersection called Assicante. These two intersections were clearly shown on aerial photographs, one of which was strapped to the Despatcher's leg.

'STANDBY', the Dispatcher shouted.

Ngwenya snapped out of his reverie and stood up with all of the others. They all paired off once again, Captain Schultz smiled at him showing the thumbs up. All still had their oxygen masks attached. Ngwenya glanced down at his altimeter; 18,000ft AGL ... jump height.

The Dispatcher placed his headset on and spoke to the pilot. He needed to identify the jump-point himself; he was giving the pilot minor heading corrections while looking out the door. He seemed satisfied.

The men stood in the door behind the crate. The Dispatcher lit the safety fuse and he and his assistant launched the crate out the door, the six men following instantly.

The crate spun violently below the jumpers. Schultz held Ngwenya's arm tightly, his contorted face still visible in the fast fading light. They raced after the crate. At 2,500ft, the crate's chute deployed and all the men pulled their

Ram's Horn Music.

ripcords simultaneously. Ngwenya could clearly see the strobe light on the crate below him all the way down. The crate hit the ground first, followed by Kumpher and Seals, Ngwenya landed about 30m away with Schultz next to him.

It was deathly quiet. The men crept carefully towards the crate. Nyandoro appeared out of the dark but there was no sign of Kachimanga. Schultz grouped the men into a tight huddle to make sure all was well and there were no injuries. Seals indicated that Kachimanga had not stabilised in freefall and had broken his grip; he had no idea where he was.

Unpacking the crate at night ran the risk of making noise, too much noise, so the plan was to wait until first light. This would also allow the group to check out their surroundings and to make sure they had not been detected.

Kumpher, who carried the TR48, silently unpacked the radio and sent the code word for a successful insertion.

The Dakota had flown on for another 40km before banking to the left for its return flight to New Sarum. Despite flying at 20,000ft, the sound of a Dakota is very distinctive, particularly at night where there is no ambient noise. The aircraft's presence was noted by at least five different groups of people spread over an area of three hundred square kilometres. The reports of the over-flight did not take long to arrive at the ZANLA HQ in Chimoio. The intelligence reports of a pending Rhodesia infiltration were confirmed! A message went out to the training bases to go on full alert.

*

Vila Salazar, southeast border with Mozambique

The sound of the 122mm Grad passing overhead at 690m/sec, rocket blast shooting from its tail, was chilling to say the least. The first rocket passed over the dinner party at Vila Salazar and burst harmlessly at least two kilometres inland. Initially the 2RR men took no notice, merely gazing up into the evening sky watching the rocket pass over. The second rocket was already on its way, four seconds behind the first.

The RLI men stood in shock as the second rocket passed overhead. None had seen a rocket attack before.

'BATTLE STATIONS,' screamed Captain John and the 2RR men disappeared into the night. Nobody said anything to the boys from the RLI.

A more familiar sound arrived, a Soviet 82mm mortar explosion. A bomb landed on the perimeter fence, then another beside it.

'Fuck, those Gooks are giving this place a rev Corp,' exclaimed Penga looking excitedly at Beamish.

Beamish was not waiting around for any instructions. He was off after Captain John in the direction of the command bunker.

'Cosmic!' shouted Kratzman over the explosions, '… now I really feel like I am back in Nam.'

'63, 63, 63 … this is 74, do you read, over.'

As the RLI men entered the command bunker, Captain John was on the big-means to JOC Repulse HQ in Fort Victoria.

'74, copied reading you fives.'

'Roger 63 we are under sustained mortar and rocket attack, request permission to return fire ... over.'

'74, ... standby.'

'Standby! ... Are you fucking crazy I am getting my arse shot off here!' Captain John's laid-back attitude was coming under pressure.

'74, ... confirm permission to return fire.'

'Roger copied ... sorry to interrupt you useless bastards sipping G and T!' Captain John threw down the TR48 handset in disgust, immediately picking up the field telephone connecting him to the mortar pits.

'*Camaradas da FRELIMO, vamos jogar alguma música enquanto.*'[76] Afonso's voice burst over the loudspeakers outside.

Lifting a weathered copy of The Who's *My Generation*[77], Afonso placed it on the record player.

> *People try to put us d-down (Talkin' 'bout my generation)*
> *Just because we get around (Talkin' 'bout my generation)*
> *Things they do look awful c-c-cold (Talkin' 'bout my generation)*
> *I hope I die before I get old (Talkin' 'bout my generation)*

The mortar and rocket barrage outside now included machinegun fire. Bullets ricocheted off steel girders on the tower outside and thudded into sandbags on the roof of the bunker.

'Fuck this for a game of darts!' shouted Captain John above the din. 'All mortar tubes, one round smoke.'

Eight mortars outside responded instantly. They had done this many times before. The TV screen accentuating the flashes from the enemy mortar tubes, but more importantly, the Grad-21 launch site.

'All tubes, four rounds HE[78] ... target ident ... Hotel Victor. Shot!'

2RR had registered a number of targets in Malvernia that were identified with code names. Hotel Victor was the railway siding, a favourite mortar firing point. The flash of the explosions of the 2RR mortars on the railway siding, were clear to see on the TV screen. Figures could be seen scurrying about in the smoke, illuminated by the few street lights still working.

A mortar bomb landed very close to the command bunker. The picture on the TV screen flickered, snowed for a few seconds, then snapped back into focus. Jumping and scratching, the needle on the record player lifted and fell back into place, The Who continued outside. The bunker shook violently, dislodging dirt and dust from the roof, making it difficult to breathe.

Captain John swore loudly.

'This is uncool man!' complained Afonso, dusting dirt off his equipment.

---

76 FRELIMO Comrades I am going to play you some great music.
77 The Who, Brunswick Records, written by Peter Townshend.
78 High Explosive.

The operator of the Grad-21 rocket battery was unprepared for the sudden arrival of mortars onto his position. He ran to the cab of the truck, leapt inside and started the engine. He engaged first gear and smashed down on the accelerator.

The vehicle, including the unfired rockets in the rack behind, took a direct hit. It exploded, lifting off the ground in a fireball. The stricken vehicle crashing down in pieces, the driver and his assistant incinerated inside.

A rocket ignited, skidded wildly across the ground towards Malvernia, eventually striking a nearby building, collapsing the wall onto the occupants inside. The burning vehicle started a bush fire that could be seen for miles around.

The mortar fire from Malvernia stopped.

> *Why don't you all f-fade away (Talkin' 'bout my generation)*
> *And don't try to d-dig what we all s-s-say (Talkin' 'bout my generation)*
> *I'm not trying to cause a b-big s-s-sensation (Talkin' 'bout my generation)*
> *I'm just talkin' 'bout my g-g-generation (Talkin' 'bout my generation)*

The record ended and a hush descended over Vila Salazar.

'I need a beer!' said Captain John to no one in particular. The men followed in silence as the Captain climbed out of the bunker to inspect the damage outside.

A man ran over to Captain John.

'Boss ... number three pit took a direct hit, the boys are totally fucked man.'

'Oh shit!'

John rushed over to where his men had gathered.

Looking down into the pit, he gasped in shock.

The bodies of three men lay in the bottom of the pit, ripped to pieces by the exploding shell. Their faces were bloated and blackened from the blast, making them virtually unrecognizable. A mortar explosion in such a confined space gave the occupants no chance.

Captain John was dumbstruck, these were his boys, he had known them for years, they were all from Bulawayo, they had been to school together. He threw his head back and screamed into the night sky, a blood-curdling scream, a scream of total anguish and despair.

*

ZANLA Saboteur Training Base, 20km south-southeast of Chimoio, Mozambique

The news of the arrival of the Rhodesian Dakota over Mozambique airspace, at the precise time it had been expected, spread very fast. All ZANLA and FRELIMO bases within a 150km radius were notified by radio to go onto full alert. At Camp Takawira[79], to the south of Chimoio, the guard

---
79 Leopold Takawira, a diabetic, was a founding member of ZANU, he died in a

was doubled. There were still fifty cadres in the camp completing their training.

The camp was situated no more than 2km off the dirt road between Chimoio and Assicante intersection, some 80km further to the south. It had a set of large barrack rooms surrounding an open quad used as a parade ground. The buildings included four classrooms used for instruction, together with a corrugated iron shed for storage of munitions, explosives and other training materials. An old colonial farmhouse surrounded by a wide veranda served as an HQ with offices, radio room and conference room.

Immediately north and east of Camp Takawira were low hills that provided excellent vantage points for observing the camp and surrounding countryside. Sited in defensive bunkers amongst the rocks and undergrowth, were two DShKM 12.7mm anti-aircraft machine guns. A bunker housing a single KPV 14.5mm heavy machine gun covered the entry road. All the guns had been carefully disguised from the air using undergrowth and camouflage netting. Pathways to and from the gun emplacements were equally well disguised to prevent detection on aerial photographs. Under trees close to the HQ building were two Soviet BTR-152 armoured personnel carriers, each mounting a DShKM 12.7mm gun, and a GAZ-63 two-tonne truck.

In the conference room attached to the HQ building were four Chinese military advisors, part of Captain Zhang Youxia's team of instructors. They had been carefully selected for their specialist skills which included long-range reconnaissance and demolition. The room had a number of large scale maps of the eastern half of Zimbabwe, as it was called, as well as maps of the area surrounding the camp and the town of Chimoio.

A short and stocky man with a scraggly beard walked into the room from one of the offices. He wore Chinese khaki uniform and badges of rank on his shoulders. He was Camp Takawira's commander, Comrade Dipuka Muponde. Muponde nodded politely to the Chinese men who did not stand. The Chinese saw themselves as superior in all respects to the senior ranks of the freedom fighters.

'Comrade Hsu, what are your recommendations for defending our camp?' enquired Muponde addressing the only Chinese advisor who could speak English. Hsu held the rank of *san Ji jun shi zhang* or Master Sergeant and was Youxia's 2IC.

'Comrade Muponde …' replied Hsu dismissively, '… intelligence reports say that the Colonists will have sent less than twenty men. Their mission is primarily reconnaissance and we are led to believe that they will seek to abduct a senior man.'

'Yes, but how can we prevent this happening?'

'I am of the view that we should seek to reverse the situation and actively try to kill and or apprehend these men. This would be very powerful and useful propaganda for the freedom struggle,' replied Hsu, leaning back in his chair, an arrogant smile played across his face.

Rhodesian prison cell from complications associated with ketoacidosis from lack of insulin. His cell had an important neighbour, Robert Mugabe.

Muponde studied the Chinese man carefully. What he was suggesting was way beyond his skill set. The camp itself was not protected by a security fence or minefield; this was deliberately done to prevent it attracting attention. The sign outside the camp on the approach road read, '*Marera Colégio Agrícola*[80]'. The camp was too big and widespread to be defended from a concerted assault, not without at least two hundred men well dug in.

'What do you have in mind, Comrade Hsu?' asked Muponde quietly, a feeling of dread suddenly deep inside his stomach.

'We need to detect their presence first. I would suggest that we dress up one of our newest recruits as a senior ranking officer, parade him about so that he can be seen and wait for these men to strike.'

'You must be joking Comrade. That is a death sentence!' exclaimed Muponde, concern now in his voice.

Then it dawned on Muponde, he was the camp commander, and, therefore, he was the prime Rhodesian 'target'. Suddenly the plan sounded inspired. He responded after a suitable period of delay … for contemplation.

'… On second thoughts Comrade, I think this is an excellent idea. I have just the man in mind. He is older than the rest and he has only just arrived. He will be perfect.'

Muponde rushed out of the meeting room to dig out his spare uniform and get his 'double' suitably attired.

---

[80] Marera Agricultural College

8

CIO HQ, Coghlan Buildings, Livingston Avenue, Salisbury City Centre

Deputy Director George Stanbridge had returned to Salisbury from his trip to London. The news that his school friend, Jeremy Hughes-Hall, had given him about a potential mole within COMOPS was disconcerting. It had been something that he had suspected for some time but he and his department had not been able to find any conclusive proof. He had discussed the problem with the local MI6 representative based in Salisbury and with the CIA man attached to the US Consulate but they had not been helpful. Stanbridge was convinced that both MI6 and the CIA had their own informers in the government and in the armed forces. There was a Cold War on after all! Rhodesia was a great place for gathering intelligence on Soviet and Chinese tactics and weapons. China, the USSR, North Korea and Cuba were Cold War enemies of the West. Not to mention the states sponsoring terrorism around the world like Libya, Egypt and Syria.

Drinking his first cup of tea for the day, Stanbridge studied the organisation chart for COMOPS as he had done repeatedly. It was impossible to pick a suitable target to go after. They were all men with exemplary military records. All were highly motivated and committed to defending their country. For any one of these men to deliberately assist the communist forces lined up against the country was unthinkable … yet fingers were being pointed.

Something had to be done, but what?

Stanbridge was convinced that the more recently planned external strikes into Mozambique and Zambia needed to be reviewed. If they had been compromised then good soldiers were going to die. The CIO spy network in Zambia was well developed, Stanbridge had two ex-British SAS agents operating, plus a lengthy list of informers. In Mozambique, however, he had virtually nothing.

While the 'horse had already left the stable' on Operation Wedza, Stanbridge felt duty bound to have a chat about his fears to Colonel Reid-Daly. The problem with talking to Reid-Daly directly was his natural distrust of the official intelligence-gathering network. He was outspoken on his opinion of COMOPS, *good officers who lacked imagination and vision*. He was also particularly critical of the SAS. He saw the SAS as trapped in the mind-set of the desert campaign in the 1940s. He thought the officers lacked the essential initiative required of special forces units and that the core skills of reconnaissance, sabotage, assassination and intelligence gathering had been relegated in favour of attacks on enemy camps and installations. The Colonel was also critical of the fact that the SAS had refused to recruit black soldiers that effectively eliminated them from pseudo operations and long-term enemy infiltration. At least these last few points were areas upon which Stanbridge and the Colonel were in complete agreement.

Stanbridge knew that Reid-Daly thought he was a 'CIO wanker', an opinion that he had allegedly shared liberally with others. The fact that Stanbridge had been educated at a private school in England and spoke with a cultured English accent did not help his cause. The Colonel was a career soldier, rising through the ranks to RSM of the RLI, later commissioned and appointed by General Walls to form the Selous Scouts. He had no time for ponsi-pretentious desk jockeys, one of whom was Stanbridge.

The other issue that Stanbridge was very sensitive about was the fact that he knew that Army Counter-Intelligence had bugged Reid-Daly's phone. They had borrowed the equipment from his department. The Army were on an internal witch-hunt looking for ivory poachers, gun running and unauthorised military expeditions … nothing had been turned up yet. Stanbridge was convinced the whole thing was rubbish, just internal army jealousies and turf fights.

In trepidation, Stanbridge picked up the phone and dialled Reid-Daly's number at Andre Rabie Barracks. He had only spoken directly to the Colonel on a handful of occasions outside of direct mission briefings.

A secretary answered and a delay ensued while she explained to the Colonel who was calling.

'Yes Stanbridge, what can I do for you?' The Colonel always direct to the point, he had no time for pleasantries.

Stanbridge was not on first name terms with the Colonel so he replied politely.

'Colonel, I would very much appreciate a moment of your time.'

'Go ahead.'

'Well I was hoping we might be able to meet.' Stanbridge was mindful of the bugged phone.

'I am busy, speak to me now,' came the clipped, irritated response.

'It is a matter of some sensitivity.' Stanbridge knew he was starting to sound like a 'wanker'.

'Look Stanbridge I don't have time to pussyfoot around. Tell me now man!'

'I am afraid I cannot Colonel, I must insist on a meeting.'

There must have been something in Stanbridge's voice that rang an alarm bell.

'Is this urgent?'

'Yes, I believe it is.'

'Okay tonight … the main bar at the Meikles Hotel … your round.' The phone went dead. The Colonel had spoken.

*

Water Hole, Gona-re-Zhou, Southeast Rhodesia, approximately 87km due south of Buffalo Range

Group Chitepo had successfully completed the first leg of their mission. The walk from the border fence to the waterhole near the village of Tswiza on the railway line between Malvernia and Rutenga had been tough. The heavy load and the soft sand meant that it had taken all night to reach the RV point. The men had collapsed under a tree after refilling their water bottles from the trough next to the wind-pump. It was too dangerous to set up a cooking fire so the men ate the meagre dry rations they had brought with them, stale bread and a few hard biscuits. They were to be completely reliant on being fed by the local villagers.

Within an hour of first light two young boys, no more than nine or ten appeared on the other side of the waterhole. The boys looked about apprehensively. This was a national park full of wild animals including lion, leopard and hyena. Hanging about near a waterhole in the early morning was not the safest thing to be doing.

Edward Sibanda watched the boys carefully to make sure that they were alone. When he was satisfied, he stood up next to the tree his men were sleeping under and gestured for the boys to approach. They ran across the bare ground surrounding the waterhole as soon as they saw him.

'*Mhoroi Sawubona*? Hello, how are you?' said Sibanda gently to the boys as they approached. They were barefoot, their clothing torn and threadbare.

'*Ahoi ... Mangwanani*, Hello ... Good morning,' replied the older of the boys clapping his hands in front of his chest, averting his eyes as is the custom when addressing adults or people with high rank.

'Are you to take us to the road?' asked Sibanda, impressed at the bravery the boys had shown in coming deep into the national park all alone.

'Yes ... it is over there,' the boy pointed to the north. 'Over there' meaning 20km away.

'*Mota irikupi*? Is that where the vehicle is?'

'*Yaa!*' replied the boy excited by the adventure. He looked around at the men with weapons under the tree, his eyes shining.

Sibanda ordered his men to get ready to move out. It was only 6:30 in the morning. Already stiflingly hot, no hint of a breeze. It was going to be another gruelling 20km hike to the waiting vehicle.

The band set off, following the two young boys who seemed totally at ease. The chances of detection by Security Forces in the middle of the national park on a hot day were remote.

*

Operation Wedza DZ, 14km south of Chimoio, Mozambique

Captain Schultz and his Selous Scouts had been up at first light, hastily unpacked the crate, distributed as much as they could and hid the remainder, mainly food and water, under rocks and undergrowth. They had collectively consulted maps and aerial photographs to pinpoint their exact position. It seemed that they had landed approximately 3km from their intended DZ, probably caused by an undetected change in the wind direction.

Sgt. Ngwenya and Sgt. Seals had covered a 360° search of the immediate vicinity with no sign of Kachimanga The decision was taken to continue the mission. Kumpher transmitted a sitrep reporting that Kachimanga was missing to their support team at Grand Reef (FAF8) airport near Umtali, approximately 120km to the west. In the back of his mind, Schultz prayed that the man had not had second thoughts about changing allegiance. He thought about asking Ngwenya his opinion, but decided against it.

They had positively identified a few farmhouses and other features on the photographs.

A team of intelligence and Air Force liaison officers supported all external operations performed by Selous Scouts. They manned the radios and plotted the progress of the teams as they progressed through each stage of the mission. A support team of Selous Scouts were also on hand to help with extraction if the mission became compromised or the external team ended up in a firefight. The Air Force could also provide close air support and helicopters to perform the extraction.

The Scout team were all dressed in FRELIMO uniforms. The plan was for them to make their way towards the target as clandestinely as possible, but if they were spotted, they would look just like any other FRELIMO soldiers out on patrol. Tpr. Nyandoro had enough knowledge of Portuguese to get by and he was familiar with the local tribe dialect called *Ndau*.

Schultz led the men off in the direction of their target. The area was mainly subsistence farmland, crisscrossed with tracks and minor roads and quite densely populated. It was slow going as the team followed thick patches of bush rather than walking along paths or across cultivated fields. The risk of detection increased the closer they got to the target. Schultz called a halt at midday. The men went into all-round defence in the cover of a thick canopy of trees.

As evening approached, Ngwenya and Nyandoro were sent forward by Schultz to reconnoitre a route to the target and establish a position from where the camp could be observed. The plan estimated that it might take as long as two days to get into position and maybe even longer to choose a target for their 'snatch'.

This was the work that Ngwenya loved, operating deep in a foreign country; the rush of excitement of being in the midst of the enemy without their knowing. He and Nyandoro crept forward towards the place referred to as Marera Agricultural College. They were approaching from the north, the sun had set and the stars were out. The half-moon was expected to rise at about 8pm, which would provide more than enough light. A 33kV power line bisected the agricultural college in a north-south direction; that made keeping on the correct bearing very simple. As is the case with all high-voltage electricity transmission lines, the bush had been cleared underneath, making a clearly defined path.

The two Selous Scouts easily identified the low hill immediately to the north of the camp. They also identified an eroded streambed coming off the reverse slope, entering it to begin the short and gradual climb to the top. As they neared the top of the slope, the bush became increasingly sparse, reducing the amount of cover. The two men slowed their progress, creeping forward carefully, placing each foot carefully in front of the other as silently as possible.

No more than forty or so metres in front of the Scout's position a man began speaking loudly. Ngwenya tapped Nyandoro gently on the shoulder and they went to ground. Leopard crawling in the direction of the voice, the men inched forward. Then another man began speaking, followed by a third. It was not possible to hear exactly what they were saying but the language was unmistakable, seShona. They had found their ZANLA camp.

Then, clearly silhouetted against the night sky, a man came into view. He was talking animatedly to another man who was sitting down. The third appeared from down the opposite slope, walking towards the men having the conversation. They were standing next to what appeared to be a large bush. As Ngwenya and Nyandoro crept closer, the unmistakable outline of a 12.7mm anti-aircraft gun came into view.

There were no anti-aircraft guns in the aerial photographs! Ngwenya thought to himself. A feeling of uncertainty washed over him. He and Nyandoro listened to the conversation for over half an hour but they got no information other than stories of girlfriends in the surrounding villages, and how disenchanted they were about double guard duty. One man played with the machinegun, spinning the barrel around on the tripod, giving off a metallic squeak as he did so. A faint smell of cigarette smoke was in the air.

Despite the darkness of early evening it was still hot and humid, the two Selous Scouts were sweating profusely, their uniforms plastered to their backs.

Ngwenya decided that they should try to move more to the east to see what else the aerial photographs had missed. They skirted the side of the hill, then crossed a narrow saddle to the adjacent high ground. It was now quite dark, the moon had still not risen and the bush on the eastern hill was much more dense. This provided excellent cover, but made moving quietly doubly difficult.

'*Zviri kunakaka?* Is everything all right?' said a man in seShona, stepping out from behind a rock directly in front of Ngwenya, '… why are you creeping about? Are you two trying to avoid guard duty?'

Ngwenya's heart leapt into his throat, he was paralysed from the shock of being discovered.

'*Aiw*, No Comrade we are trying to see if you were alert,' replied Nyandoro.

'Who sent you to check on my position?' the man asked, agitation in his voice. 'Those useless officers will never leave us alone. I am sick of this bullshit!'

The man was about the same height as Ngwenya and judging by his voice quite a bit younger.

'No … No Comrade I was only kidding. We were trying to hide away to get some sleep,' continued Nyandoro with a conspiratorial giggle.

'Who are you? I don't recognise your voice.'

Ngwenya recovered quickly from being thrown off balance by the sudden appearance of the ZANLA cadre. He realised that he only had seconds before the man sounded the alarm. He brought his hand up, smashing down hard onto the side of the man's neck, at the same time clamping a hand over his mouth. The force of the blow to the neck stunned the man, his legs giving way beneath him.

Both the Selous Scouts pounced on the man, Nyandoro pinning his legs. Ngwenya felt feverishly for his hunting knife to slit the man's throat. Still shocked and disorientated, the man began a panicked struggle. The slightest sound from the man was bound to alert others on the hill. Holding on to the man's head with one hand, his other clamped over his mouth, Ngwenya could not free a hand to get the knife. Nyandoro sensed the danger, grabbed his rifle and smashed down onto the man's forehead. The man's body went limp.

The two Selous Scouts sat back sucking for air, trying desperately not to make any more noise.

'Are you okay Simon?' whispered Ngwenya, breathing hard, sweat burning his eyes.

'Yes ... shit, that was close. What are we going to do now? Do you want me to kill him?'

'If they find the body they will know something's up. We will have to take him back with us.'

'*Tsere* is going to be pissed off,' commented Nyandoro, fearing the wrath of Captain Schultz.

'Nothing we can do about that now ... come on, let's get back.'

The limp body of the ZANLA cadre was bound up, a gag tied tightly over his mouth and then hoisted onto Ngwenya's shoulders. The man's head was bleeding profusely from the blow from the rifle; Ngwenya could feel the blood saturating the back of his shirt.

It took nearly three hours for Ngwenya and Nyandoro with their hapless prisoner to return to the staging point set up by Schultz.

'What the fuck is this?' came the hiss of disbelief when they arrived.

What the fuck indeed!

9

Vila Salazar, southeast border with Mozambique

The shock of the vicious rocket and mortar attack on Vila Salazar and the deaths of the three 2RR mortar men, cast a deep depression over the camp. The bodies of the three dead men were zipped into body-bags and laid on the veranda of the HQ building. Captain John and his men drank heavily. Afonso and many of the others got heavily into their stash of dope to the point where FRELIMO could have just walked across the border and taken over, nobody would have been any the wiser.

The RLI men uncharacteristically refrained from drinking. They were equally shocked by what they had seen. Although hardened to death and mayhem, the sight of men killed in such a brutal and destructive fashion was hard to accept.

The heartbreak felt by Captain John was infectious; nobody could be immune to his grief.

The next day was a morbid depressing affair. One of the RLI vehicles had taken the brunt of a mortar round which had holed its diesel tank and cut the fuel lines. That meant that they could not leave to drive back to Buffalo Range. They had to wait for 2RR to send a vehicle to fetch the bodies and to escort the serviceable RLI vehicle back to Mbalauta. Nobody drove on those roads with only one vehicle.

At midmorning, a massive explosion rolled across the bush from the north. The Engineers, inspecting the minefield, had struck the boosted TM46 laid the night before. Two Sappers were killed; the unfolding drama could all be heard on the 2RR HF radios.

No vehicles were available to drive to Vila Salazar to collect the 2RR bodies so eventually a helicopter was sent from Buffalo Range. Captain John had his men paraded next to the LZ, all still in their standard uniform of rifles, helmets and shorts.

The LZ was just to the north of the perimeter fence. Captain John arranged six pallbearers for each of the bodies and the small procession began the slow walk to where the helicopter was waiting. Leading the procession was Captain John wearing his 2RR beret and his camo-shirt with the three black pips on each shoulder. His rifle was held stiffly at shoulder-arms.

Afonso played Paul McCartney's *Mull of Kintyre* over the public address system.

Beamish had his men drawn up next to the helicopter, a lump in his throat as the bagpipes lifted their lament. He closed his eyes as memories of his brother's funeral came rushing back; the Scots Guards had played *Flowers of the Forest*[81].

The lonely parade watched as Captain John led the pallbearers along the dusty path. It was hot and the men were soaked in sweat.

'Parade, ATTEN… shun!' bellowed Captain John. The men slapped their

81 The traditional lament for the fallen in forces of the British Commonwealth.

rifles into the shoulder. Beamish instinctively responded to the command, impressed with how smartly the men of 2RR had reacted. Captain John marched forward to the door of the helicopter, then turned to address his men.

'We are sending Jones, Van Jarsveld and Fitzgerald home to their families. These men were brothers to us; we have served together since our national service. They will be sorely missed. We, that are left behind, must carry on this business so that they may not have died in vain ... smartly now ... PRESENT ARMS.'

The men forced their rifles to a vertical position in the centre, slapping the handguard of the FNs loudly. It was perfectly quiet as the bodies were gently loaded onto the helicopter. Captain John stood next to the door giving instructions in a soft voice ... Beamish watched him handle his men with deep compassion. The pallbearers returned to take up their places next to the others standing with their rifles at present arms.

The pilot and choppertech stood next to their machine, watching respectfully as the sad farewell ceremony came to an end. Once it was done, they climbed into the helicopter, started it up, and flew off to the north.

Afonso played *House of the Rising Sun* by The Animals over the public address system.

> *There is a house in New Orleans*
> *They call the Rising Sun*
> *And it's been the ruin of many a poor boy*
> *And God I know I'm one ...* [82]

The exact reason for the song choice was unclear but all the 2RR men sang the words with gusto. They remained at the salute until the clattering helicopter was lost in the distance.

Watching the helicopter disappear over the horizon, Penga turned to Corporal Beamish, frustration in his voice, 'Corp ... we need to fuck those Freds[83] up across the border!'

'Shut up Penga ... don't be ridiculous. We will end up in DB or dead. Bluudy fool!'

'Penga is right ... lets go and keel some Gooks Corp,' Le Beau added in support. '*Sergeant* McIntyre would theenk it was a good idea.'

'That's bullshit and you know it,' Beamish snapped back.

'I agree Corporal ... lets take out a few of them Gooks over yonder,' added Kratzman helpfully.

'Fuck off Yank, who the fuck are you making suggestions?' Beamish was getting upset.

'Mister Beamish, I would count it a personal favour if you could bring me back one of those FRELIMO bastards,' added Captain John, who had been

---

82 The Animals, Columbia Records, American folk song, the authorship of 'The House of the Rising Sun' is unknown.
83 Rhodesian slang, FRELIMO.

listening to the exchange through a violent hangover.

The 2RR men, hearing their Boss's suggestion, gave a loud cheer of support. They broke into excited chatter as to what support they could offer the planned 'external'.

'We can provide fire support Corporal Beamish, including a diversion. That will keep their heads down while you go in to snatch a Freddy, preferably an officer!' Captain John's excitement was building.

'But Surr, I cannot just go over there and capture an enemy soldier. I would get court martialled. I could go to jail for the rest of my natural life,' Beamish complained.

'Nonsense Beamish, I am giving you authority. I outrank you and I have instructed you to complete a very important mission.'

'But Surr ...' Beamish was surrounded by excited faces. He was trapped.

'Afonso, play me *Summer Holiday* ... I am starting to feel better,' shouted Captain John, happy that the decision had been taken. 'We are going to teach those bastards a lesson to remember,' he announced triumphantly to the smiling throng.

Corporal Arthur Beamish was thrust into very unfamiliar territory ... planning an invasion of another country ... aided and abetted by people from the Planet of Dope.

Afonso and Captain John took Beamish over the maps of Malvernia, where FRELIMO had mortar pits, barrack rooms and most importantly, where the most likely place would be to snatch an officer.

'That is where you will find your Fred officer, Beamish my good man,' yelled Captain John, pointing excitedly at the railway siding. He was almost his old self again.

My Fred officer! Why is he all of a sudden my Fred Officer? Beamish thought to himself, trying not to be caught up in the whirlpool of excitement. He put on his characteristic scowl, but it was lost on Captain John who interpreted it as the expression of a focused, highly professional soldier.

2RR men were coming up to Beamish slapping him on the back, wishing him good luck ... it was as if he was spearheading the D-Day landings. Penga, Le Beau and Kratzman basked in the reflective glory ... Beamish was a true war hero, the epitome of the Steely-eyed killer.

Mafuta cooked a great meal to send them on their way. The four RLI men camo-creamed up, checked their equipment and prepared to cross the wire.

Darkness fell as the heroes of the hour crept out towards the border fence guided by the thin man Frik, who knew the way. An almighty mortar barrage was initiated by Captain John to cover their infiltration, instantly responded to by FRELIMO on the other side. Green and red tracer swopped sides across no-man's land.

'The Eagle has landed,' radioed Beamish to Vila Salazar once they were through the fence and on the outskirts of the town. This was the code word insisted upon by Captain John, '... it has a nice ring to it' he had said.

*

Meikles Hotel, Stanley Avenue Salisbury

'Stanbridge, you remind me of a retired bank manager,' commented Colonel Ron Reid-Daly as George Stanbridge entered the bar of the Meikles Hotel. He had walked from Livingston Avenue down Fourth Street, right into Baker Avenue then across Cecil Square to the hotel.

Colonel Reid-Daly was a well-known public figure in the country and many of the people in the bar acknowledged his presence with a nod or a wave.

'Thank you for meeting me Colonel, I appreciate it,' replied Stanbridge ignoring the observation of his old unkempt suit. He ordered two beers and they moved to a table well away from the other hotel guests.

The men were of a similar age but their backgrounds could not have been more different. Stanbridge, born to a wealthy family, English public school education, a degree from Cambridge and a long and distinguished career in the public service. Reid-Daly by comparison, was born to a middle class family, joined the army from school, C Squadron SAS, fought in Malaya, joined the newly formed RLI, rose to the rank of RSM, promoted from the ranks, ultimately to form one of the world's best special forces, counter-insurgency, units.

'So what have you spooks come up with?' asked Reid-Daly caustically. He really did not like desk-jockeys.

'This is very difficult Colonel, but I am concerned about some information that I have come across in the past week,' replied Stanbridge, politely ignoring the Colonel's early jab.

'Get to the point man!'

'I think COMOPS have a leak.'

'So what's new! … They have been leaking for years. The word is, you work for MI6 Stanbridge,' laughed Reid-Daly, pointing at Stanbridge.

Ignoring the implication and the obvious bait, Stanbridge continued 'No this is serious, we believe this leak is directly to ZANLA HQ in Mozambique.'

Reid-Daly's face flushed, his quick temper already evident, 'I knew this was a problem! You fucking desk jockeys haven't got a fucking clue!'

'Colonel, I fear our current external operations may have been compromised,' Stanbridge continued trying to keep the conversion on an even keel.

'What? … I have three external operations under way at the moment!' the concern in Reid-Daly's voice was palpable.

'I am concerned about the Wedza operation in particular.'

'Fuck … Stanbridge you people are useless, you are supposed to be watching our backs!'

'Colonel its not helpful to get into a debate on this at the moment. The important thing is that we warn your people as soon a possible without alerting our enemies.'

'I just cannot believe this. I have good people in harm's way, giving their best … while you people are asleep at the wheel,' spat Reid-Daly. The frustrated Colonel was on a roll.

'I don't have any details but my source is excellent. That is all I have for you Colonel. I will leave you to decide on what you are going to do about this.'

With that, Stanbridge downed the rest of his beer and got up to leave.

'Believe it or not Colonel, we ARE on the same side. I will leave no stone unturned until the mole is found.'

'You do that Stanbridge! You just fuck off, leave it to us poor fuckers to pick up the pieces! We are the ones getting our arses shot off!' Reid-Daly snapped back.

Stanbridge left the hotel; he knew that the Colonel was right; they had dropped the ball on this one. He felt sick inside, hating the feeling that he had let the side down, smarting at the vicious reaction from the Colonel.

10

Worker's Compound – Triangle Sugar Mill, Triangle

Comrade Edward Sibanda sat in the darkness of a single room in the worker's compound less than 600m north of the sprawling expanse of the Triangle Sugar Mill. He had two of his men with him. The other three were in the next room.

The mission had gone faultlessly thus far. The young *mujibas* had taken them to a waiting vanette just outside of the village of Boli on the edge of the Gona-re-zhou national park. From there, the vehicle had driven past Mbiza Siding, up through the back roads in the fruit and sugarcane fields of Hippo Valley, then dropping them right outside the rooms in the mill compound. The gate-guard had been bribed with liquor. He was told that the vehicle was smuggling beer and women into the compound, information he found to be totally acceptable.

Sibanda felt exhilarated that his mission was so close to completion. He just could not believe how well it had gone thus far. The planning had been brilliant; Comrades Zhang and Hamadziripi knew their business. All he had to do now was complete their work.

It would be dark in only a few more minutes. The members of Group Chitepo sat in silence, each man alone with his own thoughts, reviewing the plan over and over in their minds. It was a complex plan in that they needed to penetrate the outer perimeter fence of the mill which was patrolled by members of the Rhodesian Guard Force. Thank goodness they did not have guard dogs, that would have been an enormous limitation. The mill was at the height of the crushing season so there were mill workers and management on the site 24hours a day.

Edward Sibanda took out the worn bible he had been given by his grandfather. His thoughts momentarily returning to his blissful childhood in the family village near Chisumbanje. Every evening his grandfather would gather the children around the fire and read passages from his bible … the very same bible Sibanda now held in his hand. He flicked to Psalm 33 … whispering the words to himself as he read.

> *… Happy is the nation whose God is the Lord, the people whom he has chosen as his heritage …*
> *… A king is not saved by his great army; a warrior is not delivered by his great strength.*
> *The warhorse is a vain hope for victory, and by its great might it cannot save.*
> *Truly, the eye of the Lord is on those who fear him, on those who hope in his steadfast love, to deliver their soul from death, and to keep them alive in famine.*
> *Our soul waits for the Lord; he is our help and shield.*

Our heart is glad in him, because we trust in his holy name.
Let your steadfast love, O Lord, be upon us, even as we hope in you.

The words provided Sibanda with comfort on the eve of his great endeavour. The men had changed from their Hippo Valley overalls into overalls sporting the distinctive Tongaat-Hulett logo on the pocket with 'Triangle Sugar' embroidered across the shoulders.

The time came for the men to move out. A group of nightshift workers had collected near the exit of the compound. Group Chitepo had put their weapons and explosives in haversacks which they carried over their shoulders as they moved off with the mill workers towards the mill. Fortunately, much of the mill was badly lit at night.

They approached the rear gate of the mill. A single guard, holding a torch, stood next to an open boom across the road. The men had plastic ID cards in their pockets which they flashed in front of the guard who was clearly bored, paying very little attention to the workers filing past. The poor lighting did not make his task any easier. A worker called to the guard, asking about his girlfriend, distracting him for the few seconds that it took for the Group Chitepo men to file past.

The nightshift workers passed through the gate without any difficulty. Sibanda had memorised the layout of the plant from satellite photographs so he knew exactly where to go. He led his men past the maintenance sheds on their left, followed the compacted gravel service road. Directly in front of them appeared two enormous storage tanks, surrounded by a concrete bund. There were very few people about. Most of the road and surrounding buildings were in darkness. Group Chitepo ducked behind the bund and divided into two pre-rehearsed groups. They then crossed over to the two tanks, careful to stay on the dark shadow of the northern side.

Sibanda took out four 1kg square packs of plastic explosive, Soviet PVV-5A. He placed them against the base of the tank; each had a detonator and timing device that had been pre-set. The other team finished their work and both groups moved to the next target, another set of smaller liquid storage tanks. The process was repeated.

The task had taken no more than fifteen minutes. It was time to make their escape through the hundreds of hectares of sugarcane to the west of the mill.

'What are you men doing?' a voice came out of the darkness. A man, wearing white overalls and a white hardhat stepped out in front of the men.

'We are cleaners, Ser,' responded Sibanda submissively, putting on a strong seShona accent.

'Which area are you cleaning?'

Sibanda was lost for words, he did not know all the names for the parts of the plant.

'The storage shed, Ser.'

'Which storage shed?'

The man's suspicions were clearly aroused.

'That one Ser,' replied Sibanda, pointing to the nearest building.

'Let me see your ID,' the man said, taking a step forward.

Sibanda realised the game was up. He dropped the sack he was carrying, in the process grabbing his AK. In one fluid motion, he raised it and shot the man with two rounds, directly into his chest.

'RUN,' he shouted to his men and the six of them ran towards the west, crossing over the railway lines leading out of the mill site. The railway lines were not protected by the security fence. Nobody stopped them.

The wail of a siren carried through the night. Security lights flashed from all directions. Group Chitepo dived into the nearest sugarcane field running for their lives.

The night lit up in a massive fiery explosion as the fuel ethanol tanks blew up. Seconds later, another explosion rocked the ground, sending a shock wave through the earth like a small earthquake. The men of Group Chitepo turned, gazing in awe as pieces of corrugated iron flew in all directions. A bright orange flame had shot skywards, turning night into day. Black billowing clouds of smoke could be seen rolling high into the atmosphere, illuminated by the intense fire burning below. The siren continued to sound it's warning … too late.

Group Chitepo laughed in nervous excitement, this was beyond their wildest imaginings. They talked excitedly slapping each other on the back. What a spectacular success!

At the mill, the fire raged completely out of control, spreading to the piles of sugarcane awaiting the crush and the mountain of bagasse used for firing the boilers. The enormous heat generated by the ethanol fire was more than enough to reach the bagasse ignition temperature. More explosions rocked the night.

Group Chitepo's escape now depended on reaching the Matibi TTL in the south. They needed the safety provided by the villages. Sibanda signalled to his men, they had another eight hours of darkness for their getaway.

*

Camp Takawira, 17km south of Chimoio, Mozambique

The team making up Operation Wedza knew they had a problem on their hands as soon as Sgt. Ngwenya and Tpr. Nyandoro returned with their captive ZANLA cadre. Ngwenya explained what had happened as best he could but that did not succeed in placating Captain Chris, *Tsere,* Schultz one bit.

They retired into the thickest bush they could find in order to base up for the day. The place was crawling with Mozambican villagers going about their business. It would have been impossible to move about without being noticed and their FRELIMO uniforms could only take them so far.

'Ngwenya, see what you can get out of this gook,' suggested Schultz; trying to figure out how much time they had before the man was missed.

The black soldier slid across to where the captive lay tied up, his gag in place, but very much conscious. In the light of day, the cadre was a lot younger than expected, no more than nineteen. His eyes were wide showing the sheer terror he was experiencing. Eyes flashed left and right trying to take in the horror of these men, the stuff of the worst nightmares. His head was a mass of caked blood with a nasty gash across his forehead that needed to be stitched. It continued to weep blood onto the ground below his head.

Placing his mouth next to the man's ear Ngwenya whispered in seShona, 'Now Comrade it is very important that you answer my questions truthfully.'

The man nodded vigourously.

'I am going to take off the gag and my friend here will hold his knife next to your throat. If you try to call out or make any noise, he will slit your throat. Is that clear Comrade?'

The man nodded again even more enthusiastically. Nyandoro removed his knife from the scabbard and placed it firmly against the man's neck.

'It is important that you tell me the absolute truth or I will have to hurt you very badly. Is that also clear Comrade?'

The eyes widened even further. Ngwenya gently removed the gag, placing his hand over the man's mouth holding his finger to his lips in the universal sign of 'quiet'.

'Now what is the name of your camp commander?'

'Dipuka Muponde.'

'How many men are in the camp?'

'Forty, plus two Chinese.'

'What training have you received?'

'Just military training, shooting, running ...' the man was starting to relax, the first white lie.

'What do the Chinese teach you?'

'Just shooting and how to use all the weapons, RPGs, mines, mortars ...'

'Have you seen Comrade Tongogara?'

Just the mention of the leader's name got a reaction. The cadre shook his head from side to side, fear again written all over his face.

Ngwenya put the gag back over the man's mouth and went back to speak to Schultz.

The man watched his departure relieved that his answers seemed to be accepted. Nyandoro kept the knife in place.

After a brief exchange, Ngwenya returned once gain whispering to the man.

'Comrade, I am in a hurry and I cannot wait for you to tell the truth. As I said before, I will have to hurt you now.'

Ngwenya nodded to Nyandoro who grabbed the man's left hand holding it against a rock, splaying the fingers. Holding his knife like a cleaver with both hands, Ngwenya neatly chopped the top of the index finger off at the distal joint.

The young freedom fighter lurched as if struck by a 1,000-volt charge, his body arched up, his head lifted off the ground, the silent scream plain to see. Holding his hand tightly over the man's mouth, Ngwenya put his finger to his lips again, for the man to be quiet. The man struggled violently, the pain was excruciating. Nyandoro held the bloody hand up which was spurting blood from the amputated finger.

The other members of the team sat watching disinterestedly. Kumpher had fallen asleep.

It took a good five minutes before the man regained his senses. Nyandoro put disinfectant on the wound and bound it with a bandage.

For the next hour and a half, the cadre spoke almost without taking breath. By the time he was finished Ngwenya had a sketch map of the camp, noted the gun emplacements, the senior officer's quarters, the armoury and, most importantly, where the camp commander and Chinese advisors were quartered. He explained the demolition training, the missions planned and the dates and times that senior ZANLA leaders, including Tongogara himself, visited. The man gave a detailed account of his year's training in Libya with other terrorist groups, the PLO, IRA, ETA and the South African *Umkonto-we-Sizwe*, the military wing of the ANC. Ngwenya meticulously recorded all the information in his notebook.

After the interrogation was complete, Ngwenya replaced the gag on the cadre and injected him with an ampoule of morphine to settle him down.

Captain Schultz was delighted with the results of the interrogation; the mission was already a success. He congratulated Ngwenya on his work but made the point that it was sloppy and unprofessional to have captured the man in the first place.

'*Yebo Tsere*,' Ngwenya and Nyandoro responded, there was no point arguing.

Now it was time to make the snatch. It had to be that night as the captured cadre was bound to be missed. His comrades would be searching for him!

Down in Camp Takawira Comrade Dipuka Muponde, camp commander, was in an agitated state. A man was reported missing and no explanation could be found. He paced up and down his office, trying to figure out what to do ... *the Skuz'apo*[84]*, Selous Scouts, must already be hiding in the hills above!* He had sent people into the neighbouring village to see if the young man was visiting his girlfriend but nothing was found. The camp and surrounding bush had been thoroughly searched.

Muponde concluded that if the missing man had been captured and interrogated, then the security of the camp had been compromised. In desperation, Muponde went to consult with the camp spirit medium, Mutumwa. In seShona her name meant, *a person who carries a message or goes on an errand for another.*

Muponde was a well-educated man, enlightened to the modern world, but when the chips were down his deep-seated tribal and religious instincts took over. He was not a deeply religious man, but he was given to superstition. The

---

[84] Shona derivative nickname for the Selous Scouts. Broad meaning, 'excuse me for what I have just done'. This is a play on the fact that the Scouts stealthily infiltrated terrorist bands, pretending to be friends, killed mercilessly, and then vanished.

medium Mutumwa had a formidable reputation for predicting the future. She was one of many spirit mediums recruited to the liberation struggle to provide spiritual and ideological leadership. The political influence that had been invested in the spirit mediums by the ZANLA leadership meant that Muponde was obliged to use Mutumwa's powers as part of the education of the freedom fighters.

Mutumwa believed that she was descended from *Mbuya Nehanda*[85], one of the great Shona spiritual leaders of the First Chimurenga of the 1890s. She was a woman of indeterminate age, but her croaked speech, wrinkled skin and her slow and deliberate gait indicated a person of advanced years.

Arriving at Mutumwa's compound located outside the camp complex, Muponde hoped that some divine inspiration would show him the answer.

He stood outside her hut and clapped his hands to announce his presence.

'*Manheru*, good evening ... what is it that brings you *Mukoma*, Brother? *Upenyu*? How is your life?' asked the woman from inside the hut. Her speech was measured, with a hint of suspicion.

'*Tatenda*, thank you Mutumwa, I am much troubled, I am in need of your guidance.'

'Come in Brother,' she beckoned.

Evening was approaching and the hut was in almost total darkness except for the flames of a small fire set in the middle. The smoke had a strange sickly-sweet smell that seemed to permeate into the lungs, making Muponde feel slightly lightheaded. Mutumwa was dressed as she always was in a full-length black coat, many heavy necklaces hung from around her neck, made from different colour beads, bones, seashells and leather.

Mutumwa sat on her haunches next to the fire, when she looked up the faint light played across her grizzled features. Muponde felt a shiver down his spine.

'You are expecting trouble Brother?' said the woman, more of a statement than a question.

'A cadre has gone missing and we have word of a pending attack by the Colonists.'

'Sit Brother,' Mutumwa whispered, closing her eyes.

The woman began a gentle rocking motion back and forward, her eyes closed, her lips slightly open. Still sitting on her haunches, she raised her hands up as if reaching for something, her knarled hands twisting and writhing in the smoke from the fire.

An eerie sound came from her throat, building slowly until it burst into

---

85 Mbuya Nehanda a.k.a Charwe Nyakasikana (c. 1862-1898) was a traditional religious leader who opposed the colonial expansion. Nehanda, along with her Spiritual husband Kagubi, were both charged with murder for the death of an African policeman, and Nehanda for the death of the Native Commissioner Pollard. They were summarily sentenced to death by hanging. Nehanda's dying words were, 'My bones shall rise again'.

a loud whooping, incredibly loud to be coming from such a frail woman. Muponde shied back from the sound, struck by a sudden disorientation, his head spinning.

The whooping sound stopped, then a new voice could be heard ... a man's voice.

'You are in great danger Comrade! The menace is already in your midst. These are not men, but shadows ... They move as silently as the snake, their deadly poison attacks the mind and soul of their victim, reincarnating that person into the most hideous, evil spirit.'

Muponde looked behind him in fright, to see if someone else had entered the room.

'The *Skuz'apo* pigs will attack tonight ... they will attack with great force!' The voice was coming from Mutumwa.

Muponde had many previous consultations with Mutumwa, seeing her in a trance-like state, but this was something completely different.

'They are after YOU, Comrade!' croaked the voice.

The shock of the revelation was too great; Muponde's worst fears had been answered. He collapsed onto the floor of the hut moaning in despair. His head felt like it would split apart. Not waiting to hear more, Muponde dragged himself up and ran from the hut his mind numb with terror. He stopped after a few paces and threw up, his body tormented with fear ... *the Skuz'apo ghosts are here, they are after my soul!*

Running back to his office, Muponde began to babble orders to the men waiting there. The first thing he did was to make sure that his 'double' was sitting on the veranda of the HQ building dressed in his best uniform. He then changed into his oldest and most stained fatigues, the exact opposite of what a camp commander would be expected to wear.

He ordered a sweep over the hills surrounding the camp and made sure that every man was on high alert. The barrack rooms were emptied and each man was placed on the perimeter, in all-round defence. He left the lights on in the HQ building.

To his surprise and distress, the Chinese suddenly decided that they had business in Chimoio, leaving in the GAZ-63 truck. As Muponde watched them drive away, it was final confirmation of his isolation. He was visibly shaking in fear.

The two BTR-152s were placed on the road leading out of the camp. Muponde took command of one of these vehicles. His substitute was given strict instructions to stay in the office building. The man was perplexed at why his commander would want him to wear his uniform.

Nothing was found during the sweep that was conducted across a 2km radius. As night began to fall, Muponde gazed up into the hills hoping desperately that his trap would work. This could seal his future career path; he would rise to high rank and be given the best farmland when the struggle had been won ... alternatively he would be dead!

The night closed in on the men from Operation Wedza as they inched forward through the thick bush to the north of the terrorist camp. They had watched the ZANLA sweepline pass by them earlier in the afternoon. They were clearly looking for their missing cadre. The night was pitch black, there was no moon and the stars were obscured by high cloud. The only sounds were clicking cicadas and cattle moaning in the distance.

Tsere Schultz led the way, his men in single file behind him. Painstakingly the men moved through the bush, careful with each step so as not to make any noise. It was slow and excruciatingly painful with the strain of balancing lightly on each foot while carrying a heavy pack and weapons. They were all sweating profusely, trying desperately to control their breathing.

Ngwenya felt his heart beating at such a rate that he was sure someone could hear it. His ears pounded with the blood pulsating through his head. He was sweating so hard that it was starting to block his vision and he was dabbing his face constantly with his face-veil. He had reflected only briefly on the necessity for killing the young captive. It was impossible to let him loose, impossible to leave him alive and impossible to take him with them. Nyandoro had simply slit his throat as he lay sleeping. It had to be done.

The plan was to enter the camp compound from the north where the cover was at its thickest, then to use the shadows of the barrack rooms to reach the HQ building to make the snatch. Kumpher and Seals were to provide covering fire support and act as lookouts for Schultz, Nyandoro and Ngwenya as they made their entrance via the front doorway.

Schultz was confident that they still had the element of surprise. That was why the plan was so bold. Get in ... get out ... simple!

The camp came into sight through the trees. A few lights were on and a diesel generator pounded away some distance off. Previous raids by the Rhodesians had knocked out electricity to most of rural Mozambique. The HQ building was easy to spot with its wrap-around veranda. A man stood smoking on the steps of the veranda, leaning against the balustrade. The bright red flare lit up as he sucked on the cigarette.

It was perfectly silent. Schultz could not believe how silent. This was a camp with more than seventy people in it; *surely there should be some noise?* He thought about aborting the mission and waiting for another night, *bugger it ... we are here now!*

Seals set up the RPD facing the courtyard in front of the HQ building and Kumpher lay next to him facing back into the bush. On Schultz's signal, the three men designated for the snatch, stepped out from behind the barrack room and walked casually across the short distance to the HQ building. They had discarded their packs and each had their AKs held loosely by their sides.

'*Manheru,*' Ngwenya called in seShona. He tried to modulate his voice so as not to give the man a fright.

'Who are you?' the man was startled by the sudden appearance of these men.

Ngwenya saw that the man was wearing a uniform with badges of rank on the shoulders and on his chest.

Ignoring the question Ngwenya spoke confidently, 'We are looking for

Comrade Muponde ... is that you?'

'No ... he is in the tank over there,' the man replied, pointing out into the darkness across the quad.

All three turned to look in the direction the man was pointing, totally flummoxed by the unexpected answer.

The night sky lit up as a 12.7mm machinegun opened up from across the quad. Bright tracer rounds stretched across the night, lifting high over the HQ building. The pressure wave from the bullets flying close overhead thumped in the chest. More rounds hit the dirt next to where the three Selous Scouts had been standing; they were already running across the quad towards their packs and the support team. Seals opened up with the RPD in the direction of the 12.7, a sustained burst which had the effect of temporarily halting the fire. A diesel engine started up and began to move in their direction.

'Fuck, it's the BTR ... come on boys time to get out of here!' Schultz urged his men who were all firing in the direction of the diesel engine. They lifted their packs and ran as best as they could away from the camp, to the north. The night filled with flashes of gunfire coming from all directions as the occupants of the camp, and those in the surrounding hills, started shooting at shadows.

Rifle muzzle flashes lit up in front of the escaping Scouts. All fired in the direction of the flashes ... they stopped.

The panicked gunners on the 14.5mm fired into the sky at ghostly aircraft, tracer rounds arched overhead, disappearing into the stars.

The Selous Scouts ran for forty-five minutes without stopping. They slowed markedly as the weight of their equipment and fatigue set in. Eventually Schultz called a halt, the men collapsed to the ground completely spent.

'Is everyone Okay?'

'I am hit,' replied Nyandoro.

'Let me have a look,' Schultz slid over to where Nyandoro was sitting. He held up his arm and Schultz flashed his penlight torch at it. It was a mass of blood; he had taken a round through the arm above the elbow.

'Looks like it passed through,' commented Schultz as he studied the arm, wiping away the blood with a first-field dressing. The arm also looked broken, the bullet must have hit the bone and then exited.

'Fuck, this is all we need! Does anybody have any idea what happened back there?'

'They were waiting for us,' replied Kumpher without hesitation.

'Yes Sir,' added Seals, 'the whole fucking camp was waiting for us to arrive. They were waiting in the BTR.'

'Dennis, get on the big means and send a sitrep. Tell them we were compromised, we don't have a captive, tell them we will be making for the LZ,' instructed Schultz. 'We are going to have to wait here while I try to sort Simon out ... Cephas, go back along our trail and make sure we weren't followed.'

Extracting the TR48 from his pack, Kumpher set up the aerial and began to code up his message.

Ngwenya crept back down the trail for 300 metres and lay down to wait, his mind racing with what had happened, *they were waiting for us! How could they have known? ... They were well prepared. Surely not just because the cadre went missing? Cadres go missing all the time, they run away; they stay with girlfriends, they get sick and go to see the Sangoma. The camp had been empty ... the commander was waiting in the BTR!* As he lay next to the trail concentrating on the bush ahead the enormity of their predicament dawned on Ngwenya, *they know we are here. They will come looking in large numbers!* A sinking feeling gripped his gut ... *we are in deep shit!*

At first, he thought it was his imagination, the slightest of sounds. He turned his head gently left and right to try to zero in on the direction.

Silence again.

Then another noise, maybe the sound of a tree moving in the breeze. Ngwenya's heart stopped, a stifled cough no more than a few yards in front of him ... *we are being followed already!*

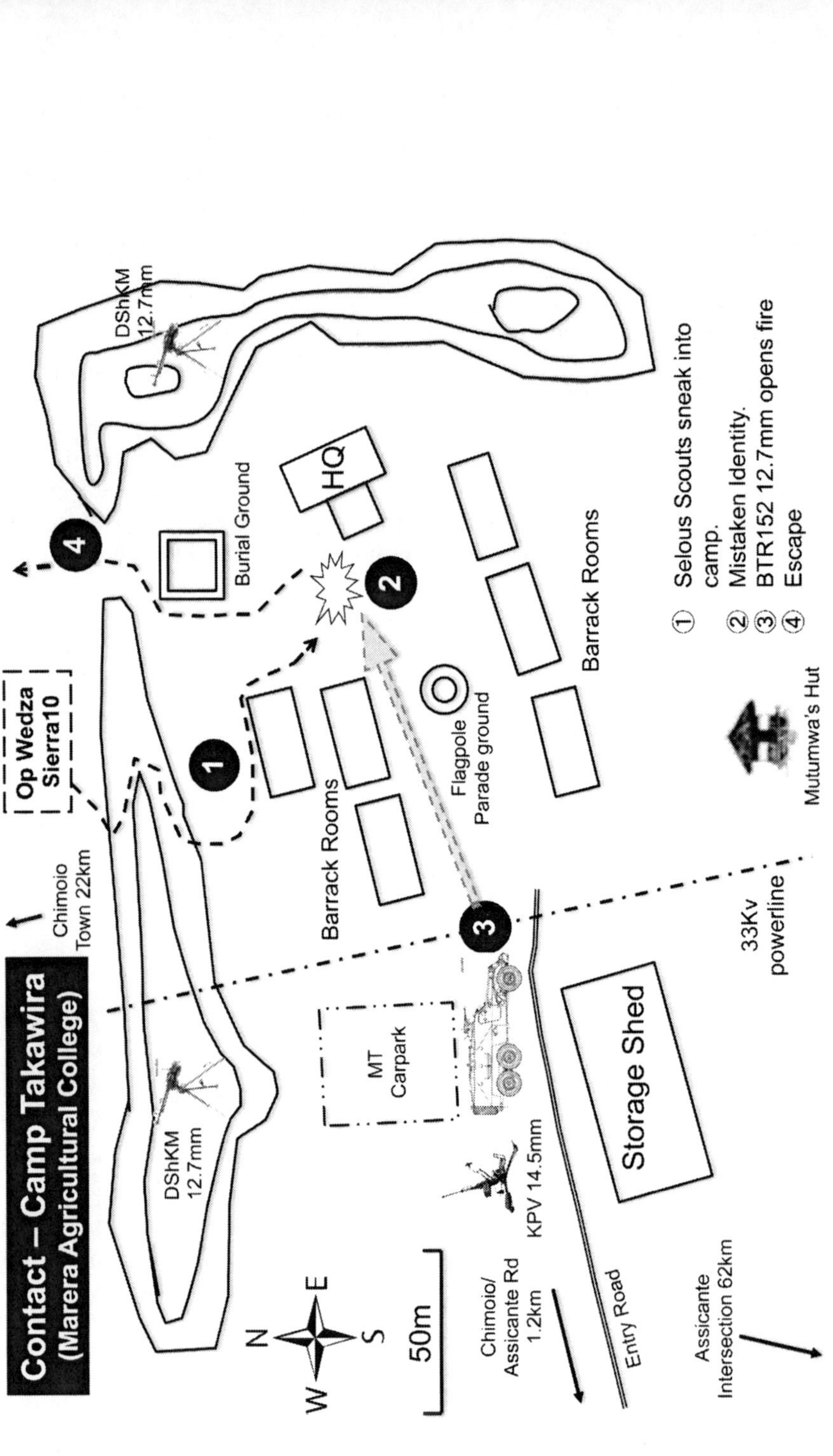

Contact – Camp Takawira
(Marera Agricultural College)
Chimoio Town 22km
Op Wedza Sierra10
DShKM 12.7mm
DShKM 12.7mm
Burial Ground
HQ
Barrack Rooms
Barrack Rooms
Flagpole Parade ground
MT Carpark
KPV 14.5mm
Storage Shed
33Kv powerline
Mutumwa's Hut
N
E
S
W
50m
Chimoio/ Assicante Rd 1.2km
Entry Road
Assicante Intersection 62km
1
2
3
4
① Selous Scouts sneak into camp.
② Mistaken Identity.
③ BTR152 12.7mm opens fire
④ Escape

*

Birmingham Road, Workington, Salisbury

A pale blue Peugeot 504 drove slowly south down Paisley Road, crossed over the railway lines, and continued towards the intersection with Birmingham Road. It was just after midnight and the streets of the industrial area were deserted. Streetlights provided isolated pools of light as the car approached the fuel storage depot. A 2m concrete wall, topped with barbed-wire, surrounded the storage complex. Bright orange security lights illuminated the huge silver fuel tanks making the area inside the depot as bright as day. Rows of fuel transport tankers were lined up in the yard.

The Peugeot continued on its way, turning right into Birmingham Road travelling to the west, the driver was the only occupant. The car passed the main entrance to the depot 70m down on the right. The entrance had a heavy steel gate across it and was patrolled by two armed security guards. The Peugeot drove on to the end of Birmingham Road, slowing at the intersection with Lobengula Road. The car performed a neat u-turn.

Returning east along Birmingham Road the car decelerated almost to a walk as it approached the fuel depot. The car's lights were turned off and it rolled to a stop in the darkness, the engine was still running. The driver could be seen looking up and down the surrounding streets, there was still nobody about and no other vehicles on the road.

The driver, wearing a dark brown, almost black tracksuit, with a black knitted balaclava, jumped out of the car moving swiftly to the boot, where the button was pushed to open it. Two men sprang out of the boot carrying, what looked like large tubes.

The RPG-7 anti-tank grenade launcher is robust, simple and lethal. The warhead has a propelling charge that screwed onto a stabilizing pipe that has four stabilizing fins folded around it with two additional fins at its rear. A cardboard container encases the back end of the stabilizing pipe. Inside the cardboard container, a squib of nitro-glycerine powder is wrapped around the stabilizing pipe and a primer of gunpowder is stuffed into the end.

The two men had already loaded the warheads into the front end of the two RPG launchers. Their assured movements showed that they were practiced users of the weapon. Ahead of them was a line of fuel tanks, at a range of only 50m. Another group of much larger tanks could be seen further away, at 360m.

The nearest fuel tanks filled the iron sites used for aiming the weapon. Simultaneously they pulled the trigger mechanism. The force of the built-up gases threw the grenade out of the tube at approximately 117m/sec. The abrupt acceleration of the grenade leaving the launcher triggered a piezoelectric fuse that ignited the primer, a pyro-retarding gunpowder mixture. This then ignited the squib of nitro, thereby activating the rocket propulsion system to carry the grenade to its target.

Two bright flashes lit the night as the rockets left the launchers; bluish-white smoke billowed out the back-blast. After one tenth of a second, the booster ignited accelerating the rocket to 294m/sec, crossing the short distance in an instant. The high explosive anti-tank rounds, the latest PG7-VL, could penetrate 500mm of armour-plated steel. The thin skin of the storage tanks was no match.

Both tanks convulsed into flame, throwing a billowing, churning bright yellow plume high into the sky. Two smaller adjoining tanks exploded as the intense heat burnt through the sidewalls. The whole street and surrounding area was lit up in bright orange light.

The heat from the blast washed over the attackers, forcing them to avert their eyes.

The two men, helped by the driver, expertly reloaded two more projectiles and corrected their aim towards the set of tanks further away. As they drew their aim onto the new target, a police Renault 4, with its blue light flashing, turned into the top of Birmingham Road. Its siren burst out, surprising the three saboteurs who were still standing in the dark, 600m further down the street.

Another rocket was launched at the depot; it flew towards the tanks in the distance, the target was impossible to miss. The two policemen in the patrol car saw the flash from the rocket ignition. They accelerated down the road, the headlights weaving side to side as the driver fought the torque from the front-wheel drive.

Seeing the approaching police car, the man with the unfired rocket, took aim down the street, waiting calmly as the car swiftly covered the distance towards him. The policemen could have had no idea, that in the darkness ahead, a deadly missile was aimed at them.

The warhead skidded off the bonnet, striking the windscreen just below the roof, enough to ignite the 730g of HMX explosive. The glass, shrapnel and extreme heat killed the two policemen instantly. The roof of the Renault 4 was ripped off, as if by a giant claw. The impact of the rocket lifted the tiny car off the ground, spinning it wildly into the concrete security wall of the petrol depot. The momentum of the vehicle whirled it around after the impact, throwing one of the policemen out of the passenger seat into the road, his body twisting in flame. The gyrating wreck then bounced off a streetlamp sending it back into the middle of the street where it burst into flames.

The three attackers jumped back into the Peugeot, spun into a U-turn down Birmingham Road, turning right into Lobengula Road, then north towards Rugare Township.

Flames and smoke lifted high into the night, sirens blared. The citizens of Salisbury had been sent another message ... the war was on their doorstep.

Attack – Oil/Petrol Storage – Salisbury

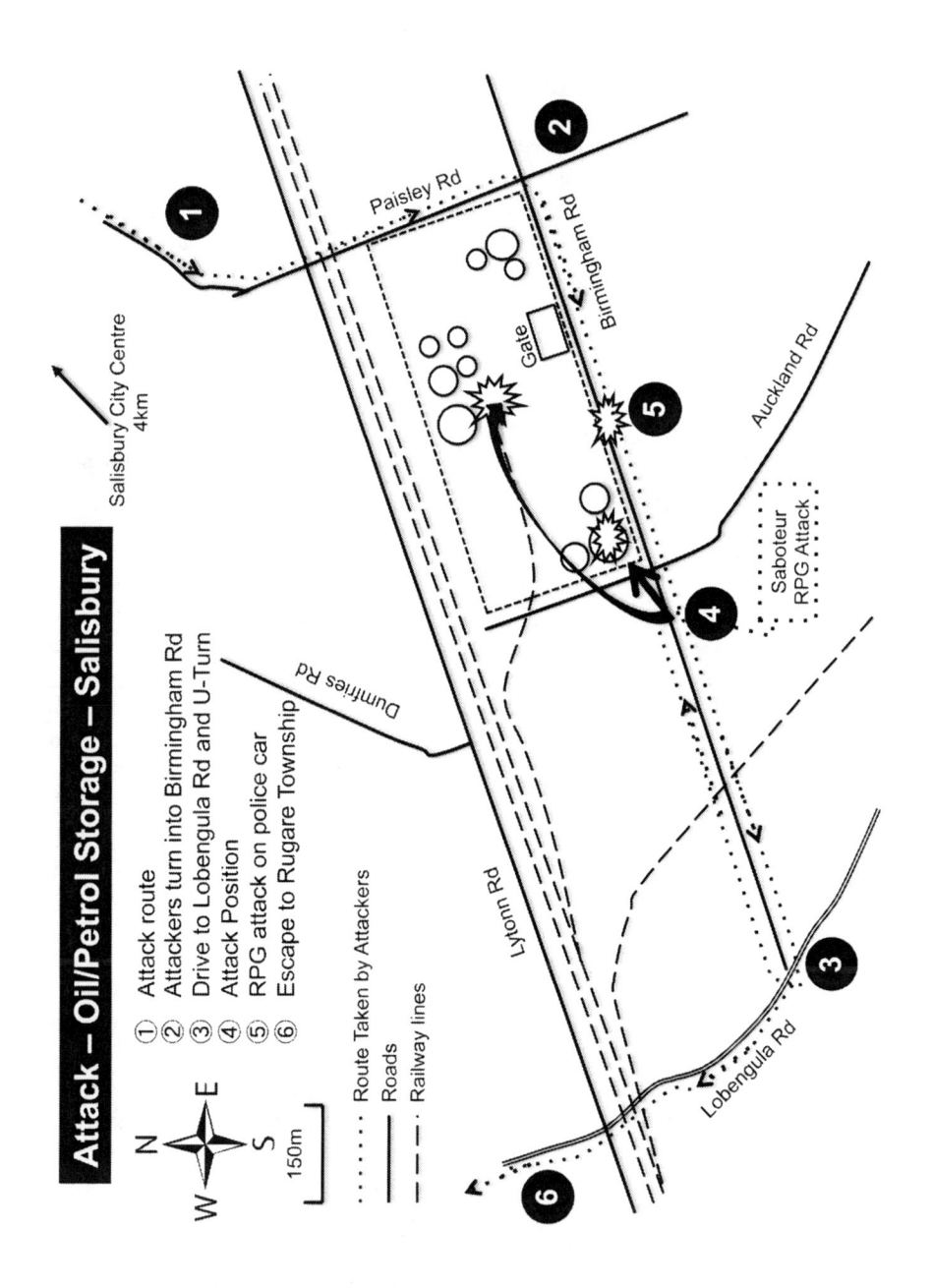

① Attack route
② Attackers turn into Birmingham Rd
③ Drive to Lobengula Rd and U-Turn
④ Attack Position
⑤ RPG attack on police car
⑥ Escape to Rugare Township

····· Route Taken by Attackers
——— Roads
- - - Railway lines

*

Thurston Lane, Avondale Salisbury

George Stanbridge woke up from a deep sleep to a strange sound; the windows in his bedroom were vibrating as if in a gale force wind. At first, he could not assimilate the sound. He lay on his back trying to remember whether the RBC weather report had forecast a storm. He glanced over to his wife who was still sleeping soundly, *what time is it?*

The vibration increased slightly and then subsided, *bloody strange*!

The telephone began to ring in his study. Swinging his legs out of bed, Stanbridge saw the bedside clock read 12:30am. A strange feeling of foreboding washed over him as he climbed out of bed and walked down the passage to the study. A phone ring in the middle of the night can rarely be good news.

'Hello, George Stanbridge.'

'George it's Ken, the shit has hit the fan, somebody has blown up the fuel storage depot in Birmingham Road.' It was Ken Rose the Director of the CIO.

The windows began to vibrate again, the result of a third massive explosion only 6.7km away as the crow flies.

'Bugger!'

'The PM is bouncing off the ceiling; he wants to see both of us and the Police Commissioner, ASAP. We are to go to 8 Chancellor Avenue[86] immediately.'

'Yes Ken, I'll get over there right away.'

The phone went dead, clearly Ken Rose had a lot on his mind. Stanbridge stood looking out the window into the darkness outside, the enormity of the news sinking in. Petrol was the lifeblood of the country; it all had to be trucked by road from South Africa. Sanctions had cut all other sources of supply. This could bring the country to a standstill.

He returned to his bedroom.

'Is everything alright?' his wife asked, alarm in her voice.

'I am afraid not. They have blown up the petrol depot. I have to go to see the PM.'

The telephone began to ring again. Stanbridge returned to his study and in trepidation picked up the receiver.

'Hello ...'

'George it's me again, you're not going to believe this but they have blown up the sugar mill at Triangle as well.'

'Fuck!' was all Stanbridge could say, a man not normally given to swearing. All the petrol in the country was blended with ethanol to reduce the reliance on imports. Ethanol was made from sugarcane at the two large sugar mills in the Lowveld, Triangle and Hippo Valley near Chiredzi.

'George you had better bring in all your files on this Operation Wedza business. We are going to have to explain it all in detail.'

'Yes Ken ... Okay, I will swing past the office to collect them.'

---

86 The Rhodesian Prime Minister's Official residence.

Once again, the phone went dead. The feeling of shock gave way to one of panic, ZANLA had pulled off part of their sabotage plan and he had been powerless to stop them. As he dressed, his mind raced through the list of other targets, the key points of infrastructure, *please God let the Scouts get us all the intelligence on this!*

Faye Chan drove quietly into the driveway; her house was only 1½km from the petrol storage depot. She had borrowed the car from her father who would have been horrified to hear for what purpose. As she opened the back door to the house, the rumble of another explosion split the night, so close it felt like it was outside the door. The enormity of the sound was hard to believe … *we have succeeded!* Looking out the window, to the south the night had been lit up by the burning depot, thick black smoke rose high into the sky. Sirens wailed in the distance.

A smile of deep satisfaction passed across her face … *we have struck another great victory for the cause …*

*

Malvernia Mozambique

The invasion of Mozambique by a stick from 11 Troop, 3 Commando, RLI was progressing well. The heavy diversionary barrage by 2RR had worked a treat. A few fires were burning in the town. The FRELIMO counter-barrage had subsided into a few sporadic mortar rounds.

Corporal Arthur Beamish and his men had skirted to the west of the town circling around to strike the railway line south of the abandoned siding. Amazingly enough a few streetlights were still working. A once magnificent Portuguese colonial railway station dominated the siding. It now lay derelict in disrepair. An 80m long station platform stretched its entire length. The building had wide, arched, covered verandas along the full length of both the track and carpark sides. Waiting rooms and station offices led off the verandas. The main entrance, facing the car park, had a sweeping stairway leading up to a central vaulted vestibule. The domed vestibule housed the dilapidated ticket office, a canteen, toilets and an open waiting area. The walls, in the building's heyday, would have been cladded from floor to ceiling with light-green ceramic tiles but most had been stripped off. Bullet holes pockmarked the walls inside and outside and most of the glass was missing from the windows. While the building was neglected and run down, it still served as offices for the local FRELIMO garrison.

Beamish studied the lay of the land with his binoculars, not very helpful in pitch dark. It was possible to see a few people walking around the streets and a small group of men were clustered in the car park in front of the station building. Two lines of rusting railway wagons stood in the siding. A GAZ truck was drawn up next to the steps leading up to the main entrance of the railway station.

His stick was in the unique position of having two MAG gunners; neither

Le Beau nor Kratzman would relinquish their guns. Beamish had made this suggestion to vehement objection from both men. He had pointed out that they might have to carry their captive once they had made the snatch. 'No problem,' he was told. Penga was way too small to carry a grown man any distance and, frankly, Beamish did not feel too confident on that score either.

The TV camera at Vila Salazar had a clear uninterrupted view of the northern side of the railway station 1.4km away, directly down the railway line. Afonso had shown Beamish all the features to look out for. The TV camera was at that very moment trained on the railway station buildings and the line of broken carriages.

A row of low straggly bushes lined the edge of the railway line providing limited cover as the RLI commandos crept forward. The ground was dry and sandy, completely devoid of grass or other vegetation. This made moving quietly much easier, but the four men progressed slowly and carefully to make sure they made no sound. They were not carrying any weight other than their webbing; weapons, water bottles and Beamish had the A63 VHF radio.

Afonso was keeping up a steady running commentary on the VHF net, describing what he could see on the TV screen. Beamish hissed at him to keep quiet, his incoherent babble was too distracting.

After what seemed an age, they reached the first line of railway wagons. The deep shadow thrown by the wagons stretched all the way to the edge of the railway platform.

A man appeared on the station platform, he was smoking and talking loudly to someone inside one of the offices. A light was flickering inside the building, probably from a paraffin lamp. He was speaking in Portuguese so it was not possible for Beamish to follow the conversation. Penga set himself directly behind Beamish with the two gunners bringing up the rear. Still hidden in the deep shadow of the railway wagons, Beamish held his hand up to stop. Slowly the men dropped to their haunches. The conversation went on and on, forcing the RLI men to stay perfectly still, trying not to breathe. Eventually the man finished his cigarette and went back into the building. He continued to talk loudly, breaking into raucous laughter.

Beamish signalled to move on, painstakingly they crept forward, eventually reaching the edge of the platform. He then had to figure out how to get his men up onto the platform without making any sound. It was at least a metre and a half off the ground, at the height of a passenger carriage. Deciding to lift Penga up first, Beamish, with the help of Kratzman, carefully lifted the lighter man onto the concrete platform. Penga remained on his stomach. They waited for a few moments to make sure that they had not been heard. Penga then carefully lifted the MAGs, gently placing them on the platform. Then Beamish, Le Beau and finally Kratzman were helped up onto the platform.

At the extreme southern end, the platform was deep in shadow, while towards the middle, flickering light splashed the platform from a few of the office windows. Beamish positioned Kratzman with his gun covering the marshalling yard, while Le Beau covered the length of the platform. He and Penga, with their backs to the wall, crept forward, glancing into each office as they progressed slowly down the platform. They reached the central vestibule without seeing anyone.

A loud laugh came from inside the vestibule. Beamish slid up next to a pillar and edged his head around to take a look inside. Three men were sitting on wooden benches drinking what looked like beer. A hissing gas lamp lit the room, throwing wavering shadows on the walls. He recognized one of the voices as the bloke they had watched smoking earlier.

Beamish slipped silently into the vestibule, the men were engrossed in their conversation clearly not expecting any form of attack. Penga stepped inside behind him and they made their way forward.

'Hands up!' Beamish demanded, impersonating John Wayne.

The three men turned in complete surprise to see the blackened ghouls pointing FN rifles at them. Beamish held his finger to his lips to make sure the men did not make a noise. They all blinked in astonishment, all lifting their hands in the air.

'Who is the highest rank?' Beamish asked, trying to sound gruff but keeping his voice low at the same time. His Lancashire accent, difficult to understand even for people who spoke English.

They all looked at him quizzically, trying to understand the question.

'Corp, the one in the middle seems to have more bird shit on his shoulder,' whispered Penga helpfully.

'You! ...' Beamish pointed to the man in the centre, 'Come here,' he indicated for the man to step forward.

'*O que você quer comigo?*' the man asked, his voice quivering slightly. The other two looked on, their eyes flicking between Beamish and Penga.

'Are you the man in charge?' asked Beamish, trying to use his charades skills by tapping his hand on his shoulder and raising his hand up to indicate 'big'.

The man shook his head and shrugged his shoulders in that unique continental fashion, meaning, *I don speaka de English.*

'Fook this!' Beamish hissed in frustration.

Seeing Beamish's momentary hesitation, one of the other men made a run for it. He jumped in behind his mate and ran for the entrance. Penga got him with his FN before the man had moved two metres, then corrected his aim and took out the other man as well. The man in the middle now defaulted to the 'target' for the snatch by process of 'Penga elimination'. The remaining man waved his hands in the air, screaming for mercy, no further translation was needed.

The gunshots carried across the border to Vila Salazar, no more than 1½km to the north.

'Fooking hell!' Beamish exclaimed as his three potential prisoners were instantly reduced to one. 'Penga help me catch the bastard.'

The FRELIMO man promptly put two and two together. Realising he was to be captured, he tried to back away from his abductors. A brief standoff ensued as the protagonists circled each other, like Clint Eastwood in *For A Few Dollars More*.

'Fook this, you Pora bastard!' Beamish exclaimed, now worried about making their escape. He swung his rifle at the man, who ducked, only to be caught by Penga's rifle coming from the other direction. The man let out a loud grunt as he fell to his knees.

The two men grabbed their prisoner by the arms and dragged him out onto the platform. He slid easily along the smooth concrete surface. The gunshots from the railway station had been the cue for the 2RR boys at Vila Salazar, sparking a barrage of smoke shells. In no time the station compound was covered in thick choking smoke that hung in the air like a toxic cloud.

The night lit up again as the FRELIMO garrison returned fire from bunkers scattered all over the town. The barrage eliminated the need for stealth. Beamish jumped off the edge of the platform, he and his men trotting to the west through the car-park, then down a side street, dragging their half conscious prisoner with them. Ramshackle houses lined the street, dogs were barking from all directions. A group of men appeared in front of a house on the left. The disorientated captive, shouted out loudly in Portuguese, '*AJUDA!*'

Kratzman swirled his gun on his hip and fired a long burst at the men, supported by Le Beau. Penga rammed his rifle into the base of the man's skull knocking him out cold.

Rifle shots cracked over the top of the RLI from behind them, near the railway station.

'Fooking Hell!' Beamish yelled out again, as he looked at his captive prostrate in the dirt. 'Penga you bluudy fool.'

Penga knelt down to lift the man onto his shoulders. Le Beau was now firing back down the street towards the railway station, red tracer streaking away, returned with gusto by the defenders.

Completely exposed, Beamish took in the situation. Penga was trapped beneath the captive who was way too heavy for him. Kratzman and Le Beau returning fire. 'Brigadier' Beamish needed to make a rapid appreciation.

'Yank ... you carry the Fred, Penga ... take the gun, Le Beau cover us.'

'74, 74 this is 31Charlie ... fire mission, over,' Beamish called into the radio as the four men struggled away, Kratzman had the captive across his shoulders in a fireman's lift.

'31Charlie, 74, copied.'

'Roger I am going to shoot a mini-flare, suppress enemy to my east ... over.'

Beamish already had a mini-flare loaded in his pocket; he took it out with his free hand and pointed it straight up. It popped out and flew into the sky in a clear arc towards the railway station.

'31Charlie, we have you visual.'

The area behind turned into a maelstrom as 2RR pounded the road next to the railway station, correcting slowly to the west a degree at a time, all eight tubes working in unison. The noise was deafening. A thick cloud of dust rolled across the town, reducing visibility to nil.

The border fence was no more than a 1,000m in front of them, Beamish ran forward with his men huffing and puffing from the exertion. Kratzman initially kept up, Penga had the MAG slung across his shoulders, his own by his side. Le Beau covered their retreat. The thick bush and soft soil soon took its toll. Kratzman's chest was heaving from carrying the deadweight of the man. Eventually he was reduced to staggering forward one step at a time, pushing through the undergrowth, his legs wobbling as his muscles went into spasm.

FRELIMO had not given up the chase; they could be heard shouting as they shook out into a sweepline. Beamish did not want to fire back towards the sweepline for fear of giving his position away, fortunately the thumping mortars were making so much noise that the enemy could not hear them crashing through the bush. Kratzman eventually could go no further, he crashed to his knees dropping the stunned captive onto the sand. He knelt over, coughing loudly, spiting saliva as he gasped for air.

'No Problem, hey Yank?' spat Beamish.

'Sorry Corp ... why did you choose the heaviest Gook in Mozambique?' Kratzman retorted, struggling to regain his senses, his voice laboured as he tried to get air into his lungs.

'Fook this ... Le Beau you and Penga grab this man under y're shoulders. Yank ... take back your gun, Le Beau give me your gun.'

The two shorter men hoisted the captive between them and staggered off, the captive's feet dragging in the sand behind.

Kratzman heaved his gun back onto his shoulders and waited a few seconds to let the others get in front, then followed. The FRELIMO sweepline was now very close, he could hear them calling to each other.

The 2RR mortar fire stopped.

FRELIMO troops came crashing through the undergrowth; they knew that they were chasing a small group of men. They would be able to trap them against the border fence.

Standing his ground, Kratzman braced for the onslaught, his gun at his waist, a belt of 100 rounds in the breach. The first FRELIMO cadre appeared in the darkness only a few feet in front of him. CRACK ... CRACK, down he went ... then another burst of 7.62 into the next man. FRELIMO were now confused, their sweepline began to break up as men started falling in a hail of machinegun fire. Their response was to shoot wildly in the general direction of the border fence. Bullets whizzed and cracked overhead like angry bees.

Breaking out of the bush, Beamish found the border fence in front of him. Le Beau and Penga collapsed next to him gasping, trying to regain their breath. Peering into the darkness left and right Beamish tried to spot the gap in the fence, he had no idea where it was.

'74, 74 ... 31Charlie ... I am at the fence can you indicate your position,' Beamish struggled to get the words out.

Frik, the thin man, heard the desperate call and fired a mini-flare vertically into the night.

'There it is,' called Penga jumping back to his feet. The tiny flare arched out to their north.

'Run you bastards!' Beamish called out, the three men ran along the track next to the fence towards the hole.

Kratzman saw the mini-flare to his north; he estimated about two hundred yards. Problem was, so did most of the FRELIMO army. It seemed as if 1,000 AKs were firing at that spot. The FRELIMO sweepline changed direction towards the flare; impossible to identify friend or foe in the dark. His legs feeling like lead from the exertion, Kratzman could not go any faster than a shuffling walk.

The weight of the FRELIMO captive was now beyond carrying. Le Beau and Penga resorted to dragging him along by his legs, each tucking a boot under the arm.

'Over here!' called a voice from the darkness near the fence.

In the gloom three 2RR men appeared, grabbed the captive and pulled him through the hole in the fence, splitting his skin as it caught on the barbed wire, his shirt wrapped about his head from being dragged backwards. The three RLI men dived through the hole and began to shoot back into the bush behind them. This had the effect of focusing the FRELIMO attention more acutely, sending down a fearsome barrage.

Smoke bombs again descended from the 2RR mortars, trying to provide cover for the escaping RLI.

'YANK... where the fook are you?' Beamish screamed into the night.

Smoke filled the air, making it difficult to breath. As if by magic, a para-illuminating mortar round burst above, bathing the border fence in a milky light as it penetrated the smoke.

Out of the gloom, like some ghostly apparition, Kratzman appeared, dragging his feet in the sand, hunched over. He was backing towards the fence firing his machinegun back into the night.

'COVER HIM' Beamish bellowed and every man fired into the bush beyond the ethereal figure. He eventually arrived at the fence and collapsed, anxious hands hauled at him, pulling him through.

'74, 74, Hotel Lima Zulu, fire for effect,' Frik called in the mortars. The Mozambique side of the fence disappeared in a cloud of dust as the 2RR mortar-men went about their business.

'74 ... 31Charlie ... Puff the Magic Dragon, I say again ... Puff the Magic Dragon.' Beamish sent the code for mission complete.

'31Charlie, copied ... Puff the Magic Dragon,' replied Captain John.

The four RLI men lay exhausted next to their comatose captive, sucking in air, listening to the sweet sound of the mortar barrage. *Captain John will be pleased.*

Snatch Operation – 11 Trp external Mozambique

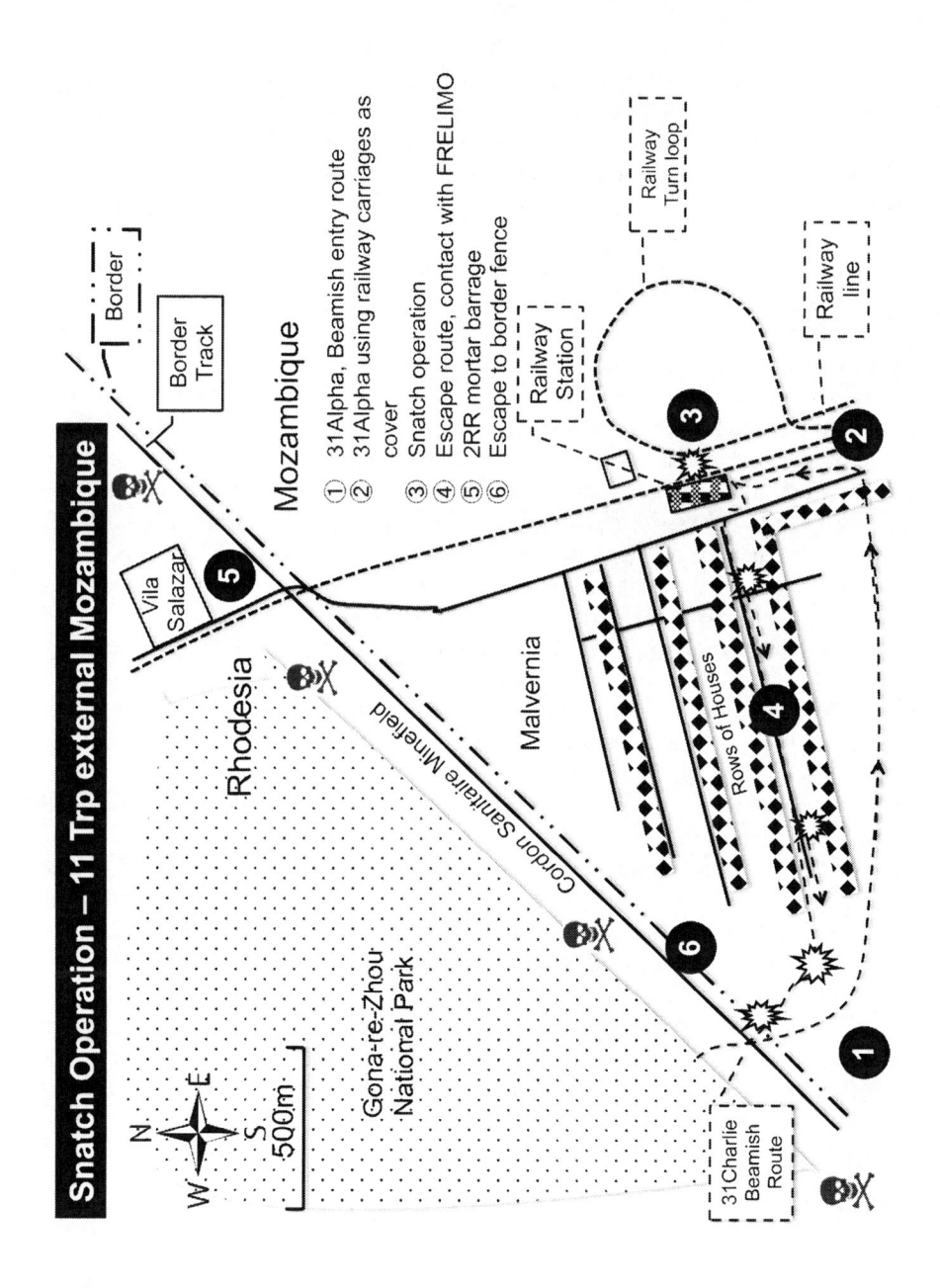

Mozambique

1. 31Alpha, Beamish entry route
2. 31Alpha using railway carriages as cover
3. Snatch operation
4. Escape route, contact with FRELIMO
5. 2RR mortar barrage
6. Escape to border fence

11

CIO HQ, Coghlan Buildings, Livingston Avenue, Salisbury

George Stanbridge and Ken Rose sat in the conference room on the sixth floor of their HQ building. It was 9am, both felt like they had been put through a concrete mixer. The interview with the PM, that included the Minister of Defence, had not gone well. The whole government establishment was in a state of shock. The war had again been brought into downtown Salisbury; what's more, two of the most vital installations had been attacked with impunity – simultaneously!

News from the Selous Scout fort at Grand Reef was equally disturbing. The mission, Operation Wedza had been compromised. The team had not made their LZ for extraction. They had not communicated since 9pm the previous evening. The assumption was that they were on the run, moving towards the secondary extraction point. They reported that they had not been able to take a high value prisoner.

Looking out of the window to the south the giant black cloud of burning petrol and diesel covered the skyline. The fire had spread to neighbouring buildings and every fireman in the city was trying to put it out. Fire engines from Salisbury Airport had been called in, spraying tonnes of foam onto the fire, in a few hours exhausting the country's supply of fire retardant. This attack was not something that could be covered up.

'The PM is rampant,' Ken Rose commented, gazing in disbelief out of the window.

'COMOPS phoned, they have been ordered to put in reprisal airstrikes on infrastructure in Mozambique and Zambia,' replied Stanbridge, also looking fixatedly out the window.

'What are we going to do George?' Rose was at a loss, what had happened was unprecedented.

'I think it's time we stopped fart-arsing about and went after the ZANLA and ZIPRA leadership … starting with Tongogara and working down the list.' Stanbridge had anger in his voice, not common in a man renowned for his cool, unflappable temperament.

'The Poms will never agree to that, they told you already.'

'I know, but we need to take the gloves off. If we don't we are sitting ducks!'

'What do you propose?' Rose sat forward in his chair, his face a picture of stress and bewilderment.

'For the first time, the politicians have a taste for the real situation we are in. They will be casting about for scapegoats, and the finger is already being pointed at us. We need to turn that energy to our advantage.'

'Yes?' Rose sat forward, completely focused on Stanbridge's words.

'My staff have been working on a plan to assassinate Nkomo, Masuku and Tongogara for some time. It only needs a few more refinements.'

'We have had a crack at Nkomo and Tongogara already and failed dismally. What could we possibly do differently?'

'That's true, but this plan involves a coordinated attack on multiple targets simultaneously.'

'What about Mugabe?'

'The problem is that he is holed up in a strongpoint in Maputo and guarded by his mate Samora Machel with half the FRELIMO army. To get to him would need an armoured division. No ... we think that if we can start taking out members of the leadership one by one the others will be more inclined to negotiate with us ... Mugabe included.'

'Aren't the others equally protected?' Rose was playing devil's advocate.

'Yes they are ... but nowhere near to the same extent. We know exactly where they stay ... the camps they visit, the roads they use. We have been able to plot Tongogara's movements very accurately ... we have informants planted in the leadership. Frankly, we could have got him long ago. Now our lily-livered politicians will have something to chew on.' Stanbridge pounded his fist into his hand for emphasis. His mind was back in the game.

'Okay ... let's present this ASAP. We need to get the heat off our backs. You will need to find a way around your friends at MI6. The Poms will definitely try to block us, they are big fans of Messrs Tongogara and Masuku.'

'Leave that to me ... I have a few ideas on that front.' George Stanbridge got up to leave; he had plenty of work to do.

'Keep me informed of your progress George.'

'No problem. You will take care of the PM?'

'Yes ... leave that to me.' Ken Rose returned his gaze out the window at the distant black cloud spreading across the city, an undeniable beacon, demonstrating the failure of the intelligence organisation.

As Stanbridge reached the door, a senior staffer knocked and entered.

'You wouldn't believe this. 2RR and the RLI at Vila Salazar have captured a FRELIMO Colonel who knows all about our saboteurs. He is squealing his head off apparently.'

'How do we know this?' asked Rose, a hint of excitement in his voice.

'I don't know exactly ... just that JOC Repulse have received a two page sitrep from the boys at Vila Salazar spelling it all out.'

'Fuck me gently!' Ken Rose jumped to his feet. 'Get that Fred up here ... send a bloody Canberra if you have to.'

*

Chimoio District, Mozambique

Sergeant Cephas Ngwenya was afraid. He was in the unfamiliar position of being lost and alone deep inside enemy territory. Lost was probably not strictly correct in that he had an estimate of his position, just nobody else knew where he was. He had watched his friend and colleague Simon Nyandoro cut down by the enemy that had overrun their position. There was nothing he could have done for him, Nyandoro was caught in a crossfire, his body twitching from many hits. Ngwenya saw him go to ground, his uniform a mass of blood. He had then watched in horror as the frenzied terrorists had bayonetted Nyandoro's body. The memory sent a shiver down his spine ... *being captured alive was not an option.*

There was no sign of the rest of his group, Kumpher, Seals and Schultz. Ngwenya had his own A63 radio but it had limited range and there were no obvious high points to climb to get better reception. He had tried calling the rest of his team but there was no answer, just the frustrating, sizzling static. Deciding that using up battery on calling people that may no longer be alive was a waste of time, he packed the radio into his backpack.

The terrain was undulating as far as the eye could see in all directions.

He sat in the shade of a huge Msasa tree, his back to the trunk, rifle across his knees. Most of the previous night had been spent on the run, dodging groups of ZANLA that were out looking for them. The searchers were still close by; he had seen a band of them on the opposite ridge to the one he was sitting on. Fatigue had made it impossible to continue, he needed to rest up to regain his strength. The chase had forced him to throw kit out of his Bergen pack and most of his food. Water was also going to be a problem; the only water he had left was two water bottles attached to his webbing belt. Two or three days in this heat would take care of that. The only radio battery was the one in the radio and that was on its last legs. The situation was desperate.

Cephas Ngwenya's mind passed to thinking of his wife and son back on his small farm near Tjolotjo north of Bulawayo. His family had lived in the region, now called Nata Tribal Trust Land, for many generations. His clan had been part of the Zulu invasion of southern Matabeleland by Mzilikazi in1838. All of his ancestors had been warriors; they fought the Shona tribes, Kalanga, the Shangaan, the white man and each other. It was a natural thing that Ngwenya had become a policeman; his father had spent thirty years in the BSAP before a ZIPRA landmine killed him.

Ngwenya's position in the police had given him a good income that had allowed him to raise *lobolo* for his wife, Nomsa. His family still thought he was in the police force; they would have been horrified to hear he was in the Selous Scouts. That information would have put his family in grave danger from the ZIPRA terrorists operating in the Nata region. Tjolotjo was the centre of the Nata TTLs. The fact that he was a policeman and from a respected family meant that the terrorists left him and his family alone. In any event, many of the ZIPRA cadres were friends of his from school; they were neighbours, herded cattle together as children, playing amongst the granite koppies that surrounded the district. Two had come out of the bush to attend his father's funeral. The war had so many contradictions - that's just the way it was.

Nomsa was the daughter of a headman and had high status. The cost of the *lobolo* had been high, six cattle, ten goats and $100 in cash. It was still the best decision of his life. He loved Nomsa more than life itself. His son Matthew was only two years old, he wanted to watch his son grow. Ngwenya considered what would become of his family if he were killed.

The thought was too appalling to contemplate ... *I have to get out of this mess!*

The fugitive Ngwenya looked at the sky ... it would be dark in two hours. Once it was dark he would make his move to the backup extraction point that he estimated to be 6kms to the southwest. The distance was no problem, but his route was through a densely populated farming area with hundreds of ZANLA and FRELIMO looking for him.

*

Selous Scout Fort, Grand Reef Forward Airfield (FAF 8), Eastern Rhodesia

Each of the Forward Airfields around the country had a Selous Scout 'fort' built near it. The description 'fort' was a bit of a misnomer; it was really a group of buildings surrounded by a corrugated iron or concrete Insta-rect wall. The idea was to give the Selous Scouts privacy from prying eyes, to keep the identity of the members as secret as possible, and to prevent the leak of information about Selous Scout activities. The fort had communications equipment; operations rooms, accommodation, mess halls and an MT yard.

The Selous Scouts' primary function was that of pseudo-operations, which involved infiltrating terrorist cells, and intelligence gathering. This included manning OPs and calling in Fireforce onto terrorist targets. External operations were also a speciality that included destroying enemy infrastructure, assassination of senior enemy officers, snatch operations, and raiding terrorist training camps. The fort was the control point for all operations in their respective areas. In the case of Grand Reef FAF 8, located to the south of the city of Umtali, it was also the hub for Selous Scout external operations into Mozambique.

The news of the compromise of the Operation Wedza team spread like wildfire. The Selous Scouts HQ at Andre Rabie Barracks near Salisbury was informed, who in turn informed Army HQ and COMOPS. The task of finding the men and arranging an extraction fell to the local Scout commander, Captain Tony Warren. The standard operating procedure for all external operations was a scheduled radio communication every two hours. This corresponded roughly to the length of time a team would move before taking a break. The communication was via the 'big-means' TR48 HF radio. The messages involved codes and passwords for each stage of the operation. This saved time instead of coding up messages using shackle and button codes. As soon as Wedza missed a scheduled radio sitrep, an alert went out warning of a problem. Two missed radio scheds meant serious trouble, three, meant potential catastrophe.

Captain Warren had two Selous Scout sticks available at Grand Reef to support an extraction effort but he figured he was going to need more firepower. A 2 Commando RLI Fireforce were stationed at Grand Reef but they were all out on various operations. All that was left at his disposal were cooks and bottle-washers. He picked up the phone to speak to his opposite number at the fort at Chiredzi. The answer from the duty NCO described how the disaster caused by the destruction of the ethanol processing facility at the Triangle sugar mill had sucked up all available manpower. A massive manhunt was underway for the perpetrators, including the Selous Scout men who were already on OPs in the Sengwe, Matibi and Ndowoyo TTLs. The duty NCO suggested contacting 3 Commando. Captain Warren duly got through to the RLI base at Buffalo Range.

'Hello, can I speak to Major Tomlinson please.'

'I am sorry but Major Tomlinson is on operations. The only officer we have is Captain Liversedge,' replied the clerk in the Operations Room.

After a short delay, Captain Liversedge came on the line.

'Ian, its Tony Warren from Scouts fort at Grand Reef. How are you?' The two men had been friends since their days on the Regular Officer's Course at the School of Infantry. Tony Warren had also started his career in the RLI before going on to do the Selous Scouts selection course.

'Tony ... you useless bastard! I am fine. How are things amongst you baboon-eaters,' Liversedge had a laugh. Part of the Selous Scout selection was trapping and eating wild animals including baboons.

'Not well. We have a little predicament and I may need some of your men to help.'

'Always a pleasure to get the Selous Scouts out of the poo, but I have to tell you the shit has hit the fan down here. The gooks blew up the bloody sugar mill and we have had to deploy every man we have on follow-up. The brass are freaking out.'

'I can't go into the details Ian but we have a call-sign trapped in Mozambique and I may need to put men on the ground to help get them out.'

'Well I can muster a stick including myself now and I am waiting for another stick to return from Mbalauta any minute.'

'That will have to do. I have asked the Blue Jobs to send a Dak to fetch you ... should be there in an hour.'

'Fuck Tony ... you boys really are in the shit!'

The phone went dead.

Warren had called the air force as soon as Operation Wedza missed its second radio sched. He had arranged to get two Lynx and a Hunter to overfly the area in which the call-sign might be hiding, to raise them on their A63 VHF radios. Each Lynx took an observer to try and help spot the Selous Scout men on the ground. So far, nothing had been heard, no radio contact had been established.

A clammy, sick feeling entered Captain Warren's stomach.

*

3 Commando RLI, Fireforce base, Buffalo Range Forward Airfield (FAF 7), South-east Rhodesia

Corporal Arthur Beamish and his intrepid adventurers drove back into their camp at Buffalo Range exhausted and in need of a square meal, shower and sleep. They had been up before first light to drive the FRELIMO prisoner out to Mbalauta in their only serviceable vehicle. Beamish had raised every argument possible of why it was impossible to drive out in a single vehicle. Captain John insisted that all would be fine, as he had arranged for an escort to be sent from the 2RR base at Mbalauta. 'Beamish my old son ... you will be fine,' Captain John had said.

As it turned out Beamish and his crew drove all the way to Mbalauta without any sign of a 2RR escort. They drove onto the airfield to a large reception committee. The news of the high value prisoner caught wandering around outside the Vila Salazar perimeter fence, dazed and confused, had spread. A Brittan-Norman Islander stood parked next to the 2RR tents on the far end of the runway. The RLI Four-Five stopped next to the tents and was immediately surrounded by soldiers.

Nothing was said to Beamish, no questions were asked. Everyone watched in silence as the FRELIMO Colonel was unloaded. He was bound and gagged, with a first field dressing wrapped around his head. The Colonel, 'Colonel Pora' as Captain John had called him, had been tied down onto one of the bench seats. The tightness of his bonds had cut off the circulation to his feet. Kratzman removed the bindings then dragged the man feet first to the back of the vehicle where waiting hands lowered him to the ground. He wobbled unsteadily with the pain as the blood rushed back into his feet and legs; he collapsed onto the ground moaning in obvious agony through the gag. His eyes flashed with tears of pain as he rolled back and forth kicking out with his legs to reduce the 'pins and needles'.

No attempt was made to help the man. Instead, the crowd studied him in morbid fascination.

Four men wearing civilian clothing, but with pistols in shoulder holsters walked purposefully up to the back of the vehicle and took possession of the prisoner.

'*Adios amigo*,' said Kratzman in Spanish, not being conversant in Portuguese.

One man grunted something in Beamish's direction but he could not hear what the man had said. The delegation marched off with the prisoner supported between them. They climbed into the waiting aircraft and it immediately took off.

Beamish and his stick completed their trip from Mbalauta to Buffalo Range. By the time they got back Beamish was in a filthy mood, hot and tired. As soon as the vehicle came to a stop he jumped off, walking determinedly towards the barrack room, he had had enough. All he wanted was a meal and a sleep.

'BEAMISH!' came a call from across the quad.

He turned to see who was calling, his face immediately taking on the countenance of a thundercloud. It was Captain Liversedge standing on the veranda in front of the Ops Room ... *fooking hell what does he want!* He walked slowly towards the officer giving a good impression of a man returning from a 42km route march.

'Corporal Beamish, congratulations on your work in the capture of the

FRELIMO Colonel. I have a signal from Vila Salazar saying you did great work,' commented Captain Liversedge, his usual smile lighting up his face.

'Thank you Sur,' replied Beamish, studying the face of the Captain to seek out any sinister intent ... *Officers always had sinister intent, giving with one hand, taking with the other.*

'You will have to tell me all about how this Colonel just happened to be aimlessly strolling around Vila Salazar in the dead of night, Beamish?'

'Yes Sur.'

Beamish was still unsure of how much detail Captain John would have given. They had both agreed that the details of the 'external' should be kept between themselves, but Captain John could have been carried away by the excitement.

'We will have to leave that to another time Beamish. I am afraid that you, your stick and I, are needed at Grand Reef. Get down to the CQMS and draw your replacement kit. Carry extra ammunition and rations for five days.'

'But Surrr ...' replied Beamish, shocked, he could not believe it. He stood in front of the officer, as if to make sure he had heard right.

'Carry on Beamish ... no time to waste ... our aircraft is expected any minute.'

Liversedge turned on his heel, leaving Beamish standing flabbergasted in the dusty road. His men stood some distance back waiting to get the nod to take a shower.

'We are going to fooking Grand Reeef!' was all he could say. The boys were not happy ... *bloody officers, always a sting in the tail!*

*

Combined Operations HQ, Milton Buildings, Salisbury

Faye Chan bounced, metaphorically, into work on the morning after the attack on the fuel storage depot. To anybody watching, her elation and excitement would not have been at all noticeable. She walked at the same pace, her head held erect, her eyes fixed in front. When greeted by her colleagues in the typing and secretarial pool she smiled politely and went directly to her desk. This was her routine. Faye then took out pens and pencils from her draw and flipped through the papers in her in-tray. Satisfied that there was nothing particularly demanding, she walked down the passage to the staffroom to make herself a cup of tea. A large stainless steel hot-water urn stood on a table in the corner. She took a teacup out of the cupboard and made herself a strong cup of Tanganda Tea. A Rhodesian Herald newspaper lay on one of the tables; a black and white picture of burning fuel tanks dominated the front page. Taking up the newspaper, she sat down to read the main story.

Outside the staffroom, there was a great deal of activity. Senior officers were hurrying from meeting to meeting; the overnight attacks had certainly stirred the pot.

Faye finished her tea and walked back to her desk. As she entered the passage, she bumped into the elderly gentleman, George Stanbridge, dressed, as always, in his aged threadbare suit.

'Excuse me, I am sorry,' apologised Stanbridge politely.

'It's no problem, it's my fault I really must look where I am walking,' replied Faye, averting her eyes.

'You are one of the shorthand typists aren't you?' said Stanbridge gently. The girl's Asian features struck Stanbridge. She was very attractive indeed, reminded him of a girl he knew at Cambridge.

'Yes, I am, I have taken notes in a few of your meetings,' replied Faye suddenly fearing that she had said too much.

'Ah well, keep up the good work … must be off … have a good day,' Stanbridge nodded. Clearly very distracted, he went off down the passage, a large file of papers under his arm.

'Thank you,' Faye replied but the man was already too far away to hear … *I must be more careful!* She knew all about George Stanbridge, as she did all the senior CIO personnel, she had made it her business.

12

Chimoio District Mozambique

Cephas Ngwenya had watched in desperation as a Lynx had passed overhead his position. By the time he had got the radio out of his pack and switched it on the aircraft was too far away. He had it set on the emergency frequency and cursed himself for not having the radio ready. There was always a delay while the radio warmed up anyway. He kept the radio inside his pack so as not to arouse suspicion. The local FRELIMO cadres did not carry radios. He could not leave the radio switched on for fear of running the battery flat ... *at least they are looking for me*, he thought.

The escape from Camp Takawira had been disastrous. The ZANLA follow-up had been upon them almost immediately. Ngwenya had opened fire, mainly to warn the rest of his call-sign. In the ensuing confusion, with bullets flying in all directions, grenade and RPG explosions, Ngwenya had been separated from the others, left to fend for himself.

On studying the maps and aerial photographs more closely, Ngwenya concluded that he was probably 15km from the alternate extraction point. The escape from the ZANLA hunting party had dragged him further north than he had expected. The set of 33kV powerlines that ran south from Chimoio through the ZANLA camp were an excellent guide. He had to move southwest on a bearing of 228° which he set on his compass. The bearing would cross the road between Chimoio and Candeeiro, then across, mostly cultivated land, for about 7km. Rescue was tantalisingly close.

The extraction point was on the top of a granite outcrop, the result of an ancient lava intrusion that had filled a fault in the earth's crust. After millions of years of erosion, what was left on the landscape was a distinctive granite whaleback-shaped ridge, running almost exactly north-south. It was approximately 2kms long and about 30m wide at the top, its highest point being about 50m above the surrounding countryside. The top of the outcrop was mostly flat and relatively easy for a helicopter to land on. It also commanded a 360° view of the surrounding farmland. These unique geological structures were found all over that part of Mozambique, making excellent landmarks, very easy to pick up from the air. This granite ridge went by the name of *Zembe* by the local people; its Selous Scout code name was '*Chenjere*' or 'danger' in seShona.

Walking out of his deep cover on a long dogleg, Ngwenya began his quest for safety. He was wearing the flat rubber-soled 'clandestine' boots that left no tread but a very distinctive *spoor* for someone who knew what they were looking for. He cursed the fact that he had not chosen a pair of FRELIMO issue boots with their unique chevron pattern. He had not been able to find a pair to fit. The thought of pushing up blisters seemed a small problem now.

Darkness fell over the bush as Ngwenya made his way towards his first and most important waypoint, the road south from Chimoio. The going was not difficult. Low undulating hills crisscrossed with streams and watercourses, most were bone dry. The moon was up early, bathing the country in an eerie light. Hill ridges were clear to see, the moon making navigation straightforward. His progress was slow as he avoided crossing open ploughed land, choosing instead to keep in the shadows of the bordering tree lines. It was tempting to take one of the many cattle tracks that crossed his path but the risk of his pursuers seeing his spoor was too great. On one occasion, the path was tempting so he removed his boots and walked barefoot for a kilometre, enjoying the feeling of the soft sand between his toes. His thoughts inevitably returned to home and the familiar pathways between the villages, of herding cattle as a child, of following his mother as she walked 5km every day to fetch water.

Movement in front of him snapped Ngwenya out of his reverie.

He knelt down, straining his ears to pick up any sound ... *it must be cattle moving in the bush.* He listened for the distinctive sound that animals make when grazing ... *no sound at all, not cattle.*

Deciding to wait a few moments, Ngwenya moved off the path and silently slipped his boots back on. No sooner had he done so than the sounds of animated conversation came towards him along the path. He ducked down, lying flat in the grass no more than a few feet off the path. The voices were indistinct at first, then, as they came closer, he could tell that they were speaking Ndau, one of the Mozambican languages ... *maybe local tribesmen returning from a beer-drink in the neighbouring village.* The distinctive sound of a rifle scratching against a water bottle dispelled any theory of local villagers moving about, these men were FRELIMO.

The conversation came closer and closer; Ngwenya could pick out at least four voices although judging by the sound of the men walking down the path, there were more than that. The clinking of equipment was now very clear, these men were making no effort to move quietly. They came around a bend in the track, Ngwenya held his breath as the men filed past, the dust from their boots filling his nose. He did not look up, keeping his face buried in the grass ... *if they see me now I am dead!*

A man called out and the file stopped.

Ngwenya's heart missed a beat; he wished he could understand what they were saying. Then he heard the sound of a man peeing in the grass not far away. The loud conversion carried on, the men seemed in a jovial mood. Another man started to piss, this time much closer; Ngwenya could smell the nauseating odour. His mind raced as he tried to assimilate all the options ... *get up and run, shoot it out, stay still, try to bluff my way through pretending to be a lost ZANLA cadre.* Any movement would more than likely frighten the FRELIMO men into shooting wildly ... *the only option is to stay still and hope they pass by, if they find me I will take as many of them with me as possible.*

Someone shouted instructions and the men started to move off. A boot appeared right next to Ngwenya's head, he could smell the man's perspiration. His body tensed ready to spring, his stomach cramped in anticipation. The boot moved away and as quickly as they had arrived, the noise of the men faded away. Ngwenya continued to lie perfectly still. Bathed in sweat, he could feel it pooling in the small of his back. The nervous tension made his whole body ache. He tried to bring his breathing back under control, his heart still pounding in his chest.

It was half an hour before Ngwenya trusted himself to get up. He slowly got to his feet, remaining crouched over, ready to react. He scanned the path left and right, twisting his head to pick up even the slightest sound. Losing concentration for a split second, he stepped back into the path, his boot left a telltale mark in the soft soil. Unaware of his mistake, he glanced down at the compass, the luminous dial marked the bearing to follow and he moved off through the bush, going as fast as he could without making any sound. His primary focus was on anti-tracking, making frequent direction changes and backtracking on his own spoor. This slowed his progress but would hopefully delay any hunting party ... *please God that FRELIMO don't have any good trackers.*

The dirt road to Chimoio appeared through the trees, red dirt shining in the moonlight. Ngwenya crept forward, keeping bent over as close to the ground as possible. He stopped next to a large tree on the side of the road and studied the bush on the other side. FRELIMO would almost certainly be checking the road for spoor; it was an obvious barrier for the Rhodesians to cross. He removed his boots again to cross barefoot. Waiting for half an hour Ngwenya continued to study the road. It disappeared into the distance north and south, straight as a die with large trees and bush on both sides. Satisfied that there was no one close by, he began his dash across the road.

'*Quem é que?*' someone called out in Portuguese.

Caught in the middle of the road, Ngwenya stopped.

'Hello friend' Ngwenya called out, using the only words in Portuguese he knew.

'Where are you going?' the voice demanded.

Ngwenya twisted his head, still not exactly sure where the voice was calling from. He continued to walk across the road his AK held loosely in his arms finger on the trigger.

'Stop!' the voice shouted, leaving no doubt that the man was serious.

The shout pinpointed his position.

The AK in Ngwenya's arms bounced as he let loose with a spray of bullets on fully automatic. He ran off the road continuing to shoot at the point the voice had called from. No gunfire was returned.

Ducking behind a tree, puffing from the shock of being discovered, Ngwenya waited. There was no sound ... *the man must have been alone.* Waiting to get his breathing back under control, Ngwenya sank to his knees, propping his back up against the tree. He gently slipped his boots back on and tied the laces tightly.

Another voice called from up the road, a man appeared walking down the road from the north. Deciding not to try to ambush and kill the man, Ngwenya moved off into the bush, once again moving as fast as he could without making noise. As he did so, he heard the sound of a truck in the distance, his gunshots had alerted his hunters. He had three hours before daylight, needing to put as much distance as he could between himself and the follow-up that must now surely come.

As first light lit up the horizon Ngwenya could see in the distance his RV point, *Chenjere*. He checked his map and the aerial photograph, convinced now that he was in the right place.

In the distance, came the drone of an aircraft engine, the distinctive sound of a Lynx. This time he had the radio out in a flash, turning it on and waited the agonizing seconds for it to warm up.

'Cyclone, Cyclone, Sierra20, do you copy,' called Ngwenya, Cyclone being voice procedure for air force.

No response.

He waited a few more seconds.

'Cyclone, Cyclone, Sierra20 ...' Ngwenya called urgently, willing the pilot to respond.

'Sierra20 this is Blue50 ... reading you threes.'

Ngwenya wanted to scream with relief, he could not remember seeing anything more beautiful than the twin tail-boomed aircraft as it appeared above at 5,000ft.

'Blue50 ... Kilo, Alpha, Romeo,' Ngwenya called the required daily code, confirming his identity.

'Sierra20 copied ... call me in.'

'I have limited radio life ... figures five.'

'Copied.'

The Lynx pilot could only see endless miles of bush and cultivated fields below him, he could not pinpoint Ngwenya from that height. The engine note changed as the aircraft lost altitude. Spreading his 1:50,000 map out on the ground Ngwenya placed rocks on the edge to hold it down.

'Roger, Blue50 go left ...' he began to call the aircraft in over his position.

A bright white streak of smoke lifted from the ground, plus what seemed like hundreds of rifles firing at once. The streak chased towards the Lynx, then passed by its tail racing high into the sky, a thick white cloud of smoke marking its course.

'Sierra20 I must abort that was a Strela[87] ... proceed to *Chenjere* ... I say again ... proceed to *Chenjere*! ... Charlie Tangos to your east,' called the Lynx pilot. The threat from the heat-seeking missile was too great.

The Lynx banked sharply and disappeared back the way it had come.

Ngwenya watched in despair as the aircraft faded away to the west ... *at least they know I am alive ... for now!*

*

Airspace over Eastern border of Rhodesia

The Alouette III G-car could travel at a speed of 84 knots if it was only carrying its pilot, tech and a full fuel load. With a stick of four men fully

---

[87] SAM-7 Soviet, shoulder fired, ground-to-air, heat-seeking missile.

loaded, its speed was reduced to 65 knots (120km/hr.) with an endurance of approximately forty-five minutes. The distance from Grand Reef to *Chenjere*, the RV point for Operation Wedza, was over 90km one way. That, with time needed over the target and the return trip, meant that helicopters were required to refuel. The operation had as a standard requirement a refuelling stop. How this was achieved was to drop 44-gallon drums of Avtur by parachute from a Dakota onto an island in the middle of the hydroelectric dam called Chicamba. This dam was located roughly halfway between the terrorist camp at Marera Agricultural College and Grand Reef (FAF8) with the entry point into Mozambique over the Vumba Mountains, near Leopard Rock. The helicopters could follow the course of the Chicamba River, with its source in the Vumba Mountains, then directly east to the island. A small team of Selous Scouts manned the refuelling point that was protected by the rough terrain and the enormous stretch of water.

Three Alouette III G-cars and a K-car crossed the border at 5,000ft AGL heading east in the direction of Chicamba Dam. In one of these helicopters was the stick commanded by Corporal Arthur Beamish of 11 Troop. He still had his two MAG gunners that, despite his earlier protestations, he was now grateful for. The plan was to wait at the refuelling point until the planned extraction of the Selous Scouts. They would not be required if the helicopters could get in, uplift the men and get out again. What was unclear to Beamish was the alternative. He had asked Captain Liversedge who had dismissed the question by implying loosely that they may be required to secure the LZ.

Beamish and his stick were issued with strange looking contraptions the Choppertech described as Pegasus harnesses. He had given Beamish and his men a short briefing on how to use the harness, describing it as important for purposes of a 'hot extraction'. Beamish was slightly perplexed by the jocular fashion in which the tech described the process, as the man shook his head and giggled throughout. Beamish had heard of a 'hot extraction' before, it was a sling hung from beneath the helicopter from a long rope. The idea being that the stick could attach themselves to the sling using the harness without the helicopter landing. 'Hot' in this case Beamish felt must mean 'difficult'.

As the helicopter bumped through the early morning thermals Beamish had pause for thought on the events of the past few days. The 'snatch' operation had been harrowing; he could not believe that he had actually gone through with it. Captain John had a very disturbing effect on him. It was a sort of intangible bond, difficult to define. The feeling was somewhat surreal, like the rest of the world did not exist at all. The isolation of Vila Salazar and the constant bombardment from both sides seemed to consume everything. In a way, Beamish was sorry he had to leave. He felt that it was almost like he would have followed Captain John through the gates of hell and yet he had only known the man for 48 hours. The only other soldier to elicit the same emotional reaction in Beamish was Troop Sergeant Jock McIntyre. Beamish was convinced the Captain had the same effect on the other three men in his stick.

The treatment of the Freddy Colonel by Captain John had been bizarre. When the man came round after the crack on the back of the head, Captain John had marched up to him and saluted smartly. He had Afonso next to him and insisted that a cordial welcome be extended in Portuguese. The man could not take his eyes off the weird sight of 'John Lennon' in a camo-caftan extending him a welcome in Portuguese.

Colonel 'Pora' as Captain John christened him, immediately went into a rage shouting and screaming, pointing determinedly back towards Mozambique. Afonso had difficulty keeping up the translation of the tirade. Captain John, surrounded by his men, had waited patiently for the man to finish. He then asked Afonso to ask the man politely for any information he may have on FRELIMO or ZANLA.

It was a general sort of question, something like, 'can you give me any information on FRELIMO and ZANLA?'

Afonso translated and the man tilted again, into a vicious verbal assault swinging his arms about in all directions. Captain John had then held his hands up in submission, shaking his head from side to side as if sympathising with Colonel Pora. He then asked Afonso to enquire whether the man 'would like a swim.' It was now ten o'clock at night. When Afonso posed the question, the man blinked in disbelief shaking his head, *'No I don't want a swim!'*

Captain John ignored the man's objection and called for a beer and one of the white plastic pool chairs. He then took the chair, placing it on the edge of the pool and sat down. Once his beer arrived, he asked Frik to throw the man in the pool, Frik obliged. Colonel Pora now really screamed blue murder. Flapping about in the pool, the man gained the edge, then was whipped out by the excited spectators who placed him gently back on his feet. Everyone, including Beamish, was now finding this process amusing and vaguely intriguing.

Beamish, also beer in hand, had taken a chair to sit next to Captain John.

Captain John then asked Afonso to repeat the previous question, which he duly did. Colonel Pora was now in such an agitated state that he simply refused to answer, shaking his head with his hands held in front of him, waving briskly from side to side; in that distinctly European fashion meaning … *I no longer wish to answer any questions.* He stood unrestrained on the edge of the pool, dripping wet. No more questions were asked of him. Instead, Captain John seemed to go off at a tangent.

'Who can hold his breath underwater?' called out Captain John to the surrounding men.

A number of excited hands went up.

'Off you go then,' he said pointing to the pool.

Four men jumped into the pool disappearing beneath the surface, only a few bubbles popped to the surface. One by one, the men came back to the surface gulping for air, Frik called out how long each had taken.

Colonel Pora looked on, thoroughly perplexed. He was not being held or restrained in any way, just dripping wet on the side of the pool.

'Excellent! Who was the longest?' asked Captain John excitedly, like watching children at a swimming gala.

'Davidson Boss, one minute thirty seconds.'

'Colonel Pora ... you can do better than that?' said Captain John, addressing the Colonel encouragingly, waving at the pool. The man looked at him as if he was a ghost, his dark complexion went grey. He once again shook his head violently from side to side ... *no I cannot do better than that!*

'Frik, help the Colonel,' instructed Captain John.

Frik and three others grabbed the Colonel by the legs. After a moment of spirited resistance, he was twisted inverted, then dunked headfirst into the pool. There was much shaking about under the water as the Colonel tried to exceed the record set by Davidson.

The spectators called out their support ... 'Come on Colonel Pora!' they called.

Up he came, spluttering and coughing, shouting a whole different set of words. Captain John enquired from Afonso as to whether there was anything interesting. Afonso shook his head. Down went the man again, slightly longer this time.

Up he came, still resolutely defiant, repeating many of the words from the previous dunking.

Down he went. Held for a suitable period, then up again.

'Frik, how long was that?' asked Captain John, waving towards Colonel Pora who was still being held upside down, gasping desperately, his arms hanging loosely below him.

'One minute.'

'Davidson I think you are safe. I don't think Colonel Pora has got it in him. Afonso, please tell Colonel Pora that this time we are going to try for one minute and ten seconds,' instructed Captain John conversationally, holding up his fingers to show what he meant.

'*Coronel! Você está indo ao abrigo de um mais um minuto e dez segundos,*' explained Afonso slowly, as if instructing a small child.

Before the Colonel could voice his acceptance of the challenge, down he went.

Colonel Pora failed hopelessly; he seemed to pass out after only fifty seconds. He was lifted from the pool, coughing up water convulsively. He was then lowered gently to the side of the pool, to allow him time to recover.

Lying on his side, the man looked across in terror at Captain John sitting opposite.

Once he had caught his breath, Colonel Pora sat up, waved his hands resignedly, and started to talk, '*Suficiente, irá dizer-lhe tudo!*' the words tumbling out, between bouts of coughing and spluttering.

Captain John looked across at Afonso to see if these words were more useful. Afonso nodded enthusiastically. Captain John instructed for a chair and a beer to be brought for their guest.

The Colonel did not miss a beat, words just flowed out of him, his hands flying about expressively as if to emphasise each point. Captain John sent for pen and paper so that Afonso could get it all down. The man jabbered on for an hour and a half, still gulping air at every opportunity, glancing furtively back at the pool from time to time, clearly not wishing for another crack at Davidson's record.

The 2RR men sat silently in rapt fascination, as kindergarten children being read a story.

It took Captain John ages to compile the signal that was sent to JOC Repulse in Fort Victoria.

Beamish smiled to himself as he went over his experience with Captain John, he secretly hoped to see him again. He watched as Chicamba Dam came into view. Beamish had the helicopter headset on so he could hear the pilots talking to each other and the Selous Scout call-sign on the ground at the LZ. The helicopters gently descended until they were skimming just above the surface. It was to be a beautiful cloudless day, but stinking hot, probably 38 – 40°C.

The island appeared directly ahead and without any orbit the helicopters landed on a wide, open patch of ground. Out from a clump of thick bush came four men, rolling a 44gallon fuel drum towards the helicopter. The engines were shut down and all the men climbed out to stand in the shade of the trees. There was nothing else to do except find a comfortable place in the shade to escape the heat and try to get some sleep. Beamish was asleep in seconds, totally exhausted and happy in the knowledge the Selous Scouts had his back.

At 3pm, a Lynx passed over the island at high altitude.

'Okay boys,' called Captain Liversedge.

The two sticks of RLI men, the pilots and three of the Selous Scouts gathered under a tree while Captain Liversedge went over the plan again.

'Right, at exactly four pm the target for uplift is going to be at the extraction point, he will pop smoke as soon as he hears us coming. As far as we know there is only one man to be picked up. There were supposed to be five. We don't know where the other four are at this time. The flying time is only seventeen minutes. One helicopter with two Scouts in it will land at the LZ and pick up their man. We will remain in orbit unless a problem arises at the LZ. If there is a problem, we will be dropped to secure the LZ. If there are no Gooks about we may not need to be dropped at all.'

'What happens if there are Goooks about Sur?' Beamish enquired.

'The K-Car will engage the Gooks; suppress their fire while we go in to secure the LZ. The Lynx will also provide support with mini-golf bombs and fran.'

Beamish nodded his understanding. Liversedge looked into the faces of the other men to check whether they understood.

'Right, let's mount up.'

Liversedge took up the seat normally occupied by the Fireforce Commander in the K-car next to the pilot facing backwards, while one of the Selous Scouts took his place in the RLI stick in the other G-car.

The helicopters were made ready, their turbines racing, blades-a-blur, dust kicking up into the faces of the waiting men. The pilot of Beamish's helicopter gave the thumbs up and they dashed forward, crouched over. Beamish took the seat next to the tech, Kratzman next to him at the right-hand door, Penga opposite facing inwards next to the pilot, Le Beau next to him at the left-hand door. The helicopter lifted into the afternoon sun. There was a loud click as the tech cocked the .303 Brownings. Beamish slipped the headset on once again, the clipped voices of the pilots crystal clear in his ears.

It was only a few minutes into the flight when Beamish realised that this was not going to be simple. The Lynx reported that he had hundreds of the enemy visual at the base of *Chenjere*; there was no sign of the target, Sgt. Ngwenya.

A new call-sign came up on the radio. Blue Section, he called himself. The pilot glanced back at Beamish pointing upwards, clicked the internal intercom, 'Two Hunters' he said.

The unpredictable always happens, one of the G-cars reported engine trouble and had to turn back. That left two G-cars and the K-car. Beamish felt as if his stomach had a hoard of vicious butterflies inside, trying to get out ... *sods law*! He looked across at the rest of his stick all blissfully unaware of the drama unfolding, Penga smiled at him ... *fook'n mad bastard ... at least he's my mad bastard!*

'Blue Leader, Blue Leader ... Sierra20 do you copy?' the weak crackle from Ngwenya's radio. Ngwenya was calling the Hunter pilots circling at 20,000ft.

'Roger Sierra20 I have you threes, can you throw smoke ... over?'

'Negative, I am hiding in rocks half way up the side of *Chenjere* ... I have CTs visual all around me.'

'Copied ... I will strike the base of the gomo. I will call you to mark FLOT. Do you copy that ... Over?'

'Roger, copied,' replied Ngwenya, bullets thumping into the rocks around him, deadly ricochet's whining and spinning viciously.

Blue Leader was the call-sign for the leader of the Hunter section, Blue 1 was the K-car.

'Blue Leader, Blue 1 ... accelerating to target,' came the voice of the K-car pilot. With his lighter load, his top speed was markedly higher, he moved ahead of the two remaining G-cars.

Out in the distance, Beamish saw the rocky ridge that was *Chenjere* come into view. The helicopters dropped altitude as the huge rock face loomed up.

'Sierra20, Blue Leader ... on my mark, throw smoke.'

'Copied.'

The Hunter could clearly be seen in the distance diving towards the hill. As it reached the bottom of its dive, two bombs dropped from beneath its wings. A cloud of dust and smoke lifted into the sky. The two 450kg, double skinned, ANFO[88] filled percussion bombs, each filled with 71,000 pieces of

---

88   Mining explosive plus diesel fuel and prilled ammonium nitrate fertilizer. ANFO, when confined in a steel container with a pentolite initiator, ignites spontaneously to generate enormous amounts of high-pressure gas in a heaving

10mm steel bar cut a patch across the field, clearing 90m of ground, killing all in their path. Those not directly in the killing-ground were stunned, blood streaming from their nose and ears from the compression and shockwave over-pressure. The survivors now faced the 30mm Aden cannon that chased men into the rocks, throwing up lines of dirt high into the air as the shells exploded. Still, there were enough survivors hiding in the trees to keep a concentrated fire onto the side of the hill that Ngwenya was trying to climb.

'Sierra20, Blue 1, get up to the top of the hill,' K-car called to Ngwenya.

No reply.

'Blue 1, Blue Leader ... he has thrown red smoke, I have him visual. He is surrounded by CTs. I am strafing with cannon. Over.'

'Blue Leader, Blue 1, copied, I am thirty seconds out, Over.'

Ngwenya had thrown the red smoke canister and immediately began to climb the rest of the way up the hill. It was steep, requiring him to go down on all fours to keep traction on the smooth rock surface. There was no cover other than a few stunted trees and bushes growing through cracks in the granite. The Hunter strike had scattered the FRELIMO follow-up group at the base of the hill. They had been trapped in open ploughed ground that came up virtually to the edge of the granite outcrop.

The K-car arrived overhead, seeing the remains of the red smoke canister.

'I have Sierra20 visual,' called Liversedge.

Climbing up the hill was taking too long. Bullet strikes on the granite were clearly visible; from the air, it seemed only a matter of time before he was hit. Liversedge had no sooner taken in the danger than Ngwenya went down, sprawled flat on the rock face.

'Sierra20 is down ... Sierra20 is down, Blue 2, drop Stop 1 on my smoke ... over.'

'Blue 2 copied.' Blue 2 was Beamish's helicopter while Beamish's call-sign was Stop 1.

Liversedge instructed the pilot of the K-car to orbit a point on the top of the hill and promptly dropped a green smoke canister out of the door. Green tracer was now zipping past the K-car as it tightened its orbit.

Beamish, Stop 1, felt the blood rush to his head as the pilot dived the helicopter at the green smoke cloud. The rock strewn LZ raced up at them only to disappear again as the pilot flared for the landing, the G-force pulling at the gut. Tearing off the headset, Beamish shouted at his men to de-bus, he and Kratzman to the right, Penga and Le Beau to the left. On the top of the hill, they were in dead ground with the bullets from below passing high overhead. An RPG-7 burst on a rock close to where the helicopter had accelerated back into the air, shooting out millions of razor sharp rock fragments.

'Stop 1, go forward to the edge of the rock face,' Liversedge called Beamish. Beamish shook his men out into a line and advanced to the eastern edge of

---

explosion which forces air outwards from the generated gas bubble. The gas cools immediately, creating a void into which air flows at supersonic speed, causing an implosion. The effect on a person in the killing ground is shrapnel and exploding lungs.

the rock face. It soon became impossible to go any further, ricocheting bullets and rock fragments were creating an impenetrable barrier. Climbing down towards where Ngwenya lay was suicide.

'Sunray, negative ... I say again negative, we cannot advance any further.'

'Copied,' was all Liversedge said in reply, seeing the problem clearly from the air.

'Blue Leader, Sunray, can you suppress the fire coming from the trees to the east of the field ... over.'

'Sunray, Roger I will throw fran.'

The leading Hunter dived once again, this time firing SNEB rockets into the trees as he dived. At 2,000ft he pulled up, releasing two 50gallon frantan canisters. They tumbled, then struck the ground, throwing a wave of superheated flame forward over the trees and all in their path. The screams of agony, as the FRELIMO men burned, carried to Beamish on the top of the hill. The incoming fire reduced instantly. The second Hunter followed with 30mm cannon. Then the Lynx dived on its attack run, chasing the panicked FRELIMO with .303 machine guns and a 30gallon frantan canister.

Moving into a wider orbit, the K-car began picking off running men on the ground with the 20mm cannon. The two remaining G-cars followed in the same orbit, the door gunners firing the twin .303 Brownings. Those FRELIMO left in the field, ran in terror towards the base of the rocky ridge. Unable to climb it, they ran along the base, easy targets for the K-car. The explosive shells were doubly effective as they impacted on the granite rock.

To the east, still more FRELIMO men could be seen converging on the rock *Chenjere*.

'Stop 1, get down the hill and recover Sierra20,' ordered Liversedge.

'Let's go boys,' Beamish called, the four of them disappeared over the crest of the hill, slipping and sliding down the sheer rock face to where Ngwenya was lying. They slid down next to him, Kratzman firing the MAG down the hill at the CTs dashing about looking for cover from the K-car. A few shots were returned.

Ngwenya was unconscious, his face a mass of blood, making it difficult to see the head wound. One eye was swollen shut. His uniform was covered in blood indicating that he had other injuries as well. Looking at the bulging purple face, Beamish felt his stomach turn.

'Lift him Penga,' Beamish called out urgently, 'Yank, Le Beau cover us.'

The two RLI men grabbed Ngwenya beneath the arms and tried to drag him up the rock face. Bullet strikes again zeroed in on them.

Le Beau and Kratzman, lying on their backs, holding the MAG on their knees, returned fire, concentrating on the far tree line.

On the top of the hill, three men in FRELIMO uniform appeared, standing next to the last remnants of the green smoke canister. The K-car saw them approach and pulled into a new orbit ready to take them out. All three men threw up their hands in surrender one of them throwing red smoke. It was Schultz, Kumpher and Seals, back from the dead. They had taken off their caps waving frantically, Schultz's long brown hair, clear for all to see.

Liversedge could not believe his eyes; he had temporarily forgotten Schultz's call-sign.

'I have Schultz, Sierra10, and his team visual on the top of the hill, their radios must be out,' he called waving at the men below reassuring them that they had been recognised. As Liversedge watched, Schultz moved to the edge of the rock face, looking down towards where Beamish and Penga were struggling desperately to lift the wounded man. The granite face was too steep for them to lift him and still keep traction against the rock. They were hopelessly trapped in the open, unable to climb up or climb down. Puffs of dust appeared on the rock as bullets from the approaching FRELIMO struck. They were too far away for accurate shooting, well over 200m, but with their sheer numbers they were bound to find their mark eventually. Another RPG-7 sailed over the top of the rock impacting against a tree.

'Blue 3, drop Stop 2 on the hill to support Stop 1,' Liversedge was racing through his options in his mind. Stop 2 was a stick of Selous Scouts. He had only two serviceable G-cars plus the K-car to pull out eleven men and one stretcher case ... someone was definitely going to be left behind.

'Sunray, Blue 2, I have five minutes before I have to return to refuel ... Over,' called the helicopter that had dropped Beamish, the other G-car was also going to have to leave shortly.

All of the available men were now on the ground to secure the LZ. The height of the rock over the surrounding countryside, the steep sides and the domed, rock-strewn crest, made for a good defensive position.

'Roger, all Stops we are returning to refuel, Blue 4 will remain to provide support,' the K-car peeled out of its orbit followed by the two G-cars, in moments they were gone. The two Hunters from Blue Section also called in that they were out of ammo and needed to rearm. This left the Lynx, Blue 4, the only air support. He had one fran canister and a dozen 37mm SNEB rockets left.

On the ground, Captain Schultz commandeered the radio from the leader of Stop 2. He had the men spread out in all-round defence of the LZ, while he Kumpher and Seals lay flat on the top of the rock edge looking down at Beamish and Penga struggling with the wounded Ngwenya. Out in the distance, a wide sweepline of FRELIMO soldiers was approaching the trees to the east of the ploughed land. The 200m of open ground could not be covered to the edge of the rock without being seen and taken out by one of the three MAGs on the hill. This did not stop them shooting towards the hill at extreme range which put Beamish and his men in mortal danger.

The base of the rock was in dead ground because of the slightly domed shape of the rocky outcrop. Those FRELIMO that had survived the Hunter strikes, now took the opportunity to escape. The rock *Chenjere* was in the shape of a whaleback, this meant that the north and south edges were a very gentle rising slope to the centre of the whaleback. FRELIMO now intended assaulting the position by climbing the north and south points and trapping the Rhodesians stuck on top. They knew that the helicopters and Hunters would be back so they needed to act fast.

It took Captain Schultz only a few minutes to figure out what was going on. He could see the FRELIMO soldiers moving off through the trees to the north and south.

'We need to get down to help the RLI with Ngwenya,' he said to his two men. 'Take your webbing belts, tie them together and strip a bivy to make rope, we are going to have to haul Sergeant Ngwenya up.'

The men worked speedily, chopping up a bivy and then twisting the pieces into a crude rope. Kumpher then slid down the slope to where Beamish and Penga lay flat against the rock. The webbing belts were slipped over Ngwenya's shoulders, then attached to the bivy rope. Ngwenya began to regain consciousness, moaning under his breath.

'Lie still Mate, we are going to pull you up,' Beamish whispered reassuringly.

Tying the bivy rope around his waist, Kumpher went back up the hill like a rock rabbit. Once the rope was fully extended, he called to Beamish to start pushing Ngwenya from behind. Crawling on all fours, gripping the rock with his hands, Kumpher strained with his legs, like a draft horse, he began to pull the wounded man to the top of the hill.

With the extra pulling power, plus Penga and Beamish pushing, Ngwenya was slowly dragged up the hill, leaving a slippery thick bloody smear on the rock behind him.

'Yank, Le Beau get to the top of this fook'n hill,' Beamish shouted to his gunners who were still taking pot shots at FRELIMO in the far trees.

The two gunners slung the MAGs onto their backs and hastily climbed back up the hill on all fours. Finally, the wounded Ngwenya was dragged over the top of the hill. Exhausted by the climb the rescuers lay panting, sweating profusely, camo-cream running in streaks down their faces.

One of the Scouts was a trained combat medic and he went to work on Ngwenya. The first thing the medic did was plunge an ampoule of morphine into his arm. Using alcohol and a first field dressing, he dabbed at the face revealing a wide gash, probably caused by a rock splinter. It had cut deeply into the cheek and nose. Blood immediately saturated the dressing and he opened another. A hurried inspection revealed another deep shrapnel wound on Ngwenya's left side. He rummaged in his pack and pulled out a drip, plugged in the catheter squeezing out the air until the needle spurted liquid. A tourniquet was wrapped around the left arm and held tight while the medic tapped at the vein in the forearm. As soon as the vein bulged slightly he expertly slipped in the needle and the drip began to run. The needle and catheter were then taped in place and the medic went to work to stop the bleeding.

'Stop 2, Blue 4, you have CTs climbing *Chenjere* north and south of your position. I am going to throw fran and then I have to leave to refuel,' the Lynx pilot called.

'Roger, Blue 4, copied, any chance of a replacement?' Schultz replied.

'Stop 2, I have contacted 60, they confirm another Lynx on its way ... ETA thirty minutes ... Over.'

60 was the call-sign for Grand Reef. The Lynx pilot banked to the east at 3,000ft then began a dive; at 1,000ft, he opened up with .303s mounted above the cockpit, then at less than 500ft released the fran. All the way down he was met with ground fire from the FRELIMO men climbing the hill. The frantan exploded in a cloud of white smoke, blanketing the rock with lumps of burning gel. The Lynx climbed out to the west, continuing until it disappeared over the horizon.

The fact that there was now no air support, gave FRELIMO renewed confidence. They pressed the attack.

Kratzman and Le Beau were positioned in rocks facing south while the other gunner faced north. Penga and Beamish were also in position to cover the south. They did not have to wait long. The top of the hill was only 30m at its widest. The vegetation was limited to stunted trees and bushes surviving on rainwater trapped in the cracks and crevices. The first of the enemy appeared, skirmishing forward. A RPG-7 landed in rocks only a few metres in front of Beamish and his stick, showering them in pieces of rock. Kratzman and Le Beau began double tapping on targets as they appeared. The rock increased the effect of the bullets tenfold, spraying pieces of rock into the advancing men.

The first 82mm mortar round sailed overhead to crash harmlessly over the hill. The second was much closer, forcing all the defenders to lie flat on the rock. A blizzard of rock fragments and shrapnel spread over the top of the hill as the FRELIMO mortar men found their mark.

'I'm hit Corp,' called out Penga.

Beamish, his head flat on the rock, twisted to look at Penga only two metres away, his head was a mass of blood.

'I can't see Corp ... fuck there's blood everywhere,' a hint of panic in Penga's voice.

Slithering across the rock Beamish came up next to Penga. It was no use calling for the medic; he would be cut to pieces in seconds.

'Fook'n Hell!'

'Is it bad Corp?'

'It's a scratch man.' Beamish pulled at his kidney pouch for a first field dressing. Ripping it open, he shoved it onto Penga's forehead over the six-inch wide gash; the skull was clearly visible, as if the skin had been peeled like an orange.

'Hold that in place ... It's nothing ... you will be just fine.' Beamish's reassurances were unconvincing.

The mortar attack was joined by more RPGs. FRELIMO clearly intended to sweep from the south and drive the Rhodesians into their own stop group hiding in rocks to the north.

'Stop 2, Stop 1, I have a man down.'

'Copied Stop 1, there is nothing much we can do, hold your position, casevac is in figures fifteen,' Schultz replied.

Fifteen minutes ... we could all be dead by then ... Beamish thought to himself. It was impossible to look up, the crack of bullets and the whizzing rock seemed inches over his head.

The whaleback shape of the rock provided the greatest protection from the bullets and RPGs shot from below, causing them to sail high. The 82mm mortars were a different proposition. They had the LZ bracketed and their fire was now on target, effectively supressing any defensive fire from the Rhodesians on the top of the hill.

FRELIMO crept ever closer from the south, using the cover provided by their mortars. It was unclear whether FRELIMO had radios as part of their command and control but when the mortar barrage lifted, they pressed their attack instantly. When Le Beau and Kratzman lifted their heads the first wave of enemy were less than fifty metres away, coming forward fast.

CRACK … CRACK, the MAGs opened up spraying 7.62mm into the rocks. Beamish took out a white-phos grenade from the pouch under his arm, pulled the pin and hurled it forward as hard as he could. David Lloyd could not have done better from the boundary at Old Trafford. The grenade burst on the hard rock throwing burning phosphorous over the stunted vegetation, setting it alight. The burst of flame and smoke slowed the advance and obscured the Rhodesian position.

Looking behind him Beamish could see the Scouts firing to the north.

'Corp!' Kratzman called out urgently, '… I am down to my last belt.'

'Choose your targets Yank … Fook sakes!'

Beamish pulled open his kidney pouch and extracted the 100-round belt inside, then rummaged for the belt in Penga's pouches. He then hurled them the 5m to where Kratzman was positioned.

'Are you okay Le Beau?' called Beamish, as he could not see where the Frenchman was hiding.

'*Oui Caporal*,' grunted Le Beau, concentrating hard on trying to pick off enemy soldiers creeping ever closer.

Out in the distance the familiar clatter of helicopters carried over the sound of gunfire. Beamish turned slightly to look out to the west and there they came in line abreast, a beautiful sight.

The K-car came over first, banking tightly into a left-hand orbit.

'Stop 2, prepare to load wounded,' called Liversedge.

The G-car was already making its way into the LZ; the FRELIMO now had a much bigger target, green tracer raced past the helicopter as it flared for the landing.

'Sunray, Stop 1, I have one wounded as well,' Beamish called anxiously.

'Roger … get him loaded immediately.'

'Le Beau, help me with Penga.'

The helicopter touched down facing to the east.

The door was no more than thirty yards away. Beamish grabbed Penga by the webbing harness throwing an arm over his shoulder, Le Beau did the same on the other side. Penga was starting to lose consciousness from loss of blood. He stumbled forward trying to carry his own weight. The three men crouched low beneath the flying blades, dashing forward as fast as they could. Reaching the door of the helicopter, Beamish threw Penga inside, headfirst. Le Beau pushed his legs hard, wedging his body in behind the pilot's seat.

On the other side of the helicopter, the tech had thrown out a stretcher. The Scouts were loading Ngwenya onto it. Incoming bullets were flying past the canopy, zipping and cracking. The stretcher had to be brought around to the right side of the helicopter as the left was blocked by the twin-303s. The medic was holding the drip, Schultz, Kumpher and Seals the stretcher handles. The medic jumped in first, the others shoved the stretcher in behind him. Penga lay still, overcome by blood-loss.

The pilot applied full take-off power. As he did so, Beamish saw bullet strikes hit the perspex canopy. The howling engine took over and the aircraft lifted off, the nose tilted forward as maximum power took the helicopter away.

The position in the LZ was now untenable. FRELIMO were mortaring again making it impossible for another helicopter to get in.

The K-car was their only hope; they had to kill the mortar position.

The other G-car attacked the FRELIMO to the south of the LZ forcing them to break off back down the hill.

'We have to get the fuck off the top of this koppie,' Schultz called to Beamish.

Beamish had no idea who this person was, dressed like FRELIMO, his face pitch black topped with wavy brown hair.

'No complaints from me Sur!' Beamish replied, assuming the man was an officer, *you can never be too careful.*

'Sunray, Sierra10, we are going to move to the west we will RV at that dam you can see two clicks west,' Schultz called the K-car.

'Copied Sierra10,' Liversedge replied, '... we will keep their heads down.'

All the men left on the hill collected in a tight group next to a rock.

'Okay, if you look out to the west you can see a farm dam, that is our RV point. We are going to slide down this gomo and run like fuck to that dam. Is that clear?'

Nobody replied, the look of intense strain was on all their faces. They were beyond thinking. The fact that someone had taken charge was enough.

'Right let's go!'

As Beamish looked out to the west, the dam that the man had pointed out was clearly visible.

Down the edge of the rock they went. The only way was to sit on the bum and let the legs act as a brake. The bottom of the rock came up; Beamish lost control of his legs and crashed into the dirt at the bottom, ripping his shorts to shreds, grazing away the skin to leave a bleeding mess.

Their escape had not been seen by FRELIMO who were more focussed on avoiding the helicopters. As everyone collected at the base of the hill, another Lynx passed overhead.

At Schultz's signal, the men took off towards the dam. The sound of the K-car 20mm cannon was reassuring; Beamish could hear Liversedge excitedly taking out the mortar position and now focussed on clearing the remaining

FRELIMO on the top of *Chenjere*. The bush was open and relatively flat making progress at a steady trot possible. The MAG gunners were the first to tire, the heat and the weight of the gun and ammunition just too heavy to sustain a run.

Anxious to keep everyone together, Schultz called a halt to allow the gunners to catch up. Everyone knelt down pointing left and right panting in the heat of the late afternoon. The gunners re-joined and were given a short time to catch their breath. The gunfire on the top of *Chenjere* stopped suddenly.

The K-car and G-car now returned to the task of uplifting the men on the ground.

Liversedge called Schultz, 'Sierra 10, Sunray, we will have to lift in stages, four and four, I will come down to collect one of you.'

Through the trees, the farm dam came into view.

'Roger, Sierra 10 I have you visual we will lift from the open field a hundred metres to your west.'

The G-car was already coming in to land as the men came out of the trees into the clearing.

'You first,' called Schultz, pointing at Beamish.

'Negative my two gunners will need to secure the LZ,' replied Beamish.

Schultz and his two Scouts nodded. Taking one of the other RLI troopers with them, they ran towards the helicopter. As its wheels touched, they jumped in and it instantly lifted off again. Then the K-car came in to land, Beamish signalled a trooper from Liversedge's stick and he ran to climb into the K-Car. Beamish, Le Beau, Kratzman and the last man in Liversedge's stick, were left in the trees waiting for the G-car to return. The K-car and Lynx continued orbiting above.

'Sunray, Blue 4, I have CTs visual approaching from the east … Over.' The Lynx pilot had spotted the regrouped FRELIMO still chasing the escaping Rhodesians.

'Roger, we will try to slow them down,' replied Liversedge. The K-car extended its orbit to take in the approaching FRELIMO.

A heavy machinegun came into action against the K-car; tracer from the gun chased the helicopter across the sky.

'Sunray, Blue 4, a BTR with a twelve seven on the back is shooting at you from the road in the south.'

'Can you take him out?'

'I am too slow, he will get me long before I can drop my fran.'

The sudden arrival of the BTR changed the game completely. The DShK 12.7mm machine gun can fire 600 rounds per minute; it was designed for killing low flying aircraft. The arrival of the 12.7 forced the K-car to move away, thus protecting the FRELIMO sweepline.

'Stop 1, Blue 2, I am one minute out, prepare for uplift.' The G-car was returning for Beamish. The sweetest news Beamish had all day.

'Blue 2 copied.'

'Okay boys ready to go home for a beer,' Beamish called out, the smiles on the faces of Kratzman and Le Beau told the story.

The G-car came in low from the west, just above the trees. The FRELIMO were too close, they opened fire, forcing the helicopter away.

'Stop 1, I cannot get in, prepare for hot extraction.'

Beamish and his men had fitted the Pegasus harnesses as instructed. They ran desperately through the trees, following the helicopter as it hovered slowly forward, just above the trees. The downdraft threw up dust and leaves, the trees swirling wildly as the helicopter passed overhead. All the time, rounds whipping past as the enemy continued their chase.

The helicopter pilot and his choppertech frenetically searched the ground for an extraction point. The tree cover was just too thick. The airmen knew that if they did not extract these men immediately they would almost certainly be killed. The pilot glanced back at his choppertech. With a look of resignation in his eyes, he nodded his head.

The tech threw out the bench seat with the rope attached ... it was now or never. It fell through the trees, if it snagged, the helicopter and its crew would die just as certainly as the men they were trying to save.

'Stop 1, GO, GO ... GO ...' called the pilot on the radio.

The pilot fought to keep the helicopter steady in the hover. More bullets flew past, the crack of their passing audible through the helmet.

Racing through the trees, the four men reached the bench seat, suspended just above the ground. They each tried to clip on their harness, pulling the seat left and right, making it impossible.

'Fook sakes one at a time!' screamed Beamish, helping the Selous Scout man to hook on.

Moving forward again, the pilot had swung the helicopter through 90° to give his gunner a field of fire. Firing into the bush towards the oncoming FRELIMO, the gunner held his finger on the trigger. Spent .303 casings were raining down on Beamish from above as he struggled to get hooked onto the seat.

The helicopter was now sideslipping in the hover, pulling the only man attached off his feet, dragging him along in the dirt.

'Come on Yank, you next,' shouted Beamish pulling at the big man's harness, clipping it on.

Le Beau was shooting into the trees, holding his gun on its strap over his shoulder. Beamish grabbed him hard by the webbing strap, almost pulling him off his feet. The clip went home.

The helicopter moved again, faster this time, the pilot was battling to keep it in position with the sudden extra weight attached.

Above them, the choppertech waved his arm frantically to make sure they were all attached. Beamish clipped himself on, lifting his hand, thumbs up.

Misjudging the effect of the weight, the pilot pulled forward. As he did so, the helicopter dropped. All four men went crashing onto the ground on top of each other, scraping along in the dust. The rapid forward acceleration of the helicopter pulled them even faster; all Beamish could do was hold his arms across his face as dirt flew up, filling his eyes. Kit was ripped off his webbing. Kratzman's gun hit Beamish full in the face, his already badly broken nose gushing blood. His gut wrenched as the helicopter rocketed upwards, like being on the end of a giant swing, he couldn't bear to look as the pilot continued to pull full power.

Trees flew past; a huge thorn acacia tree loomed up. They crashed though it, Beamish felt the thorny branches tear at his arms as he tried to shield his face ... then up and clear. The helicopter pulled ever higher, the four men clinging to the harness for dear life as it spun uncontrollably.

Arthur Beamish closed his eyes and said a silent prayer ... *thank God for Blue Jobs!*

Fook'n hot extraction ... that's a bloody understatement!

> *A spirit, ay, a god, ascended he,*
> *Spread in a moment to the stormy wind*
> *His noble wings, and left the earth behind,*
> *And, ere the eye could follow him,*
> *Had vanished in the heavens dim*[89].

---

[89] *Pegasus In Harness*, Frederick Schiller, last stanza, lines 8-12.

Contact – Chenjere Mountain – Mozambique

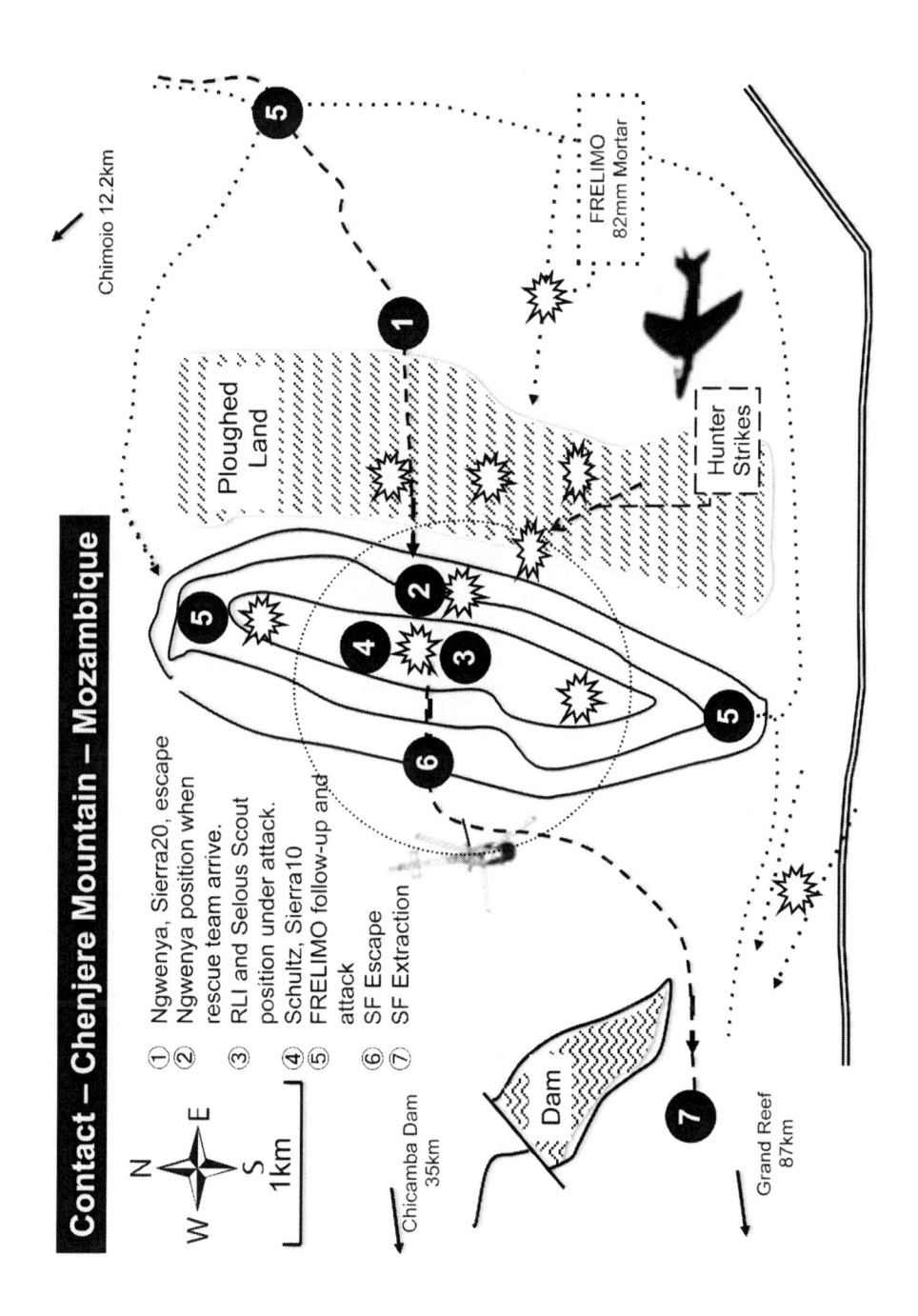

① Ngwenya, Sierra20, escape
② Ngwenya position when rescue team arrive.
③ RLI and Selous Scout position under attack.
④ Schultz, Sierra10
⑤ FRELIMO follow-up and attack
⑥ SF Escape
⑦ SF Extraction

FRELIMO 82mm Mortar

Hunter Strikes

Ploughed Land

Chimoio 12.2km

Chicamba Dam 35km

Dam

Grand Reef 87km

1km

13

Camp Takawira (Marera Agricultural College), south of Chimoio, Mozambique

The news of the failed attack by the Selous Scouts on Camp Takawira spread fast. Comrade Josiah Tongogara decided to pay a visit himself. He had driven south along the road from Chimoio with his escort of two BTR-152s, accompanied by his Chinese advisors that included Comrade Captain Zhang Youxia, who had returned from Jorge do Limpopo in the south.

With much fanfare, the motorcade drove into camp. Comrade Colonel Peter Muponde had his men lined up in three ranks on the parade ground. All were wearing their newly issued Chinese khaki uniforms. These were the men of the ZANLA elite and Peter Muponde was justifiably proud. The bodies of two dead Rhodesians were on display on a canvas tarpaulin on the veranda of the HQ Building.

As the vehicles came to a halt, Tongogara stepped out of the Landcruiser he had been travelling in. He marched smartly towards where Muponde had his men drawn up.

At a signal from Muponde the men called out in unison, '*Pamberi Nechimurenga, pamberi ne hondo, pasina neRhodesia.*[90]'

The cadres called out to Tongogara, hailing him as their leader, promising to fight to the death. Muponde then called the men to sing their anthem, *Ishekomborera Africa*.

> *Ishekomborera Africa*
> *Ngaisimudzirwe zita rayo*
> *Inzwai miteuro yedu*
> *Ishe komborera,*
> *Isu, mhuri yayo ...*[91]

The introductions were completed and Muponde proudly led his leader to the veranda where the bodies were laid out.

'This one was killed when we chased them away Comrade,' said Muponde pointing to Nyandoro's body. 'This one we found with his parachute still attached ... he must have died when he landed ... see his neck looks like it is broken.'

---

90 Forward with the revolution, forward with the war, away (down) with Rhodesia.
91 God bless Africa,
 Let her fame spread far and wide!
 Hear our prayer,
 May God bless us!
 Come, Spirit, come!
 Come! Holy Spirit!
 Come and bless us, her children!

George Kachimanga's neck was twisted at an unnatural angle, *rigor mortis* locking it in place.

'This is well done Comrade Muponde. I recognise this man,' Tongogara pointed towards Nyandoro. 'This is Simon Nyandoro one of our brightest prospects for leadership in ZANLA. He was taken by the Colonists and with their *murungu* magic they changed him into a monster.'

'*Aaie!*' the watching men exclaimed. They had heard of these strange things happening.

'Comrade Muponde, call for Mutumwa the *n'anga*, she must purge these bodies before they are laid to rest. These were brave soldiers; they were trapped by Whiteman's tricks and magic. They must be honoured in death,' instructed Tongogara in a soft voice, always showing respect for the dead.

Tongogara intimately understood the power of traditional religion. While he was not a very religious man himself, he had seen first hand the impact that the spirit mediums had on morale within the guerrilla army. Morale, in the face of repeated cross-border raids by the Rhodesian forces, causing thousands of casualties, was a precious commodity.

Muponde issued some clipped instructions and a man ran off to summons the powerful spirit medium Mutumwa, the great-great grand daughter of *Mbuya Nehanda*.

'Is the camp secure Comrade Muponde?' asked Tongogara looking into the surrounding hills.

'Yes General, it is, all the men have been put on alert,' replied Muponde respectfully, bowing his head.

'Nyathi!'

'*Yee Nyenganyenga,*' replied Godfrey Nyathi stepping forward.

'Send your men and sweep these hills carefully, if they find any men not in their correct positions bring them to me.'

'*Aiee,*' saluted Nyathi, firing off instructions to a section of his men. They doubled off towards the hills, kicking up dust as they went.

Within a few minutes of being summoned, Mutumwa arrived at the front of the HQ building. She had a retinue of twenty women cadres with her.

'Welcome, Mutumwa,' said Tongogara, bowing his head and clapping his hands as a sign of respect.

Mutumwa averted her eyes as is customary when addressing a male of high rank.

'What brings you *Nyenganyenga?*' she asked respectfully, bowing her head. Using Tongogara's nickname was a sign of the deepest respect, but more importantly, placed her relationship with him above that of others. While Tongogara had a nickname, only his closest friends and confidants were allowed to address him directly by the name *Nyenganyenga*.

'We have had a great victory against the *Skuz'apo*, but as you can see, two of them were our brothers. Their death, I believe, is the result of *Ngozi*[92].'

---

92 seShona, avenging spirit. Death amongst the Shona can come in many ways, it is not so much the 'how' that is important but the 'why?' Tongogara is suggesting that the deceased died because they offended the spirits.

'They must be laid to rest immediately *Nyenganyenga*, it has been two days,' replied Mutumwa. She knew that unless the spirits of these dead men were buried very soon they may never be satisfied, left to haunt the land of the living for ever.

'Where are these men from *Nyenganyenga*? Do you know their totem?' asked Mutumwa, aware of the danger of presiding over a funeral for a person of a different or opposing totem.

'This one,' said Tongogara, pointing to Nyandoro, 'is a Karanga from near Mushandike, his father worked on Gaths Mine, I don't know his totem. This one ...' pointing to Kachimanga, 'I have no idea.'

'It is well *Nyenganyenga*, I have the power to divine their totems. I will make sure their spirits are put to rest,' replied Mutumwa, expelling air from her chest, in a way that created a low whistle, like a person with asthma. Mutumwa did not have asthma, in fact she had lungs as good as a person half her age. This was her way of showing that she had the spirit of another deep within her soul.

'So be it Mutumwa. We will have the ceremony tomorrow, at first light,' said Tongogara in a more commanding voice. He respected the spirits, but in times of war, sometimes things needed to move more briskly.

'May I speak with you *Nyenganyenga?*' asked the old woman softly, her head bowed.

'Speak now Mutumwa,' replied Tongogara equally softly.

Mutumwa looked about her, obviously uncomfortable with the people that could overhear their conversation.

Realising her dilemma, Tongogara indicated for the woman to follow him as he walked into the shade of a large scented thorn acacia tree, *umNqawe*. Mutumwa, pulled at the leaves of the tree, rubbing them in her hand, holding them to her nose as they gave off a sweet scent. Nyathi followed at a respectful distance.

She did not wait to be invited to speak.

'You are in great danger *Nyenganyenga*. I have seen the great crocodile in a dream ... you know the crocodile is the tool of the most evil of all spirits,' whispered the old woman. 'I have also thrown the dice, *hakata*, to divine the future and the truth of this dream is clear.'

'Yes Mutumwa,' said Tongogara, 'is there more?'

'My dreams have included the great Owl. An evil witch is in your midst,' hissed the old woman, using the superstition of the owl as the embodiment of a witch sent to bewitch and betray its victim.

'I have always been in danger Mutumwa. The *murungu* have tried to kill me many times. I am happy that I might die in battle.'

'It is not only the *murungu* to be feared,' replied Mutumwa, concern etched on her face. Her concern was that Tongogara was not taking her warning seriously enough. '... I have spoken,' she said, a hint of frustration in her voice.

'Thank you Mutumwa, if the dreams can be more specific that would be most helpful,' said Tongogara, now bowing his head in respect to the old woman, his hand open towards her as a sign of dismissal.

Mutumwa took the command with deference, clapping her hands as she backed away from the great man, her head bowed. As she made to return to her entourage, the woman looked straight into Nyathi's eyes, as if she could see the inner-most workings of his soul. He felt a cold shiver that made his forehead suddenly bead with sweat.

A slight tilt of the head by the old woman sent the women forward. They wrapped the dead men in blankets and hoisted them onto their shoulders. Mutumwa began a soft resonant chant, joined by the other women as they carried the bodies away. The male cadres made a path for the women, bowing their heads as the procession passed. The funeral song grew louder and louder until the women were in full voice, breaking into unreserved, high-pitched ululation which sent a shiver down the spine of even the most hardened soldier.

The sun began to set over the hills in the west, the dark reds, purples and oranges of an African evening.

'We must drink *hwahwa*, beer, Comrade Muponde,' called out Tongogara loudly, breaking the melancholy in the air.

'*Aiee*!' called out the men; it was time to drink to their great victory.

The celebrations went late into the night. Goats were slaughtered and the men were treated to fresh meat for the first time in many weeks. The prospect of fresh meat added to the feelings of euphoria brought on by smoking *mbanji*[93] and drinking the strong traditional opaque sorghum beer.

One of Comrade Tongogara's weaknesses, despite the fact that he was a loving husband and father, was his interest in the many young female freedom fighters housed in the ZANLA training camps. Tongogara, like many of the senior commanders, demanded the sexual favours of the young female cadres who had joined the freedom struggle. In this sense, the General practiced his own code of morality based on the traditional tribal system. This meant that he was opposed to both contraception and abortion and felt free to enjoy sexual favours at every opportunity, whether the woman was a willing participant or not. This practice put him at odds with the younger and more educated members of the leadership, but they largely suffered their opinions in silence. Any criticism of the great leader would have resulted in severe punishment or death.

The ZANLA hierarchy saw the seduction of the women cadres as part of the spoils of leadership, or, to go one step further, as an inalienable right. Tongogara's power base within the liberation movement came from the old style 'veterans' of the struggle. These supporters were unquestioningly loyal to Tongogara and the established military leadership. The veterans were mostly hardened soldiers with very little formal education. In addition to the rival power brokers lead by Felix Mhanda and Peter Hamadziripi, a new

---

93   seShona, cannabis, dagga, dope.

opposition movement called the *Vashandi*[94], saw the veterans as ignorant peasants who lacked a proper plan for the future and betrayed the Marxist-Leninist ideals of the revolution. The ultra left-wing *Vashandi* leadership was made up of mostly young guerrilla officers and their educated university-trained leaders who were diametrically opposed to any negotiations, *détente*, with the Smith regime. They were adamant that the creation of a communist state in Zimbabwe was of paramount importance. It was not only colonialism that they were fighting; they were equally against the bourgeois, capitalist form of government.

The deep philosophical differences between the veterans and the Vashandi, added to by the sexual exploitation of women, set the Tongogara leadership at odds with the progressive thinking *Vashandi*. The seduction, or more accurately, the rape of women freedom fighters, was also deeply opposed by the traditional religious leaders. The fact that the *Vashandi* espoused their suspicion and distrust of traditional religion, calling it the 'opium of the people', meant that, despite the religious leaders opposition to the sexual exploitation of women, it was tolerated as the lesser of the two evils.

The veterans and the religious leaders saw military victory over the Colonists as the primary goal and as Tongogara promised this result, he was supported wholeheartedly. The head of the political leadership, Robert Mugabe, had no powerbase amongst the veteran military and he, therefore, was obliged to support Tongogara despite his own Maoist leanings, and despite the fact that Tongogara was his greatest threat for the future presidency.

In the same way that Tongogara had crushed the Nhari rebellion in 1975, he now faced the naked ambition of Peter Hamadziripi, the Marxist *Vashandi* movement and his enemies in the *Dare de Chimurenga*.

Having had a belly full of beer Tongogara called out to his camp commander.

'Comrade Muponde, it is time for you to call for our 'warm blankets'!' Tongogara used the euphemism the leaders used to describe their female 'camp wives'.

Muponde counted himself amongst the more enlightened leaders of the revolution and was not in favour of the sexual abuse of his dedicated young female cadres.

He tried to dissemble.

'Comrade, it is late … they will be sleeping.'

'Rubbish they must be available for 'night duty', they should be ready to take up their swords.'

Tongogara burst into laughter at his joke; the other leaders joined him as he lolled over, tears running down his cheeks. 'Come on Muponde, fetch me some women.'

The camp commander realised he was cornered. He called two of the younger cadres to look for some women. They returned almost instantly

---

94   seShona 'worker', as in a Marxist-Leninist worker's revolution.

to report that there were no women in the barracks. The reputation of the Tongogara leadership team had clearly preceded them and the women had taken to the hills.

'What? This is bullshit!' shouted Tongogara instantly angry. 'You take your men into the bush and find them, bring one of them to my room.'

The young cadres rushed into the surrounding bush in search of the women who were hiding. The darkness and the shock of the recent attack meant that the women had grouped together for their mutual comfort and protection. They heard the men coming and ran for their lives.

A fearsome fight broke out in the surrounding bush as one by one women were captured. Screaming and shouting could be heard for miles. The women were giving as good as they were getting, kicking, biting and scratching, all to brain-piercing screams. Also racing around in the bush, Tongogara found it great sport urging the men on, using a short thin stick to whip any who were not giving of their best.

Eventually a young woman was subdued and presented to the leader for his pleasure. She was sobbing loudly, tears awash down her face, sucking in short breaths. Her left eye was already almost swollen shut, turning black from a blow from a fist. Her whole body shook in terror; this was clearly not her idea of the glorious revolution. She was tiny in relation to the six-foot bulk of her leader, the contrast not lost on the surrounding observers. Tongogara took her gently by the hand and she followed reluctantly to his room.

Her screams shook the night.

Comrade Dipuka Muponde went around the back of the HQ building and threw up, his revulsion at the evening's end was too much to take. Fortunately for him, the other leaders ascribed his sudden illness to too much beer.

*

Combined Operations HQ, Milton Buildings, Salisbury

A very sombre group of men waited in silence in the passage outside the main briefing room on the second floor of the COMOPS HQ. A very loud conversation was taking place inside the room; in fact, it was more like a screaming match. They had been summonsed to attend the meeting at short notice. Each branch of the armed forces was represented, including Military Intelligence, the SAS and the Deputy Police Commissioner responsible for Special Branch (SB).

The door burst open and Colonel Reid-Daly stood in the doorway.

'You fucking idiots better get your house in order ... our country is going down the tubes because you people cannot do your jobs.' Reid-Daly was pointing accusingly at two of three men in the room, his shaking finger testament to the rage he was in. The years since his time as the RSM of the RLI had not reduced the penetration of his voice or his ability to vent his anger. He glared into the faces of the men waiting outside, then marched off smartly down the passage, his boots ringing on the highly polished parquet flooring.

'Come in gentlemen,' called one of the men inside.

The group filed in and took up seats around the large wooden table. An overhead projector stood on the one side of the table, pointing at a portable screen set up in front of one of the walls. The screen was lit up with the word 'Briefing' the only information displayed. Still nobody spoke. At the top of the table facing the screen was Lt-Gen Peter Walls the commander of COMOPs. The other two men sitting to his right were George Stanbridge and his deputy, John Sutcliffe from the CIO. Flanking the General were large-scale maps of the eastern border of Rhodesia, with most of western and central Mozambique on the one side and Zambia on the other. There was no secretary or stenographer in the room.

'My apologies for the outburst from the Colonel but he is understandably upset at the loss of two of his best men and the fact that he nearly lost the whole of the Sierra call-sign on Operation Wedza,' said General Walls quietly. 'We will get straight to it, George Stanbridge and John Sutcliffe will brief you on a project they have been working on. Please carry on gentlemen.'

John Sutcliffe got to his feet and walked around next to the overhead projector. He had a small pile of transparencies next to the machine; he removed the first slide and slipped on the next.

'Gentlemen this is the first briefing on a project we have tentatively called Operation Hippo. To cut a long story short, this is a mission to assassinate, Joshua Nkomo, Lookout Masuku and Dumisa Dabengwa from ZIPRA and Josiah Tongogara, and Rex Nhongo from ZANLA.'

There was a collective intake of breath as the enormity of what was being suggested was absorbed.

'Has this been discussed with the PM?' the senior policeman asked looking towards the General.

'This mission has been sanctioned by the PM and the Cabinet, we have their full support,' Gen Walls interjected. 'Please carry on Peter.'

'General, we have had a crack at assassination before ... we failed dismally every time,' stated the SAS Major. 'Why would this time be any different?'

'It's true that we have tried before, but we never really got the full buy-in from the political leadership so we could never apply the right level of resources ... this time will hopefully be different. Please carry on Peter,' replied Walls in his characteristically soft-spoken voice.

Sutcliffe then spent the next two hours explaining the various options for the assassination attempts. The men mostly sat in shocked silence as the broad basis of the mission was explained. The complexity of such a mission was mind-boggling. The CIO men answered the few questions that were asked and then the representatives from the army, air force and police, who would prepare the detailed plans, were selected.

At the end of the briefing Gen Walls addressed the men, 'Gentlemen, let's be under no illusions as to the reasons we have to go to such great lengths on this mission. It is because the perception in political circles is that we have lost the initiative.'

There was a murmur of agreement from around the table.

Walls continued, 'the on-going negotiations with the external leaders of the Patriotic Front are not going well. To reach a settlement with them will take a great deal of effort, but the feeling is that if they see their leaders being systematically taken out, they will more likely come to the party. Let's also be clear, the days of thinking that we can win this war on the battlefield are over. We need to lay the military foundation for a political settlement. This mission supports that objective.'

The men around the table all nodded their agreement. There was no doubt in all their minds that the General was right.

Gen Walls got up, wished the project team the best of luck, and offered his help if it was needed. The meeting broke up and the men prepared to leave the room.

'George can I have a word,' asked Major Ben Wallis the representative of the SAS.

'Yes Ben, what is it?'

'George we just don't have the resources needed to pull this off. Certainly not in the concentrated time frame that you have laid out.'

'I know Ben, but the fact is the effectiveness of this mission depends on these men being killed in short succession.'

'The point is that virtually all these targets are in suburban environments in Gaborone, Lusaka, Beira and Maputo. We would need months to insert the operators needed for the mission.'

'Yes Ben, fortunately, we have a few people already in place, as has SB. It should be fine. Plus we can call on the Scouts.'

'Come on George, this is beyond the kick-the-door-down shoot-em-up capability of the Scouts. They would be hopeless in an urban environment.'

'Leave that with us for the moment. We have a few ideas that should help,' replied Stanbridge trying to remain patient with the obvious inter-service rivalry. It never ceased to amaze him how the Special Forces units refused to cooperate with each other ... *kick-the-door-down shoot-em-up indeed, that described the SAS perfectly.*

*

Ward B4, Andrew Fleming Hospital, Salisbury

Tpr Dudley 'Penga' Marais slowly came out of the anaesthetic. A thick cloud seemed to be covering his eyes, his nostrils full of the smell of disinfectant. His mouth felt dry as if his tongue was stuck to the roof of his mouth. As the haze began to lift slightly, the pain in his throat began to throb ... *I need water badly*. While he knew he must be awake, he could not see anything. He tried to lift his left hand but it seemed to be tied down, a sudden feeling of panic washed over him. His right hand was free, he lifted it to touch his face, but it was covered in bandages.

Then the pain in his side struck like a punch in the kidneys. Penga winced ... *why is someone pushing a needle into my side?* His whole body seemed stiff and sore.

A vision of Beamish appeared, pushing a field dressing onto his face and swearing at him ... *'I can't see Corp.'* The door of the helicopter was in front of him, the sound of the engine so loud. Le Beau was saying something to him, *'what is it?'*

'Dudley, stay still ... its okay, you are in hospital.'

Who is that? Nobody calls me Dudley. Except ...

'Now now, soldier no more thrashing about, you will pull the drip out,' said another voice with a hint of a Scottish accent.

Who are you?

Trying to speak, nothing would come out. His throat felt like it was on fire. Someone held a glass of water to his mouth, supporting his head.

'Drink this son, you will feel much better.'

The water was cool in his mouth, providing instant relief. The flow of the water into his throat, coursing all the way into his stomach was like Heaven.

'I can't see.'

'Not surprising your head is in bandages, the doctors have patched you up right as rain.' The Scottish voice was speaking again.

The pain in Penga's throat gave way instantly to a throbbing headache, like the worst possible hangover. Stars and flashing lights appeared in front of his eyes.

'Dudley it's me ... its Lily, thank God you are alright.'

'Lily ... I ... I.'

'Don't try to speak Dudley. Go back to sleep I will be back to visit. They tell me that they will take your bandages off tomorrow.'

'Lily ...'

'The kids are looking forward to visiting you; I have to go now ... to fetch them from school. You are going to be just fine. Sleep now.' Lily had taken the young soldier's hand and squeezed it tightly.

Lily is here ... things are going to be all right ... Lily is here.

'Now then, you need to rest. I am going to give you something to help you,' said the Scottish voice and instantly a warm feeling flowed through his body.

The pain in his head dulled away and Dudley 'Penga' Marais went back to sleep.

*

In another part of the same hospital, in a private ward, lay Sgt Cephas Ngwenya. He was conscious and had already eaten a light meal His head was also covered in bandages but they did not cover his eyes. Sitting upright propped up by pillows, he was stiff and sore from the effects of being held rigidly in one position. A drip was still attached to his left arm.

A rock splinter thrown up by an exploding RPG had caused the wound in his head. It had cut into his forehead, but more of a glancing blow that had done enough to render him unconscious. While the splinter had not cracked his skull, it had caused an enormous facial swelling, almost closing both his eyes. His eyes were orangey-purple slits that were painful to open. He had a vicious case of concussion with a thumping headache. The wound in his side had also been caused by an RPG, this time a piece of shrapnel. It had entered his side just above the left kidney, missing it by a few centimetres and then lodged against the ribcage, miraculously missing all his vital organs.

The door to his room opened and three men walked in. They were all dressed in camouflage uniform with the distinctive green stable-belt and light brown Selous Scout beret. Their hair was long and unruly, pushing out from beneath their berets; one had a thick bushy beard that covered most of his face.

Ngwenya painfully opened his eyes, not able to see all three men at once.

'*Mangwanani*, good morning, Cephas. It is good to see that you are going to make a full recovery,' said Captain Chris Schultz.

'Bloody well done Cephas,' added Dennis Kumpher, a man of few words, placing a hand on Ngwenya's shoulder.

'Did we all get out?' Ngwenya asked trying to twist his head to see all the men in the room.

'Nyandoro and Kachimanga are still missing, we hoped you may be able to tell us if you saw them,' replied Dave Seals.

Ngwenya closed his eyes again trying to think back.

'I did not see Kachimanga ... but I did see Nyandoro.'

'Can you remember where that was Cephas?' asked Schultz gently.

'We were together, when the *makandangas* overran our position. I saw him hit many times. I could not get to him. I ran for my life. I am sorry *Tsere* ...'

'It's okay Cephas ... we all had to run that night, to stay would have been certain death. We were just worried that Nyandoro may have been captured alive.'

'No *Tsere*, Nyandoro is now amongst the *nyikadzimu*, the world of the departed ones.'

'Thank you Cephas, stay well. The doctors tell us that you were very lucky. You will be able to plough your lands and make many more children,' said *Tsere* Schultz with a broad smile.

'*Tatenda*, thank you *Tsere*, I am anxious to kill many more Gooks.'

'So you shall my friend. You are welcome to work with Recce Troop anytime. Rest well ... The Boss sends his respects. He will visit you soon. You will go on R and R as soon as the hospital lets you out.'

'*Chisarai zvakanaka*, Goodbye my friend,' said Schultz bracing up slightly as a sign of respect to the wounded soldier. The other two men said their goodbyes and they left the room.

Outside the door, a Regimental Policeman (RP) stood up and saluted the Captain.

'You look after that man Corporal,' said Schultz.

'Yessir!' replied the man bracing up smartly. He watched as the three living legends of the Selous Scouts walked smartly down the corridor.

*

3 Commando RLI, Fireforce base, Buffalo Range Forward Airfield (FAF 7), South-east Rhodesia

Corporal Arthur Beamish with Troopers Jean-Paul 'Le Beau' D'aubigne and Jim 'Yank' Kratzman III arrived back at Buffalo Range, exhausted beyond measure. The past four days had been a whirlwind of gut-wrenching terror. They stumbled out of the Dak under the weight of their kit and shuffled off towards their barrack room. Beamish had a plaster over his nose and he limped painfully from stiffness after the skin had been scraped off his bum sliding down the granite koppie. Beamish was both sore and in a foul mood.

The news of their recent exploits had travelled throughout 11 Troop who had now all returned from various follow-up operations after the attack on the Triangle sugar mill. 11 Troop had been pulled out as it was their turn to go on R&R. 14 Troop were due back any minute to take their place in the line ... so to speak.

An impromptu piss-up was underway in the troopie mess as the boys celebrated the end of another bush trip with the bright lights of Salisbury beckoning. Kratzman had not been introduced to the rest of the troop, so Beamish felt duty bound to take him down for a beer. Despite his initial misgivings, Beamish was now of the opinion that the big Yank had some potential, although he certainly was not going to tell him that ... *Fookin Yanks are way too cocky anyways.*

The three men dropped their kit on their beds and hit the showers.

Kratzman was in a buoyant mood, albeit a bit shaken from the hot extraction from Mozambique. He was, as with Le Beau and Beamish, covered in hundreds of cuts and scratches having been pulled through the thorn acacia tree. The combat shirt that he had taken was covered in blood, torn to shreds. He picked it up and threw it into the corner of the room to be disposed of later.

To anyone meeting Jim Kratzman for the first time, the immediate impression was a man with a jovial, happy disposition. He had a ready smile and was happy to enter into conversation with anyone who had a mind to. As with so many Americans from country towns, Kratzman was exceedingly polite and respectful of his elders and senior ranks. For a man in his early thirties he was in excellent physical condition, he made it his business to keep fit and 'pump a bit of iron' when he had the opportunity. As there was no such thing as a 'gym' in Rhodesia, certainly not on a Fireforce base, Kratzman used the only thing at his disposal, the MAG. He lifted it from every conceivable angle, above his head, out to the side, up and down in endless repetitions. He was so strong he could twist it in front of him, like cadets drilling at West Point.

Like many of his countrymen who had been sent to Vietnam, Kratzman had been conscripted, 'drafted' as he called it. He came from a small country town in Virginia, Maces Springs. The family were poor, scraping a living off a tiny farm. He had no prospect of going to college, he was needed on the farm to help his aging disabled father. Jim had both a younger brother and sister so the family looked to him to take over the farm. His Dad, also named Jim Kratzman, had been with the 101st Airborne at Normandy, fought through France, to be wounded in the leg at Bastogne. The leg never really healed properly. One doctor said there was still some German shrapnel inside. The injury became increasingly debilitating, as 'Big' Jim got older. The father and son were both enormous men, called 'Big' Jim Senior and 'Big' Jim Junior by the neighbours. Big Jim Junior had that nickname since the fifth grade; he stood a head taller than his classmates.

When the draft papers arrived 'Big' Jim took his son to one side and said simply, 'your country needs you more than I do.' The whole family stood out on State Highway 614, just opposite the Carter Family Fold in Poor Valley, waiting for the bus. Jim never did see his Dad again; he died of a cerebral aneurysm before Jim finished boot camp. It was something that Jim just never got over, the vision of his family standing on the side of the road waving at him, imprinted on his brain. His Dad's parting words simply, 'good luck son.'

When Richard Nixon decided to attack NVA ammunition caches and other enemy sanctuaries inside Cambodia, Jim's company, Charlie Company 2nd Bn, 7th Cavalry was the first unit choppered in. LZ X-Ray in the 'Fishhook' was only about 90km northwest of Saigon; in the middle was a major NVA resupply and assembly area. No sooner had they hit the ground than Jim's troop started taking intense small arms, mortar, and rocket fire from an enemy force that vastly outnumbered them. It was the day that Jim lost his three best buddies in all the world, Dan Bradshaw, Nate Konomacki and Pete 'Slick' Angelis. The horror of their loss meant that Jim did not sign up for a second tour; he had fully planned to do so.

Upon returning to the United States, he landed at Fort Bliss where he was discharged. He decided to visit New York before returning home to the farm, so he caught a plane from El Paso via Dallas. He had no civilian clothes so he travelled in uniform. He noticed that most people refused to look him in the eyes; they seemed to avoid him despite his usual disarming smile. When he arrived at LaGuardia, he took a bus into the City. The bus dropped him at the Port Authority Bus Station in 42nd Street; he then decided to walk the few blocks to Central Park via Times Square. He slung his bag and started the walk, in what was a cool, November afternoon. As he approached Times Square along 7th Avenue, he noticed a large crowd had filled the square. It was at this moment that Jim Kratzman's world came apart, and destroyed his faith in his country and its people.

His size and the smart uniform stood out in the crowd. People were carrying placards, chanting, a man stood on a stage shouting through a megaphone. Jim noticed a young kid holding a placard that read, 'Children are not born to burn.' Someone started to shout at him, a young woman ran up to him and spat on his uniform. He tried to step away, they followed him, another woman hit him with a placard that read, 'Love not War.'

The sound was deafening, the shock of the attack and the screaming of the people disorientated him. He stumbled through the crowd, trying to get away.

A detachment of policemen on horseback were lined up on the other side of 7th Avenue, they saw him in obvious distress and three rode into the crowd to pull him out. This seemed to infuriate the crowd still more and they started pelting the policemen with placards and bottles, anything they could get their hands on. One of the policemen was pulled from his horse and a man started kicking him on the ground. Jim's mind cracked. He lunged at the man smashing him hard in his face, splitting his nose apart. Blood burst over Jim's uniform that was now covered in spit. He bent down, grabbed at the policeman, throwing him over his shoulder in a fireman's lift and ran for the line of horses.

He ran ... every step carrying him away from the people of his country. The vicious words, the hate, the sight of women screaming at him, would haunt him for the rest of his life ... *your country needs you more than I do* ... his father had said.

When Jim Kratzman read about the war in Rhodesia in Time magazine two years of heartbreak later, he left his country swearing never to return. UN sanctions, the arms embargo and US foreign policy, meant that what Jim was doing was illegal in his country, if he had returned, he would likely have been jailed.

'Jeezz Corp I haven't seen this much action in four days since I was in the Fishhook in Cambodia,' said Kratzman.

Beamish had heard of the war in Vietnam of course, but the nuances of the US activities in Laos and Cambodia were lost on him. A student of history, Beamish was not ... *it was a war against communist chinks wasn't it?*

'Yank, you haven't seen anything yet. Wait until you get into a contact with a few hundred of the fookers on an external raid in Mozambique. I must tell you about the raid on Chimoio sometime,' replied Beamish, with the superior tone of an 'old soldier.'

Beamish had concluded that a sunny, happy disposition in the army was a recipe for disaster. It resulted in being singled out for all sorts of things. Looking miserable and unhappy tended to keep senior NCOs, and more importantly, officers at bay. That was the 'Beamish Philosophy' on the army, and he was happy to share it with anyone who would listen. It had been more difficult in The Fusiliers as most of the soldiers were miserable and unhappy, but in Rhodesia, there were piles of people with a happy-go-lucky disposition. Beamish figured it was the weather or the beer or something.

The three intrepid invaders of Mozambique, although that was strictly on the QT[95] between them, walked into the mess. The party was well on its way. The celebration of pending R&R was added to by the welcome of the new Troop Sergeant, Colour Doug Barker. Barker had been in the RLI since the age of seventeen, starting in 1 Commando, a short period with Support

95 The slang term 'qt' is a shortened form of 'quiet'.

Commando, then various courses at the School of Infantry and now given his own Troop. The inexperience of the Troop Commander 2nd Lt 'Dick' Van Deventer meant that the powers-that-be had chosen another veteran to help the young officer find his feet.

'Corporal Beamish! You useless piece of Pommie shit,' shouted Barker from the bar. Beamish knew Barker quiet well; they had been on the same para-course together in the old days. It seemed a lifetime ago, although it had only been two years. Barker had never impressed Beamish, he though he was a bit of a 'tosser'.

'Evenin' Colourr,' Beamish replied, with what would pass for a smile. 'Welcome to 11 Troop … Congratulations on your promotionnnn.'

'They gave you another stripe Beamish … shit they must be getting desperate,' added Barker with a laugh.

'Yes Colour … they must be getting desperate,' replied Beamish, his attempt at irony lost on Barker.

Beamish introduced Le Beau, who Barker already knew by reputation, and the new man Kratzman.

Ignoring Le Beau, Barker looked across at Kratzman, '… my, my, you are a big unit, can you shoot son?' Barker put some emphasis on the word 'son' to stamp his authority on the new man.

'I can shoot as well as the next man Colour,' replied Kratzman, still with his winning smile.

'You see action in Vietnam?' sneered Barker; he had plenty to drink already.

'Yessiree I surely did. Charlie Company, 2nd Battalion/7th Cavalry, 3rd Brigade, 1st Cavalry Division,' said Kratzman confidently.

'How the fuck does anybody in that army know what's fucking going on with all that shit to explain … got your arses kicked in Nam didn't you?' stated Barker disparagingly, a smirk on his face.

Barker studied the giant of a man through slightly glazed eyes. He was just over six foot but he gave at least six inches to the American. Despite the difference in rank, they were probably the same age.

Kratzman held the sergeant with a steady gaze, the smile on his face suddenly gone.

'Colour, the Yank did well in our first contact in Mozambique, they sent us to get some Scouts out the shit,' Beamish chipped in; he didn't like the way Barker was behaving towards the new man.

'Come Yank, lets get a beer,' said Le Beau. He had already decided that he didn't much care for the new Troop Sergeant.

Barker watched the two men walk away, clearly unsure of whether to have another crack at the Yank … or the ugly Frog.

'Come on, Colour,' said Beamish disarmingly, 'let me buy you a beer.'

The two troopers moved to the bar and Le Beau loudly announced the new man to those gathered about. 11 Troop, like so many other Troops in 3 Commando, in fact the whole Battalion, had men from all parts of the world. They came from Australia, New Zealand, Canada and the USA, but mostly from the UK. There were a few men like Le Beau from France, as well as Germans, Italians and Dutch.

Selection of recruits to the RLI paid no heed to the man's past. There were social misfits, criminals, rogues and psychopaths amongst them, but once they joined the RLI their past was forgotten, in the same way that it is forgotten in the French Foreign Legion.

Most of the Americans and Canadians were in Rhodesia fighting for mostly philosophical reasons. They saw the war more in the sense of defending the west from the advance of communism. The wounds of the Vietnam conflict were still wide open for these men and they saw the defence of Rhodesia as the next front line. Most did not discuss their previous experience except amongst themselves, but all, like Jim Kratzman, carried the scars of their treatment at the hands of the anti-war demonstrators that vilified them when they returned home from Vietnam. Their previous military experience made them older than the vast majority of homegrown Rhodesian recruits.

Recruits from Australia, New Zealand and the UK were a different kettle of fish. These were often rough and tough men from the lower strata of society in their own countries. Beamish was a typical example. They were drawn from the Regiments of Foot, Marines, the Paras, and the Guards, where the military was a way of life. Often their fathers and grandfathers had served in the same regiments before them. Their motivation for fighting in Rhodesia could be described in one word, 'adventure.' A few, like Beamish, were there because of experiences in Northern Ireland. The horror of open suburban warfare, against people that Beamish would have described as fellow countrymen, was too much to accept.

In addition to the regular contingent of the RLI, the ranks were also supported by the addition of National Servicemen. The constant demand for more men, plus the severe impact of soldiers killed and wounded in action, meant that school-leaver NS recruits had to be added to the mix. These men had been conscripted into the army, providing them with no choice. The choice of joining the RLI, as opposed to any other unit, was, however, theirs. This made for a mainly highly motivated group of, mostly, very young troopers.

The NS recruits were by no means welcomed with open arms. The 'old soldiers' had set a very high standard of operation, and they feared the impact that a large number of green 'fresh poes' would have on the performance of the unit. This suspicion and distrust was renewed every time a new NS intake was integrated into the Commandos.

The nature of the environment and the constant exposure to intense violent battles, of mostly very short duration, created a sort of stress that was not well understood. The combat stress that is found in all armies in time of war was superimposed over the fundamental stress of fighting to save their own country, their way of life. This stress manifested itself in many ways, but mostly excessive drinking, drugs and violence. So it was that night at the canteen at Buffalo Range.

'So Beamish, our little lunatic Penga Marais took a bullet, did he?' smirked

Barker, wobbling slightly on his feet.

'He was hit in the head, there was blood everywhere, the chopper pilot told me he took a round through the floor of the helicopter as they pulled out. It was a totalll fookin mess.'

'He will be okay from what I hear?'

'The medic told me that the wound in his head is just a big scratch but it only just missed his eye. The bullet in his side passed through without hitting anything.'

'Well I am adding one of those new nasho arrivals to your stick until Marais gets back,' said Barker pointing at one of the three men sitting alone at a table.

'Noo Colour, I haven't got the patience to baby-sit. They look twelve years ooold.'

'Well, there it is. As they say in Russia, *tough ka-shit-ski*. His name is Francis. That's his surname, his first name's Rob I think.'

'Noo Colourr ...'

'... and you can't have two gunners in your stick. Choose one to carry the gun and be done with it.' Barker staggered off to chat to the other NCOs in 11 Troop.

Beamish looked across at the three new NS arrivals. As an old soldier, he had little sympathy for them. Part of him resented their presence; they were the living representation of the good men that had been lost. The NS replacements sat huddled together nursing a beer, trying not to make eye contact with the other RLI troopers who were all drinking heavily and talking loudly. The new men were being completely ignored.

As if on some silent command, Troopers West and Bolton together with the others, rushed at the three unsuspecting nashos who were given no time to react. The largest of the three saw Bolton coming and tried to push him away, to no avail, as he was dive-tackled to the ground. A few rabbit punches were issued. Excited hands grabbed at the three and carried them bodily from the mess. The NCOs egged them all on ... 'come on lads, lets get these nasho *fresh poes* cleaned up.' The procession carried the three struggling men into the night. The raucous laughter brought the few officers in camp out of their mess onto the veranda.

Just to the south of the hardstanding in front of the control tower was a muddy drainage pond ten or so metres in diameter. The group arrived at the edge of the pond and the three nashos were dropped unceremoniously to the ground. Beamish appointed himself the master of ceremonies.

'You three fresh poes will race across the pond,' ordered Beamish, waving expansively at the fetid pool.

Not wanting to seem like poor sports, the three men enthusiastically jumped in, clothes and all. As it was late October, the rainy season had not yet begun so the water was foul, giving off a putrid rancid stench. What the young NS troopers could not have known was that the various 3 Commando Troops stationed at Buffalo Range had thrown all manner of road-kill into the pond. This would have included dead goats, jackal, and pieces of donkey amongst other things. To spice it up, buckets of kitchen slop had been added. The pond would have been no more than two metres deep at its deepest point but the mud on the bottom was thick and sticky.

Realising that wading across wasn't going to work, the three initiates began various forms of doggy-paddle eventually crawling out the far end. The watching troopers were very impressed and in no time, a book was begun with money placed on the participants. A coach was appointed for each swimmer to huge applause from the spectators. As nobody knew the names of the new men, Beamish issued them names that the spectators could easily remember, Chico, Harpo and Groucho ... as in the Marx Brothers.

Beamish shouted the rules to the three men, who were already coughing and spluttering to try and remove the acrid taste and stench from their mouths and noses.

'Right you wankers; this is the best of three races. Winner get's to be first out the door on the next Fireforce drop.'

The three new men blinked at the dubious fruits of victory. They were stripped of their uniform as the various coaches went to work preparing their respective charges.

Beamish raised a mini-flare projector and out popped the signal for the first race.

In dived the participants, now with a much higher level of urgency, not wanting to let their coaches down. There was much flapping and splashing as the three men crossed the stinking broth. Groucho came out first to much clapping and shouting from his supporters. His odds shortened markedly.

'Okay Race 2, is an underwater race, on your marks ... GET SET ...' Pop went another mini-flare, in went the men. Harpo was clearly far better under water; out he came the other side. Poor Chico had been forced to surface halfway across so he was ordered to start again. All three swimmers were now vomiting violently as the primordial soup took its toll on their delicate constitutions.

'Okay Race 3, the decider, Groucho and Harpo only, ... one addition ... helmets on.' Helmets were produced and placed on the heads of the two surviving gladiators. 'The helmets must be seen to go below the surface at least twice ...'

Pop went the start for the final race, in went the helmeted swimmers. Of course the steel helmet trapped air inside, making it almost impossible to get below the surface completely, made doubly difficult by the fact that the participants were fatigued and throwing up at the same time. Groucho emerged the winner crawling out of the quagmire; too exhausted to stand, he lay in the mud next to the pond, joined by his mate.

'Who else is new to the Troop?' demanded Colour Barker, who had been looking on. He turned mischievously to the giant American.

The troopers enthusiastically advanced on the American who stood his ground.

'Go quietly Yank,' Beamish whispered to Kratzman helpfully.

Quietly was not how things progressed. Kratzman floored the first man with a punch to the nose, 'Get him,' went up the cry. Down went another man, then another, Kratzman let out a blood curling scream and charged at his pursuers. Beamish winced as more of Kratzman's blows found their mark. Four more men were rendered senseless before he was brought under control. He lay in the dirt with three men on each arm and the same number on his legs. They hauled him up, carried him to the edge of the pond and threw him in.

Completely at ease, resigned to his fate, the giant then swam purposefully across the pond, using a stroke that Jim Montgomery[96] would have been proud of. He emerged as an apparition similar to the *Creature from the Black Lagoon*[97]. The crowd stood in awed silence, then broke into spontaneous applause. The reputation of Jim Kratzman had begun.

Delighted with the outcome, the crowd joyously returned to the mess, two of their number still senseless from a Kratzman blow, supported on the shoulders of their *mukkas*.

The three NS *fresh poes* lay stark naked next to the pond all covered in black, gelatinous goo, too exhausted to move.

'Welcome to 3 Commando, RLI!' shouted one of the revellers back at them.

'Which one is ours?' Le Beau asked Beamish on the way back to the canteen.

'Chico I think,' he replied.

*

Camp Takawira (Marera Agricultural College), south of Chimoio, Mozambique

Immediately after death, the Shona believe the spirit of the deceased is unpredictable and dangerous. Consequently, the rites that are performed by the living relatives are based on the belief that the deceased's spirit leaves the body and continues to live. Death is frightening and brings with it confusion and uncertainty, not only to the family, but also to the community at large. In this case, it was the community of ZANLA cadres at Camp Takawira.

Comrade Tongogara had said that he felt that the two men, Nyandoro and Kachimanga, had died because of *ngozi*, they had offended the spirits. Mutumwa the *n'anga* needed to take this very seriously because the consequence of not divining the reason for their death correctly was dire. It is believed that when an individual dies, his or her spirit wanders the Earth until it is invited to return home to protect its descendants. When a spirit becomes extremely angered or seeks revenge against someone, it is known as an *ngozi* or evil spirit.

The *ngozi* may attack its victim in various ways, causing serious sickness, death or disaster in the family. If the two men had died because they had offended *ngozi*, the offended spirit had to be appeased by first discovering the

---

96 1976 Olympic Gold Medalist in the 100m freestyle, 4×200m Freestyle relay, 4×100m medley relay.
97 Horror movie by Jack Arnold (1954).

cause of its anger and then doing restitution by prayer and funeral offerings. Mutumwa's task was made more difficult because the families of the men were not present and, therefore, she needed to ensure that their spirits could still find their way home.

Mutumwa was a very powerful *n'anga;* this task was well within her capability.

Immediately after she had collected the bodies, she and her attendants had carried them to her hut where they were washed and cleaned in preparation for *kurova guva,* the funeral rites[98]. The women in the hut wept and wailed to mourn the loss of these men. Despite the fact that they were not related in any way, their grief needed to be genuine or the spirits would think they welcomed the men's death. They needed to act the part of mourning and weeping so they would not exact the dead's vengeance.

The next task was for Mutumwa to divine which of the spirits had been offended and why they had taken these men's lives. This process is called *Gata.* Under normal circumstances, Mutumwa would have been able to divine the problem without the need for throwing the dice or *hakata.* The circumstances of the men's death, particularly the man who's neck was so cruelly twisted, meant that she needed to use all the means at her disposal. She took a pouch of *hakata* from her leather belt. They consisted of a series of four miniature tablets, made of bone, each with a distinct design motif inscribed on one side.

The mighty *n'anga* began a low nasal chant, rocking backwards and forwards as she sat on her haunches. With a flourish, she threw the *hakata* onto an intricately woven grass mat on the floor of the hut. The bodies were laid out in the hut on straw mats covered by blankets. It was important for their spirits to witness the divining process. The women attendants sat quietly in a semi-circle in front of the great *n'anga.* They took up the soft chant. This was the favourite chant for the spirit that would take possession of Mutumwa.

As the chant grew in intensity, Mutumwa's body went rigid, sucking in air through her narrowed larynx with a loud, high-pitched squeal. Her neck muscles become taut, standing out, the veins in her neck could be seen throbbing. She threw her head back convulsively. Gurgling noises came from her throat. Mighty shudders racked her body and the squeal transformed into a deep-throated groan as if she was in great pain. The gyrations slowly dissipated and Mutumwa became calm and relaxed, her eyes rolled back in her head as the spirit of *Nehanda,* that now possessed her, began to speak. The words tumbled out of her mouth in a strange deep voice, completely different to her own.

Yes, it was true these men had been tricked by the white-man, the *murungu.* A powerful spell had been cast upon the spirits of these men, forcing them to offend the *ngozi.* The spirit *Nehanda* spoke of a great battle. Giant birds would descend to kill the children of *Mbire* [99]. The people needed to beware of the

---

98 In reality the funeral rites are spread over the period of a year.
99 The ancestors of the Shona. The Mbire took over the land north of the Limpopo somewhere between 1000 and 1050 AD. Their invasion from across the Zambezi

spirit of the treacherous crocodile, who could not be trusted.

Mutumwa's eyes rolled back and she shuddered as the strange voice left her. Her body visibly relaxed as the possession faded away, leaving her chest heaving from the enormous physical effort.

Once the spirit had left her and she had recovered her breathing, Mutumwa took freshly brewed beer, pulled away the blankets and sprinkled it over the bodies. Speaking soothingly and with great reverence, she informed the spirits of the men that they were about to be inducted into the family and the world of the ancestors. The ritual of *kurova guva*, the burial ceremony had begun. Mutumwa sent a messenger to Comrade Tongogara to tell him that all was well and that the bodies must be laid to rest first thing in the morning.

She would wait to warn the great leader in person of the other messages sent by the spirits.

Before first light Mutumwa called for two live goats to be brought to her hut. These were to be the sacrifice offered to *ngozi*. She pulled the goats one after the other into the hut to introduce them to the deceased. The women attendants sitting outside the hut began to sing. This was the signal for the men in Camp Takawira to begin the funeral procession to the grave. The two graves had been dug the previous day in the small graveyard behind the HQ building.

Navigator:	Okay. We're coming up to the *Gomo*[100] now. Zero-eight-five.
Green Leader:	Zero-eight-five we've got. We're crossing now. Check.

A short delay ...

Navigator:	Roger, flight level ... one zero five, come left to zero-nine-zero, speed two thirty knots.
Green Leader:	Check. Go left five degrees ... set one zero one nine[101].

Green Leader then spoke to the other aircraft in the formation ...

Green Leader:	Green Section speed up ... keep formation ... maintain two thirty knots.
Green 1:	Copied
Green 2:	Copied ... speeding up.
Green Leader:	Roger, confirm approaching IP[102] in ninety

---

marked the beginning of the dynasty of the Mbire Empire, also known as the Mutapa Empire.
100 Chimanimani Mountains on the eastern border between Rhodesia and Mozambique.
101 1,019 QNH altimeter setting, 4,500 feet.
102 Initial Point for a bomb run.

	seconds.
Navigator:	Affirmative ... Make your level zero one six ...

Three Rhodesian English Electric Canberras, in a tight V formation, were passing through 10,000ft above the sawmill at Tilbury, at the foot of the Chimanimani Mountains on the eastern border with Mozambique. They began a rapid descent to 1,600 feet AGL to avoid Mozambican radar coverage.

A group of men arrived outside Mutumwa's hut carrying two crudely made wooden stretchers made by lashing wooden cross beams between two poles. The men entered the hut and gently lifted the blanket-draped bodies onto the stretchers. Outside the hut, the stretchers were lifted onto their shoulders. The women took up their station behind the procession and they all began the slow walk to the graveside. The sun pushed up over the surrounding hills, promising a beautiful day.

The birds were singing in the trees, that made Mutumwa very pleased. If she had made a mistake in her divination, the birds would not be singing. An African Hawk Eagle, *Gondo*, turned high in the sky above. It gave a loud *kwee-oo kwee-oo* as if to welcome the day.

Green Leader:	Descend to level zero one six, make your speed two forty knots. Maintain zero-nine-zero.
Navigator:	You should be coming up to the bridge on your right.
Green Leader:	Roger I see it ...
Navigator:	Ten seconds to your turn.

The Canberra bombers had now descended to 1,600 feet AGL or about 4,000ft above sea level. They had increased their speed slightly. Their flight bearing was taking them east into Mozambique. The voices on the radio were calm and professional but the violent buffeting at such low level forced the air out of their lungs, making them sound out of breath.

Navigator:	Come left to bearing, zero-four-nine.
Green Leader:	Copied.

Comrade Tongogara and his entourage waited patiently at a short distance from the graveside. Before anybody approached the grave, the ritual friend, *sahwird*, appointed by Mutumwa, sprinkled the grave with water mixed with medicine. The purpose of this ritual was to re-sacralise the grave that may have been desecrated by witches the night before. Once this was done, the procession approached the two neatly dug graves.

The two sacrificial goats were brought forward.

Navigator:	You should be coming up on the IP at the dam in fifteen seconds.

| Green Leader: | Yes I can see it. Roger Green section, I am rolling out … now, come round to two-eight-five. Increase speed to two seventy knots. Make your level zero one zero. |

The leader of the Canberra section, called Green Leader, was turning the aircraft through 236°. They were flying in a flat echelon, 100m apart, one stacked 100ft, the other 200ft, above him. The new course was to bring them onto their target directly from the west. They had dropped to a height of 1,000 feet AGL. A slight hint of excitement was now audible in their voices.

Mutumwa carried a knife, a ceremonial knife, that she used for slaughtering animals needed to appease the spirits. The first goat was brought forward its neck twisted back to allow her to cut its throat.

The eagle flying above called again.

Mutumwa hesitated. She looked up at the bird, at the same time tilting her head slightly as if trying to discern a noise she was unsure of. The presence of the bird was the best possible omen as the eagle carried very powerful spirits. She held this strange pose for a few seconds, the other mourners watched in fascination, unsure of what she was doing.

Navigator:	Okay, we should begin to accelerate in five seconds.
Green Leader:	Are you happy for me to go?
Navigator:	Accelerate! Green Section aircraft … accelerate!
Green Leader:	Okay. I am on two-eight-five. Speed now three zero zero knots.
Green Leader:	Road coming up. Shit, we are exactly on time!
Navigator:	We should open the doors.
Green Leader:	As soon as my speed is up.
Navigator:	Go left a bit … go left … go onto two-eight-two.
Green Leader:	Is my speed OK?
Navigator:	Yes, its fine. I have the target! Steady … Steady.
Green Leader:	Switch on the doors.
Navigator:	Roger … Go left … Steady … Steady! … Steady!

The Canberras were accelerating onto the target at just over 300knots, 300ft above the ground.

Still unsure of what she had heard Mutumwa bent down again to slaughter the goat.

Comrade Tongogara shifted on his feet, a little irritated at the delay.

| Navigator: | I am going to put the bombs right in the middle. Fuck, they are grouped next to the buildings. Steady … Steady! BOMBS GONE! … Beautiful man, bloody |

beautiful!

The screaming, reverberating sound of the approaching aircraft, struck Tongogara like a punch in the gut. It was a sound, heard once, would stay in nightmares for a lifetime. He dived into one the open graves as the first of the aircraft passed overhead.

Each of the aircraft dropped three hundred Mk2 Alpha bouncing bombs. The bomblets struck the ground bounced up and exploded, killing or maiming everyone within an area of 1,000m×300m. The first blast threw Mutumwa into the grave on top of Tongogara. The massive collective explosion killed everyone standing in the open next to the grave. Their bodies were literally torn apart making them unrecognisable as human beings. Blood and flesh dripped from the surrounding trees. The camp buildings looked like they had been spray-painted in red.

Comrade Dipuka Muponde lay where he had stood, one arm amputated at the shoulder, his body a mass of wounds, his eyes staring vacantly at the bodies of Nyandoro and Kachimanga that still lay on their stretchers peacefully undisturbed. There were now many tortured souls to be put to rest.

Perfect silence followed the attack as a cloud of choking dust lifted into the morning sky, billowing upward covering everything for hundreds of metres in a thin dusty film. The DsHK 12.7mm guns in the surrounding hills fired forlornly after the rapidly disappearing aircraft.

High in the clear blue sky the African Hawk Eagle gave another loud, urgent cry, *kwee-oo! kwee-oo! ... Giant birds would descend to kill the children of Mbire.*

On a hill above the base at Marera Agricultural College, Godfrey Nyathi watched in shocked amazement as the Canberra strike decimated the camp. He had slipped away at first light on the pretext of checking security in the surrounding hills. The percussion of the bombs and the shock wave had struck him in the chest like a hammer. He felt slightly winded, riveted to the spot. The cloud of dust and smoke drifted over his position on the early morning breeze.

Could it be possible that Nyenganyenga is dead? ...

He broke into a run down the hill, his mind churning with the enormity of what he had just witnessed. A feeling of conflicted confusion washed over him at the thought of Tongogara being killed ... a man he has spent every hour with for two years.

The radio messages to Rhodesia were detached ... unemotional ... his instructions issued in simple coded text ... witnessing the effect of these words translated into complete devastation was unnerving ... his stomach went into a knotted spasm.

Nyathi ran on ... *is the General dead?*

14

CIO HQ, Livingston Avenue, Salisbury

Colonel 'Pora', in fact, was Colonel António Borges Santos the Commander of the FPLM[103] Southwest region. The Colonel described, through his interpreter, his treatment at the hands of the 'crazy' men at Vila Salazar. He demanded to be given access to the Red Cross and to be taken back to his country or handed over to the United Nations. He denied all the information that had been recorded so carefully by Afonso of 2RR.

George Stanbridge and his staff had listened patiently to the initial three-hour ranting and raving by Colonel Santos. They had not asked any questions but simply asked him to explain his relationship with the ZANLA leadership. Stanbridge had intended, as his core plan, to 'turn' the Colonel into an informant and send him back into Mozambique. This had to happen relatively soon or otherwise the man's arrival back in Mozambique would be difficult for him to explain. Plus the complication of his alleged abduction had to be considered. Stanbridge's other thought was that the Colonel might be able to play a role in the CIO's recently created RENAMO[104] resistance movement against FRELIMO in Mozambique.

The Colonel had been treated with great respect thus far. He had been fed, the room he was given was well appointed and his uniform had been dry-cleaned. He was referred to by his title and there had been no attempt to intimidate him. Unfortunately for the Colonel, he interpreted the respectful treatment as a sign of remorse on the part of the Rhodesians for his illegal incarceration. He pounded the table and gave his questioners a mouthful at every opportunity. After a day of this, Stanbridge decided he would have to change strategy. He called in his friends in the Police Special Branch.

At first light the following morning, Colonel Santos was roused from his slumbers with a cold bucket of water. The shock of the sudden and quite brutal awakening removed the Colonel's bravado. He jabbered away in Portuguese but, as the interpreter was not present, he realised that nobody was listening to him. This made him panic, and he started pleading with his captors.

The Colonel was stripped to his underpants and led into a cold dark room in the basement of CIO HQ. Three masked men held him down while a forth filled a syringe from a glass vial. The Colonel screamed in terror as the man came towards him. It seemed obvious to Stanbridge, looking through the observation window, that the Colonel was more willing to talk. The Colonel was injected with Thiopental (Sodium Pentothal), a class of barbiturates designed to decrease higher cortical brain functioning. The theory is that

---

103 *Forcas Populares para o Libertacao de Mocambique*, the military wing of FRELIMO.
104 *Resistencia Nacional Mocambicana*, The Rhodesian CIO and their equivalent in South Africa created this resistance movement as a counter for the support FRELIMO was giving ZANLA. RENAMO went on to conduct a violent civil war in Mozambique that only came to an end in 1992.

because lying is more complex than telling the truth, suppression of the higher cortical functions may lead to uncovering the truth.

The four masked men left the room, and the interrogator and interpreter entered. They wrapped the Colonel in a blanket and a fresh pot of tea was produced. The FRELIMO officer had shown an appreciation for Tanganda Tea. The Colonel was immediately chatty and cooperative. He began, without prompting, talking about his childhood living in Lorenco Marques, his years at Catholic school, how he had escaped from the Colonial Portuguese to Tanzania where he had been trained as a soldier. The words tumbled out of him. He spoke of the great victory over their colonial masters and the independence of Mozambique, the creation of the Marxist state and his pleasure at being appointed as a battalion commander. Much of this early information matched what he had told 2RR, under slightly different circumstances.

'Do you know Comrade Hamadziripi?' asked the interrogator in a conversational fashion.

The Colonel seemed to hesitate for a second, 'Yes' he answered.

'Do you know where Comrade Hamadziripi lives?'

'He lives in a house in Sao Jorge do Limpopo, but he travels to Maputo and Chimoio a great deal.

'Do you know Comrade Tongogara?'

Once again, a cloud came over the man's eyes as if he was struggling to find an answer.

'Yes I know Comrade Tongogara.' The man seemed to be relieved by giving the answer. He added, 'We meet once a month to discuss matters of cooperation.'

'Where are these meetings held Colonel?'

'The meeting is always held in Aldia de Barragem because there is a particular woman that Comrade Tongogara likes to visit in that town ... the next meeting is on the 24th.'

The information struck Stanbridge, and those watching the interrogation, like a thunderclap. He could hardly believe his ears, it was more than he would have expected in his wildest dreams.

The interrogator did not miss a beat, he continued in the same friendly conversational fashion. 'Who attends this meeting Colonel?'

'The meeting is attended by the ZANLA area commander, Comrade Hamadziripi, Tongogara, his second in command, Rex Nhongo, and his Political Commissar Josiah Tungamirai, ... on our side it is General D'Almeida and myself and our intelligence officer.'

The crucial question was next.

'Where is the meeting held and what time Colonel?'

This was not information that the 2RR men had obtained. Captain John had not even thought to ask such a question, he was much more interested in the distribution of enemy forces in front of his position at Vila Salazar.

The FRELIMO Colonel hesitated again. There was a battle going on inside his brain, he was fighting the effects of the drug. He shook his head refusing to answer.

The interrogator did not push the point, returning instead to why the Colonel had been in Malvernia the night he was kidnapped. He seemed to relax again and gave a detailed account of his monthly visits to the various FRELIMO military outposts in his region. He detailed the weapons he had at his disposal, where they were positioned including the GRAD-21 launchers that had recently arrived from the Soviet Union. He appeared not to be particularly enamoured with the Soviet advisors he had met, preferring the Chinese. This was because he had been trained in China in the 1960's and he preferred the Chinese focus on the power of the people and their philosophy of focussing on the peasantry. The Soviet weapons were very welcome, however, particularly the new Strela ground-to-air heat-seeking missile. These, he said, were held at all FRELIMO and ZANLA bases. This all accorded closely with information provided by 2RR.

'Where is the meeting held with your ZANLA comrades Colonel? What time is the meeting?'

'It is not at our base. It is in a house that the woman lives in, it is a big house built by a Portuguese colonist. The meeting normally starts after lunch as many of us have to drive from some distance.'

Bingo! Stanbridge could not believe his luck. This information would have taken years to gather. The problem he now faced was what would be FRELIMO's reaction when their man was reported missing. They were bound to change all their plans.

First, the information Colonel Santos had given needed to be further substantiated. The unfortunate Colonel was then subjected to a vicious beating using a rubber hose on the pads of his feet. During this excruciating experience, he confirmed all the information he had previously given.

*

BSAP HQ, Montague Avenue, Salisbury

Despite the close co-operation of the various intelligence-gathering units within the Rhodesian security forces, that co-operation was not necessarily forthcoming at the most senior level. The CIO maintained a network of informers and spies in neighbouring countries and within the security forces themselves. The BSAP Special Branch also maintained a network of informers and spies, in particular within the liberation movements in Mozambique and Zambia. Both the Rhodesian SAS and the Selous Scouts had placed spies in neighbouring countries for intelligence gathering purposes in support of their planned missions. Rhodesian Army Intelligence and Counter-Intelligence also developed a network of spies and informants. All this, coupled with the fact that ZANLA and ZIPRA had their own intelligence agencies operating in Rhodesia, meant that there were a great many spies knocking about. Superimposed over the top of these spies were the CIA and MI6 who both maintained offices in Salisbury.

As to be expected, each service jealously guarded its networks and the names and codenames of operatives. It was rare that the intelligence from the deepest buried spies made it into the planning rooms at COMOPs and if it did, it was heavily sanitised.

The Police Special Branch had been at the spy game much longer than everybody else. They were formed in the early 1950s and they operated during the Federation of Rhodesia and Nyasaland and subsequent to the breakup of the Federation. The threat offered by the various liberation movements in the 1960s meant that Special Branch had to increase the intensity of its activities. Some farsighted and highly strategic thinkers led the Special Branch. One of the outcomes of their planning was the Selous Scouts themselves who grew out of Special Branch pseudo-terrorist operations.

It was in early 1971 that a landmine killed a Police Senior Constable. He was driving an unprotected Land Rover while operating from his police station in Runde Tribal Trust Land near Shabani. The Senior Constable had spent thirty years in the force and was highly respected by his peers and his superiors. The dead policeman had three children; a boy of twenty-one and two girls aged seventeen and eighteen. The eldest son, who was attending a teacher's training college near Fort Victoria, felt the loss of the father very deeply. After the funeral, this young man presented himself to the Victoria Provincial Special Branch Officer, a Chief Superintendent, at Police Headquarters in Fort Victoria.

The young man was obviously highly intelligent, making a strong case to the Special Branch officer for helping to catch the people who killed his father. The officer immediately seized on this opportunity, sending the man to the police station in Shabani as a cleaner/tea maker and cook. He was provided with one-roomed accommodation in the local black township, where he began the painstaking process to understand the local terrorist network.

In the early seventies, there were likely no more than a few hundred terrorists in the whole country, so it took the man two months to make contact with someone who could lead him to the terrorist band. This was under the guise of wishing to be recruited and sent overseas for training. Eventually the contact man led him to a cave in the Chironde Range of hills just 25km south of Selukwe, facing east over the Runde TTL.

The meeting with the terrorist leader went very well. There were only six men in his band. The leader was very free with information and boasted of killing policemen with his landmine. He was pleased to hear that the young man was a Karanga, as were he and his men. Details of recruitment were outlined, it was established that all recruits had to make their way to Botswana where they would be transported to Zambia or Tanzania for training. They explained in detail exactly who the recruitment agents were and where they were located in Francistown. The terrorists showed him how to strip and assemble their AK47s; it was all very impressive indeed.

After the briefing, the excited young man left with a promise to bring food before he started the arduous overland trek to the Botswana border. Two days later, the police, supported by the RLI, killed all six terrorists, and over the following month, using the intelligence gathered by the young man, they killed or arrested ten more. After this operation was over, the young man convinced his SB handler that he should be allowed to infiltrate the ZANLA army and become an agent. This audacious plan was put into action and the man was given intensive training on communications, morse code, light weapons and intelligence gathering.

It was over a year later that this agent resurfaced. The Special Branch, Projects Section, HQ in Salisbury received a short Morse-code message in seShona, 'The Owl was in the Tree.'

The agent, known by the Shona word for Owl, *Zizi*, had been working diligently for two years, feeding vital information to the Rhodesians. The Owl had been largely responsible for the success of the first attack on the ZANLA base north of Chimoio, where many hundreds of cadres were killed and vital equipment destroyed.

The SB member, who had been put in charge of managing *Zizi*, pored over the most recent message received. *Zizi's* secret message to his controllers in Salisbury had confirmed that Josiah Tongogara would be at Camp Takawira. It appeared that Comrade Tongogara had escaped the air strike with only a slight wound and had returned to Chimoio. *Damn!* ...

*

Ward B4, Andrew Fleming Hospital, Salisbury

Lily McIntyre and her two children, Matthew five, and Amanda four, walked down the long corridor towards Ward B4. The children chatted excitedly; they were going to see Dudley. Dudley was the most ideal playmate. He played hide-and-go-seek, he swam in the pool, he helped with drawing and painting, building blocks, tea parties, making mud pies ... he did everything with them.

Ward B4 was full of wounded soldiers. Some had lost limbs, some had been badly burnt, most had various forms of gunshot and shrapnel wounds. At the entrance to the ward, Lily asked to see Dudley and she and the kids were led down between the rows of beds. Many had curtains drawn around them, the voices of visitors filled the room with sound. The nurse stopped in front of Dudley Marais's bed and announced that he had visitors.

Lily sucked in her breath when she saw the swollen face; Amanda began to cry ... *this wasn't Dudley*. A thick line of stitches stretched from his hairline down to just above his right eye. Congealed blood had collected in his eyebrows and the wound had been covered in anti-septic. Both eyes were swollen almost shut, making Dudley a formidable sight for a young child.

'Amanda, I told you that Dudley had been in the war and he had been hurt, don't be afraid,' Lily tried to sooth the child.

'Don't cry Amanda,' croaked Dudley, his throat still raw and painful.

The young girl held her mother's hand even more tightly trying to figure out what she was looking at.

Matthew stood at the foot of the bed and looked around at all the patients. 'My Dad was in the war!' announced Matthew loudly to no one in particular, in the way that five-year olds do.

'Your Dad was a very brave man,' said the man in the neighbouring bed.

'My Dad had a gun and he shot terrorists!' Matthew told the man.

'Matthew come closer so I can see you,' Dudley called to the boy. Matthew walked up bravely next to the man with the swollen face ... *the voice was Dudley.*

'Don't be afraid, my face is just swollen 'cause I bumped it,' announced Dudley as loudly as he could, to try and settle the children.

Lilly lifted Amanda and placed her on the bed next to Dudley, she took his hand and squeezed it.

'I will be better soon and we can go swimming,' said Dudley, 'We can play catchers too.'

'I am going to big school next year,' said Amanda. 'I will have a school case just like Matthew.'

'I am playing cricket,' Matthew informed the ward to make sure he was not left out.

'What's that?' Amanda asked pointing at the blood that had seeped through the bandage strapped around Dudley's torso.

'I scratched myself and it's still bleeding a little, don't worry I will be better soon.' Dudley's familiar voice had now put the children at ease although both stared at his swollen face.

Seeing the children brought all the memories flooding back, all the good times with Jock, Lily and the kids ... his family. A tear ran down Dudley's cheek, these were the only people he had in the whole world.

'Thank you for coming Lily. I ... It's so good to see you and the kids,' he whispered, the stutter of emotion in his voice.

'Why are you crying?' Amanda asked in the forthright way that only young children can.

Lily leaned forward and pulled the curtain around the bed. Then taking Dudley's hand she whispered in his ear, 'don't get upset Dudley, we are here for you. We will visit until you are better, and then you can come and stay with us until you are completely well again.'

The stress of the past few weeks, the painful memories and the joy of seeing the children, were too much for the nineteen year old. He wept, tears streaming down his face, too overcome to speak.

Lily sat on the bed next to him and held his hand tightly, talking softly about all the domestic subjects expected of a young mother. Dudley closed his eyes, lay back on the pillows, and let the sound of her soothing voice wash over him.

The children went to speak to the man in the bed next door who offered them some chocolate cake that he said his wife had made for him.

*

Le Coq d'Or nightclub, corner of Kingsway and Baker Avenue, Salisbury

'What the fook happened to you?' Beamish inquired.

On the pavement on Baker Avenue were three young troopers from 4 Troop RLI. Their faces had been bashed; one had a badly bleeding nose. They didn't look too good at all. Beamish was surprised they were still on their feet, particularly the one whose nose was clearly broken, bent to one side and distorted. He sat propped against the wall, his head down between his knees, the blood pooling on the pavement; he spat more blood out of his mouth.

'Only fucking asked the DJ to play ABBA's *Dancing Queen*, that's all,' replied one of the soldiers.

'Well no wonder!' replied Beamish. 'You better get to hospital with your mate to get that nose seen to, you useless one commando prick.'

Middle of the Road's, *Tweedle Dee, Tweedle Dum*[105] filled the air from inside the nightclub.

> *Do you recall some years ago?*
> *Up in the mountains that were white with snow*
> *Inside a cavern*
> *McDougal he was plannin' ...*
> *There's gonna be a showdown with somebody he knows ...*

Cpl. Beamish led his two gunners, Le Beau and 'Yank' Kratzman up the stairs into the notorious Le Coq d'Or nightspot in the heart of Salisbury. Their boots splashing in pools of blood dripping down the stairs of the narrow, dimly lit staircase.

> *Oh, Tweedle Dee*
> *Oh, Tweedle Dum.*
> *... The tune McDougal always used to hum*
> *While he was fightin' his rival clan McGregor*
> *Dishonour, he would never,*
> *The tartan of his clan ...*

Beamish smiled to himself, remembering the hit song from 1971, just before he was sent to Northern Ireland. His memory flashed to the few Scots in his regiment who sang the song at every opportunity.

> *... Soon you'll hear the sound of people shouting*
> *you will see the claymores in their hands*
> *if you knew the reason for their fighting*
> *you would never understand.*

---

105 Middle of the Road, RCA (1971), Songwriters Capuano, Mario and Stott.

Oh, Tweedle Dee
Oh, Tweedle Dum ...

Le Coq d'Or was one of the places in Salisbury 'owned' by the RLI, along with the Lion's Den Bar attached to the Windsor Hotel a little further along the street. The nightclub and bar, was located in a relatively modern, 1960s building that had, no doubt, started life as an office block. It was constructed of concrete and glass, instead of the bricks, mortar and sandstone of an earlier period. The building was like many that had sprung up in Rhodesia's boom times following World War II when the world wanted the country's minerals and tobacco. The building was looking a little jaded, in need of rejuvenation. An American-based religious sect owned the building, but they had pulled out of the country when Rhodesia defied the world by declaring UDI. The sect had laid down strict conditions that banned the selling of alcohol and tobacco in their building. Dancing was also prohibited. The major tenant had told the sect that the building was being used as a library. In a sense, Le Coq d'Or was a place of learning, ... fighting, drinking, dancing and virginity, maybe a little praying as well ... to get lucky!

At the top of the stairs, two large bouncers met Beamish and his gunners. Both were ex-RLI PTIs[106] who Beamish knew well. He exchanged nods with the men, and the three 11 Troop soldiers strode purposefully into the nightclub which was packed solid. Kratzman used his bulk to push through to the bar, followed by the two shorter men.

'Three *Shumbas*,' he called to the barman.

The Yank had already learned the local term for Lion Lager. Kratzman would normally have drunk Bourbon Whisky, but with sanctions, imported hard liquor was virtually unobtainable. The locals made gin and cane spirit but the American was not partial to either.

Without any ceremony the three downed their first beers, Le Beau didn't even take a breath, just holding up the bottle and sucking out the contents. It was not strictly speaking their first beer; they each had downed half a dozen at the Oasis Hotel earlier. Beamish had decided that they needed to show Kratzman some of the local sights. The Oasis was the most popular meeting place in Salisbury on Saturday lunchtime, crammed full of *punda*[107]!

Elbowing room at the bar, the three 'old soldiers' held the beers in their hands as they silently surveyed the scene in front of them. It was loud, bawdy, boozy, bare-knuckled and bra-less. Most of the men in the room were soldiers, predominantly RLI predominantly drunk, predominantly looking to 'shape' as speedily as possible. These men lived with life and death. The imminent possibility of death, used as a common form of 'persuasion'.

The dance floor was full of gently swaying bodies, completely out of time with the music, clutching girls in a 'shuffle', not so much in a dance, but more for physical support. Their eyes were blank and their minds numb. It was

---

106 Physical Training Instructors.
107 Rhodesian slang, women. The implication, when using the word, was that the women were 'available'.

head thumping, reverberating, pulsatingly noisy, the DJ putting on record after record without a pause. Manfred Mann's Earth Band was playing *Blinded by the Light*.

> *Blinded by the light,*
> *revved up like a deuce,*
> *another runner in the night*
> *Blinded by the light,*
> *revved up like a deuce,*
> *another runner in the night*

The strobe lights illuminated two men dressed in jeans and khaki standing at the bar. One was wearing a sleeveless bush jacket or fishing vest with many pockets, the sort reporters wear. They were watching the three RLI men at the bar. Kratzman scanned the room from his lofty height and noticed the men.

Beamish was relating a story to his two companions, having to shout above the music. It related to the time some nameless RLI troopie, who thought it might be really cool to sneak into the lady's loos and doctor the toilet paper with Buffalo Bean. The result was bedlam; they had to call the police and ambulances. With tears running down his cheeks the animated Beamish explained, with some input from Le Beau, how the Buffalo Bean comes from a plant that grows wild in the bush, that had been accidentally encountered by many an unsuspecting troopie squatting with his pants down! The fibres from this plant have the same effect as itching powder, only a million times worse. The only cure is from the mud from around that plant's roots, or thick dabs of camomile lotion. Any form of mud would have been scarce in the loo that evening! Beamish had a very good sense for a story and, by the time he finished, he had his companions laughing heartily. Kratzman's laugh was an infectious loud booming affair that got louder as Beamish demonstrated the poor victim's 'dance of the infernal itch'.

'Can we buy you boys a beer?' a man with an American accent asked. The two men in khaki had moved along the bar to stand next to the three soldiers.

'Whose asking?' enquired Kratzman with his own distinctive Appalachian drawl.

'My name's Sharp and this is my friend Bentley,' replied the man with the fishing vest, he had a posh English accent.

'You look like reporters,' observed Kratzman.

'I 'ate reporters more than anything in the world,' said Le Beau.

'Why don't you two fook off and leave us alonne,' added Beamish, who was clearly of the same opinion.

'We don't mean trouble friend,' said the American Bentley. 'We are new in town and would like to meet some of the locals.'

'Well we are not locals, so fook off,' Beamish was starting to get agitated.

'You boys mercenaries?' asked Bentley flippantly.

'That's enough buddy!' Kratzman moved in front of the two reporters who had their backs against the bar. 'You two gentlemen should now leave before this gets outa hand.'

'So you are mercenaries! Why are you so defensive?' said the Pom cockily. His accent was enough to tilt Beamish, all English public school ... *the poof probably went to Oxford.*

'What?' Beamish was now ready to plant one of these pricks.

'It's okay Corp, I will handle this,' said Kratzman, pushing his arm, more like a tree trunk, in front of Beamish. He pushed his face inches from the Pom Sharp. 'For the record I get paid a hundred and fifty Rhodie dollars a month, I am a volunteer and I am here to fight for the freedom of these people from Communism.' Kratzman waved his arm indicating all the drunken dancers in the nightclub.

'Have you killed women and children in refugee camps in Mozambique?' pressed the Pom Sharp who refused to be intimidated by the American giant.

Le Beau ducked beneath Kratzman's outstretched arm and punched the Pom squarely on his pointy nose, following up with a full-force blow to the solar plexus. The Pom Sharp's nose burst into a spray of blood and spittle. He slid to the floor under the bar, gasping for air, completely winded. Sucking, whimpering sounds came from his mouth as he tried to regain his breath, sucking more blood into his throat, slowly drowning in his own blood.

Beamish took the opportunity to grab the American Bentley by the throat, holding it so tight that no noise could come out, his other hand crushing the man's balls. Bentley's face went crimson, then purple, as the effect of his crushed gonads became more pressing than being able to breath.

One of the bouncers tapped Kratzman on the shoulder.

'Have we got a problem here?'

'No Sir! This man has had too much to drink and has fallen down,' said Kratzman, pointing at the Pom under the bar.

Beamish released the neck of the American Bentley, just to allow some air in, before clamping down on the throat again. The man was now bent backwards over the bar, his feet kicking involuntarily.

'What's wrong with that one?' asked the Bouncer, pointing towards the man Beamish had over the bar.

'Ah, he swore in front of that lady,' replied Kratzman indicating a young woman watching the altercation a few feet away. The Pom on the floor of the bar let out a stifled yelp. Blood was now frothing at his mouth as he tried to throw up and breath at the same time. Le Beau gave him a vicious kick in the chest breaking a rib.

That was enough for the bouncer.

'That's it. All of you out ... NOW!' He signalled to his mate at the door who rushed over.

The American Bentley was still firmly in Beamish's grip, his face changing alarmingly to a puce colour, his legs kicking back more urgently against the bar. Bentley was trying ineffectively to pry Beamish's hand away from his crushed genitals.

The bouncer leaned over to grab Beamish by the collar. His hands were still holding Bentley's extremities, refusing to let go. The rough jerk on

Beamish's collar forced him to release his grip on the throat.

Bentley gave out a blood-curdling scream as he fell to the floor holding his balls. The pain was like a knife through the brain. He rolled backwards and forwards in the foetal position.

With both hands now free Beamish gave the bouncer a push.

'Leave us alone. We were minding our own business when these journalists starting asking us questions,' shouted Beamish self-righteously.

The shout of the word 'journalist' was enough to bring the party to a grinding halt. International journalists were seen as the scum of the earth, misrepresenting Rhodesia's struggle to the outside world.

'Kill the bastards!' someone roared from the back of the crowd.

The bouncers were now in the difficult position of trying to protect the two reporters, both writhing on the floor, from a now very angry crowd.

Kratzman bent down and grabbed each reporter by a foot, dragging them both across the floor towards the staircase. The two bouncers barred the way for the other revellers as Kratzman went down the blood soaked staircase to the pavement below. The journalists slid helplessly down the stairs behind him, banging their heads hard on each stair as they went.

Beamish and Le Beau stayed at the bar to finish their beers. A cheer went up from the soldiers inside the bar for the successful eviction of the two despicable journalists. Beamish threw up his fist in triumph ... *we showed those two reporters a thing or two!*

Outside on the pavement Kratzman propped the two men up against the wall. The Pom was holding his nose that was till spouting blood; his shirt and fishing vest a sticky mess. The American Bentley lay in a tight shaking ball, making short sucking sounds, willing the pain to go away.

Kneeling down in front of the Pom who seemed more *compos mentus*, Kratzman gave a short piece of advice, 'If I see either of you again, so help me, I will kill you myself ... with my bare hands.'

The strains of Status Quo's *Rocking all Over the World*[108] echoed through the street.

> *Here we are*
> *here we are and here we go*
>
> *all aboard*
> *and we're hittin' the road*
> *here we go rockin' all over the world!*

Men came piling down the staircase out of the nightclub led by Corporal Beamish.

'We are going to visit Penga in hospital,' announced Beamish. It was now midnight.

An old Bedford RL used to transport men into town from Cranborne Barracks was commandeered and the driver instructed to drive to Andrew

---

108 Status Quo, Vertigo Records (1977), written by John Fogarty of CCR.

Fleming Hospital. It looked like Beamish had managed to get about fifteen men together for the impromptu visit. The truck careered in the direction of the hospital, the men singing Mike Westcott's version of *Tipperary* in the back.

> *It's a long ... long way to Mukumbura.*
> *It's a long way to run ...*
> *And we're going up there to stir ... stir... stir*[109].

The RL pulled up in front of the main entrance to the hospital and the men tumbled out. They rushed in a knot at the door, which was instantly barred by an enormous, formidable looking nurse. She was flanked by a group of medical orderlies and a student doctor. Somebody at Le Coq d'Or had the presence of mind to phone ahead of the visiting party.

'Now what would you lads be looking for this time of night?' the nurse demanded with a broad Yorkshire accent.

Corporal Beamish, the senior rank, took one step forward, 'We are here to visit a wounded friend Ma'am,' he replied respectfully.

'Yes,' shouted the entourage.

'Well lads visiting hours start at ten in the morning I'll be seeing you then,' the matron replied.

'We've cum a long way Ma'am,' Beamish ventured.

'You lads go 'ome to bed, I'll not be having any trouble with you tonight, we have many a sick person in here that don't need the likes of you running about creating havoc.'

'But Ma'am,' Beamish was desperate not to let the matron get in the way of a good idea.

The matron stepped forward inches from Beamish; she was certainly a very big woman, '... you Corporal take one step forward and I'll knock your block off,' she hissed. She looked like she could and she meant it. 'Now bugger off!' she pointed to the car park.

Perplexed by the matron's aggressive response, Beamish's addled brain sought an alternative.

'Right boys, form up in the car park,' ordered Beamish.

In the light of the street lamps, the small contingent of RLI formed up in three ranks in the car park. Beamish ordered them to attention and then conducted a loud inspection to the amusement of the men themselves and the now large crowd of night-duty nurses that were collected at the front door. Beamish, after a skin full, had a great feel for the theatrical.

'Parade ... PARADE stand at EASE.' Boots were driven into the tar.

He began to sing Clem Tholet's *Rhodesians never die* in a deep resonant voice.

---

109 Rhodesian slang, stir means to cause trouble, to make a nuisance. Mukumbura was a tiny village on the northeast border with Mozambique. It was Rhodesia's version of Timbuktu, bloody far from anywhere.

> *'cause we're all Rhodesians*
> *And we'll fight through thick and thin*
> *We'll keep our land a free land*
> *Stop the enemy coming in*

The other men on parade took up the song ...

> *We'll keep them north of the Zambezi*
> *Till that river's running dry*
> *And this mighty land will prosper*
> *For Rhodesians never die.*

They sang with real gusto to the applause of the nurses who had stepped through the doors onto the steps.

Then Beamish, flushed with the success of the first song, sang the RLI marching song, *The Saints*, sung to the tune of *When the Saints go marching in* ...

> *Oh when the Saints,*
> *Oh when the Saints go marching in,*
> *I want to be in that number when the Saints go marching in.*

The song was another huge success; patients and nurses were now leaning out the windows above.

> *Oh when 3 Commando ...*
> *Oh when 3 Commando ...*
> *Oh when 3 Commando go marching in,*
> *I want to be in that number when 3 Commando go marching in!*

'MORE' the crowd cried.

In the distance, sirens could be heard approaching. The singers remained in their ranks ... *the bloody matron has called the Fuzz*, thought Beamish.

'As you were!' he called to the men.

If they had to 'face the music' there was safety in numbers.

The first ambulance raced up into the entrance to the Casualty Ward. It came to a halt and the driver rushed around the back to open the doors. Two stretcher patients were removed, both had drips attached. Two other ambulances arrived in quick succession.

Beamish wandered up to one of the drivers.

'What's going on mate?'

'Some bastard threw a grenade into La Boheme Nightclub, it's a bloody mess.'

*

Tjolotjo District, central Matabeleland

Sgt Cephas Ngwenya recovered very quickly from his wounds. The head wound healed without too much discomfort although he did get headaches from time to time. The scar across his forehead gave his face a more sinister look. A few facial scars were part of being a warrior, so Ngwenya felt satisfied with his new 'look'. The wound in his side was much more uncomfortable, forcing him to walk with a stiff measured gait as it hurt if he tried to walk fast or lift a heavy weight.

He caught the train south from Salisbury to Bulawayo and then waited in a long Shu Shine Bus queue to take him out to his home near Tjolotjo. The country had a well-developed bus system that transported migrant workers and their families from the rural areas to the major towns and cities. The transport was rough and uncomfortable. The buses had hard bench seats and the suspension left much to be desired. As was customary for a trip home, Ngwenya had purchased two 20kg bags of maize meal (mielie meal) as well as presents for his wife and son. These were all loaded onto the roof of the bus amongst a huge conglomeration of luggage including bicycles, crates of beer, live animals like chickens and goats, and all manner of general household items. The luggage piled on the roof was almost as high again as the bus itself.

Communication home was a challenge as the only reliable means was by way of letter. Ngwenya had written to his wife as soon as he was able, telling her he was coming home on holiday. The logistics of getting the letter to her were, however, considerable. The letter was sent care of the local trading store, called Naidoo's General Store, where 'local' meant a 15km walk. She did not go to the trading store more than once a month to buy provisions; it was then that she would collect her mail. This was the situation for almost all the people in the TTLs as post offices were few and far between. Mr Naidoo, who owned the store, kept all the mail in batches, one for each of the many villages spread around the district. Often a representative of the village would collect the mail on a weekly basis and distribute it on behalf of all the residents.

There were public telephones at the trading store and at the police station but these lines were notoriously unreliable and often long queues of people waited to make calls.

The trip from Bulawayo to Tjolotjo, via Nyamandhlovu, was excruciatingly painful. Every jolt on the corrugated road was like a hot needle in his side. He rued the fact that he had left the hospital so early against the advice of the doctor. The repeated jolting opened up the wound and it soaked the bandages around his waist. When the bus pulled up outside the police station at Tjolotjo, it was mercifully time to get off. The police had set up a roadblock and they were checking *sestupas*[110]. Ngwenya still carried his police ID card,

---

110 The law required each black person to have identification. They carried a pass or

as carrying an army, or much less, a Selous Scout ID, would have been suicide if it became generally known.

The police still commanded a high degree of respect in the rural areas, and while terrorists targeted policemen on leave, this was rare. Cephas's status as a policeman gave respect to the Ngwenya family, meant that he was relatively safe when he was on leave.

Instead of waiting in the queue to pass through the roadblock, Ngwenya approached the white Patrol Officer in charge of the roadblock. Ngwenya did not recognise the man so he must have been new to the district. Ngwenya made an effort to meet all the policemen stationed in Tjolotjo.

'*Uxolo Ishe*, excuse me Sir,' Ngwenya addressed the young policeman in siNdebele.

'*Litshone njani*, good afternoon,' the PO replied, also in siNdebele.

Ngwenya passed him his police ID.

'I am on leave, Sir, and I have a Tokarev pistol in my baggage plus five clips of ammunition.'

One of the black policemen working on the roadblock looked up and immediately recognized Ngwenya.

'*Kanjani*, Cephas,' he shouted and walked over to shake hands.

'You know this man Constable?' the PO asked.

'Yes sir, he is from Jelume,' replied the Constable, pointing out to the west.

'Good to meet you Cephas,' said the PO respectfully, handing back the ID. 'I would be happy to drive you home myself but your area has been frozen.'

When Selous Scout pseudo operations were in progress in a district, the area was 'frozen' by making it off limits for any other SF units including the police and Intaf. This was to prevent any inadvertent contacts between friendly forces, as, when on operations, the Selous Scouts were virtually indistinguishable from the insurgents. Each Selous Scout operation was kept on a strictly need-to-know basis and, therefore, there is no way that Ngwenya would have known that an operation in his home district would be under way. What he did know for certain, however, was that the Selous Scouts on this operation would be from his own troop. This is because his troop, 3 Group, specialized in operations against ZIPRA. The team would all be siNdebele speakers and almost all were ex-RAR from Bulawayo.

A shiver of excitement flowed through Ngwenya. He could not help but look up into the surrounding hills where his brothers would be hiding. It was common knowledge that ZIPRA used the Nata River as a transit route from Botswana into the Tjolotjo TTL and further east towards Nkai and south to Bulawayo.

After a short negotiation, Ngwenya engaged the services of a donkey scotch-cart made from the load-box of an old 1954 Chev truck. The goods were loaded and they started on the slow 20km journey to Ngwenya's kraal (homestead). There was a 6pm to 6am curfew in all the TTLs so they stopped on the side of the road for the night.

The next day Ngwenya finally arrived home to great excitement from reference which gave permission to travel from place to place.

his wife, his aged mother and his sisters. It was always a great moment to take his son in his arms and look into his eyes. Those eyes were the same as his father's, and Cephas took great comfort in knowing that the spirit of his father was still present through his son. The arrival of extra food and presents of sewing needles, colourful material for making clothing, plus a new cooking pot, brought great pleasure.

Cephas had purchased his mother a new transistor radio with a pack of batteries. She began to cry when he gave it to her. She had never had a radio of her own. He showed her how to turn it on, and the old woman cried even more when the sound of the RBC siNdebele service came through on medium wave. A goat was slaughtered, sorghum beer was brewed, and the celebration of the return of the first-born son went well into the night. The sound of the celebration carried to the local ZIPRA Political Commissar who was visiting the neighbouring village. Sound travels so well at night.

Cephas Ngwenya slept well that night in the arms of his beloved Nomsa, listening to the gentle breathing of his son as he slept.

*

Malvernia, Mozambique

The African Spotted Hyena has a symbiotic relationship with vultures. Their feeding habits revolve predominantly around carrion and the one can lead the other to a kill. There are, however, well-documented accounts of family groups of hyenas working together to hunt prey, and they have been known to chase lion off a kill. Surprisingly, the hyena does not have a particularly acute sense of smell, relying more on eyesight for hunting. Circling vultures are enough to pique the curiosity of any hyena; particularly one that is hungry and feeding pups.

The huge area on the southern border of the Gona-re-zhou National Park in Mozambique is virtually devoid of human habitation. It is a hot, dry, forbidding land, without permanent water other than the Limpopo and Nuanetsi Rivers and their few tributaries. The wildlife lived in isolation as the war had eliminated organised poaching, now limited to the few local people hunting for the pot.

On this day, a large female hyena, the matriarch of her clan, was patrolling her territory along the border fence. She had recently given birth to a litter of pups and they were very hungry. She looked up at three Lappetfaced Vultures circling above. As she watched, Whitebacked Vultures joined them. This was a good sign. She sniffed the air, but nothing triggered in her brain. In the familiar economical gait of the hyena, she set off in the direction of the circling vultures.

It was not long before the distinctive smell of dead flesh carried to the hungry animal. She increased her pace, anxious not to miss out, there were other hyena clans that encroached on her territory. Then another familiar scent entered her nostrils, it made her hesitate. She became more cautious. While the stench of rotting flesh became overpoweringly inviting, she inched forward. Warily surveying her surroundings, she came upon the dead impala. It had been dead for at least two days; the body was swollen and distended. The gut had been sliced open attracting a swarm of flies.

The hyena looked up quizzically at the impala hanging from a tree by a rope. Beneath the tree lay a man. He sat propped up; his left trouser leg was covered in blood. She watched pensively, the distinctive scent of humans was everywhere. Every instinct in her body was telling her to flee. Carefully, one step at a time, she crept forward. The hunger in her stomach overcame her caution.

Sniffing the air, she could tell that there were other humans close by. Her ears folded against her head, mane flattened across her back, a sign of fear and uncertainty. She lifted her tail and rubbed her anus against a stunted tree, releasing a pungent soapy-white substance, 'pasting' it with her scent. At the same time, she scratched the ground with her front paws, releasing scent from glands between her claws. Taking another step forward, she sniffed the air again trying to determine how close the other humans were.

A vulture landed close to the tree, announcing its arrival by flapping its wings loudly, kicking up puffs of dust. It rushed forward with its neck outstretched, grabbing at the man's face, tearing away a chunk of his cheek. The need to protect the kill overcame her fear, she chased forward biting into the bloody leg, pulling the body after her.

The man's eyes were open and blinking. An arm moved slightly. When she sensed it move, she dropped the body in surprise. After a brief hesitation, she carefully approached the face, sniffing at the mouth. She could smell the breath coming from the man's lungs. Shaking her head to clear her senses, she looked up again, scanning her surroundings. The vulture on the ground watched her every movement. Two others flapped down to join it. They beat their wings loudly, high pitched squeaks showed their excitement and anticipation. Jumping forward, their wings outstretched, the vultures became more determined.

The hyena, anxious not to lose her kill, bit down hard on the face, a sickening crunching sound. The strongest jaws in Africa crushed the cheekbone easily. The second bite broke the jaw that tore away.

A gunshot burst over her head. The terrifying sound was enough to make her drop the body and escape into the bush. She ran for a hundred metres before stopping. Looking back, she realised that nothing was following her. The hunger in her stomach was intense.

Four men dressed in torn and battered clothing came out of the bush next to the body. One cut down the dead impala. The others picked up the mangled remains, still dressed in the uniform of a Colonel in the FPLM, his nametag still in place. They carried the body a few yards to a bush track then placed it in the road, careful to brush away any spoor. One man, wearing the same boots as the Colonel, recreated his movements by walking the path to the point of the attack, dragging his leg, as any wounded man would do. A Tokarev pistol was placed in the dead hand after two more shots were sprayed in the air. The four men then melted back into the bush to wait, taking the dead Impala with them.

The shots were heard in Malvernia less than two kilometres away. A patrol was sent out and the body of their Colonel was discovered. The four Selous Scouts watched to make sure that the patrol did not investigate any further. It was obvious that a wild animal, a hyena judging by the spoor, had attacked the man. The story was clear ... he had been wounded in the Rhodesian attack two days before, then chased by the wild animal, he tried to shoot it but he was too weak and the animal killed him.

The vultures were still circling high above. They shared the dead impala, left at the border fence, with the Hyena.

15

Audley Street, Cranborne Park, Salisbury

Lily McIntyre lived in a neat and spacious house that she and Jock had purchased together. Jock's salary from the army had not allowed for saving for a deposit so her parents had helped by lending them the money. She had worked for the Ford dealership, Dulys, before they had kids, so between the two salaries they got along fine. Since Jock died, things had tightened up enormously. The army were paying her a widow's pension but it was nowhere near enough. She had been forced to go back to work and was leaning heavily on her parents for help.

The house in Audley Street was only half a kilometre north of the RLI Depot at Cranborne Barracks; Jock had walked to work in the early days when he was in Training Troop. When the war intensified after 1972, he spent most of his time away from home. The only time they spent together was during the R&R every six to eight weeks. She had nagged Jock to take the opportunity as a National Service Officer's Course Instructor at the School of Infantry in Gwelo, but he refused point-blank. He wanted to be in the thick of things, jokingly stating often that the only way they were going to get him out of 11 Troop was in a pine box ... *and so it was.*

At only twenty-eight Lily was in her prime. She was petite, not a sexily attractive girl in the way one would describe Brit Ekland or confident and precocious like Goldie Hawn. She was homely and reserved, more like Julie Christie. She had the same straight blond hair as Julie Christie and similar blue eyes. Lily was a quiet girl; a little introverted, unlike Jock who loved a party. She was the sort of person who was reserved amongst people she didn't know. With friends, she was animated and effervescent. She loved her home and her children and was most happy working in the garden and pottering about the house.

Lily had fetched Dudley Marais when he was discharged from hospital and taken him home to recuperate. Dudley did not take long to get better. His youth and natural fitness speedily brought him back to health. Lily fed him royally, enjoying the distraction of having someone else around the house.

Dudley played endlessly with the children, he had as much energy as they did and then some. The three of them were in bed and asleep by seven every evening. She had bought a case of beers which she put in the fridge, offering Dudley one every evening. He steadfastly refused. 'I should not drink' he would say, 'it makes me crazy'. Being in Jock's house was something almost spiritual for Dudley. His respect and love for the man were such that he did not want Lily to see him drunk or badly behaved. He was just so happy sleeping in a comfortable bed, three meals a day and time to play with the kids. This was Dudley Marais' own personal heaven.

Beamish had brought Le Beau and the new man Kratzman over for a braai and the three of them polished off the beers. Jock had always invited the ex-pats home for meals during R&R. Most had no family in the country to spend time with, and R&R was way too short to fly overseas. During times when the Troop or the Commando was in barracks, there was a constant stream of soldiers through the house.

A plan for home projects was stuck on the fridge and when the Troop were home, she would enlist the help of the men to help. Jock was not hot on gardening or home projects, happy instead to sit on the veranda drinking beer, playing with the kids and issuing unsolicited advice to the 'workers'. The distraction of digging rockeries, or painting rooms or putting up fences was a sort of therapy for the men and they threw themselves into each project with great enthusiasm. Lily understood intimately the pain and suffering many of the men were going through, the mental strain and pressure, and the difficulty they had in coping with it. In her own way, Lily played her part in giving the men a taste of normality, a haven they could visit without qualification or judgment. All men were equal in Lily McIntyre's house.

There was no shortage of advice for Lily who had to stand her ground on a few things; the house could have been a bright fluorescent yellow if Le Beau had his way. Lily worked alongside the men, enjoying their company, and loved listening to their stories of home. She was kind of like a 'big sister' away from home, although many of the ex-pats like Le Beau and Kratzman were older than her. Most of them wrote letters to her, especially after Jock had died; they all wanted her to know that they were thinking of her.

Lily was not much of a drinker herself. She enjoyed a glass of wine when on holiday in South Africa but she couldn't drink the Rhodesian plonk that was hopeless, preferring gin and tonic instead. The party was great fun and the four of them got quite merry. Dudley enjoyed himself immensely but did not have anything to drink, 'I am at home!' he declared. Dudley loved Jock's record collection, and the house always had a record on the Pioneer Stereo when he was home. They played Elton John, Albert Hammond, ABBA, David Bowie, the Beatles, Manfred Mann amongst others. Jock's favourite was *Free Electric Band* by Albert Hammond, all would sing it at the top of their voices when it was played.

> *'Cos all I need is music and the Free Electric Band.*
> *Well they used to sit and speculate upon their son's career*
> *A lawyer or a doctor or a civil engineer*
> *Just give me bread and water, put a guitar in my hand*
> *All I need is music and a Free Electric band ...*

Jim Kratzman, the consummate gentleman, helped Lily wash and clean up afterwards. He seemed to be able to drink vast amounts of alcohol without any visible effect at all. Beamish and Le Beau on the other hand were legless, the two of them passed out on the veranda.

'When Dudley is well, I need you to look after him Jim,' Lily said as she put the kettle on to make coffee.

'Yes Ma'am, but Jock did a good job with him, he is a damn fine soldier,'

Kratzman replied.

'You did not know Jock, but he had to put a lot of time into keeping Dudley on the straight and narrow, he is still a young kid.' Lily had given up asking Kratzman to stop calling her 'Ma'am' she felt like a fifty-year old schoolteacher when he said it. Plus he was older than her anyway.

'They are all young. It's hard to believe that they do what they do, half of them look like they are fourteen years old,' added Kratzman as he dried the last few plates in the sink.

'Dudley has some real issues about his past, he was abandoned at birth, you know ...' Lily looked up at the giant American who seemed to fill the whole kitchen. '... It's just that he will be very vulnerable emotionally with Jock gone. He has a problem with violent behaviour as well as alcohol and he used to smoke pot. Jock managed to a put a stop to that.'

'Ma'am there's more dope being smoked in the RLI than in New Orleans. We smoked our fair share in Nam but, man, its got these youngsters beat. The problem is that the Gooks smoke it, nearly every dead Gook we find has got the stuff in his pockets.'

'Well I am asking you as a friend to please keep an eye on Dudley for me, I will speak to Arthur and Jean-Paul before you boys go back.'

'Yes Ma'am.'

*

COMOPS, Milton Buildings, Salisbury

It was early evening when Faye Chan was called in to take notes for a meeting of one of the COMOPS project teams. The operational tempo at COMOPS had increased substantially since the blowing up of the key installations and the staff were asked to put in more hours. They were reviewing aerial photographs of a number of terrorist training camps. There was a general discussion before the meeting started on the effect of the bombing on the camp called Takawira. The photographs showed that many of the buildings had been destroyed. The hope was that if the bodies of Nyandoro and Kachimanga were in the buildings, they would have been incinerated by the frantan delivered from the second wave of bombers.

Faye had not been privy to the fact that the camp was to be bombed so she could not have sent a warning. All the talk was about Operation Hippo. It was difficult to understand the gist of the conversation as code words were being used to describe the various targets. She waited patiently for the meeting to start, concentrating hard on memorising the code words people were using. It would have been highly suspicious to be seen taking notes before the meeting started.

The senior man, a Major from Military Intelligence, called the meeting to order.

'Please start taking notes Faye, and by the way, thank you for working late, I really appreciate it,' he said politely.

She nodded her understanding and began swift shorthand. The meetings generally followed a set format that covered the status of the planning of each part of the operation concerned. Each military operation followed a sequence of orders that would eventually be synthesised down to specific instructions to each unit and sub-unit on the ground and in the air. The status of each part of each operation was then recorded and circulated to the COMOPS leaders based on the distribution list. As so many operations were in different stages of development, it was a challenge to keep all the various operational leaders informed.

'Okay people, let's get an update on the situation regarding our target code name Sting.'

The representative from the CIO, George Stanbridge's 2IC, began with describing in detail the movements of target 'Sting'.

It became clear to Faye that their target was a person not a place; this was a first in her experience. She blushed slightly when the enormity of what was being discussed sank in – *this is an assassination*! Keeping her head down over her writing pad, Faye concentrated as hard as she could on the conversation. The man described towns, houses and training camps that were each given code names. Unless she had the list of codes, Faye would never be able to figure out who and where the target was. The date for the operation was referred to as Oscar Bravo (OB). Faye knew that the code for the date would likely refer to the button code numbers for the month in question. The permutations were exponential in number. What she found particularly shocking was the sources of information the man was referring to. It appeared that either the CIO or SB had an informer within the senior ranks of ZANLA, who was feeding information to the Rhodesians. Once again, no names were mentioned, the information was so secret that codes for the names of the informants were withheld. This fact alone was of major importance to the ZANLA leadership.

The Major then listed the units that had been allocated to Operation Swallow. They included the Selous Scouts and 3Cdo 1RLI. The air force included 7 Sqn (Alouette) 3 Sqn (Dakotas) 4 Sqn (Lynx) and 1 Sqn (Hunters). From all accounts, the target was very deep inside Mozambique as the plan included an Admin Area. This meant that the helicopters would be refuelled 'in-country' at a temporary base. The mission was complex because the target could be on the move, requiring great flexibility in the planning.

From what Faye could gather, the plan was for the Rhodesians to cover two places at the same time. There was also to be a mobile unit to cover a third area with some sort of ambush. The intelligence pointed, with a high degree of certainty, to the target being in one of the three places.

The Major concluded the meeting at 8pm. He thanked Faye for her help, directing her to type up the notes the next morning and to let him review them before they were distributed. He offered her a staff car to take her home that she gratefully accepted. As she was leaving the room, one of the officers commented on the good news that SB and PATU had tracked down and killed the CTs that blew up the oil storage tanks in Mtoko TTL. The sole survivor had squealed on his comrades and had confirmed his training by the Chinese at Camp Takawira.

This news shocked Faye as she thought of the brave young men who she had transported on that mission. *Thank God Rugare was not on that mission ... it was too terrible to contemplate!*

Upon arriving home, Faye went straight to her room to type up the notes she had memorised. The ZANLA leadership needed this information urgently.

*

Tjolotjo District, central Matabeleland

Julius Moyo, the Political Commissar for sub-sector Nata in the ZIPRA Southern Front Area 3, decided to pay a visit to the Ngwenya kraal to find out what the festivities were about. He had a section of eight men with him who acted as his bodyguards and liaised with his network of informers and *mujibas*. He ran a tight ship in his operational area and was confident that the people overwhelmingly supported the struggle against the white colonists. Julius, in some cases, had to break a few heads to reinforce support for the struggle.

Moyo had been born and raised near Nyamandhlovu, attending Catholic mission school before deciding to leave the country for military training. He had shown much promise during his training and was therefore selected for political training at the Higher Komsomol[111] School in Moscow. This was an institution of higher education attached to the Central Committee of the All-Union Lenin Communist Youth League (VLKSM); the school trained cadres for work in youth organisations, for editorial work in youth newspapers, radio, and television, and for other political occupations. Moyo had the great privilege of being educated in communism by the Honoured Test Pilot of the USSR, G. K. Mosolov, a Hero of the Soviet Union, who headed the sub-department of military and patriotic education. Moyo had great hopes for high political office once the war was won and his leader Joshua Nkomo was installed as President.

The Moyo band entered the Ngwenya kraal in the early afternoon. They were not concerned at concealing their movement; no SF had been reported in the area for many weeks. Not even the police had been seen. This, in itself, did not concern Moyo because his policy was one of consolidation. He did not wish to provoke the SF by attacking farms and other soft targets, preferring instead, to build up arms caches and train new cadres for the great conventional war that would be launched across the Zambezi once the necessary forces were built up in Zambia. His men would then rise up and crush the enemy in one fell swoop.

Cephas Ngwenya was not in the kraal at the time of the arrival of Comrade Moyo. He was with the women in the fields, preparing the ground for the first rain. Only his aged mother and the small children were present. The

---

111 The Communist Union of Youth usually known as Komsomol was the youth division of the Communist Party of the Soviet Union.

children had seen the soldiers before and crowded around them, fascinated by these great men with guns. They stood staring at the men, their bright shining faces looking up expectantly. The men spoke to the children in gentle voices, joking with them, showing them their guns and weapons. These were truly great men.

Moyo signalled his cadres to spread out through the village, then he walked up to the old woman who was listening to her new transistor radio. She did not get up, she knew who he was.

'*Litshone njani Ugogo,*' Moyo greeted the old women in siNdebele.

As is the way with very old people who have no interest in being disturbed, she completely ignored him

'You have a nice new radio, where did you get it?' asked Moyo politely, he was a powerful man but he felt respect for the old people was still important.

'My son,' she spat at him defiantly. She was not impressed with this freedom fighter with his uniform and guns.

'Ah, so Cephas is back on leave!' commented Moyo, bending down to pick up the radio.

'Leave it,' she croaked pointing a finger at Moyo accusingly. These freedom fighters stole everything from the people.

He ignored her, turning it over in his hands. It was playing music from a station in Botswana.

'Very nice Ma ... I think I will keep it. Please thank Cephas when he returns ... it is a great gift for the struggle,' said Moyo sarcastically.

Moyo knew perfectly well that Cephas was in the police force. His cadres were from this area, they knew Cephas from school and all had known Joseph Ngwenya, his father killed by the landmine.

The old woman started to cry, this in turn upset the young children who crowded around her, suddenly frightened of the men with guns. The wailing cry aroused Cephas' brother-in-law, Gibson Sibanda, who was working in his woodworking shop behind the village. The sound of the crying was disturbing, so he went into the village to investigate. He saw the ZIPRA men standing around the old woman and shouted to them.

'Leave the woman alone!' he demanded.

'Who are you to give orders? You are a coward. You should be fighting with us in the struggle for freedom!' replied Moyo with disgust in his voice.

Sibanda was not afraid of these men, he knew them all, he knew their families and their villages. 'You call me a coward, but here you are robbing on old woman of her radio ... it is the first radio she has had in her life,' shouted Sibanda, pointing at Moyo accusingly.

Comrade Julius Moyo was not accustomed to uneducated peasants questioning his authority. The attitude of this man annoyed him. His hand stirred towards the Tokarev pistol in the holster at his waist.

One of his cadres saw the movement and jumped between Sibanda and his leader.

'No Comrade, ignore this man, he is just a useless peasant. Who cares what he thinks?' the man said, trying to distract Moyo.

Now Moyo's notoriously short temper was aroused. He rounded on his man, swinging his arm violently, back-handing him across the face. The metal bracelet on his right wrist caught the man's lip, ripping it open. The man staggered back holding his bloody mouth, shocked at the sudden and vicious outburst.

Snatching at the pistol in his holster, Moyo cocked the weapon loudly and held it up against Sibanda's forehead.

'You can die now or you can run with your tail between your legs!' demanded Moyo, his eyes wild, spittle flying from his mouth.

The old woman seeing the danger, tried to get to her feet, 'Take the radio, take it ... leave us alone,' she cried.

Gibson Sibanda was a proud man, his dark brown eyes showed no fear, he stood resolutely in front of the freedom fighter, refusing to move. The children were now all crying in fear, not understanding what was going on. Gibson's tiny son, only two years old, ran to his father, clinging to his leg.

Moyo pulled the trigger, the bullet exploded out the back of Sibanda's skull. For a split second, he remained standing, before toppling over into the dust, his son trapped beneath him, the boy screaming in terror.

The gunshot carried to Cephas Ngwenya working with Nomsa in the fields. He knew instantly that this was trouble; he dropped his badza and ran towards the village.

Moyo ignored the crying woman and ordered the men to look for food. The two unopened bags of mielie meal brought by Cephas were found and the band left the kraal very satisfied with their afternoon's work.

Cephas Ngwenya found his mother lying across the body of his brother-in-law. The children were wailing in fright, tears running in streaks through the dust on their cheeks. When they saw Cephas approaching, they ran to him, clinging to his arms and legs. Gibson's son was hugging his grandmother in shocked, uncomprehending silence. The old woman was inconsolable. The tears would not stop flowing; she rocked back and forward, her cries increasing in intensity. The other women arrived back at the village, running forward, sprawling in the dirt next to Gibson's body. They too began to cry; they called out and ululated, almost at a scream. Cephas' sister held her hands to the sky, God, *Nkosi* had taken her husband.

Eventually, through the sobs, the old woman managed to get out what had happened. Ngwenya felt a deep rage build in his gut. Seeing his brother in law so brutally murdered and his mother so distressed was too much for him. He went to his bag that he had buried in a hole behind his hut, took out his hunting knife and his Tokarev pistol with spare clips and set off for the surrounding hills. His wife Nomsa chased after him, pleading for him not to go, hanging onto his arm trying to pull him back. Cephas stopped and turned to her.

'We cannot allow these animals to kill us. They will come for me one day,' said Cephas, fierce determination on his face.

Nomsa stood in front of him, tears running down her face, knowing that what he said was true ... they would come for Cephas one day ... he was their enemy. She stood back from him and bowed her head.

'I shall pray for you Cephas,' she said softly, then turned and walked slowly back to the kraal.

Cephas Ngwenya knew Julius Moyo by reputation; the police and Selous Scouts had been looking for him for years. He was known as a ruthless bully that had killed a great many tribal leaders in his quest to subdue the local population. He now had a much more personal enemy added to the, already very long, list.

It was obvious to Ngwenya that if the Selous Scouts had set up observation posts (OPs) in his area, there were only three likely places. Ngwenya set off for the first of these. To the casual observer he would have looked like any local tribesman traveling from one place to another. The fact that he was alone would not attract any interest or attention. To the trained observer his normal fast confident stride would have attracted some attention so instead he shuffled along with hunched shoulders. He wore an old threadbare jacket, once his father's, to conceal the pistol in his belt and the knife strapped to the small of his back.

The challenge was to make contact with his colleagues in the hills without being killed in the process. The risk of compromise was so great that the Selous Scouts made great efforts to conceal their presence; anyone getting too close would be killed silently and brutally. Ngwenya approached the first of the hills, a high granite koppie that sat two or three hundred feet above the surrounding countryside. He made no attempt to hide his approach, confident that if his people were in the hills they would already have him under observation. Even with powerful binoculars, they would likely not recognize his face under the wide straw hat he was wearing.

The evening was fast approaching so Ngwenya decided to lie up at the base of the hill. It was too dangerous wondering around at night with Selous Scouts in the area.

After an uncomfortable shivering night, where the temperature dropped close to freezing, Ngwenya began the slow and careful climb up the hill. It was thickly wooded with trees growing between the huge granite boulders. He took great care with every movement, knowing that if his men were present they would be alert and vigilant. It would have been much faster climbing over the top of the rocks, instead he crept through the dense undergrowth around the sides. This was full of nettles and thorn scrub that was difficult to avoid. It took at least two hours before Ngwenya reached halfway. The fact that the koppie was a bald granite dome meant that the OP would not be near the top. The sun was now beating down strongly and the day got progressively hotter and hotter. Ngwenya started to rue the fact that he had not brought water with him; his anger had got the better of him.

The Selous Scouts had turned observation into an art form. One person manned the OP at a time, hiding in a heavily camouflaged lookout. Each man kept a careful log of all that he saw, noting vehicles arriving and leaving, people living in the villages, each got a descriptive name based on their clothing and routine. At times, depending on the wind, it was possible to hear the villagers talking to each other, as they called across fields or roads. To the trained eye, village life had a very defined routine, early rise in the morning, cooking of food, working in the fields, fetching water, herding cattle, visiting neighbours, cleaning and preparing for the evening meal. They particularly noted the movement of young kids, especially boys in the age group seven to sixteen, as they were the eyes and ears of the CTs, the *mujibas*. It was common for the CTs to insist that the *mujibas* herd cattle, or if that was not possible, climb over the surrounding hills to look for SF OPs. This was most often the way OPs became 'compromised'.

Each OP had a 'base' where the off-duty team members could sleep or eat. This was where they kept their radios and other equipment. There was no cooking of meals or boiling of water for tea, as cooking and gas can be smelt a long way off. All possible sources of sound were carefully considered, opening food cans, scraping of spoons, checking of weapons, cleaning weapons and the like. Talking was in hushed tones and only when absolutely necessary. Most communication was done with hand signals.

Ngwenya was looking for the OP admin base that would likely be in the deepest undergrowth.

'*Igama lakho ngubani?*'

The question was asked in a soft but unmistakable voice. A gun barrel was pushed into Ngwenya's back.

'*Ngiyajabula ukukubona Umnewethu*, I am very pleased to meet you brother, I am Sergeant Cephas Ngwenya, 3 Group, Selous Scouts,' replied Cephas in a soft whisper.

'Cephas what the fuck are you doing here?' the voice hissed. It was Corporal Stu McCloud, a territorial member of the Scouts on one of his 'six-weeks-in' call-ups.

'I am on leave but I thought I would pay you a visit,' replied Ngwenya. 'Can I have a drink of water please?'

The four men on the hill were flabbergasted. Shaking their heads in total amazement, they fired a frenzy of questions, all in the softest of whispers. He told them of the deaths of Nyandoro and Kachimanga. The horrible scar on his forehead also caused some comment.

'Comrade Julius Moyo is in the valley,' said Ngwenya matter-of-factly, pointing out into the distance.

'How do you know Cephas?' whispered McCloud, his blackened face showing streaks of sweat.

'He has killed my brother-in-law for a transistor radio and two sacks of mielie meal,' replied Ngwenya, his eyes suddenly hard.

The four men did not comment, their silence was enough ... words were meaningless.

'Moyo has killed a District Commissioner and three policemen in the past month,' said McCloud. 'We also found the bodies of two Headmen near Sikende to the west.'

'I am here to help you find this man, but it must be left to me to kill him,' hissed Ngwenya, the unmistakeable, steely determination in his voice.

'I don't care Cephas, as long as we get the bastard, and soon,' replied McCloud.

'I have some better news, the radio the *makandanga* stole from my mother has a tracking device in it. I got it from the CQMS to save myself some money,' added Ngwenya, his face softening slightly into a grim smile.

The Selous Scouts and SB often left doctored transistor radios code-named 'road-runners' in places that CTs were likely to find them. Often they were left in trading stores likely to be robbed by CTs looking for food and provisions. The radios were normally overpriced to prevent one of the locals actually buying one. The radio emitted a VHF signal on one of the least used air channels. The low-powered signal could be detected from some distance using Becker homing equipment that brought an aircraft virtually straight to the target. The radio was designed to continue to transmit the VHF signal for at least ten minutes after it was switched off, as, in most cases, the CTs would turn off the radio when they heard an aircraft approaching.

A signal was sent by the Selous Scout call-sign to JOC Tangent in Bulawayo announcing the arrival of Sergeant Ngwenya and the news of Julius Moyo and his new transistor radio.

Comrade Julius Moyo was pushed to the top of the 'Hit Parade'.

*

ZANLA HQ Chimoio, Mozambique

Comrade Josiah Tongogara returned to his operational HQ at his house in Chimoio. His arm was in a sling from the shrapnel wound he sustained at Camp Takawira. Godfrey Nyathi, code name *Zizi*, could see that his General's mood was sour; he was angry and frustrated, complaining that his arm was throbbing with pain.

On the drive back to Chimoio, the General had spoken bitterly about how the work they had undertaken in training up saboteurs had been undone. Dipuka Muponde, the Camp Takawira commander, had been killed with many others. It was a miracle that anyone had survived. All the Chinese advisors led by Captain Youxia had escaped injury because they had not attended the funeral, choosing instead to help patrol the hills above the camp.

The camp itself had been all but destroyed by the Colonists with bouncing bombs, but worse, they had sprayed the area with delayed-fuse bombs which made it too dangerous to stay. The camp had to be abandoned completely; explosions were still going off two days later. Tongogara had survived by diving into one of the newly dug graves. The spirit medium Mutumwa had also survived completely unscathed, adding to the power of her already formidable reputation. The same could not be said for the forty odd cadres and support personnel who were killed. Many more were injured.

As soon as the vehicles stopped outside the house, the General got out and went straight to his room, ignoring all those waiting to see him. Nyathi placed the guard at the door of the bedroom with strict orders that the General was not to be disturbed.

Nyathi felt an inexplicable sense of relief that Tongogara had survived the Rhodesian attack. Spying and leaking information had always seemed removed, now the reality of being instrumental in the death of Tongogara was unsettling. Yet, he knew in his heart that one day the instruction may come that he, Godfrey Nyathi was to kill the General. It was a thought he pushed to the back of his mind.

A junior Political Commissar, who manned the radios in the house, came to Nyathi with a decoded message.

'Comrade, the General must see this message urgently,' said the young man respectfully, clearly frightened to death of Nyathi.

'Give to me, I will see that the General gets it. He has been wounded and he is in much pain,' demanded Nyathi brusquely, putting out his hand to take the message.

'The message is from our agents inside Zimbabwe Comrade, I have orders to give these messages to *Nyenganyenga* personally,' replied the Commissar, his voice starting to waver.

'Who are you to refer to the General as *Nyenganyenga?* Who do you think you are? Where is your respect?' Nyathi took a menacing step towards the man, who was now visibly shaking.

'I am sorry Comrade, I mean no disrespect, please give Comrade General the message,' replied the man, thrusting the piece of folded paper into Nyathi's hand and fled back to his post in the radio room.

Nyathi unfolded the paper and glanced down at the message. It was written in English, in long hand, in neat capital letters. He felt a sudden tightening in his stomach.

Definite spy in ZANLA leadership ... stop. New plan to assassinate senior members of ZANLA leadership ... stop. Operation Hippo stop. Operation Swallow ... stop. Multiple strikes ... stop. Dates to be confirmed ... stop.

There followed a half-page of other information, including the fact that the oil storage tanks in Salisbury were still burning.

The news was appalling, somehow he had been compromised, or maybe there were other Rhodesian spies at work in the ZANLA leadership? The shock of reading the message made Nyathi's heart race. He was overcome by a sudden feeling of panic ... he took a few deep breaths and a long drink of water from a water bottle in a pouch on his webbing belt.

Composing himself, he walked to the door of the General's bedroom and gently knocked.

'Urgent message *Nyenganyenga.*'

'Come in,' came the instant reply.

Nyathi handed over the message and immediately left the room, closing the door softly behind him. There was silence from inside the room, Comrade Tongogara was not a man to rant and rave.

What Nyathi did not know was that the information concerning the presence of an informer was not new. On all the previous occasions, Tongogara had been able to trap the spies and kill them. Tongogara knew that the spy had to be in the senior ranks of ZANLA as the Rhodesian attacks were normally well timed and lethal. The deaths of thousands of his comrades in the attacks on Nyadzonya, Chimoio, Madulo Pan and Mapai by the Selous Scouts, SAS and RLI, still haunted him. The day would come when he could round up the members of the hated *Skuz'apo* and execute them in the same way that he had executed Thomas Nhari and his rebels. The General knew that the spy had to be one of his 'loyal' veterans. He had to set a trap … but how?

As Nyathi waited patiently for instructions from his General, the Political Commissar returned with another message. This time the report was of the death of Tongogara's FRELIMO friend and ally, Colonel António Borges Santos.

After reading the message, Nyathi delivered it, but this time, waited in the room while the General read it. The report read that the Rhodesians had attempted to kidnap the Colonel. He had escaped but wounded in the process. After being overcome from loss of blood, he had been killed by wild animals. Santos had been a great support to ZANLA, providing equipment and logistics to help successful infiltration into Rhodesia. He had also been a great personal friend. Comrade Tongogara shook his head; this had truly been a very bad week indeed.

'Get me something to eat Nyathi, we have work to do,' said General Tongogara quietly, clearly deep in thought.

As he walked through to the kitchen to give instructions to the cook, Nyathi reflected again on his mission. He had not lost faith, his father's death still haunted him, but the fact was, if the freedom struggle was to be won, then, maybe … just maybe, Tongogara was the right man to lead the new country?

Being in such close contact with the man for so long, Nyathi felt a begrudging respect in his heart. *This man is a giant compared with the other snivelling leaders I have met!*

*

Audley Street, Cranborne Park, Salisbury

Dudley 'Penga' Marais had walked the kids to the nearby café to buy ice cream and then took them for a swim in the neighbour's pool across the road. The neighbours, the Baxter's, were also an RLI family, they had no problem with the McIntyre children swimming in their pool. Dudley noticed a car pull up outside the McIntyre house but did not give it any thought. The kids were playing underwater games, fetching stones from the bottom of the pool.

The three finished their swim and walked back across the road. The kids ran ahead to tell their mother what they had been doing. Dudley opened the front door and entered the lounge. He was shocked to find Colour Doug Barker sitting in Jock's chair holding a beer.

'What are you doing here?' he demanded indignantly.

'What do you mean, what am I doing here? I am visiting Lily,' replied Barker, upset at being asked such a question by the young trooper. Barker was aware of Dudley's relationship with Jock and Lily.

'You can't sit in that chair. That's Jocks chair!' Dudley pointed accusingly.

'Fuck off Penga. I don't care that you caught a bullet, piss off.'

Lily heard the loud voices from the kitchen and rushed through. Barker had stood up out of the chair and was advancing toward Dudley who was standing his ground.

'What are you two doing?' she cried.

'He's sitting in Jock's chair. Why is he here?' asked Dudley who was clearly very upset.

'Who the hell do you think you are you little prick?' shouted Barker, equally upset.

'Both of you calm down! Dudley, Doug Barker was a friend of Jock's and he is a friend of mine. He can sit where he likes.' Turning to Barker she said, 'Doug, Dudley is a member of this household, he is family, and you will treat him with respect ... I don't need any RLI bullying in my house!'

Barker blushed brightly at the admonishment so swiftly issued.

Dudley was visibly upset, totally unhappy with seeing another man alone in Jock's house.

'Dudley, you will call Doug 'Colour' or 'Sarge' when he visits here. I know you can't be on first name terms ... Doug I don't care what you call each other in the bush but you will call Dudley, Dudley, when you visit here ... Is that clear to both of you?' demanded Lily, her faced flushed.

The concern in her voice was unmistakable for both men. They nodded their acceptance, Barker sat down again and Dudley went to his room. Lily went back to the kitchen where she was making sandwiches, then, after quick reflection, went through to Dudley's room. He was sitting on the bed looking visibly distressed. She went in and closed the door behind her.

'Now Dudley you must understand that Jock is gone. I have cried now for weeks and weeks ... I can't cry any more. We have to think about the kids. They are struggling to understand all of this,' she said gently.

'But he was sitting in Jock's chair,' pleaded Dudley, still refusing to accept that there was another man in the house visiting Lily. His emotions were all over the place; he couldn't hope to explain his feelings.

'Its not Jock's chair anymore Dudley, its just a chair.'

'Why is Barker visiting you?' asked Dudley, trying to understand.

Suddenly the real impact of Lily being visited by other single men dawned on Dudley. *She was still young – she could find a boyfriend – she could even marry again, where would that leave me!*

'Do you, do you ... like ... him?' asked Dudley almost inaudibly, pointing in the direction of the lounge, the intonation in his voice showing that he dreaded the answer.

'No ... No, of course not!' cried Lily. 'Doug is just a friend, I promise you.'

The look of relief on Dudley's face was profound.

'I have to get on with my life Dudley. I have the kids to think about. You have to get on with your life. You are still so young; your whole life is ahead of you. Jock is a happy memory for both of us. We can both cry from time to time, we both miss him, but we have to move on.'

The discussion was upsetting Lily; tears welled up in her eyes.

Dudley looked up at her, even more upset at seeing her tears.

'Please don't cry Lily. I am sorry if I have made you cry.'

She sat down on the bed next to him and put her arm around his shoulders hugging him tightly.

'We just have to get through this together. I know you miss him and its worse when you are out in the bush. You relied on him so much ... Doug Barker was a friend of Jock's and he is just coming to say hello ... Now come on, don't be silly, come through and have some tea, I've made scones,' she said, brushing the tears away from her eyes.

'Please don't cry Lily. I'll behave,' whispered Dudley, his eyes also filled with tears.

Lily understood exactly what it was that had upset Dudley so much. He felt threatened and the fear of being rejected or worse, abandoned, was overwhelming him. His lack of maturity and the deep emotional scars he carried, meant that he was not coping. Lily knew she had to tread carefully with him, to get him through this.

After a shower, Dudley did come through for tea but he just sat at the table and listened to Lily chatting comfortably with Barker. She avoided any discussion on 11 Troop or the RLI or anything to do with the army.

Dudley made an excuse to get up to read the kids a story. He could read the most basic of children's stories, many of them as new to him as they were to the children.

Lily watched him as he got up from the table. A profound sadness washed over her. This tormented young man was completely emotionally reliant on her. As he stood up, he nodded at Barker, still quite obviously very upset at the man's presence. Barker nodded back without making any comment.

As he walked down the passage to the kid's room, tears filled his eyes, running down his cheeks.

'Right, let's read *Noddy and Big Ears!*' he called out, wiping his face with his sleeve.

After Doug Barker had left and Dudley and the kids had gone to bed, Lily made herself some tea and walked through to the lounge. She looked at Jock's chair and her eyes filled with tears. Flicking through the rack of LPs in the hi-fi cabinet, she lifted out Diana Ross & the Supremes, *Reflections*[112] and placed it on the turntable. The title track on side one began with its distinctive tambourine beat.

> *Through the mirror of my mind,*
> *Time after time,*
> *I see reflections of you and me.*
>
> *Reflections of ...*
> *The way life used to be*

---

112 *Reflections*, written by Holland- Dozier-Holland, Motown 1967.

Reflections of ...
The love you took from me.

Lily turned the sound down so as not to disturb the children ...

Oh, I'm all alone now
No love to shield me
Trapped in a world
That's a distorted reality

She walked across the room and stood in front of Jock's chair, tears running down her cheeks.

Happiness you took from me
And left me alone
With only memories ...

... Reflections of ...
The love you took from me.

Lily McIntyre cried for Jock ...

... Everywhere I turn
Seems like everything I see
Reflects the love that used to be ...

She cried for her children ... she cried for Dudley ...

In you I put
All my faith and trust
Right before my eyes
My world has turned to dust...

... she cried for herself ...

Reflections of ...
The way life used to be ...

16

Tjolotjo District Central Matabeleland

The windfall of having a traceable transistor radio in the hands of one of the most important ZIPRA leaders in Matabeleland was not lost on the powers-that-be. The Selous Scout support team, positioned at 1 Brigade HQ at Brady Barracks in Bulawayo, arranged for a Lynx to fly over Tjolotjo to see if Comrade Julius Moyo was listening to the radio. As the battery-life was limited, and procuring replacement batteries difficult, the CTs would only listen to the radio in the early morning and in the evening.

The Lynx flew over at 15,000 feet so as not to alert anyone on the ground, sure enough, the Becker homing device picked up the radio signal. The pilot was careful not to look like he was flying a search pattern so he flew straight on an east-west heading, marking the position of the signal on the map strapped to his knee. The tracker was only accurate to within a kilometre or so but that was enough to give the Selous Scouts an approximate location. They could complete the search on foot. The plot was radioed through to the two Selous Scouts call-signs on the ground and they set off in search of Comrade Moyo and his band.

As the area was 'frozen', there was no risk of running into any other SF. The two Selous Scout call-signs approached the general area identified by the air force in broad daylight. They were all dressed as ZIPRA cadres except for Ngwenya who played himself, a local tribesman. The Nata River drains from the east to the west, providing a major transit route in and out of Botswana. The local people were used to the coming and goings of ZIPRA freedom fighters.

The pseudo team made a special effort to be friendly and they stopped and spoke to local people they came across on the way. Ngwenya slotted into his role as an informer with ease. He gently questioned the people about other ZIPRA bands that they had seen in the area. Most of the people were delighted to meet the pseudo team; enthusiastically pointing out areas that other ZIPRA bands had been seen. Ngwenya asked about Comrade Moyo but only one person knew who he was by name and he pointed to an area further to the west. This confirmed the radio tracker information.

It was always confronting for the Selous Scouts, especially the white members, to see the level of support within the rural population for the freedom fighters. They were, in many ways, the only unit in the army that saw this grass-roots support first hand.

Pseudo operations in ZIPRA-held areas were much more difficult and dangerous than in other parts of the country. The primary reason was the superior training given by the Soviet and Cuban advisors and the tighter command and control of the ZIPRA leadership. They were also intimately aware of the Selous Scout pseudo operations and had developed a complex set of countermeasures. These entailed verbal codes, hand signals, clothing and other subtle nuances that even the most accurate intelligence gathering would miss. This made infiltration into the ZIPRA gangs a very high-risk business, unless it was done with a recently 'turned' ZIPRA cadre who knew all the coded messages.

The importance of capturing or, alternatively killing, Comrade Moyo meant that it was too risky to try and infiltrate his tight-knit band. He was way too intelligent and in touch with his region, to accept a new group of ZIPRA cadres that he knew nothing about. The plan, therefore, was to identify his location and set up a snatch or, if that failed, to call in a Fireforce strike.

Possible OP sites were non-existent. The landscape was flat, criss-crossed by sandy river lines. The area was densely populated with large tracks of land cleared for subsistence agriculture. As the rains had not yet started, the land was parched and cracked, almost completely devoid of grass cover. A few scanty clumps of acacia trees had survived the woodcutter's axe. Away from the dry streambeds, where the land was more broken and rocky, the bush was thicker, but still very open and easy to walk through. Cattle had grazed the land for a hundred years and their trails were everywhere. A few isolated boreholes with slowly turning wind-pumps provided the only permanent water for miles in any direction. Cattle and goats shared the shade under the few larger trees, otherwise nothing moved. It was hot, well over 38°C.

The Selous Scouts entered the dry bed of the Nata River, settling under an overhanging tree to rest until darkness fell. Ngwenya and the stick commanders checked their maps estimating that Moyo was about 15km further to the west, probably also hiding in the riverbed. The TTL bordered a hunting reserve and Wankie National Park to the north. Game migrated through the area between Wankie and the Tuli Block wildlife area, bordering Botswana, in the south. Elephants would enter the dry riverbeds and with their keen sense of smell, identify water beneath the sand. They dug, sometimes very deep holes into the sand to find water. This not only sustained themselves but also the other wildlife on the migration. These waterholes in the riverbeds also sustained ZIPRA CTs, so it was common to find base camps in the thick undergrowth bordering streambeds.

The plan was that Ngwenya and one other man would walk in the direction given by the tracking device to try to identify Moyo's hideout. Once that was done, the others would join them and they would then plan their attack in more detail. To save time, they called the JOC in Bulawayo to do another over-flight that evening to make sure Moyo was still in the area. The eight Selous Scout men and their 'informer' slept soundly in the soft sand beneath the shade of the tree.

As late afternoon approached, Ngwenya and Corporal Nechena had a final briefing with the other men in the riverbed. Once all was agreed, they set off. Ngwenya was still only armed with his knife and Tokarev pistol. As the river was such an important source of water, game and cattle trails followed its course on both banks. Deciding that creeping about would only arouse suspicion, they walked along a path next to the river. Ngwenya had borrowed a map and a compass and he navigated his way towards the point where they expected Moyo to be based. The moon, still in its first phase, rose, bathing the bush in a pale light. The white sand of the path reflected the light like a ribbon through the undergrowth.

The faint sound of an aircraft flying very high could be heard approaching from the east. It remained on a steady course, its engine getting louder as it approached. An aircraft flying at high altitude at night was not something that would alarm a band of CTs. The aircraft passed overhead.

Almost immediately, Ngwenya heard the message from the pilot that the radio was in the same position as it had been the previous day. Ngwenya and Nechena pressed on.

The sound of singing was the first indication that the two Selous Scouts had of the presence of a ZIPRA camp. The river ran a predominantly east-west course with a few broad meanders. In places, the river had created sand islands from flooding in the distant past. These islands were thickly wooded, throwing an impenetrable canopy over the top. Anything moving on the island would be invisible from the air.

It seemed to Ngwenya that it was most likely that the CTs were on an island in the riverbed. The two men followed the path along the river to establish just how large the island was. It was marked on the 1:50,000 map, as about 1km long and about 200m at it's widest. It tapered to a point at each end.

As they got closer, it was clear that the crowd were singing revolutionary songs. The sound of women's voices meant that this was likely a meeting arranged between ZIPRA and the surrounding villagers. The ZIPRA leaders called these meetings to discuss the progress of the war, but also for political education and matters of logistics, including the supply of food and shelter for the freedom fighters. There would be no doubt that the CTs would have struck up romantic relationships with the local womenfolk. The nearest village was a kilometre to the south, so Ngwenya and Nechena moved around to the south of the island looking for the path to the camp.

Just as expected, the well-worn path wound its way from the village into the riverbed and then across to the island.

The two men lay down to wait.

Within a short space of time, a group of villagers could be heard approaching. They were chatting away loudly and seemed in a jubilant mood. As they passed, the two Selous Scouts slipped in behind them and followed the path down into the riverbed through the thick sand and up the steep bank onto the island on the other side.

There seemed to be hundreds of people gathered in the darkness. The ZIPRA cadres could be distinguished by the AKs strapped to their shoulders, the metal barrels reflecting in the moonlight. A large clearing had been cut out of the thick undergrowth with a fire blazing in the middle. The people sat next to the fire in a semi-circle. A man with an AK strapped across his back was leading the singing. Ngwenya counted twenty ZIPRA men reflected in the light of the fire but there could have been many more mingled with the crowd.

The man in the middle held up his arms and the singing slowly subsided. He called for silence and then loudly introduced Comrade Julius Moyo to the crowd.

Ngwenya looked at the man, his feelings of hate and the need for revenge overcame him as he felt for his pistol. Nechena, grabbed at his arm, squeezing it tightly ... *be patient, take your time* ... the message was clear.

A hush spread amongst the people as Comrade Julius Moyo stepped forward. He was not a very tall man maybe 5ft 9, slightly built, dressed in a new East German *reis-fleck* uniform[113]. He wore a *reis-fleck* combat cap with the insignia of a Regional Command Commissar on his shoulders.

Moyo held up his arms and bowed his head as if in prayer. The people sat watching him in perfect silence. After a long pause he began to speak.

For a slightly built man he had a deep penetrating voice. He began with great praise for the surrounding villagers for their support in the struggle, for the food and blankets. The people clapped their hands. The speech then continued, explaining the fruits the people could expect from a ZIPRA victory, education, healthcare, land taken from the white farmers, but most importantly 'Freedom': freedom to say and do as they wished, freedom to create political parties, freedom to vote for their representatives. The power of the State would be harnessed for the good of the People; everyone would have food and housing. The people were ecstatic; they called out and sang their praises to the ZIPRA leader. Moyo was clearly delighted at the response to his speech. It was a speech he had given many times. He had learned what it was the People wanted to hear. This was great preparation for the day when he would take his place in the Revolutionary Government of the People.

Moyo held up his hands, calling for the people to be quiet.

'Comrades, we must still be very vigilant. There are still traitors in our midst.' He quoted his great leader Comrade General Lookout Masuku, 'An informer is more dangerous than someone who is carrying a gun.'

The People shouted their agreement.

Then Moyo called again for silence, 'Comrades, victory is now within our grasp; it will take one last effort from all of us. Send your sons and daughters across the border for training. We need them now ... the time for going to school will come, we need our freedom first, then our youth can go back to school.'

The crowd clapped again, but slightly less enthusiastically. Sending the children to school was seen as vitally important for the villagers. They worked hard in their fields to make sure that their children could be educated. To take them out of school was not something the people were willing to do. The older people in the crowd were clearly not happy at the request that had been made. The teenagers in the crowd, on the other hand, were delighted. They clapped and sang out their willingness to fight for freedom.

'We will be taking volunteers across the border to Botswana tomorrow,'

---

113 ZIPRA used a variety of uniforms. As many had been trained in East Germany they wore the East German, 'Rain' or 'Strichtarn' camouflage pattern, referred to by the Rhodesians as 'Reis-fleck'.

Moyo called out. 'Send your children to us' he urged. Children spontaneously ran forward to volunteer. The ZIPRA cadres efficiently placed them in lines according to their ages. Those below the age of fourteen were rejected.

The meeting broke up and the people started the walk back to their villages. Ngwenya could hear the unhappiness in the voices around him. The older people were not happy with their youth being taken away, but they were careful not to make their objections too loudly or run the risk of being accused as traitors.

The two Scouts mingled with the crowd as they left the meeting, returning to the place where they had hidden their radio. Time was of the essence; an early morning strike on the camp was vital if this large ZIPRA group were to be caught.

Ngwenya called up the other Selous Scout call-signs on the A63 radio and told them what he had seen. They in turn called JOC Tangent in Bulawayo to call in a Fireforce strike in the morning.

After he had made all the calls on the radio and he was satisfied with the preparations, Ngwenya spoke to Nechena.

'Nechena I must avenge the killing of my brother,' he whispered. 'I must go back into the base camp to kill Moyo myself.'

'Cephas, it is madness, there are too many, you will be killed yourself,' replied Nechena.

'I am dead anyway if this man should survive, he knows my family, he knows my village, he will eventually come for me. I cannot run the risk of him killing my wife and son. We have to make sure he is killed. If the attack on the camp fails it will result in reprisals amongst the local people, these pigs could kill hundreds.'

'I will come with you, you cannot go in alone, I can help,' said Nechena earnestly.

It was no point arguing with Nechena, his mind was made up; he was a brave man who had survived many dangerous missions.

'Alright, we go together,' replied Ngwenya and the two men melted back into the bush following the same route back to the base camp.

From the airfield in Bulawayo to Moyo's base camp was approximately 168km as the crow flies. From Bulawayo to the airfield in Tjolotjo was approximately 100km. This meant that the Fireforce helicopters would need to be refuelled at Tjolotjo before flying on to the target. The Paradak could loiter for an hour or so before going in, as could the Lynx. The Selous Scout Fort at Brady Barracks alerted the local Fireforce, that was manned by the men of D Company, 1RAR.

Before first light, the K-car and two G-cars plus their respective sticks lifted off for the airstrip at Tjolotjo. The police at Tjolotjo were asked to drive their trailer carrying drums of Avtur to the airstrip to help with the refuelling. An hour later the Paradak and Lynx took off to wait overhead Tjolotjo until the strike was called by the K-car commander. Unfortunately, no Hunters were available at that time as they were already tasked for an early morning strike into Zambia. The Fireforce strike was in the hands of the sixteen men in the Paradak plus the eight men in the G-cars together with the Selous Scouts already on the ground. Two platoons of D Company 1RAR had been loaded on trucks at three in the morning to drive to Tjolotjo as part of the 'land tail'. They would also supply men for the second wave if that were required.

The Selous Scouts, because of their pseudo-garb, could not take part in the strike as the risk of them being attacked by friendly forces was very high. They set up a stop line 2km to the east of the camp and waited for the morning.

*

3 Commando RLI, Fireforce Base, Buffalo Range Forward Airfield (FAF 7), southeast Rhodesia

'Troop ... TROOP, SHUN,' bawled Troop Sergeant Doug Barker to the men of 11 Troop 3Cdo, 1RLI. A cool early morning breeze flicked through the ranks of men, the watery light filtered by wispy clouds on the eastern horizon.

2nd Lt 'Dick' Van Deventer marched smartly to the front of the three ranks of men formed up in front of the Ops Room. He was about to address the men when he was interrupted as an Air Rhodesia Vickers Viscount 700D, with its four Rolls Royce Dart turboprops howling loudly, landed and taxied onto the hardstanding in front of the control tower. The Viscount was over 200m away but its engines nevertheless drowned out any other sound. As the aircraft turned, the powerful prop-wash threw dust across the neatly mowed lawn between the airport buildings and the Fireforce base. The men sheltered their faces from the dust; one lost his beret and had to go chasing after it. Eventually the pilot shut down the engines and the quiet of the early morning returned.

Taking a deep breath, 2nd Lt Van Deventer began his carefully prepared speech.

'Stand the men at ease please Colour,' ordered Van Deventer nervously.

'Stand aaat ... EASE.'

The men expertly threw their feet apart, hands clasped behind their backs. All wore clean uniforms with berets and stable-belts. The contrast between the sun-bleached berets and worn stable-belts of the 'old soldiers', and the bright green of the newer men, including the national servicemen, was a stark reminder.

Barker saluted the officer and reported to him, 'Sir ... we have twenty five men on parade, two men on tracking course, one man in DB, one man recovering from wounds, one man AWOL and four men on para-course ... SIR!'

The troop, at full strength would have been roughly equivalent to an infantry platoon of thirty-six men. The troop had the full compliment on its register but that did not mean they were all available for deployment at the same time.

'Thank you Colour … Now men, we have all returned from R&R and we now need to get our heads back in the game. I hope you all had a good rest although I suspect the ladies in Salisbury did not …' He paused for the punch line … his attempt at a joke had no effect whatsoever. The men stood dead still with perfectly blank expressions on their faces.

'Fook'n officers!' hissed Beamish to Le Beau on his left. A grunt of agreement was offered in reply.

The young officer coughed slightly and continued, 'We welcome Colour Barker to the Troop. He is a man with great experience and we are lucky to have him. I expect that each of you will give Colour Barker your full support.'

The men remained impassive.

'We also welcome three national servicemen, Troopers French, Loxton and Smyth to the Troop. Trooper French will join Corporal Beamish's stick, Loxton with Lance-Corporal Parnell and Smyth with Colour Barker.'

Watching the faces of his men lined up in front of him, Van Deventer was given no feedback whatsoever.

'Many of you would have met Trooper Kratzman who joined us a few weeks ago, but I formally welcome him to our troop today. Trooper Kratzman comes to us with a wealth of experience and he already has two contacts under his belt. Trooper Marais is recovering well from his wounds and is expected back in a few days.'

Van Deventer then turned to Barker who was standing next to him.

'Would you like to address the men Colour?'

'Yes, Sir! Thank you, Sir!' replied Barker taking two steps forward. 'Listen up LADIES … I don't care about how this troop has performed in the past but all I see is a bunch of badly disciplined, poorly turned out rabble. You are slack and if we don't sort it out people are going to die. We will commence this deployment with rifle range practice … we will recheck each one of you. Any man who fails my test will be given extra duties. We will have a full kit and barrack room inspection at eight am tomorrow morning. This Troop goes back on immediate Fireforce alert as of lunchtime tomorrow. Wake up … or die LADIES! Any questions?'

The men made no reaction and no questions were asked.

'Who the fook does he think he is calling us ladiees,' whispered Beamish out the corner of his mouth. He received a universal rumble of agreement from all in earshot.

'Carry on please Colour,' ordered Van Deventer more loudly this time, happy the ordeal of addressing the men was over.

'Report in full combat order in thirty minutes. Troop, Troop SHUN! … Kratzman, Le Beau and Beamish report to the CSM immediately,' shouted Barker

The men returned smartly to attention.

'Troop DISMISSED.'

The men turned smartly, marched three paces and then walked briskly to their barrack rooms to prepare for the rifle range practice.

Beamish and his stick walked forlornly towards the CSM's office.

'You three pricks are very lucky not to be in jail,' began CSM Butch Strydom. 'Those two reporters you fucked up at Le Coq d'Or laid charges against you at Salisbury Central and they gave very accurate descriptions as well. Plus let's face it, a Pom, a Yank and a Frog in RLI uniform doesn't exactly stretch the imagination.'

'Yes Sur!' replied Beamish, always choosing to show maximum respect to match the maximum potential shit he might be in.

'The Police phoned the RPs at Cranborne but they made up some story about you three being on some external operation. That does not mean that the police have given up, it's just bought you some time.'

'Yes Sur!'

'You boys keep a low profile on your next R and R. Is that clear?'

'Yes Sir!' the three answered in unison.

'Now fuck off and kill some Gooks!'

11 Troop formed up again outside their barrack room with their rifles, webbing and packs, in the same kit they wore for a Fireforce callout. The only difference was the absence of camo-cream.

Troopers in the RLI on Fireforce carried webbing and equipment largely of their own choosing to maximize comfort and efficiency. Most wore chest-webbing or fireforce-jackets to carry eight magazines and one white phosphorus grenade, one shrapnel grenade (M962), and one or two smoke grenades of different colours. Most chest-webbing designs had pouches built in for essential kit, such as compass, mini-flare projectors, notebooks, radio scheds and maps. A lightweight pack contained one day's rations, one or two radio batteries, an extra belt of MAG rounds plus a sleeping bag, and an A63 radio if a stick leader. The gunners had large side pouches for the ammunition belts. Most carried two water bottles, or four, depending on the time of year and availability of water, that were carried on the webbing belt, together with other essential supplies such as drips and first field dressings in two kidney pouches. All men had a set of identification or 'dog' tags around the neck plus a plastic squeezable syringe of morphine.

The Troop fully expected that they would be directed to trucks to take them to the firing range. Lt Van Deventer and Colour Barker arrived dressed in their kit and instructed the men that they were to run the five kilometres to the range. Now the Troop really had something to complain about. It was a hot Lowveld day so there was a mad scramble to fill extra water bottles that were surely going to be needed.

As the men crowded around the taps on the wall next to the canteen, Beamish gave a few of his own instructions.

'I don't want to see any bullshit show-offs. We go nice and slow. Any man running off ahead will answer to me and Le Beau,' said Beamish menacingly, loud enough so all could hear. There was general approval to this suggestion. 'You NS fresh *poes*, this is not the time to show how pleased you are to be in the RLI, you run in the back. Do you hear?'

'Yes Corp,' the new men replied.

The men all shuffled back to where Barker and Van Deventer were waiting, making sure not to show any enthusiasm. The threat of a few slaps from Le Beau and Beamish was real.

The Troop were arranged in stick order, Van Deventer call-sign 31, Barker 31Alpha, Parnell 31Bravo, Beamish 31Charlie … and so on. The new recruit, still referred to by Beamish as 'Chico', slotted in next to his stick. Both Kratzman and Le Beau continued to both carry the MAG.

Slowly, so as to conserve energy, the Troop lumbered out of the camp in the direction of the rifle range. Van Deventer tried to increase the pace by urging the men on, but the troop sullenly refused to go any faster than a slow shambling jog. He increased his own pace only to find himself running on his own, well ahead of the rest.

'Come on lads, let's get a move on,' shouted Van Deventer, trying his best School of Infantry bullshit leadership skills. He was totally ignored.

'Steady boys, nice and easy,' grumbled Beamish threateningly, glaring at the new NS recruits.

Barker, the old soldier, was not massively excited about jogging in full kit either. He made a few token attempts to support his subbie by half-heartedly shouting for the boys to go faster. He knew better.

The heat took its toll on the men. Their discomfort was added to by the fact that most had spent two weeks of heavy drinking and partying. They were saturated in sweat in minutes with the weakest dropping off the back of the group. Men stood on the side of the road retching violently, their bodies not coping with the heat and exertion. Many had eaten large breakfasts that were reproduced in the dirt on the side of the road.

While Beamish didn't want to go fast, he was equally determined not to stop, no matter how bad he was feeling. He stoically kept up the pace, personal pride would not let him slack off. His stick took his lead, the two gunners jogged silently by his side. Chico, being straight out of Training Troop, was still super-fit, showing no discomfort whatsoever.

It was a very tired and hot group of men that eventually arrived at the rifle range. There was much moaning and groaning in the ranks. The range had been cut out of the bush and the butts had been pushed up using earthmovers. Barker divided the men, some to man the butts, others to take their turn zeroing their rifles. Stragglers continued to drag themselves in. A Land Rover loaded with Figure 11A targets and ammunition was parked at the 100m mark.

All weapons were zeroed for 100m and sights were set to the same range. The troopers carried eight magazines of 19, or even 18 rounds each. Most of the magazines were old so the springs could not handle a full 20-round load without causing stoppages. Most had two tracer rounds at the top of the magazine to help 'mark target' with double tracer rounds at nine and ten and then at the end of the magazine as a warning to be ready to reload. The MAG gunner carried 500 rounds in 100 round belts (2 belts x 50 rounds linked together), while each member of the stick carried an extra 100 round belt in their pack or kidney pouches.

In reality, the troopers rarely got the opportunity to 'aim' at a target in a contact. In most cases the bush was too thick and the situation, too chaotic. Instead, they adopted a technique called 'cover' or 'drake' shooting. This was a process of deliberately 'killing' probable cover used by the enemy. No actual visual sighting of the enemy was required. This saved time attempting to identify the exact location of the enemy by searching for muzzle flashes or blast, a movement or a shape. Instead, careful observation of the terrorist's position was carried out while 'killing' their cover. Most shooting took place with both eyes open looking down the barrel of the rifle. The rifle became an extension of the arm in the same way as pointing with a finger.

Troopers were taught to shoot directly into and through the CT's position, keeping their aim deliberately low, while gunners were required to aim at the ground immediately to the front of that cover. Tumbling rounds, dislodged stones, or fragments of smashed rocks and trees did great injury to those lying in cover, while the dirt that MAG's kicked up provided excellent distraction and demoralisation value. The primary action was to draw the barrel of the rifle or MAG across the cover area, usually beginning left to right, while squeezing the trigger at appropriate moments so as to 'rake' it from one side to the other. Each round or burst was fired in a deliberately aimed fashion. By aiming low, the first round was intended to skip and strike a prone target, while the second would go directly home as the barrel lifted.

Barker had the targets set up in the bush adjacent to the cleared range to help the men practice their open-sights cover shooting.

Beamish's stick waited patiently under a shady tree for their turn. The air was full of rifle and MAG fire as the men took the opportunity to get off as many rounds as they could. Barker, who was renowned as a marksman, walked along the firing line helping the men adjust their sights. As each magazine was emptied, the men left their rifles and then walked in a line towards the targets to check their respective grouping. Barker noted the results on a clipboard and berated the men with poor results. Lines of men doing press-ups appeared all over the range as Barker began issuing punishment for poor shooting.

Then Barker's attention turned to the stick of call-sign 31Charlie.

'Corporal Beamish, I see you have ignored my instructions to choose a gunner,' he said accusingly.

Beamish knew better than getting into a debate with a senior NCO. He braced up and looked straight ahead. His two gunners and Chico followed his lead.

'Do you want me to do it for you Beamish, you useless Pommie twit?'

Being called a Pommie did not normally upset Beamish but the way Barker said it made him prickle with indignation.

'Permission to speak, Colour?' asked Kratzman in his measured American drawl.

'What the fuck do you want Yank?' spat Barker, looking up into the eyes of the giant who stared fixedly at a point on the far side of the rifle range.

'With respect Colour we need a competition,' stated Kratzman reverently.

'What sort of competition,' snapped Barker, now irritated by the interruption. The shooting on the range died down as the set of men finished their magazines and made their weapons safe.

'If you can outshoot either Le Beau or myself then you can take one of the guns away,' continued Kratzman with his trademark smile.

Le Beau looked across at the American, a smirk across his face. He gave a poorly disguised wink that Barker did not see.

'So you are trying to get cute with me … Yank?' replied Barker, clearly not sure of how to respond to the challenge.

Other men in the troop were now watching the altercation; Lt Van Deventer was in the butts unaware of the challenge being issued.

Kratzman would not be diverted. He rattled on, 'We start at the two hundred, fire a belt of a hundred, run to the hundred and fifty, fire a belt of fifty, then to the hundred where we fire another belt of fifty. Two targets each. Most rounds in the square box wins.' He was referring to the square box designating the 'kill' area on the 11A target.

Barker stared at the tall American, weighing up the challenge. 'I don't need a competition I just need to order you to do what I want!' he said loudly, trying to stamp his authority on the situation. Barker looked around at the expectant faces of the men watching him. He had been effectively trapped.

'Okay set it up, I am happy to kick a bit of Yank and Frog arse, ' stated Barker confidently. While he had capitulated, the fact was that he was an expert shot with all weapons. He had carried the gun in his days as a trooper.

With great excitement, the men ran to set up the new targets, two for each of the participants in the competition. Van Deventer walked up to Barker and demanded to know what was going on.

'Just a bit of friendly competition Sir, to put these men in their place,' said Barker, with some bravado. 'If you don't mind Sir, I would ask you to adjudicate.'

Van Deventer was clearly unhappy that his range practice had been interrupted without his permission.

The three men marched off to the 200m mark, draped in the belts they would need for the competition. The Troop lined up at the 100m mark to watch, all thoughts of heat, tiredness and thirst, lost in the excitement.

Van Deventer, realising that he had to play along, held up his combat hat to the three men, they waved back and he dropped his arm.

The three dived to the ground, cocked the weapon and commenced a steady BANG … BANG double tap at the targets. Each man fired in the prone position the gun sitting on its bipod. The gun was fired with the stock pulled into the shoulder, the right forefinger on the trigger, the left hand gripping the top of the stock to steady the weapon on the target. Dust kicked up the back of the butts and the targets shivered as the rounds passed through them. As soon as the first three belts were empty, they got up and ran to the 150m mark, going down again, replacing the belt, cocking and firing. The spectators shouted their encouragement, waving their arms wildly. Up the men got again, down the range they ran to the 100m mark. The strain of the run and the weight of the weapon could be seen on their faces as they purposefully fired at the targets. The last belt finished and the three stood up.

Van Deventer sent the men off to fetch the targets.

The results were impossible to compare, the centre section of each target was a massive hole, the targets were so bullet ridden that they broke in pieces.

'Colour, may I suggest we fire from the hip using the sling?' asked Kratzman politely, not wanting to give up. 'Fifty rounds. Two targets.'

The men continued to shout their support enthusiastically.

Van Deventer decided that he wanted his range practice completed.

'No more bullshit, let's get these men finished Colour,' demanded Van Deventer impatiently.

'No harm done Sir, I can handle these two wankers. Teach them a lesson,' replied Barker, still confident.

Up the targets went again.

Once the targets were up, the three walked back over to the 100m mark to take up their positions. Once again Van Deventer called the off.

All three stood with the MAG slung at the hip. Firing at the butts from that angle was difficult to judge, dust kicked up at the base of the Figure 11As as the gunners walked the rounds onto the target. Then half way through his belt, Kratzman lifted the gun to his shoulder, holding the 11.8kg weapon rock-steady, the MAG kicking into his shoulder as he fired. The crowd cheered their support; very few men had the strength to shoot an MAG from the shoulder, more especially shooting twenty-five or more rounds.

The targets were duly produced and the result was patently clear. Thirty of Kratzman's rounds could be counted, almost all in the centre square. It was not necessary to count the others.

'You cheated, who said anything about shooting from the shoulder?' shouted Barker.

Kratzman just smiled broadly at him, victory written all over his face. There was no way that Colour Barker was going to try firing twenty-five rounds from the shoulder into a target at 100m.

'Can Le Beau and I keep our guns Colour?' asked Kratzman mischievously, still smiling.

Barker glared at him, 'I don't know why you want to carry the bloody heavy things anyway.' He rounded on the men watching on, 'What the fuck are you looking at? ... I want to see the last man around the rifle range ... GO!'

The troop gathered in a tight knot and shuffled their way around the shooting range, laughing and joking with each other, the discomfort of the intense heat temporarily forgotten. They called out their congratulations to Kratzman.

Le Beau was delighted, breaking into the Legionnaire's song, *Le Boudin*.

> *Tiens, voilà du boudin, voilà du boudin, voilà du boudin*
> *Pour les Alsaciens, les Suisses et les Lorrains,*
> *Pour les Belges, Schultz en a plus,*

> *Pour les Belges Schultz en a plus ...*

The slow, scraping trot matched the tempo of Le Beau's chant, as he sang on the top of his voice.

> *Oublions avec nos peines,*
> *La mort qui nous oublie si peu.*
> *Nous, la Légion ...*

Beamish smiled broadly, shaking his head in amusement. He was really starting to like this Yank ... but that he would keep to himself. The Frog wasn't too bad either.

The men sang all the way back to camp, a buoyant Kratzman leading the men in the song of the 1st Cavalry Division, *Garry Owen*.

> *We'll break windows, we'll break doors,*
> *the watch knock down by threes and fours,*
> *then let the doctors work their cures,*
> *and tinker up our bruises ...*

Teaching the men the chorus as they went ...

> *Instead of spa we'll drink down ale*
> *and pay the reckoning on the nail,*
> *for debt no man shall go to jail;*
> *from Garry Owen in glory.*

Finally, on reaching the airfield, the men spontaneously formed up in three ranks, rifles in the shoulder. Beamish, always enjoying a song, led the boys in an RLI lament, to the tune of *Mull of Kintyre*.

> *Far have I traveled on land and through sky.*
> *Dark are the valleys, the mountains are green,*
> *But oh our Colours fly higher than high*
> *For we are the men of the RLI ...*

11 Troop marched smartly into their camp, in step, heads held high, singing at the top of their voices.

> *Now one lies wounded.*
> *He's so far from home.*
> *All of the Troopies they pray for his soul*
> *As life leaves him. He hears a heavenly choir.*
> *As they carry him back to the RLI.*

Butch Strydom walked out onto the veranda in front of his office, his pace stick wedged under his arm. With a broad smile on his face, he threw a salute as the men marched past.

*

COMOPS, Milton Buildings, Salisbury

The planning for the assassination of senior members of the ZANLA leadership was now well underway. The Selous Scouts had been assigned to kill or snatch Josiah Tongogara and other members of the ZANU/ZANLA leadership in Mozambique. While the CIO and SB gave the broad intelligence briefings, it was up to the individuals within each team to work out the finer details. The Air Force provided liaison officers for each major task to co-ordinate the vital air element.

The officer in charge of Operation Swallow was Captain Chris Schultz, Selous Scouts. He had been allocated a team of sixteen Selous Scouts for the operation and a troop of RLI. Schultz had requested the services of Sgt. Cephas Ngwenya as soon as he returned from R&R.

Captain Schultz presented himself, as ordered by his Boss, to COMOPS to meet with George Stanbridge and his team. An air force Group Captain was added as the planner for the air element. Schultz arrived exactly on time, together with his 2IC for this operation, the recently promoted Colour-Sergeant Dennis Kumpher. Both wore camouflage uniform, green stable belts and dark brown berets with the distinctive Selous Scout silver osprey cap badge.

Stanbridge welcomed the men in his usual friendly manner, impressed at finally meeting two men with such enviable reputations. The small group took their seats and one of the secretaries brought in a tray of tea. A lever-arch file bursting with paper was open in front of Stanbridge and maps were laid out on the large table. No secretary was called to take notes.

'Thank you for coming, Captain. I thought it would be good to meet face to face on this little project of ours,' opened Stanbridge with a smile. He introduced the men to the Group Captain who nodded his greeting.

Schultz did not reply, instead choosing to remain impassive. His Boss had warned him to take everything the CIO told him with a pinch of salt.

'Well then, we understand that the detailed planning is up to you chaps but we thought we would explain a few things about the mission and the target.' There was still no response from the two soldiers so Stanbridge barrelled on. 'Our sources have confirmed the target can be in one of three places, here in Mapai,' he pointed to a house on an aerial photograph, '... or on the road here between Sao Jorge do Limpopo and Aldia de Barragem ... or in the village of Aldia de Barragem itself.'

'That narrows it down nicely, ... what is that? ... A hundred and ninety-five kilometre radius?' interjected Schultz, still sitting back in his chair, not looking at the map. As it happened, he knew the exact distance between Sao Jorge do Limpopo and Aldia de Barragem, and the distances between most other towns in northern Mozambique, off-by-heart.

'Yes ... ah ... quite, it does seem a little vague but in reality it is not. You see the target drives in a motorcade of three or four white Toyota Landcruisers that have been donated by Sweden, and, as luck would have it, we have managed to place a tracking device in one of them.'

For the first time a glimmer of interest crossed Schultz's face. He shifted in his seat slightly. Kumpher, on the other hand, looked as bored as if he was watching *The Partridge Family* on TV.

'Our contact is located at Mapai which, as you know, is sixteen kilometres southwest of Sao Jorge do Limpopo. We will know for sure whether the target is there. If he is not, then he has to be in one of the other two places.'

Still no comment was forthcoming from the Selous Scouts.

'We will put an aircraft up that should be able to track the vehicle if it is on the move, allowing you to spring an ambush on the road. If the vehicle is in Aldia de Barragem then we will know that as well.'

'There is a Brigade of FPLM at Barragem,' observed Kumpher dismissively.

'There is a company of FPLM and at least a thousand Gooks at Mapai,' added Schultz.

'Yes, that's true, but this is intended to be a surgical strike ... in ... kill ... and out. A very small team.'

'How much time will we have before we know for sure where the target is?' asked Schultz.

'In both cases, the meeting point is a house which we know about, but as you say, they are both in the middle of densely populated villages. I estimate you will have a window of no more than an hour between being told where the target is and going in on the strike.'

'That means we have to have three teams ready at a moment's notice to cover all our targets,' said Schultz thoughtfully.

'How do you propose to insert the teams?' interjected the Group Captain.

Everyone looked at Schultz who was the only person to provide an answer. It was obvious that Schultz was reluctant to discuss any sort of operational plan with COMOPS, or the CIO, after what his Boss had told him.

'I would rather not discuss that at this stage,' he replied. 'There's way too many unknowns with this mission; we will have to work through the options. Plus I am not sure how we can prepare a backup plan if something goes wrong. It's a bloody long walk back to Rhodesia from Barragem with a couple of thousand gooks chasing you.'

'It would help if you could give me some idea at this early stage, Captain,' asked the Group Captain encouragingly.

Schultz ignored the request, asking instead, 'Just how accurate are those tracking devices?'

The Group Captain responded, 'Well, as you know, VHF is limited by line-of-sight constraints but in an aircraft at ten thousand feet we should be able to pick up a signal twenty kilometres away. The battery strength in the transmitter has a lot to do with it as well. I believe the transmitter in the Landcruiser is actually inside the car radio which means it's running off the car battery. We should be able to pick it up from over thirty kilometres. The device should be accurate to within one kilometre.'

'One kilometre is a big distance inside a densely populated village at night,' interjected Kumpher, who was still not showing much enthusiasm. 'If these people are in a Landcruiser and you know where they are, why don't you just bomb the shit out of them?'

'We need to be absolutely sure that the target is dead. It's vital to the overall plan. This can only be certain if we can identify the body,' replied Stanbridge trying desperately not to get needled.

Just then, there was a knock on the door and a very troubled looking COMOPS staffer entered. He walked around the table and spoke in hushed tones to Stanbridge. The CIO man's face paled, he looked across the table at the two Selous Scouts.

'I regret to report that terrorists have attacked Chironga Mission near Mount Darwin and killed three missionaries and abducted a group of school children. I suspect that there will be a very substantial escalation in the importance of your mission gentlemen.'

The men around the table sat in stunned silence as the enormity of the news sunk in.

'We will kill this Gook for you, Mister Stanbridge,' said Captain Chris Schultz in a soft voice.

*

ZANLA HQ, Rua 3 de Fevereiro, Chimoio, Mozambique

Comrade Godfrey Nyathi was summonsed to a meeting with his leader at the house in *Rua 3 de Fevereiro* in central Chimoio. He felt a twinge in his stomach in light of the news that he had read about the identification of a spy. He knew the General well; if he had been discovered, retribution would be instant and brutal.

Nyathi sat waiting for his meeting while sitting on a chair on the veranda of the rundown Portuguese colonial-style house. A brand new dark green Chinese BJ212[114] raced up skidding to a halt in the dusty driveway. Two men dressed in FRELIMO uniforms, jumped out and walked briskly up the stairs towards the front door. Nyathi leapt to his feet to bar the way into the house. The men did not acknowledge Nyathi, instead one tried to brush past him.

'You cannot barge in here,' commanded Nyathi in English, his rifle now in his hands.

'Get out of my way!' said one of the men in heavily accented English. He had a lot of gold flashing on his shoulder. 'I want to see Comrade Tongogara now!'

Nyathi would not budge, the man tried to push him out the way.

'What is going on?' demanded Tongogara in seShona from inside.

'You have two visitors *Nyenganyenga*.'

The General came to the door. 'Yes, what is it?'

'I am Colonel Gonzalves ... we have not met General, but I have been

---

114 Jeep-type four by four utility vehicle.

sent by General D'Almeida from High Command to discuss matters of great importance,' said the Colonel, in broken English.

The door was opened and the Colonel was admitted. The other man was sent to wait in the vehicle.

A heated exchange took place inside the house between the FRELIMO Colonel and Tongogara. The conversation was in English, as Tongogara could not speak Portuguese and was not confident on the local *Ndau* dialect. It was impossible to hear the whole conversation, just a few words here and there. It was clear that the Colonel was very upset indeed. Eventually, the conversation settled down to a more subdued level and all that could be heard outside was the sound of conversation.

The men left without ceremony and Nyathi was ushered into the living room.

'Comrade Nyathi, I want to discuss your next assignment which is of grave importance,' said Tongogara, who was obviously preoccupied.

'Yes General,' said Nyathi standing to attention.

'We have news that the Colonists will try to assassinate our leadership. They have tried before and failed but they are going to try again,' stated Tongogara, who did not seem particularly disturbed by the information, in fact, he seemed at ease with it.

'Yes General,' replied Nyathi, he had learned not to interrupt the General with questions.

'You will need to increase the size of my bodyguard and we need to be even more careful with our travel arrangements. Our brothers in FRELIMO will provide you with some additional equipment.'

'Yes General.'

'You will travel with me in my vehicle everywhere I go and make preparations at each of our destinations. Is that clear?'

Nyathi nodded his understanding. The prospect of driving in the General's vehicle was not appealing, he avoided it whenever possible.

'Also Nyathi, you need to know that our comrades have attacked a mission near Mount Darwin and killed three missionaries. This has upset our FRELIMO hosts greatly. This was not authorised by me, and the men will be caught and punished, but it is guaranteed that the Colonists will mount a reprisal against us. We have blamed the killings on the *Skuz'apo* for purposes of the world press but that will obviously not work with the Colonists. You need to be very well prepared Nyathi.'

Nodding his understanding, Nyathi could not trust himself to speak. His mind in turmoil he stood up and saluted his leader … *the reprisal will be swift and deadly!*

'Thank you for your trust *Nyenganyenga*. I will not let you down,' stated Nyathi confidently, still standing to attention. Nyathi could feel the hint of uncertainty in his voice, hoping that his leader would not pick up on it.

'I have faith in your ability Comrade, *ufamba zavanaka*,' Tongogara dismissed him.

Nyathi turned towards the front door but Tongogara stopped him.

'Nyathi, there is one more thing.' The General's voice was suddenly quiet and sinister; Nyathi had heard this voice many times. 'I have been told that we have a spy in my leadership team. I cannot tell you how I came by this information, but I am convinced it is true.'

'Yes, *Nyenganyenga?*' Nyathi felt his heart sink... *I am dead!*

Tongogara studied his face. 'Are you alright Nyathi?'

' ...Yes General.' *What type of death can I expect?*

'We must be even more vigilant with our own people. Look out for anything strange or unusual. Anything at all ... report it to me instantly!'

'Yes *Nyenganyenga* ... We must seek out this pig and kill him slowly,' replied Nyathi, blood pounding in his ears. He felt certain the General could hear his heart beating.

Nyathi walked out into the hot afternoon sun, the sense of relief palpable.

The voice of Mutumwa the *n'anga* played on his mind ... *Nyenganyenga ... I have seen the great Owl ... the Owl is the tool of the most evil of all spirits.*

17

Nata River, Tjolotjo District Central Matabeleland

Sgt. Cephas Ngwenya and Cpl. Joseph Nechena were awake and ready before first light. They had not had time to return to the RV with the rest of their men. Instead, they had taken cover in thick bush on the edge of the riverbed to the east of the CT base camp. They had slept head to toe, as was the custom of ZIPRA cadres in the bush. They lay in their positions, weapons at the ready, prepared in case they had been compromised.

The eastern horizon heralded the start of the day, the soft light spreading over the ground until the trees around them gained definition. It was serenely silent like the African bush is at first light. The sun caught the tops of the tallest trees while a Blackcollared barbet called loudly in a tree above, *whoop-dudu, whoop-dudu*, answered by its mate some distance off.

Out to the east the gentle sounds of early morning were broken by the thud, thud, thud, of helicopter rotors, getting louder.

'Sierra 25, Sunray do you read?' The Fireforce Commander from D Company 1RAR was calling, his call-sign was Sunray.

'Sunray, Sierra 25, reading you fives, you are to our east. Over,' replied Ngwenya.

'Sierra 25, Roger we are twenty seconds out ... standby to mark FLOT.'

The sound of the helicopters reverberated through the bush, Ngwenya glanced out in the direction of the clattering whine but he still could not see them, they were flying at treetop level.

'Sierra 25 mark FLOT ... NOW,' came the call from the Fireforce Commander.

Ngwenya threw out a green smoke grenade to show their position and allow the K-car to line up accurately on the target. The three helicopters passed directly overhead Ngwenya's position down the line of the riverbed towards the ZIPRA base on the sand island.

As the helicopters arrived overhead, the CTs in the camp broke cover and began to disperse. The 20mm cannon in the K-car carried clearly to the Selous Scouts who were lying flat on the top of the riverbank, the smoke grenade still fizzing behind them. The Fireforce Commander immediately deployed the heli-borne sticks, one to the north the other to the south while the Paradak lined up for its drop in the west.

'Sierra 25, you have Charlie Tangos approaching your position, two hundred metres.'

'Sierra 25 copied.'

Ngwenya and Nechena waited for the oncoming CTs, who were trying to make their escape back into the safety of the densely populated TTL. Within seconds they arrived running along the top of the riverbank, running like the wind looking back over their shoulders as the helicopters circled above.

CRACK ... CRACK Nechena's AK rang out. Holding his Tokarev out in front of him, Ngwenya tried to pick off oncoming CTs. The running men had no chance against the deadly accurate fire from the Scouts hiding in thick cover. The CTs jumped to the left and right to try to avoid the men shooting at them. A few turned and ran back the way they came. Others arrived in the riverbed below, easy targets as the soft sand made it impossible for them to run at full speed.

One of the Stop groups called in a Lynx strike to try and clear the thick undergrowth on the island. In minutes, the tinder dry reeds and grass were ablaze from the 37mm rockets and frantan. This flushed out the CTs and their new recruits still hiding in the long grass. The slaughter continued as the helicopters circled round and round, spitting death and destruction. Out to the west, the CTs ran into the RAR para-borne sweepline. There was no escape.

In front of Ngwenya, a CT, who had miraculously avoided being killed, ran towards him. The man had thrown his weapon away in the hopes of blending in with the local population. Ngwenya leapt up in front of him. Swinging his pistol, smashing the man on the side of the head, Ngwenya knocked him off his feet. The man screamed in fright at the scarred apparition appearing above him. He slid backwards in the dirt pushing with his feet, trying to get away.

The vision of his dead brother and his distraught mother, flashed in Ngwenya's mind as he levelled the pistol at the man.

'No Cephas, don't kill him,' screamed Nechena, 'he may be useful.'

Standing to his full height, the pistol still aimed at the whimpering man on the ground, Ngwenya emptied the rest of the clip ... just inches from the man's head. The man wet himself, soiling his pants, wailing uncontrollably.

Within only a few minutes of concentrated battle, the gunshots died away. Only a few isolated shots rang out, as the RAR sweepline took out CTs still hiding in the riverbed. On the island, a few massive explosions sent clouds of dust high into the morning sky as the fire burnt through packs containing TM 46 landmines and RPG-7 projectiles.

Vehicle engines could be heard approaching from the northeast as the rest of D Company arrived to follow-up any CTs that had survived the contact.

Selous Scout McCloud, further to the east, gave his position to the Fireforce Commander to avoid any overenthusiastic RAR rifleman shooting at them. All were warned of the Selous Scout presence as they swept slowly forward towards the burning island. The helicopters landed in an LZ to the north where the D Company trucks had parked their refuelling trailers.

After the contact had died down, Ngwenya and Nechena took the time to study the sobbing CT they had captured. He looked very young, but then they were all very young. It became immediately apparent that there was something strange about this particular ZIPRA CT. He was dressed in Chinese khaki for openers. The man began to babble in seShona, his eyes were rolling in his head, spit running from his mouth, as if he was having some sort of fit. Ngwenya asked him questions in his home tongue siNdebele, but the man clearly did not understand. The reason became obvious, he wasn't ZIPRA at all, he was ZANLA!

The captured CT was propped up against a tree and Ngwenya gave him a hard slap across his face to stop him moaning incoherently. The man's eyes were wide, flashing from side to side in complete panic. Ngwenya took out his notebook to take some notes.

'I am not going to kill you now, Comrade. I am going to ask you some questions. If you answer truthfully you will live to father many children. If you lie, I will kill you slowly. Do you understand, Comrade?' said Ngwenya quietly in se Shona, the sinister intent clear in his eyes. He always referred to captured CTs as 'comrade', it seemed to calm them down.

The man nodded his head vigorously; he was going to tell the truth. Once he realised he wasn't going to be killed, the man visibly relaxed, smiling up at his captors. It transpired that the ZANLA group had infiltrated Rhodesia at Pafuri on the border with Mozambique, crossed the country into Botswana and then walked north to re-enter Rhodesia north of Plumtree. The CT spoke freely in seShona, without hesitation, he needed absolutely no reinforcement from Ngwenya at all. Their mission included blowing up the railway line between Rhodesia and Botswana and the railway line north from Bulawayo to Victoria Falls. The ZANLA cell had made contact with the local ZIPRA detachment.

'Where were you trained Comrade?' asked Ngwenya, a friendly smile now on his face.

'At Aldia de Barragem for my basic training, then Camp Takawira near Chimoio for specialist sabotage training,' replied the man matter-of-factly.

The mere mention of Camp Takawira shocked Ngwenya, the recent memories of his escape still vivid and frightening.

Once all the Selous Scouts had RV'd and contact made with the RAR commander on the ground, Ngwenya and his captive crossed the riverbed onto the island that had housed the ZIPRA camp.

The bush had been well and truly burnt out. The grass and driftwood bashas that the CTs had used as sleeping positions were incinerated. Bodies lay everywhere, some burnt beyond recognition. Abandoned backpacks and clothing littered the ground. Amazingly, a large pot full of boiling water still simmered undisturbed on a cooking fire in the middle of the camp. It was clear that many of the young teenage recruits had not escaped the attack. Their bodies were scattered in the riverbed and on the sandy banks of the island. The stench of frantan and burnt flesh was everywhere. Some of the trees were still burning from the frantan blast. Thick smoke filled the air.

Corporal McCloud called to Ngwenya when he saw him enter the camp, 'Cephas, I think this is your transistor radio.' He was holding up a burnt radio, the plastic melted into a blackened lump. It would have been impossible to tell that it was a radio if it wasn't for the distinctive aerial sticking out the one side.

In a shallow slit trench, only a few metres away from where the radio was found, was the body of Julius Moyo. His throat had been cut from ear to ear and his heart had been cut out of his chest.

Ngwenya handed his prisoner over to SB who already had three others tied up in the middle of the camp. He told the SB Inspector what the captive had told him.

The Inspector nodded and shook Ngwenya's hand, 'Well done man!' He then turned and shouted out, 'has anybody got any idea how this Gook got his throat cut ... and his heart cut out?'

Joseph Nechena caught Ngwenya's eye, a knowing smile spread across his face.

As a Matabele, the spirit of Cephas Ngwenya's brother-in-law, Gibson Sibanda, his *Idlozi*, had sought revenge for the premeditated and brutal way that he had been murdered. His *Idlozi*, in extreme distress, had metamorphosed into the most evil avenging spirit, *Uzimu*. The *Uzimu* needed an instrument for its revenge. Cephas Ngwenya became that instrument, through the power of possession. Cephas had accepted, in fact welcomed, Gibson's angry spirit into his body, the process of *ukuvumisa*. In this way, Cephas had crept into Julius Moyo's terrorist camp, sought him out, and killed him. The *ukuvumisa* allowed Cephas to move silently and invisibly. By cutting out Moyo's heart, Cephas ensured that his lost soul would wander the Earth forever and would never find peace or contentment. Moyo's soul would forever remain in purgatory, causing great harm to his house and to his relatives.

Cephas Ngwenya turned and walked out of the smouldering base camp. He needed to return to his village to make preparations for the burial of his brother-in-law. In an instant, with his straw hat, threadbare jacket and submissive gait, he changed from a proud and confident Selous Scout, to being a poor, subservient, subsistence farmer.

Contact Tjolojo District - Matabeleland

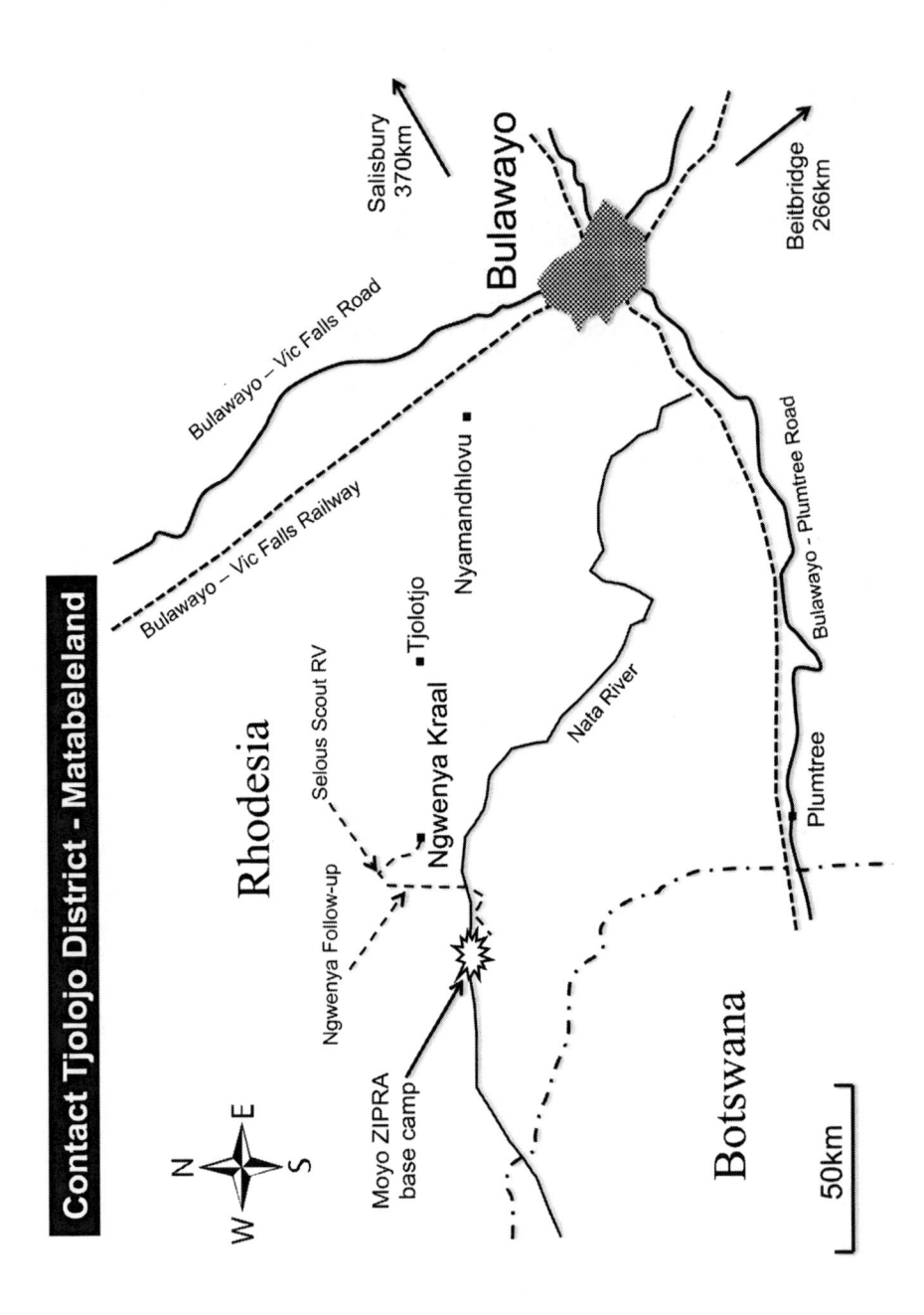

*

3 Commando RLI, Fireforce Base, Buffalo Range Forward Airfield (FAF 7), southeast Rhodesia

'Chico, I have a little mission for you,' called Corporal Arthur Beamish conspiratorially, sitting on his bunk. It was getting dark outside and the boisterous noise of a piss-up could already be heard coming from the canteen.

'Yes Corp,' replied the young NS recruit, eagerly. Beamish hadn't said more than two words to him since he had joined the stick. Those had been limited primarily to 'Fook off'.

Le Beau D'aubigne, with a twinkle in his eye, joined the conspiracy that already included Kratzman.

'Le Beau, give Chico the shampoo,' said Beamish pointing to the bottle in Le Beau's hand.

Le Beau handed the bottle to Chico giving him an encouraging slap on the shoulder.

'Now see here Chico, you need to take that bottle, go into the CSM's room while he's having a drink, and fill up his shampooo bottle with it,' instructed Beamish, as if briefing the youngster on an external raid.

Chico looked across at the other members of his stick both smiling reassuringly at him.

Seeing that Chico was a little perplexed, Beamish added,' Not to worry, we will keep a look out for you.'

'But Corp, what is in the bottle?' asked Chico trying to the read the label in the poor light.

'Don't worry about that, its to help kill lice, you'll see … the CSM will appreciate it in the end,' replied Beamish, trying not to laugh. Kratzman couldn't hold it in; he began to laugh, lying back on his bunk, the whole bed jumping up and down in time with his huge body. That set Le Beau off as well, tears of laughter running down his cheeks.

'Eet's to keel lice Chico,' laughed Le Beau, jumping from one leg to another with excitement. That set Kratzman off on another paroxysm of laughter.

Beamish, cool as ever, kept a straight face, 'Make sure you empty the whole bottle or it won't be strong enough to kill all the liiice,' he added, emphasising the importance by pointing at the bottle. 'You see Chico, the CSM is too proud to admit he has lice, so he wouldn't ask for the medication.'

That was too much for both Le Beau and Kratzman, they howled with laughter, forcing Beamish to crack the tiniest of smiles.

Chico, realising that this was some form of test, was smart enough to get the message. He needed to get into the spirit of it all, come what may. Smiling broadly, he stood up, 'Well let's go kill some lice.'

Now all three members of his stick rolled around with laugher, Beamish could only manage, 'Good lad' through bursts of giggling.

The four men went out into the darkness towards the block occupied by the CSM and senior NCOs. The CSM's room was at the end of a line of six rooms in a long block. It was the largest of the rooms, as befitting his rank. He had his own writing desk, a basin for shaving, but it did not have a shower. The CSM had to use the communal showers and toilets like the rest of the Commando.

Beamish sent Le Beau to one end of the block and Kratzman the other, while he loitered under a nearby tree.

Chico, showing great initiative, went straight to the door to the CSM's room, a stable door with only the bottom part closed. A wide veranda stretched the length of the block. The door had a spring-mounted mosquito screen in front of it that squeaked loudly as Chico opened it. He froze, looking about to make sure he hadn't been seen. He glanced across at Beamish who urged him on by waving his hand.

In Chico went, gently allowing the mosquito screen back into place behind him. A security light on the rear of the block let in enough light through the back window to allow him to find the CSM's shampoo bottle. It was a plastic triangular conical shape ... *Palmolive, for extra body and shine!* It seemed about half empty so Chico hastily removed the top and then, holding the bottles up to the light from the window, he carefully poured the contents of the lice medicine into the shampoo bottle, messing a little on his hands as he did so. He rinsed the shampoo bottle and his hands in the basin to remove the medicine that had spilled out.

Across the quad, the CSM walked out of the canteen, burped loudly, then made his way, on slightly shaky legs, towards his room.

'Chips' hissed Beamish, trying to catch Chico's attention. No response.

The CSM continued his approach. Kratzman, seeing the danger rushed around the back of the building to warn Chico. The window at the back of the CSM's room was well off the ground above the washbasin.

'Evenin' CSM' said Beamish, on the top of his voice, hoping Chico would hear.

The CSM looked across at Beamish standing in the shadows, his slightly addled brain confused by the fact that Beamish had offered a greeting. Beamish did not offer unsolicited greetings to senior NCOs, the CSM in particular.

'What do you want Beamish?' sneered the CSM, positive that Beamish was up to no good.

'What a beautiful evening Sur,' commented Beamish conversationally, looking up at the stars. He took a step towards the veranda where the CSM was standing.

Now the CSM was convinced something was up.

'Have you broken something Beamish? Are you pissed?'

A loud yelp came from inside the CSM's room as Kratzman dragged Chico bodily through the narrow window, the spike for the window latch digging into his stomach, opening a gash.

The CSM's head spun around, unsure of what he had heard, wobbling on his feet.

'Actually CSM ...' demanded Beamish, in a louder voice, his mind racing.

'I was hoping you might put my name forward for the drill and weapons course.'

'What!' exclaimed the CSM, shocked at the request from such an unlikely quarter. The CSM studied Beamish's smiling face, trying to come to terms with this strange request. 'Fuck off Beamish! You are the most uncooperative, obstinate and miserable bastard I have ever met. The fact that you have two stripes is a miracle in itself. Now bugger off and leave me alone!'

'Thank you Sur,' replied Beamish respectfully, bracing up, then turning smartly on his heel to walk back towards his barrack room. The CSM watched him go, shaking his head in total amazement ... *drill and weapons course ... hell will freeze over first!* Fortunately for the conspirators, a skin full of beer had dulled the CSM's senses.

... Mission accomplished!

Beamish was delighted, as was the rest of the stick who crowded around the youngster.

'Well done lad,' said Beamish, 'Come on, I'll buy you a beer!'

Chico smiled with satisfaction, he was being accepted into the stick ... *maybe they will stop calling me 'fresh poes'.*

Colour Barker was having a drink in the canteen, when he saw Beamish enter, he called out, 'Hey Beamish, you useless Pommie bastard, come here and buy me a beer.'

'Yes Colourr,' said Beamish with uncharacteristic enthusiasm.

Outside the CSM grabbed his towel and his toiletries and hit the showers. He was not in great shape, listing slightly to port as he stumbled along. Only one light bulb lit the showers, just enough to see. The CSM gave his hair a good scrub. He finished, towelled off, and went back to his room, fell on his bed, and was instantly asleep.

The party broke up early as the boys of 11 Troop were going on Fireforce alert at first light the next day.

Next morning, Colour Barker had the Troop up early, making sure that all the kit was in order and those on para-duty were matched up with harnesses, parachutes and helmets. After breakfast, Corporal Beamish sat his new recruit down, to give him the heads-up on what to expect on his first Fireforce action. He had insisted that both Kratzman and Le Beau listen as well. They had been designated as heli-borne for the time being, which Beamish was particularly relieved about. Jumping into a firefight with a new man, who had no previous experience, was always scary. The kid had only done training jumps, they bore no resemblance to jumping out of a buffeted Dak at 500ft with people shooting at you.

Chico was very excited about his first deployment, listening in rapt concentration to Beamish's Lancastrian explanation. Of course, Beamish had a feel for theatre; a captive audience was enough for him to exaggerate the briefing until it sounded more like Arnhem than an isolated skirmish against communist insurgents.

'Youu just stick close to me lad,' Beamish finished the briefing with the only, really useful, piece of advice.

'When we shoot, you shoot, remember your training on shooting into cover, the gooks will always be in cover,' was the advice advanced by Kratzman.

'Don't get ahead of us if we are sweeping forwarrd,' added Le Beau, who was not usually given to providing advice.

Chico the recruit nodded his head vigorously repeating every word of advice like a tape recorder.

'MEDEEEC!' A blood-curdling scream came from outside.

Beamish and his boys had forgotten about the lice medicine. They rushed to the door. The CSM, dressed only in his underpants, half his face covered in shaving cream, stood on the veranda in front of his room. His body was covered in what looked like a violent rash, streaked in bright, fire-engine red, vertical stripes. His hair also seemed to have changed colour, a kind of orangey-red.

One of the medics from the sick bay dashed across the quad with his bag. He arrived in front of the CSM out of breath, the look of surprise on his face showing his appreciation of the ferocious rash.

The loud distress call had attracted a small crowd. The boys watched as the concerned Medic looked all over the CSMs body, keeping his distance, taking great care not to touch in case the rash was contagious. The Medic had never seen such a rash. It seemed a little like zebra-stripes except the stripes were glowing red.

The crowd in front of the CSM's room grew as more men came to see what all the fuss was about. They all examined the rash from a safe distance. It looked frightening, *it must be life threatening*.

The medic stepped back, his hand on his chin, and like any self-respecting member of the medical profession, he said, 'Hmmmm.'

'What's wrong with me you bloody fool?' screamed the CSM, his distress making the veins stand out on the side of his neck.

The diagnosis was complex, the Medic walked around the CSM again, still keeping his distance. 'It looks like some sort of allergic reaction ... does it itch CSM?'

'That could be measles CSM,' chirped one of the troopers helpfully.

'No I think its chicken pox,' commented another.

'Does it burn CSM?' asked yet another.

'Fuck off ... all of you,' bellowed the CSM. His sudden illness had clearly not affected his voice, which was as loud and penetrating as ever.

Beamish and his stick did not dare leave the barrack room, they were all giggling like schoolgirls. Chico looked on with some distress. 'Is the CSM going to be okay?' he asked, starting to get really worried.

The spectacle was too much for Beamish to miss, he went out to join the growing crowd of onlookers.

The Medic, after much 'Hmming', saw a clue; the CSM's underpants also had a rash!

'Did you scratch yourself, Sir?' asked one of the troopers mischievously.

The man next to him began to giggle. More and more questions were fired off … to help with the diagnosis.

'Were you bitten by a spider, Sir?'

The conversation then unexpectedly changed tack.

'Who plays in red and white stripes?'

'Stoke City!' said Beamish emphatically; he knew for sure, Stoke-on-Trent was only 33 miles south of Manchester.

'Sheffield United also play in red stripes,' said another trooper.

The CSM blinked at the men debating in front of him.

'Yes, but Sheffield's stripes are lined in black, I don't see any black stripes on the CSM,' said Beamish, pointing at the stripes.

'Fuck off with this stripes business!' screamed the CSM, beside himself with frustration.

The Medic bent down to take a closer look at the underpants, which were tinged in red. The CSM backed away, 'What are looking at you poof?'

'I think its Mercurochrome, CSM,' stated the Medic, stepping back, crossing his arms.

'WHADAYOUMEAN?' screamed the CSM, rounding on the Medic.

The Medic had a bottle of Mercurochrome in his first aid kit. He took it out and slowly read out the label to the CSM, 'Topical antiseptic … When applied on a wound … the dark red colour stains the skin.' The Medic's explanation was given in a tone that would have been equally appropriate in a kindergarten.

'Why did you pour Mercurochrome all over yourself, Sir?' asked the Medic incredulously. It was a reasonable question to ask. As a topical antiseptic, it does not wash off easily, for obvious reasons.

'I didn't fucking pour anything on myself … ' bawled the CSM in front of, what was now, quite a large crowd, including a few officers.

Then there was a flickering of comprehension … the CSM disappeared back into his room. A howl of recognition came from inside, the CSM reappeared holding the offending shampoo bottle above his head. The outside of the bottle had changed colour to mostly red.

'How would mercurochrome get into your shampoo bottle, CSM?' asked the Medic, now completely perplexed.

Drawing himself up to his full height, the CSM let out a cry of anguish, pointing at the men standing in front of him, 'MUSTER PARAADE!'

The CSM dashed back into his room, pulled on a pair of shorts, grabbed his pace stick and was back out in the quad yelling, 'FORM UP … FORM UP' over and over again on the top of his voice.

Slowly, from all corners of the camp, men appeared, shuffling into three ranks. The trooper with the giggles had set off his mates who were standing in line, shaking in suppressed mirth.

Beamish and his stick took up position in the back row.

'PUT OUT YOUR HANDS,' screamed the CSM, and then, like Sherlock Holmes, he stalked down the ranks, his imitation Stoke City football shirt glistening in the morning light. Half his face was still covered in shaving cream, his pace-stick under his arm. He moved determinedly, bent over, studying each set of hands in turn.

Finally getting to the third rank, the CSM continued reviewing each set of hands, fixed in deep concentration. Slowly he made his way along the line towards Beamish, Le Beau, Kratzman and Chico at the end.

He stopped in front of Beamish. 'You know anything about this Pommie?' snarled the CSM, knowing this was just the sort of stunt Beamish would pull.

'Nooo Sur!' replied Beamish emphatically.

'Ahgg!' grunted the CSM, beginning to smell a rat. He leaned over, studying Beamish's hands even more closely. Using his pace-stick, he lifted each hand in turn up to the light.

'Permission to speak, Sur?' asked Beamish, in his British Army style.

'What is it Pommie?'

'If I may say so Sur ... red hair suits you.'

That was enough ... the ranks broke down into uncontrolled laughter, even the CSM was starting to see the funny side. A smile flickered across his face, immediately extinguished.

'SHUT UP!' screamed the CSM, whirling around, ' ... the next man to laugh gets a charge!'

It was the turn of the last man to be inspected. Chico kept his hands to his side.

The CSM stepped in front of Chico, 'Show me your hands fresh *poes*,' he said ominously.

The young man was blushing redder than the CSM's chest; he glanced at Beamish for support. No support was forthcoming ... Beamish was studying the horizon.

The young man's life flashed before him ... it was all over ... his existence on this earth was done. He lifted his hands ... they were a perfect match for the CSM's bright red stripes ...

The siren wailed across the runway.

The men of 3 Commando spontaneously broke ranks to collect their kit. Beamish and his stick turned to run off as well.

'You're not going anywhere, you little turd, you ...' interjected the CSM, leaning forward to grab the recruit.

'Sur, we have a callout. Can't this wait?' said Beamish, the same uncharacteristic smile on his face as from the night before. 'Come on Chico, let's go and slot a few gooks.'

Not waiting for an answer, the men doubled away to get their kit. Men were scattering in all directions. As Beamish ran towards the barrack room, he called across to Chico.

'Looks like you will be able to put your instructions into practice Chico,' said Beamish, slapping the youngster on the shoulder. The young soldier smiled back thinly ... the sudden realisation that his baptism of fire was upon him.

Stoke's *We'll Be with You*, rang in Beamish's ears, memories of his youth flashing back ... the words of the football song, strangely relevant to his current circumstances.

> *City, City , Tell the lads in red and white, everything will be alright .*
> *City, City , You're the pride of all of us today,*
> *We'll be with you, be with you, be with you ,*
> *Every step along the way .*
> *We'll be with you, be with you, be with you*
> *By your side we'll always stay ...*

The CSM stood alone in the quad, his pace-stick still in place, his red stripes glowing ... *nobody ever died from mercurochrome*. He strolled back to his room, giggling to himself ... *bloody Beamish ... I'll get the bastard!*

'We are Stop 2,' Beamish called to the others as they strapped on their webbing, then walked purposefully towards the chopper pad to get their briefing.

Cpt. Ian Liversedge was the designated Fireforce Commander as Maj. Tomlinson was away. He called the sticks together as the helicopters were being pushed out of their revetments behind him.

'Okay boys, a 6 Indep[115] stick has been ambushed on an OP in Matsai TTL here ...' he pointed to a position on the map about 62km north of Buffalo Range.

'They are on top of this *gomo* here ... and the Gooks have stonked them with 82mm mortars and then a band of about twenty have tried to sweep the 6 Indep guys off the top. From what we can gather, the 6 Indep stick is still on the top of the *gomo* but they have taken casualties ... they report one dead.'

'The weather is looking a bit dodgy Sir,' observed L.Cpl. Eric Parnell; a thick layer of low clouds could be seen to the north.

'Yes ...' agreed Liversedge, then turning to Barker he said, 'Colour Barker we may have to stand down the para-sticks, the clouds may be too low to get you boys in. If that's the case, standby for second wave if we need you.'

Liversedge then addressed the three G-car pilots and the K-car pilot listening to the briefing. They all checked the position of the contact on their maps and discussed their approach to the target. The well-practiced ritual of a Fireforce deployment began to unfold as it had hundreds of times before, the pilots and techs efficiently completed their pre-flight checks. After less than two minutes, the helicopters were starting up with blades gently turning.

2nd Lt Van Deventer was Stop 1, Beamish Stop 2 and Eric Parnell Stop 3.

The helicopters taxied out of the revetments onto the runway and took off to the north, estimated ETA to target, twenty-eight minutes. The Paradak turned onto the end of the runway and with engines droning loudly, lifted off into the approaching low cloud.

Matsai TTL was covered in high granite koppies, perfect for OPs. Good soils and rainfall meant that the area between the hills was a patchwork of

---

115 6 (Independent) Company, Rhodesian African Rifles.

cultivated land, cut by densely vegetated riverlines.

Beamish slipped the headset over his head and adjusted the arm on the mouthpiece. He sat in the middle seat, the chopper tech with the twin .303 Brownings on his left, Kratzman on his right at the door, Chico in front facing him with Le Beau at the front left hand door. The trees below were flashing past as they raced towards the target area at low level.

'62Alpha, Sunray, do you copy?' Liversedge, in the K-car, was calling the 6 Indep call-sign.

The radio hissed with static through Beamish's earphones, no response.

'62Alpha, 62Alpha, Sunray, do you copy?' more urgency in his voice.

Then a crackle could be heard on the radio as someone tried to transmit but was still out of range.

'Sunray, 62Alpha reading you twos ... Over,' the voice sounded thousands of miles away, like listening to the BBC on Short Wave.

'One minute out,' interjected the K-car pilot.

Beamish's stick (Stop 2) were third in line behind the K-car and the G-car carrying Van Deventer (Stop 1).

'Roger, 62Alpha on my call ... mark FLOT,' instructed Liversedge.

'62Alpha, copied.'

The clouds seemed to be getting lower and lower, a few spots of drizzle appeared on the perspex canopy.

'The weather is closing in fast,' commented the K-car pilot, as casually as asking for the salt and pepper.

The helicopter ahead of Beamish disappeared into the cloud, then reappeared again below them as the pilot dropped even lower. Beamish's helicopter followed it down; the taller trees now only a few feet below them.

Out in the distance a large granite koppie came into sight, its summit shrouded in cloud.

'That's our *gomo*,' said the K-car pilot.

'62Alpha, mark FLOT ... now!'

Beamish's helicopter lurched to the right as it followed the others around the hill, and then banked sharp left, the blades chopping the air in a clatter of noise. There was a pause, when time seemed to stand still, as everyone waited for something to happen.

The koppie was covered in trees interspersed with smooth granite rock, now shining slick from drizzle.

Liversedge barked over the radio, 'Roger, Gooks nine o'clock ... left, bank left, bank left now! K-car is firing!'

Dum-dida-dum, dum-dida-dum ... the loud thump of the 20mm cannon firing carried over the screaming helicopters.

Beamish felt a rush of adrenalin course through his body, a strangely warm feeling. Sweat ran down his back as he dabbed his forehead with the face-veil around his neck. The G-car gunner sent .303 rounds into the thick bush around the base of the koppie below.

The helicopter shuddered with the vibration of the guns firing, pushing Beamish to the edge of his seat. The familiar sick feeling entered the pit of his stomach, he glanced up to see Chico staring fixedly at him, his blue eyes wide, the terror of his first contact all over his blackened face.

'It'll be okay,' shouted Beamish reassuringly over the whine of the engine, '… you just stick with me.'

Chico nodded unblinking, not taking his eyes off Beamish … *time to pray.*

The choppertech was crouched over the guns firing into the bush below with deadly effect. Flashes of green and orange winked from the ground below, followed by the roar of incoming enemy ground fire. The perspex shattered just to the left of the pilot; Beamish felt the sting as a piece of plastic slammed into his arm like a hefty punch. Touching his hand to his arm, it came away sticky wet.

Chico's right cheek spilled blood from a cut as the perspex flew around the cockpit. The young man instinctively put his hand to his face, the look of complete disbelief on his face as it came away covered in blood.

Spinning his head left and right, Beamish checked the rest of his stick. Kratzman was staring at the bush below, his face a picture of concentration. Le Beau smiled and gave a thumbs up. Beamish looked down at his arm … *I'm okay and there is no time to worry about this … Chico's face … just a nick!*

The floor between Beamish's legs burst open like thin tinfoil, as rounds crashed through the aircraft. Green tracer whizzed around like wild hornets. Beamish ducked involuntarily, feeling vulnerable and stupid all at the same time. There was nowhere to take cover … *There is nowhere to hide.*

To his left, the tech was still firing. Despite the gaping hole in the canopy and jagged holes in the floor, the helicopter kept flying; there was no comment on the intercom from either the pilot or the tech.

Dum-dida-dum, dum-dida-dum … the K-car ahead fired again.

As the contact was taking place on a hill, there was only one place to drop the stops, right on top. But the top was covered in cloud.

'Yellow 3, drop your stick on my smoke,' K-car was calling Beamish's pilot.

'Yellow 3 copied,' the pilot turned to Beamish pointing vigorously towards the ground.

'I am going to have to drop you at the base of the *gomo*,' the pilot spoke to Beamish on the intercom, his voice calm and measured as if giving directions to a lost traveller.

As Beamish watched, Van Deventer was dropped at the base of the hill, his helicopter lifting off again, its nose bending forward as the pilot clawed for more altitude.

Then it was Beamish and Stop 2's turn.

The pilot banked tightly, G-forces pulling at the stomach, already alive with violent butterflies. Dropping fast, the nose lifted at the last second as the pilot flared for the landing and they were down.

'GO …GO, GO,' Beamish yelled. Out the four jumped, going to ground instantly. Bullets were flying at the helicopter as it lifted off again. Beamish looked around for any sign of Van Deventer as the next helicopter, carrying Eric Parnell, pulled in sharply to make its drop.

All the time the K-car circled above, watching.

Flashes erupted out of the bush to the east of the LZ. Kratzman had seen them and opened up with the MAG. Chico materialised next to Beamish diving down next to him shooting in the direction Kratzman indicated.

'Stop 2, move to your north fifty metres link up with Stop 1,' instructed Liversedge.

'Sunray, I am taking fire from my east, can you see the gooks, Over?'

'Roger, we have Gooks visual, standby,' the K-car pulled in at 300ft.

'K-car firing!' The 20mm once more spat out its deadly load effectively supressing the enemy fire.

Parnell dived into cover in rocks to Beamish's right. All three sticks were now on the ground. Beamish could see the faint wisp of red smoke about halfway up the hill.

The radio crackled to life, 'Contact, contact! Stop 1 we have contact!' Van Deventer had been sweeping up the hill towards where the 6 Indep men had been trapped. The CTs, making a break for it, ran into him.

Suddenly CTs were running all over the place. A billowing mushroom of white smoke erupted from the direction of the gunfire; Van Deventer had thrown a white phos grenade.

'UP ... lets go,' Beamish shouted pointing towards the white cloud. Parnell's stick joined him as they swept forward in support of Van Deventer.

'Stop 2, Stop 3 move one hundred metres north, the gooks are gapping it down the hill.' Liversedge, in the K-car, could see the CTs break off the action against Van Deventer.

Linking up with Van Deventer, Beamish's stop swept up towards the position of the 6 Indep call-sign.

It appeared that the 6 Indep men had been in an OP halfway up the hill. The top was a huge granite dome, that did not provide any place to hide, totally unsuitable for an OP. They had somehow been compromised with the result that the CTs had mortared them. The 6 Indep call-sign, which included a white national service officer with black RAR riflemen, had not been prepared for the ambush. The CTs had attempted to trap them by moving up from the base of the hill.

To get to the 6 Indep position the RLI men had to push through thick, almost impenetrable, thorny scrub. Thorns scraped their bare legs, tearing at their clothing. The faster they tried to move, the worse it became. Finally, covered in hundreds of bleeding scratches, they slid over a bare piece of rock to where the 6 Indep men had been hiding.

The sight that greeted them was appalling. A man lay on his face, a huge bloodstain on the back of his shirt. He was dead. Two others sat next to him; one bleeding from an arm, the other's head was a mass of matted blood.

'Where is your officer?' asked Beamish.

'Over there *Ishe*,' said one of the men pointing to his right.

They found the body, only twenty or so metres away in thick scrub. Beamish looked down at the man, bile filled his throat, forcing him to turn away. The dead man lay on his back; half his face looked like it had been smashed in with a rifle. Chico threw up.

Van Deventer called the K-car to arrange casevac. It was going to be a while before the G-cars would return from refuelling. Probably too late anyway, the clouds had closed in completely and it was starting to drizzle even harder.

'We are not going to get out before nightfall. This rain looks set in ... Corporal Beamish, we need to get to the base of this *gomo* in an ambush position in case those gooks come back tonight,' said Van Deventer, his voice cracked from the shock of seeing the man so brutally killed.

Working fast, the Medic sorted out the two wounded men, both could walk but the one had lost the sight in one eye and his head was covered in bloody bandages. The two dead soldiers were wrapped in their bivys to be carried off the hill.

The task of getting back down the hill was daunting. Van Deventer sent Beamish's stick with his two gunners down the hill first, to ensure they weren't ambushed. Beamish took the man with the wounded arm with them.

Drizzle had given way to pouring rain by the time Van Deventer and the rest of the RLI men got to the bottom of the hill. The men were exhausted from the effort of carrying the bodies, while the thorn scrub had torn holes in the plastic bivys, rendering them useless.

Time was of the essence in finding an ambush position. At the base of the hill a well-used path between neighbouring villages was covered by a low ridge providing a good vantage point.

'Okay boys, all-round defence covering that path. Now switch on! You saw what happened to these 6 Indep men. Beamish cover our entry point onto this ridge with one of your gunners,' instructed Van Deventer, clearly growing in confidence. 'If you are going to have something to eat, eat now, no cooking ... no smoking.'

Beamish positioned Kratzman and Le Beau covering the entry onto the ridge and an arc covering ninety degrees to the north. He positioned Chico and himself to cover the path, in line with Van Deventer and his stick. The men lay and waited as the late afternoon passed. The rain increased in intensity, soaking everyone to the bone.

Last light fell over the bush, the trees gradually losing their definition. The two wounded men had drips in them and the medic had given them morphine. The two bodies had been removed from the shredded bivys and wrapped in sleeping bags. Despite the rain and poor light, the white sand on the path below made a distinctive ribbon through the bush. After two hours, the rain began to abate, returning to a steady light drizzle. It was perfectly quiet except for the gentle drip of rain in the trees above. There was no breeze.

'Fooking army,' whispered Beamish to Le Beau next to him, rainwater dripping off his combat cap. Le Beau gave a low grunt of agreement. It was rare for the Fireforce not to recover to their base at night. The boys hated staying out at night. Most of Le Beau's camo-cream had come off, except for the cleft of his scar that remained a black line across his face, making him look even more sinister.

'You really are an ugly bastard!' hissed Beamish, his trademark scowl on his face.

Le Beau just smiled, he understood Arthur Beamish perfectly.

'I wonder if the CSM is still red?' commented Beamish with a stifled giggle. Le Beau and Kratzman grunted in agreement.

'How much shit am I in Corp?' asked Chico.

There was a faint movement in the bush down the ridge. Beamish blinked, thinking that the light was playing tricks with his eyes. He tapped Le Beau and pointed in the direction of the movement, straining his eyes in the half-light … *Bloody Hell! Gooks are approaching in extended line!*

Scrambling across on his belly, Beamish alerted Van Deventer who looked down the ridge in shocked surprise. There were sixteen or seventeen CTs, weapons at the ready, armed with AKs and one had an RPD machine gun. Directly in front of Beamish's line of sight, one of the CTs was carrying an RPG-7. Le Beau pulled the gun into his shoulder while Kratzman took careful aim. There was no time for preparation. Le Beau opening up with the MAG, the CT with the RPD spun to the ground from his double tap. Rounds sent up splatters of mud as they struck the sodden soil.

A hail of fire raced down the hill. The combined effect of three MAGs was too much for the CTs who broke and ran. The RPG man managed to point his weapon towards the top of the ridge and fire the projectile before he disappeared in a cloud of mud and spray.

Chico gave a soft sigh.

Sometimes things happen in war, inexplicable things, where the chances seem a million to one. The rocket grenade fired uphill struck short of where the RLI men lay. It exploded against rocks throwing a shower of jagged splinters and shrapnel up the hill. The tiniest piece of razor-sharp stone, no more than a few millimetres in diameter, but travelling at supersonic speed, struck Chico between the eyes, crashing through his skull into the frontal lobe of his brain. He died instantly. The young recruit had slumped forward as if he meant to put his head down to sleep for the night.

In the frenzy of battle, no one noticed Chico's passing.

> *… Death took him by the heart. There was a quaking*
> *Of the aborted life within him leaping…*
> *Then chest and sleepy arms once more fell slack.*
> *And soon the slow, stray blood came creeping*
> *From the intrusive lead, like ants on track*[116] *…*

Chico's stick had not had time to learn his proper first name, nobody even knew where he came from, or went to school, what he liked to eat, or the music he listened to.

He was gone before he could be a friend.

---

116 *Asleep*, Wilfred Owen (1893 – 1918), first stanza lines 5 to 9.

Contact – Matsai TTL

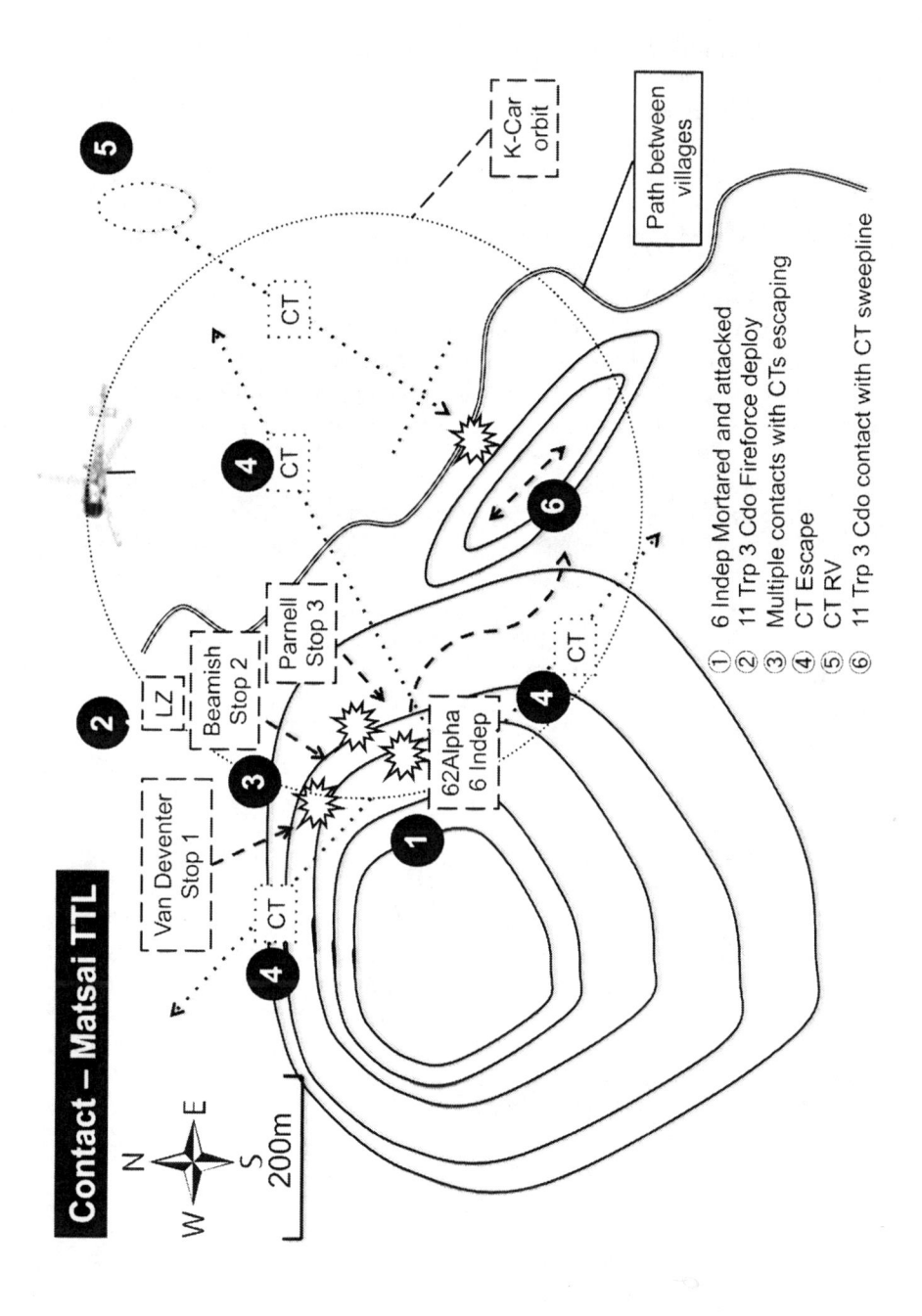

Van Deventer Stop 1
Beamish Stop 2
Parnell Stop 3
62Alpha 6 Indep
LZ
CT
K-Car orbit
Path between villages

① 6 Indep Mortared and attacked
② 11 Trp 3 Cdo Fireforce deploy
③ Multiple contacts with CTs escaping
④ CT Escape
⑤ CT RV
⑥ 11 Trp 3 Cdo contact with CT sweepline

200m

259

*

CIO HQ, Livingston Avenue, Salisbury

George Stanbridge was determined to follow through with Operation Hippo to take out the ZANLA leadership. He knew that the fall-out internationally from the assassinations would isolate the Smith regime to an even greater extent, but this was survival. The terrorist attack on the Chironga Mission northeast of Mount Darwin was another example of a terrorist atrocity that gained little traction with the foreign press. Stanbridge had visited the hospital to interview the nun who had survived the attack. She recounted the events of the terrorist attack with amazing calm. She said the terrorist leader twice shouted out the slogan 'missionaries are enemies of the people' before he gunned down the missionaries.

Stanbridge phoned the local MI6 officer attached to the British Consulate as soon as he returned to his office. It was an open secret in the intelligence community that both MI6 and the CIA operated active agents in Rhodesia. The MI6 man agreed to the meeting, but insisted that he was not prepared to be seen in public with a high-ranking Rhodesian official. The meeting was set in the car park of the Salisbury Koppie overlooking the city.

The hot afternoon temperature was starting to abate when Stanbridge parked his aged Peugeot 404 in the car park, not far from the water reservoir on the top of the koppie. It was a popular spot for youngsters to make out on warm summer evenings; Stanbridge recalled his own sexual adventures at 'the koppie' during University holidays from Cambridge. He did not have long to wait; the British representative arrived exactly on time in a new BMW 2500, a privilege of the diplomatic class.

'Hello George, I see you haven't got around to replacing that suit,' the man said in his usual friendly manner, he had been on the 'Rhodesian Desk' for a long time.

'Hello Nigel, I trust I find you in good spirits?' replied Stanbridge, he had always liked Nigel Pennefather, but trust him ... he most certainly did not.

'Shall we get down to business George? I have a game of tennis at Salisbury Sports Club at six,' said Pennefather with a smile. Clearly, the rigours of war-torn Rhodesia had not impinged on Pennefather's lifestyle.

'Quite, well, Nigel, this business of another massacre of missionaries has got our chaps in a real lather. That, with the attack on some of our key installations, is going to elicit a response from us.'

'What sort of response.'

'We are going to have another crack at the ZANLA leadership.'

'I know.'

'What do you mean you know?' asked Stanbridge, completely dumbfounded.

'Your mole in COMOPS has been busy, the Operation is called Hippo, I believe, and one of the targets is called Swallow. Now we know that Tongogara's nickname in ZANLA is *Nyenganyenga*, so it doesn't take a rocket scientist to figure out that Swallow must be him,' said Pennefather condescendingly, obviously very pleased with himself.

Not knowing what to say next, Stanbridge stood looking out over the city, his mind in turmoil.

'Come on George, you fellows are complete amateurs you know. I mean for goodness sake, using the English translation of the man's nickname! It's just as well for your lot that the other side are so disorganised and lacking in resources or they would give you a good walloping,' added Pennefather, shaking his head incredulously.

'Did you pick up another radio message?'

'Yes, we did George, and it has already been reacted upon by the opposition. They have started to increase the protection of their people.'

'Damn and blast!' Stanbridge was beside himself with frustration.

'I know what you want George. You are hoping that we will condone the assassination of the ZANLA leadership in favour of a more conciliatory opposition arriving at the negotiating table. Am I right?' The smile on Pennefather's face broadened into a knowing grin.

Stanbridge had been outflanked, 'Yes, that's exactly what I want. Can you arrange it?'

'Really George! This isn't bloody *Casablanca*; you chaps are running out of cards to play. I know that Jeremy Hughes-Hall has already warned you that we think that killing the leadership will just bring forward even more radical elements. The answer is emphatically NO! I am sorry George but your little white paradise north of the Limpopo is on borrowed time.'

Stanbridge had nothing more to offer. All of a sudden, he felt completely exhausted, isolated and alone.

Pennefather looked at the man who was obviously completely crestfallen, 'Look, George, we intercepted the radio message on the second, so you must know that the leak took place before that. I am sorry if I sound harsh ... and obviously we are in favour of a negotiated settlement without communist influence.' Then, in a vain attempt to make Stanbridge feel better, Pennefather added, '... by the way, good effort in dropping the five bridges on the road between Espungabera and Chimoio. We picked it up on satellite.'

George Stanbridge returned to his office in an absolute fit of rage. He called his team together and gave them a good dressing down. He called for every file concerning Operation Hippo, and ordered that no person was going home until they found a suspect. He picked up the phone to his opposite number at Special Branch and told him what he had discovered, being careful not to divulge the source. The policeman agreed to send over two of his best counter-intelligence investigators to help. The Special Branch man also said they needed to have a chat about something very important.

The files were piled up in the large meeting room and divided up amongst the staff. The names of all the people involved were written on the blackboard and lines drawn connecting each person to each file. Stanbridge had performed this task many times before to no avail ... *the answer had to be in the files – it had to be!*

Documents produced after the 2nd were ignored for the time being, the focus placed on meetings and notes that took place in the week before. Each document was laid out on the table in date and time order.

All operational orders were disseminated by way of a strictly managed distribution system where each hard copy could be tracked to the person receiving it. In this way, the CIO got copies of all the correspondence and orders that related to the projects they were working on. The names of the people in the meetings and on the distribution lists were familiar to all of the agents in the CIO. All had been the subject of numerous security checks, those with even the very slightest potential as a spy, had their phones tapped ... nothing had turned up.

Concentrating as hard as he could, Stanbridge studied each document, every line, and every notation.

'Who is FC?' Stanbridge asked, looking at the initials of a typist in the footer on the bottom of each page of one of the documents. Initially, nobody showed any recognition, there were at least fifteen typists in the pool at COMOPS. The typists sometimes worked in the Ministry of Defence pool when the pressure was on. All had security clearances if they worked on secret documents.

'Have we got a list of the typists and secretaries at COMOPS and MOD?'

'Yes, I have it somewhere in my office ... I will fetch it.' The staffer left the room to look for the list. He returned a short time later with a list of twenty names on it.

'We have screened everyone on this list,' the man said handing it to Stanbridge.

Scanning the list, Stanbridge found the only initials FC, Faye Chan!

'When did we last review the security status of these people?' demanded Stanbridge, pointing to the list.

'Frankly, not for a while, probably twelve months or more,' was the reply.

'Is the Operation Wedza file on the desk somewhere?' Stanbridge stood up to look for the file. After a short period of rummaging through the piles of paper he found the file and opened it, scanning the contents, running his finger down each page. The initials jumped off the pages, the sudden realisation hitting him straight between the eyes.

Dropping the file on the desk, Stanbridge looked up at the people around the table. A silence fell over the room as the staff studied his expression, trying to interpret what it was that had obviously knocked Stanbridge for six.

Leaning over, placing his hands on the table, a quiet, steely determination entered his voice, 'People, I want you to go through every file in this office for the past year and correlate every document with the typist. Use some sort of colour code to identify each typist concerned.'

The mole may have been hiding in plain sight!

18

Selous Scout HQ, Andre Rabie Barracks, Inkomo, north west of Salisbury

Sgt. Cephas Ngwenya had no sooner reported to the duty officer at Andre Rabie Barracks on returning from R&R, than he was summoned to a meeting in the Ops Room. He changed into his camo-uniform and marched smartly to the Ops Room, greeted by the RSM on his way. The Selous Scouts had two RSMs one black and one white. The purpose was to ensure the needs of all the men were adequately attended to, as befitting their respective cultures and background.

'I am sorry to hear of the death of your brother, Cephas,' said RSM Chikaka respectfully in seShona. He was old school, ex-RAR, a deeply compassionate man.

'Thank you, Sir. I just need to kill more *makandanga*, Sir,' replied Ngwenya.

'I hear you brought a young terr with you who looks like being a star recruit.'

'Yes, Sir, I picked him up in a contact, he is ZANLA and he seems only too pleased to change sides.'

'Well done Cephas, I am glad that you are fully recovered from your wounds. It looks like another big Op is on, good luck.'

Cephas braced up as was customary in addressing a warrant officer and knocked on the door of the Ops Room. Inside were the same men he had worked with on the last Op, Seals, Kumpher and Schultz, plus three other men that Ngwenya did not know. The men exchanged greetings, Schultz seemed genuinely very pleased to see him.

Not being hot on pleasantries, Schultz got straight to the point.

'Welcome back Cephas ... we are going after Tongogara and the ZANLA leadership ... Again!' stated Schultz. He emphasised the word 'again', as this would be the third attempt. Ngwenya did not make comment, he just nodded his head and waited for Schultz to continue.

'This is a complex mission because we have to be in three places at the same time,' Schultz was all business, not being a man given to levity, plus the mission was such that survival was questionable. 'Ngwenya will work with Seals, Kumpher and myself on the target in Aldia de Barragem, while you men will focus on the target at Mapai. We are getting the services of 3 Commando RLI and elements of Support Commando to help us cover the approach roads and, if necessary, ambush any FRELIMO response.'

Schultz waited for the information to sink in before he continued.

'We will also use a Scout Flying Column, as we have done before, on the road between Malvernia and Barragem. Their mission will be to support the RLI if they get into shit but also to extract us if the air support is unavailable for any reason.'

'How are we going to get in, Sir?' asked Kumpher.

'Because of the importance of surprise, the hit teams will HALO jump in on the twenty-third. The Flying Column will use the same entry route we used last time, north of Vila Salazar, on the twenty-forth. The RLI will also be dropped by Dak on the twenty-third, in two groups, one north of Jorge do Limpopo, and one south of Jorge do Limpopo at Mabalane. Our alternative targets for the Column are the newly reinforced ZANLA camp at Mapai, and the FRELIMO garrisons at Chicualacuala and Malvernia ... these last two are primarily about diversion.'

'What about the FRELIMO tanks at Barragem?' asked Seals.

'We are going in to kill one man. Fast in ... fast out. There will not be a ground attack on the FRELIMO garrison at Barragem, but the Air Force will put in a few strikes if we need support. The tanks should not be a factor.'

'How are we getting out Sir?' asked Kumpher, the question on everyone's lips.

'There will be helicopter LZs designated for both the hit teams within ten clicks of the target. If we miss either RV, then the alterative will be the Flying Column on the road between Barragem and Malvernia. That road is two hundred and eighty two kilometres long, basically north-south ... we should be able to find it.' That was the best attempt by Schultz at flippancy. 'As soon as we are out, the Flying Column will withdraw, taking the RLI with them.'

The meeting continued for another two hours. The teams then broke up to discuss their respective elements of the plan. Rehearsals were set for the whole of the following week.

*

3 Commando RLI, Fireforce Base, Buffalo Range Forward Airfield (FAF 7), southeast Rhodesia

The death of Chico on his first contact, hit Arthur Beamish hard. He took it deeply personally that the young man died in such nonsensical circumstances. The ridgeline was dead ground for someone shooting from below and yet shrapnel had somehow hit Chico. Everyone agreed that the only way he could have been hit was some sort of ricochet; it was the worst possible luck. The wound in his forehead was tiny, about the size of a five-cent piece. A thin trickle of blood dribbled from the hole in his head. The young man looked like he was asleep, his face relaxed, as if without a care in the world.

The Commando had been severely impacted with casualties in the past year. Beamish estimated that nearly 30% of the strength had been either killed or wounded and experienced replacements were rare.

Penga Marais was due back any day, but Beamish was worried about his state of mind. It was obvious to everyone when they had visited Penga at the McIntyre house that he was in pretty awful psychological shape. There was no doubt that Marais was far from over the death of Jock. Beamish was of the opinion that Penga staying with Lily while on R&R was making things worse, not better. Lily had written Beamish a long letter explaining her feelings about

'Dudley', as she called him, and she was clearly very worried herself. What was even more alarming was that Lily said she had started dating a lawyer in the city. She hadn't told Dudley because she feared his reaction. Beamish had shown the letter to Kratzman and Le Beau and they both commented on how potentially dangerous it would be if Penga couldn't get his head back in the game straight away. The situation was such that Beamish even discussed reporting the matter to the CSM or Captain Liversedge. It was pointless talking to Colour Barker; he disliked Penga intensely, so all he would do is bully the kid even more. Van Deventer was way too inexperienced to grasp the difficult situation and would probably find a way of transferring Penga out of his troop. Penga's own poor disciplinary record and his two trips to DB, made his position even more tenuous with the senior leadership in the Commando. The end result was that the three members of call-sign 31Charlie would have to deal with the problem themselves.

The bad weather reduced the number of Fireforce callouts for a week and the men were able to relax and do a bit of housekeeping around the camp. Beamish's stick was stood down anyway because there were only three of them. What Beamish did find interesting was the fact that his two MAG gunners were in great demand. The other stick commanders saw the opportunity to co-opt the two spare gunners to add firepower to their sticks. Both went out on callouts with 12 Troop who were now on the 'immediate' standby roster.

Lying on his bed trying to catch up on some sleep, Beamish felt a hard tug on his foot.

'Beamish you lazy bastard, Captain Liversedge wants to see you,' laughed the duty NCO.

'Fook'n hell!'

Being summonsed by an officer could never possibly be a good thing. Beamish just hated officers, not because of who they were, some of them were quite pleasant, it was more their status that irked him, having to bow and scrape.

Pulling on a clean t-shirt, Beamish headed off across the quad to Liversedge's office.

'Ah, Beamish, please sit down, I need some help with something,' Liversedge began encouragingly, always aware of Beamish's intransigence.

Beamish sat down on the chair, highly uncomfortable in the presence of the Captain. It never ceased to amaze him that the officers hardly ever commented on the death of one of the men. They seemed to ignore the whole episode, cut it out of their collective memory like it never happened … *Ah, well, what could I possibly help the Captain with?*

'This is still under wraps, but we have been selected for another external, it will involve both 11 and 12 Troops. Both Troops will be dropped in by Dak. I can't tell you when, but it will be soon. What I would like you to do is make a list of our inventory for the kit I have listed on this sheet,' continued Liversedge, in his normal business-like fashion.

'How long will we be in for Sur?' Beamish asked in a vain attempt to sound enthusiastic.

'I am told no more than two days, three days is the worst case,' smiled Liversedge. He really did like Beamish, despite his taciturn attitude.

Casting his eye down the list, Beamish felt a tight grip on his gut.

'There are TM46 landmines on this list Sur, and claymores, and plastic explosive.'

'Yes, how good is that, we may get to blow a few things up.'

'There are tanks on the other side Sur. How will we deal with them?'

'Good question Beamish. Support Commando are sending us a few sticks with 88mm anti-tank rockets. They are also going to refresh our memories on landmine laying and booby traps,' explained Liversedge buoyantly.

Beamish considered asking a few more questions but decided against it, they were going into Porkers[117] ... and that was that.

Walking out into the hot midday sun, Beamish decided to delay his task for a few hours, deciding instead to have a natter to Eric Parnell. Eric would be very interested in his news. As he walked past the Orderly Room, out walked Penga Marais, neatly dressed in beret and stable belt.

'Penga you useless bastard, you have decided to come back to the war,' shouted Beamish with obvious delight at seeing the young man.

'Hey Corp, I hear you couldn't hang on to my replacement,' replied Penga as they shook hands.

'Hit in the head, there was nothing anyone could do. The gooks 'bushed some NS call-sign from six Indep, fucked them up good and proper.'

'Well I'm back Corp, ready to slot a few more floppies and to look after you three old farts,' replied Penga smiling, his pleasure at seeing his Pom corporal all over his face.

'You feeling okay, Penga?' asked Beamish disarmingly.

'I'm fine. Sometimes I get a headache but nothing that Disprin can't fix. Lily says to say hello. Where are Le Beau and the Yank?'

'They are around someplace, probably eating. Put your kit down and come to the canteen.'

The two men parted. Beamish watched the younger man hoist his sausage bag over his shoulder and walk towards their barrack room. He seemed to be back to normal, no limp or sign of discomfort in his walk. It was what was going on inside his head, that worried Beamish.

The siren sounded ... something impossible to get used to, making the heart miss a beat. Beamish watched the 12 Troop men rush towards the helicopters ... relieved it wasn't his turn.

*

CIO HQ, Livingston Avenue, Salisbury

It had occurred to George Stanbridge that the attractive Asian secretary Faye Chan was a potential high-risk suspect. He had studied every file that she had been involved with, every memo she had typed, there was a very

---
117 Rhodesian slang, Mozambique.

strong correlation with the leaks picked up by his own informers within ZANLA senior ranks. The more recent top-secret Operation Wedza had been compromised long before the Selous Scouts were dropped. The correlation was very strong, but there were at least three other people that had the same connection to the missions concerned. What to do with this information was now the subject that occupied Stanbridge's mind. He deliberately did not inform his staff or his superiors of his suspicions, not until he had absolute proof.

He decided that instituting another security check of the support staff at COMOPS and MOD would potentially alert Chan and she could go to ground. The best way to trap her was to feed her some bogus intelligence and wait for it to be reported on the other side. Another option was to try to recruit her as a double agent. The risk in all of this was leaving her in position, undisturbed. There was no way of knowing how much damage she had done or was about to do. She could likely compromise any number of other operations in the works. Thankfully, the very detailed planning for the operations took place within the Selous Scouts, SAS and RLI units themselves. COMOPS was, however, copied on the plans they produced. Chan could have worked out how to access these files within the COMOPS system. The threat was very high indeed.

The Chief Superintendent from Special Branch was waiting outside his office. He was not in uniform.

'Jim, come in will you,' said Stanbridge in his usual friendly manner. 'What can I do for you?'

'George, I'm not quite sure where to begin, we have been running an operation over the past three years which we have kept very close to the chest,' replied Jim Winston, the man in charge of the SB 'Terrorist Desk'.

'Yes? ...' said Stanbridge, the hair standing up on the back of his neck.

'Well, you see George, we have a man in position next to Tongogara.'

'You have what?'

'It's a long story ... but we have a SB man in charge of Tongogara's bodyguard, he's been in this position for most of the past two years.'

'I don't believe it ...' moaned Stanbridge with a sigh, sitting back in his chair, running his hands through his thinning hair in complete shock and disbelief.

'Why have you taken so long to come forward with this Jim?' asked Stanbridge, sitting forward again, crouching over his desk, as if he was about to leap over and take the man by the neck.

'To be brutally honest, our top brass don't trust you George, or your boss, or any of your other staff for that matter,' replied Winston calmly. 'Your place leaks like a sieve, even worse than COMOPS. We felt that if we came forward it would only be a matter of time before our man got burnt.'

'That's total rubbish and you know it Jim,' snapped Stanbridge.

'Is it really George? Have a look at these,' said Winston, still in complete control. He took out an envelope from his brief case and placed a set of photographs on the desk. They showed Stanbridge talking to Nigel

Pennefather of MI6, plus the local CIA man. There was even one of him standing on the steps of the East India Club in London with Jeremy Hughes-Hall.

'These meetings were all sanctioned and reported on,' hissed Stanbridge, now visibly upset.

'Be that as it may George, but you can see from our point of view, why we have been so hesitant,' replied Winston, his face a picture of concentration.

'So where does that leave us, Jim?'

'Well, we have taken the view that if we can pull off these assassinations then, if our man is compromised in the process, it wouldn't matter too much. Plus, you are now the only person outside of my office who knows about this. If our man gets burnt we know the leak is you George,' said Winston, with a deadpan face, the classic experienced policeman.

'If it all goes to hell in a hand basket, can your man be relied upon to pull the trigger?' asked Stanbridge, his voice now in a whisper, with the enormity of the prospect.

'Unquestionably ...' answered Winston firmly, 'but the order would have to come from us, we have a set of codes and procedures in place.'

'Bloody hell!'

The shock of the disclosure from SB hit George Stanbridge hard. The fact that SB had been keeping such a close eye on him was disturbing. He felt cheated and violated. Stanbridge knew he needed a win, and he needed it soon ... *maybe exposing and turning Faye Chan is part of my solution.*

Feeling desperate, Stanbridge decided to do some old-fashioned detective work. He took himself off to Milton Buildings on the pretext of updating the staff on the latest intelligence. He was familiar with the layout of the typing pool and walked past, noting the position of each of the typists. Scanning the women he picked up the long dark hair of Faye Chan as she concentrated hard on the work she was doing. Stanbridge could see that she was typing up some shorthand notes. The speed of her fingers over the keys of the typewriter was mesmerising. Her eyes were fixed on the notes next to her, not looking at the typewriter keys, right hand flashing to slide across the return for each new line. The new-fangled Olivetti electric typewriters were still rare in Rhodesia.

Waiting for the workday to end, Stanbridge followed Faye Chan's bus on the way home to her house in Ridgeview. She got off the bus and walked the three blocks to her house in Anson Road. Stanbridge had her address on file so he knew where the house was, having driven past it a few times already. Parking under some large trees, he sat and waited.

Consistent with Faye's evening routine, it was not long before she emerged with the Labrador on her walk. She greeted a neighbour at the gate and had a short chat. Not sure what to do next, Stanbridge waited for her to turn the corner into Avro Road before starting the engine and slowly driving down the road. By the time he reached the corner, Faye had crossed over the road and the dog was running about in the bush on the other side. She was throwing a tennis ball and the dog was hunting for it in the long grass. Driving past, Stanbridge turned into Hurstview Road with the Sunshine Sports Club on the right. He drove past the clubhouse until he reached the intersection with Sunshine Road. He pulled off the road again under some trees. Climbing out of the car, he walked to the edge of the cricket ground, as if to watch the afternoon cricket training session taking place on the main oval. He then walked back to the corner to see Faye turn into Hurstview Road about 400m away.

Stepping behind some trees, Stanbridge watched her approach. He had missed her duck off the road to place the stick in the fork of the tree. Entering the grounds of the sports club, she walked to the cricket oval where the dog raced off to chase a cricket ball. There was much laughter as the cricketers chased after the dog to get the ball back. From what Stanbridge could see, this was all part of the evening ritual. The cricketers knew both Faye and the dog and it was all great fun. Stanbridge, momentarily distracted by watching the antics on the field, lost sight of Faye. He moved out from under the trees, looking expectantly left and right. She was nowhere to be seen. Frustrated with himself, he trotted to the edge of the cricket field.

'Hello Mr Stanbridge' said Faye, stepping out from behind a tree. She smiled up into his face. 'What brings you to this part of town?'

'My goodness ... what a small world! Forgive me, your name ...'

'Faye, Faye Chan, I work at COMOPS.'

'Yes, of course, hello Faye ... I am one of the Mashonaland cricket selectors and I was kind of spying on this team. They have a good opening bowler we are looking at. Mums the word hey?' said Stanbridge winking, touching his forefinger to his nose in that very English conspiratorial manner.

'I saw you in the office this afternoon,' stated Faye, still watching his face. Her deep brown eyes seemed to be looking straight through him.

'Yes ... well, you know, we live in busy times,' he replied now starting to feel awkward.

'Ah well, I must get on. If I don't take that silly dog home there won't be any more bowling this afternoon,' she laughed, touching Stanbridge lightly on the arm. Her laugh was open and infectious. Stanbridge found himself quite taken in, now a little lost for words. She was truly magnificently attractive.

She offered her hand which Stanbridge took, surprised at the firmness of her grip.

'Happy spying ... Mr Stanbridge,' she added, still smiling broadly.

Calling the dog to heel, she slipped on the leash and they made their way off the field heading for home. She stopped a short way off, turned and waved. Stanbridge returned the wave, now feeling totally ridiculous ... *happy spying!*

As Faye walked out of the main gate back into Hurstview Road, the shock of her meeting fully sunk in. She felt as if she was going to burst into tears, wanting to run as fast as she could. Suddenly yearned to speak to Rugare, she knew that was impossible. If she had been compromised ... she could lead her enemies to the man she loved ...

A feeling of desperation passed over her, a feeling of complete panic she had never felt before ... *even with my meagre knowledge of cricket, the opening bowlers for the first team at Sunrise could not bowl themselves out of a wet paper bag!*

19

New Sarum Air Force Base, Salisbury

The inside of the hanger was enormous. All the aircraft that would normally be inside the hanger were parked in neat lines on the hardstanding outside. Sets of rugby spectator stands had been built, covering three sides of a square. In the middle of the square was a gigantic map of the southern half of Mozambique, next to it were papier-mâché models of three small towns. Various lines were marked in red tape and large black dotted lines marked boundaries with equally large black arrows marking directions. On the fourth side of the square was a stage that sat about a metre above floor level. On the stage were desks and chairs running the full length. Stage lights had been set up, aimed at the map and models on the floor.

11 and 12 Troops from 3 Commando had been flown up from Buffalo Range that morning, and after a meal in the air force canteen, they were marched into the hanger where the doors were closed. MPs patrolled the outside of the hanger and no one was allowed in or out. Beamish and his stick, together with the rest of the available men from 11 and 12 Troops were placed on the centre stand facing the stage. The map in front of them was orientated to the north so the layout of Mozambique was clear to see. On their right was a large group of Selous Scouts, more than half of whom were black. On their left were elements of Support Commando as well as all the Air Force personnel involved in the operation.

The atmosphere in the hanger was charged with excitement. Men were talking loudly to each other and there was pointing and discussion around the map and models built in front of them. Groups of officers stood on the stage and Captain Liversedge stood talking to 2nd Lt Van Deventer and Major Tomlinson at the foot of the rugby stand.

'Jeezz Corp, this looks big,' said Penga Marais who was sitting next to Beamish with Kratzman on his right. Le Beau was to Beamish's left.

'Looks like it Penga,' replied Beamish not quite sure what to say.

'We look like we are invading Mozambique, half the bloody army is here, check out all the brass on the stage,' added Penga awed by the occasion. There were majors, colonels and at least one brigadier standing on the stage shuffling files full of paper.

'This is what it looked like when we went into Chimoio the first time,' commented Beamish, trying to be nonchalant.

'Waal, I reckon we are going to spoil somebody's day,' commented Kratzman in his usual understated way. Le Beau sat silently, happy to watch the situation unfolding, listening to Penga jabber away.

Eventually the briefing was called to order and a brigadier stood up to welcome the men. He made a brief introduction that covered the broad parameters of the mission, which to Beamish's mind sounded more like a giant ambush. The Brigadier then handed over to a Selous Scout Captain who continued with the detailed briefing.

The briefing began with a discussion of the mission for the Selous Scout Flying Column of twelve vehicles including two Eland 90[118] armoured cars. They were to enter Mozambique north of Vila Salazar in order to bypass Malvernia and then make their way south to a point north of Jorge do Limpopo. 12 Troop had to be dropped ahead of the column in order to ambush any FRELIMO moving north on the main road. Eventually the briefing came around to 11 Troop who were to be dropped at a point ten kilometres south of the village of Mabalane, some 145km south of Jorge do Limpopo on the same road. Their mission was to ambush the road using command detonated landmines, claymores and RPGs. They had to stop any FRELIMO movement on the road north or south. Beamish could not be sure, as the briefing went on for a long time, but it sounded like some Selous Scouts and Support Commando were to be attached to their group.

The Selous Scout Captain was thorough and professional; Beamish was impressed by the man. He had not had much to do with Selous Scouts himself, other than listening to them calling Fireforce onto targets. The Captain moved confidently around the map and the models, using a snooker cue as a pointer, addressing each group on the stands directly by pointing out their various tasks and positions. Enemy strong-points were carefully pointed out together with their strengths and equipment.

As the briefing continued, Beamish took the opportunity to study the Selous Scouts on the neighbouring stand. The black soldiers sat perfectly still, deep in concentration, their faces impassive. It had always been a concern to Beamish that his unit, the RLI, had consistently refused to admit black soldiers; it seemed such an obvious contradiction. A war in Africa, where people with the knowledge and understanding of the local population were deliberately excluded, seemed ridiculous. He had only ever raised the matter once, as a newly recruited British volunteer in Training Troop. He had been given a stern talking to by the CSM at the time. As far as he could determine, the reasons, as explained to him by others, were that the black troops could not be trusted, that they may change sides, that they were shaky in battle, and that they lacked discipline and aggression. All these reasons seemed total bullshit when he looked across at these men of the Selous Scouts ... *weren't there three whole battalions of black troops in the RAR, plus six Independent Companies! ... How did the saying go? ... Ours is not to reason why, ours is but to do and die ...*

Eventually the briefing ended and the Selous Scout Captain finished with a sincere 'Good Luck' that Beamish felt was a nice touch. The RLI men were loaded back onto trucks and driven back to Cranborne Barracks, escorted by local police and MPs. The men were warned that they were confined to barracks and that no phone calls could be made.

---

118 Eland 90s had been purchased from South Africa and were based on the French Panhard AML 60-7.

Operation Hippo (Mozambique)

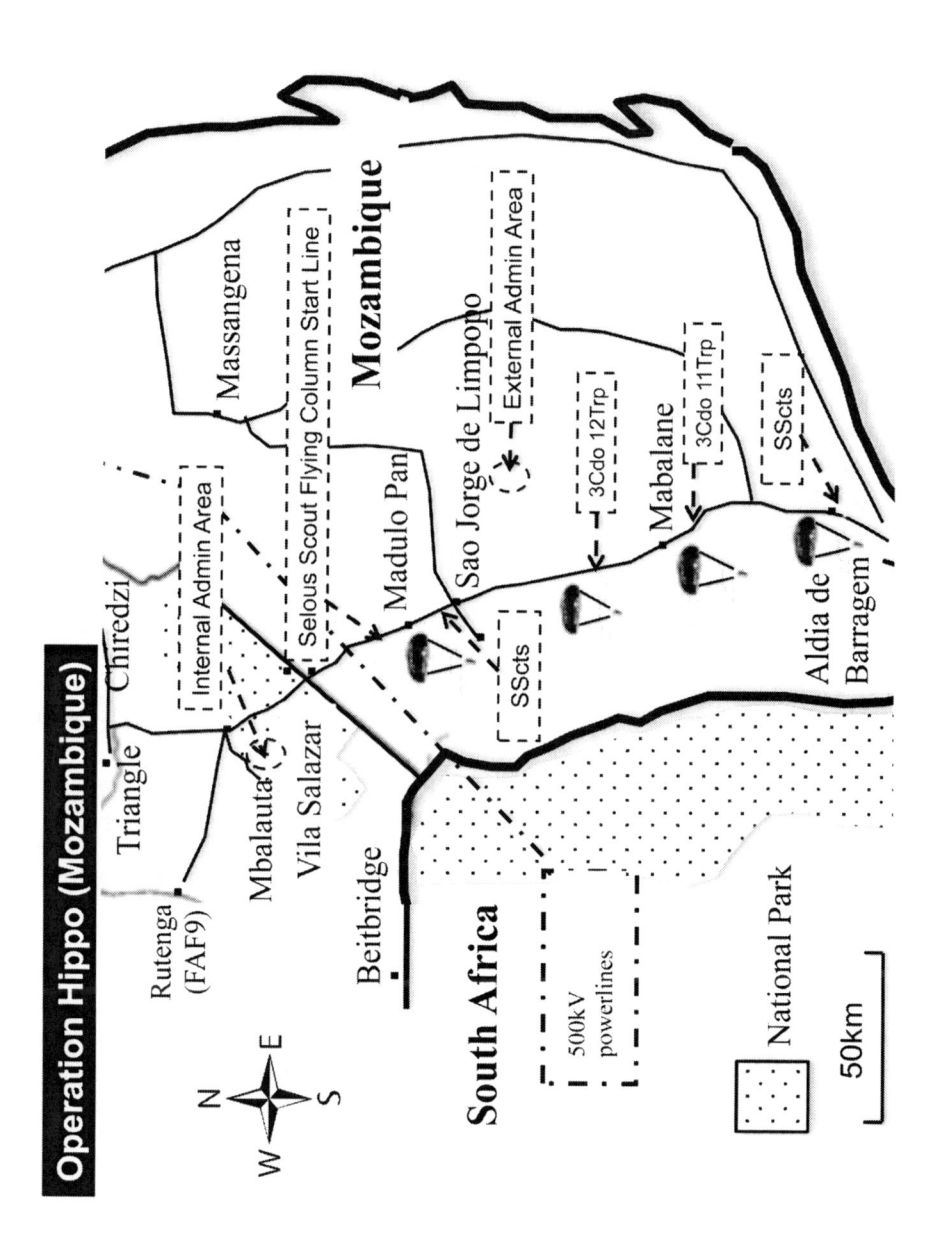

The day after the briefing at New Sarum was frenetically busy as kit was issued including 60mm mortars, 88mm rocket launchers, landmines, claymores and thousands of rounds of ammunition. All of it had to be loaded into CSPEP containers that ended up ridiculously heavy. Colour Barker confirmed the allocation of men to sticks and they were introduced to the eight Support Commando men who would accompany them. Beamish only knew one of them, Sgt Bonner, who had been on para-course with him.

Beamish studied his orders and the notes he had taken in the briefing, checking off all the items on his list; 1× sosegen (pentazocine), 1× morphine, 1× saline drip, blood group written on shirt collar, 3× spare batteries, heliograph, compass, maps, 4× water bottles, all to wear combat caps with day-glo panel, NO blacking up, length of para-cord per man for prisoners, mini-flares and codes. He made sure that his stick had taken care of their kit lists.

That night, as the sun began to set, they were driven back to New Sarum where they collected their parachutes and were then flown back to Buffalo Range. Buffalo Range had been designated as the main forward base for the mission with an internal admin (refuelling/resupply base) at Mbalauta with an external admin base some 50km to the east of Jorge do Limpopo inside Mozambique.

Tension filled the air once the Daks were unloaded and the kit was laid out on the apron. Men stood around in groups smoking and chatting nervously. Four Dakotas stood silhouetted against the stars, plus two K-cars, six G-cars and two Lynx. Beamish could have sworn he heard an aircraft pass over at very high altitude at nine that evening.

It was impossible to sleep, nerves and stifling hot. The Lowveld before the rains was insufferably hot and Beamish and his men discussed how much water would be needed over three days with no chance of resupply. Extra water was loaded into CSPEP containers but strict water discipline was going to be important. Fortunately, the walk from the drop point to the ambush site on the road was no more than ten kilometres ... *unless the Blue Jobs fook up their navigation!*

The risks associated with a night drop with heavy equipment were considerable. To mitigate this, the decision had been taken to drop at first light. The area designated for 11 Troop to be dropped in was mostly uninhabited, so the chance of being seen were relatively low. They were to be uplifted by the Flying Column when their mission was over. Beamish had deep reservations ... *what happened if they didn't make it through! 145km was a long way, with thousands of Freds*[119] *and ZANLA Gooks in between!*

'Where is Penga?' asked Beamish to Le Beau standing next to him having a smoke.

'A letter came from Lily and he asked the Yank to read it to him,' replied

---

119 Rhodesian slang, FRELIMO.

Le Beau distantly.

'Shit, why didn't you tell me, you bloody fool!' exclaimed Beamish, taking off for the barrack room. Le Beau, a little perplexed, watched Beamish run off, deciding to follow to see what all the fuss was about.

Arriving at the barrack room out of breath, Beamish saw Kratzman sitting on Penga's trunk at the base of his bed, the letter in his hand. Penga was lying on the bed, his pillow over his face.

As Beamish walked down between the rows of beds, Kratzman looked up, the expression on his face told it all.

'What did she say?'

'There's a whole lot of family stuff, but in the last paragraph ...'

'Give me the bloody thing,' demanded Beamish, snatching the letter out of Kratzman's hand. He scanned down the two pages to the last paragraph.

> ... *Dudley, you should not be upset but I thought you should know that I am seeing a man that I met when I was sorting out Jock's will. He is very nice and very gentle, he is a widower, his wife died of cancer. It is nothing serious but I do enjoy his company. I want you to know that you will always be welcome in our house. Nothing has changed ...*

'Penga look at me,' demanded Beamish.

'Noo ... she's got a boyfriend,' moaned Penga from under the pillow. He was clearly crying, not wanting the other men to see.

Le Beau took the letter from Beamish to read it.

'Come on Penga, its not a big deal,' said Kratzman gently.

'She is a young woman Penga. She was always going to find someone else. She is a good looking woman,' said Le Beau encouragingly, his French accent emphasising 'womaan'.

'She says nothing has changed,' added Kratzman helpfully.

'Everything has changed!' screamed Penga, throwing the pillow away, his eyes red and swollen.

'Look Penga, we have got a massive op tomorrow, let's all get some sleep and we can deal with this when we get back. It just a letter,' said Beamish trying to snap Penga out of it.

'Corp, what's going to happen to me? I haven't got any family. What if her new bloke doesn't like me?' pleaded Penga sitting up on his bed, his distress was palpable.

'That's rubbish Penga, she says clearly that you will always be welcome in her house.'

'What's going on in here?' shouted a voice from the door.

They all turned to see Colour Barker walking purposely down the barrack room.

'Why aren't you men asleep? You want to get your arses shot off tomorrow?' demanded Barker. 'What's wrong with you Penga, you look like shit.'

'It's okay Colour,' said Beamish, 'just a bit of news from home.'

'What news?' commanded Barker. Seeing the letter in Le Beau's hand, he snatched it away, scanning the pages.

'So Lily has found a new bloke. That's you fucked Penga, you mad little bastard,' smiled Barker.

A cloud passed over Penga's face. They had all seen it before. He stood up off his bed. Le Beau stepped in front of him.

'Come Penga, lets go and have a walk, to clear our heads before tomorrow,' said Le Beau, putting his arm around the young man's shaking shoulders.

'I think that's enough Colour,' said Beamish positioning himself in front of Barker. Yank Kratzman stood up as well, his hands on his hips just behind Beamish.

'What's this, a little mutiny have we?'

'Noo Colour, but Penga is a bit upset and you should leave him aloone,' whispered Beamish with a threatening tone that nobody had heard before, his fists were clenched white.

Barker's eyes flicked from man to man, summing up the situation. 'Fuck you Beamish!' he said crunching up the letter and throwing it on the floor.

Penga leapt from behind Le Beau, throwing himself at Barker's throat. His movement was like lightning, way too fast for Le Beau and Beamish to react. Barker threw up his arms to prevent the smaller man getting to him, but Penga had his hands around his neck, dropping his weight at the same time, forcing Barker to topple forward. As Barker fell forward, he cracked his head on the side of one of the steel bunk beds, opening up a deep cut. Blood spurted over Penga's hands but he held on with all his strength. Penga, with surprising strength, flipped the much larger man over onto his back, straddling him, gripping his throat. Barker croaked for air as Penga pushed his thumbs into his larynx.

'Pengaa!' shouted Beamish, grabbing Penga's collar, trying to pull him away. Le Beau took a grip of his arms to try and separate them from Barker's neck. Penga's grip was like a vice. All his pent up emotion, frustration and fear were now focused at one point, Barker's neck. There was no doubt that he meant to kill him. It was like trying to separate a bull terrier from its victim. Kratzman, in desperation, lifted Penga by the legs, lifting him, pulling him away. The combination of the strength of the three men eventually broke Penga's grip. Kratzman held him in a bear hug as the young man struggled to free himself, Penga's eyes wild, like a frenzied animal. The sound that came from his lips sounded like a deep-throated growl, his furious eyes not leaving Barker lying prostrate on the barrack room floor. Lifting Penga up off his feet, the giant carried him out of the barrack room.

Barker lay on the floor, blood all over his face, spreading on the floor, as he writhed about holding his throat in pain. Laboured, sucking sounds came from Barker's mouth as he tried to get air into his lungs through his crushed throat. He looked up at Beamish, his eyes wide in disbelief and pain, pleading for help.

'Now, Colour, I am sorry that you tripped and fell,' said Beamish menacingly, 'but I need your agreement that this will go no further.'

Barker's eyes blinked, the viciousness of the attack had clearly put him into a state of shock.

'Colour, I need your agreement. We all saw you fall down,' hissed Beamish putting his mouth to Barker's ear.

Unable to speak, Barker nodded his agreement, his face now going a horrible blue colour, he was suffocating.

'MEDEEC' shouted Beamish, indicating for Le Beau to help him. They lifted Barker up and dragged him towards the sickbay.

*

Gona-re-Zhou National Park, 12km north of Vila Salazar, Mozambique Border

A convoy of fourteen vehicles was drawn up in thick bush 1km short of the border fence with Mozambique. This was the Selous Scout Flying Column, used so many times before to great effect on attacks into Mozambique. The most notable success was the Pungwe/Nyadzonya raid that had killed thousands of ZANLA cadres. Most of the vehicles were two and a half tonne Mercedes Benz Unimogs, appropriately named Pigs, modified with armoured plate on the side panels to protect the troops and armed with an assortment of weapons. The lead vehicle carried one of the 20mm Hispano cannon that had been donated from the Air Force after they had scrapped their De Havilland Vampire jet fighters. Some had twin-mounted 7.62mm MAG machine guns, others .50 inch Browning heavy machine guns (50Cal) and Soviet 12.7mm machines guns. Two had 81mm mortars mounted on the rear tray. Second in line was the command vehicle, an ex-Portuguese six-wheeled Berliet troop carrier with a 20mm cannon mounted over the driver's compartment. This vehicle had been liberated from Mozambique in a previous raid and was affectionately named 'Brutus'. Immediately behind the Command Vehicle was the first of three Eland 90 armoured cars, each mounting a 90mm GIAT F1 gun plus a 7.62 machinegun. The second Eland 90 was in the middle of the column while the third took up the rear. A total of fifty-four Selous Scout officers and men manned the column plus the three Armoured Car Regiment crews.

The Unimogs had been meticulously painted in FRELIMO colours. They even had a final authentic touch, provided by Rhodesian Radio Intercept Services, who had passed on genuine FRELIMO registration numbers borrowed from vehicle strength returns radioed from Chimoio to Maputo. Number-plates of the exact dimensions were fitted, painted carefully with red letters on a white background. The vehicles were literally bursting with spare ammunition plus high explosive, landmines, water and rations.

Each vehicle was part of a sophisticated radio network. Each had a HF facility as well as several VHF channels, so that all vehicles could communicate with each other, speak to other ground forces, and air force close air support.

The commander of the Flying Column, Captain Rob Walker, who had commanded two of the previous vehicle-borne raids, sat hunched over a HF radio set in 'Brutus'. A reconnaissance team had covered the route into Mozambique the previous week, but Walker was waiting for final confirmation that the crossing was clear. Another reconnaissance team had been sent in two days before to check the crossing point and the first ten kilometres of the route. Other teams had been HALO dropped onto the main road and railway line between Malvernia and the towns to the south, to cut telephone lines. Captain Walker was aware of the basic premise of Operation Swallow. His own mission was to attack the newly rebuilt ZANLA camp at Jorge do Limpopo, then move south in support of the RLI ambush teams on the main road to Barragem, and finally to uplift the RLI and return to Rhodesia.

Strict silence was maintained by the men in the column in case a FRELIMO patrol was working along the border fence. The sound of a weapon being loaded can carry a long distance at night.

The HF radio crackled in Walker's ear, ' Oscar1, Oscar1, 81 do you copy.'

'Roger, 81, go.'

'Oscar1, Fullback, do you copy that ...Over.'

'Roger ... Fullback copied ... Oscar 1 out,' Walker chuckled to himself, the use of Rugby field positions, as code words was a nice touch. He picked up the handset for the VHF radio net, 'All Oscar call-signs, Oscar1 ... go for the try line.' He smiled again; the image of his fourteen heavily armed vehicles spread across a rugby field was amusing. *Let's hope the opposition have a weak pack of forwards*, he thought to himself.

The engines all started up and they drove towards the border, the convoy crossing over at exactly 00h15. All the men were heavily disguised as FRELIMO cadres. The soldiers were covered in thick camo-cream, with woollen balaclavas pulled down over their faces to further disguise their features, and fight the early morning cold. Sitting next to Walker in the command Berliet was Sgt. Tapson Manyika, fluent in the Ndau language, and next to him Sergeant Antoneo Guerreiro who had been borrowed from the SAS because of his Portuguese first language.

The recce party were picked up after a short distance and the column trundled on into Mozambique at a slow but steady pace. Good time was made, helped by the bright moonlight. The dimmed park lights allowed the vehicles to keep their convoy distances.

The column's progress was being monitored by the Selous Scout commanders at their base at Andre Rabie Barracks at Inkomo. They could hear snatches of the HF transmissions between the vehicles.

After winding through the bush for 19km, the column reached the Cahora Bassa[120] powerline, which ran parallel to the border. They turned southwest onto the track running under the 500kV DC powerlines. There were in fact, two sets of powerlines one kilometre apart, running across the north of

---

120 Cahora Bassa is a giant hydroelectric dam built on the Zambezi River inside Mozambique. Sets of unique 500kV DC powerlines radiated out from the scheme to feed power to all of Mozambique. A set of powerlines also fed South Africa, and these were the lines that the Selous Scouts were following.

Mozambique towards South Africa. The powerlines provided the route to the intersection with the road running south along the Maputo-Malvernia railway line. This road connected all the towns along the railway line between Malvernia and Barragem.

As the column approached the intersection with the road it came to a halt and the engines were turned off. The intersection was 22km south of Malvernia; there was still a chance that FRELIMO could be patrolling the road. The time was 02h00.

Cpt. Walker picked up the HF radio handset and called, '74, 74, ... Oscar1 do you copy.'

The response came instantly, 'Oscar1 this is 74, top of the morning to you.' The cheery welcome came from 2RR Mortar Platoon at Vila Salazar.

'Roger, 74, you may throw the ball into the lineout. I confirm ... throw the ball into the lineout.'

'Copied ... throwing the ball into the lineout, 74 out.'

2RR then commenced a bombardment of Malvernia, creeping their fire along the track and railway line out to the maximum range of their mortars, 5,000m. The rumble of the barrage could be heard clearly by the column and the trucks all pulled out onto the track and drove south towards their start-line just north of Madulo Pan. They picked up the telephone line-cutting team along the way.

*

Aldia de Barragem Mozambique, 284km south east of Vila Salazar

Captain Chris Schultz and his stick including C/Sgt Kumpher and Sgts Ngwenya and Seals, had a successful HALO jump, landing in open ground about 15km northeast of the town of Aldia de Barragem. The town derived its name from the barrage thrown across the mighty Limpopo River in Portuguese times as part of the large Chokwe irrigation scheme. The town had died during the period since liberation because the infrastructure supporting the irrigation scheme had not been maintained. A once productive valley was now dry weeds and rusting farm equipment. The town's only economic support came from the Brigade of FRELIMO soldiers stationed there with their wives and families. Barragem was also a good communications hub, being at the intersection of a number of arterial roads leading inland from Maputo.

The jump was textbook perfect. The team landed within a few metres of each other. The 'box' had been unpacked and the kit distributed between the men. Schultz had sent an HF sitrep to Selous Scout HQ at Inkomo and the Fort at Chiredzi. The immediate plan was to get a visual on the house that was to be used by the ZANLA leaders for their meeting with their FRELIMO comrades.

The house had been studied in great detail. A full size replica had been built out of wood at Andre Rabie barracks to be used for rehearsals. What was needed was absolute confirmation of the size of the FRELIMO guard around the compound and the distribution of other FRELIMO units in the immediate vicinity. The four men were dressed, once again, as FRELIMO cadres and they carried AKs, Soviet grenades, and rifle grenades. Seals carried a Soviet RPD light machine gun, while Kumpher carried an RPG-7 with a pack of four projectiles across his back. The packs they were carrying were lightweight with only essential food and water, each held a bunker bomb to be used for blasting through walls and doors if that became necessary. Ngwenya was tasked with setting the bunker bombs, so he carried two in his pack.

The men made their way towards a track, identified on the aerial photographs, that would take them into the heart of Barragem. The bush had mostly been cleared as part of the irrigation scheme and the land was criss-crossed with disused irrigation ditches and canals. The moon sat high in the southern sky, bathing the terrain in silvery light. Passing deserted huts and cattle kraals, the men approached the outskirts of Barragem. The house they were to target was on the northern edge of the town and at one time would have been a magnificent rolling colonial mansion overlooking the spectacular Limpopo River. The flood plain had no hills high enough to use as an OP so the plan required the men to observe the house from within the sandy riverbed. Fortunately, the river was full of drift wood and covered in thick vegetation providing ample cover.

Digging into the thick sand under a thorny acacia bush, the Selous Scouts took a short rest, taking the opportunity for a drink of water. First up on OP was Schultz who crawled out from under the bush, creeping closer to the house. He chose a point directly opposite the house that was in total darkness. Removing the magnified night-sight from its pouch, he focused on the house and the surrounding outbuildings. The countryside turned a dim green colour as he scanned every detail. There was no movement at all. If there were sentries, they weren't patrolling the perimeter.

Glancing at the luminous dial on his watch, Schultz noted one hour to first light.

*

10,000ft AGL above Rhodesia / Mozambique Border 50km north of Vila Salazar

The sudden drop in temperature from the heat of Buffalo Range made Cpl Arthur Beamish shiver. The shock and distress of the last few hours had him in a cold sweat. His mind was a jumble of emotions that he was having difficulty processing. They were on their way into Mozambique with all the frightening consequences of an external raid.

Colour Barker had been stuck in sickbay, the doctor had to intubate him with a breathing pipe until they could figure out how much damage was done to his throat. He hadn't been able to say a word about how he got his injuries. His forehead had taken ten stiches. The fact that he had been injured required a reassessment of all the tasks for 11 Troop. Circumstances made Beamish the acting 2IC of the troop.

Le Beau and Kratzman sat next to him in the darkness of the aircraft cabin.

Everything had got completely out of control. The gunshot had come from the showers. Men were screaming and shouting in the confusion. Beamish got to the shower stall too late.

Penga Marais had stuck his Tokarev pistol into his mouth and blasted the top of his head off.

Blood and gore covered the shower stall. Beamish had sat down next to the dead man, the young man he felt so responsible for. The accumulated emotion of losing Chico, and the death of the NS 6 Indep officer, closed in on him. For the second time in his life in the army, Arthur Beamish had wept. The first was at his brother's funeral.

Le Beau and Kratzman stood above, trying to comprehend the horrific sight in front of them. Beamish rocked backward and forward, his arms crossed in front of his chest. These men had witnessed the most unspeakable scenes in their military lives but this was something they were unprepared for.

CSM Butch Strydom arrived, taking in the horror of the situation. He, unfortunately, had seen this all before. He spoke to the men calmly and compassionately, giving instructions.

'Come on Beamish, get up son,' he said leaning down to help the stricken man to his feet. 'Let's take Penga to the sickbay, come on, let's get this place cleaned up shall we.'

Beamish got to his feet, struggling to regain control, shaking like a leaf. The CSM called for men to lift Penga's body.

'No Sir,' said Le Beau, 'he is ours.'

Le Beau and Kratzman gently lifted Penga's body as if they were holding a new born baby. A stretcher had been brought from sickbay and they lowered him onto it. A small procession followed Le Beau and Kratzman across the quad to the sickbay.

It was all over ... Penga's pain and anguish, his tortured life, was over. The thought of being abandoned by Lily and the kids had been the final breaking point. In his tormented mind, he had nothing left to live for.

The mission needed to be completed, there was no time for reflection, within only a few hours they were loaded into the aircraft.

As the aircraft turned to taxi to the end of the runway, standing at attention in a pool of light on the hardstanding was Butch Strydom, dressed for the parade ground, a red sash across his chest, his pace stick under his arm. As Beamish's aircraft passed, Strydom threw up a salute ... *I want to be in that number when the Saints go marching in.*

Snap out of this ... you have these men to look after. It's up to me to get them through ... was the thought that occupied Beamish's mind, as he tried to push the sight of Penga's body out of his mind. *It was for the best ... Penga is in a better place.* Beamish now had to think about his own life and how he was going to survive the next few days.

The Dak sat stable in the airstream with not a hint of disturbance ... *what a pleasant change for this fook'n vomit comet?* The blast of cold air through the door was soothing after the hot sweaty wait for the final equipment check by the dispatchers. The weight of the CSPEP containers meant that each man needed assistance climbing into the aircraft. The loading took a long time after a great deal of swearing and complaining from the men.

Outside in the darkness stacked at 1,000ft intervals were three other Daks carrying the men of the RLI. The cabin was in total darkness except for the dim light coming from the cockpit. The men sat in silence, all in fearful contemplation. Beamish checked Le Beau and Kratzman sitting next to him and reflected on how lucky he was to be with two men such as these ... *there was nothing quite like an early morning jump into hostile territory to focus the mind on one's own mortality.* In many ways, he regretted that he could not tell his men just how much he appreciated them. Showing true feelings in front of your mates is not something soldiers do. Just a nod, wink or smile is all that is given and received ... *it means everything.*

A sudden lift in his gut indicated to Beamish that the aircraft was starting to lose altitude; they had been told the drop would be at 500ft. First light streamed through the door. Out to the left of the aircraft the other three Daks came into view as the pilots tightened their formation.

What a sight it was, majestic in the morning light the sun bouncing off wings and propellers, a feeling of immense pride washed over Beamish, his spirits suddenly lifted ... *So what if I die today. Everyone has to go sometime!*

'STAND', the Dispatcher called. As he struggled to his feet, Beamish glimpsed two of the Daks outside peel off ... *12 Troop were going in.*

'Hook up.'

Beamish's stick were second out the door, 2nd Lt Van Deventer would be last. The CSPEP container weighed a ton, Beamish had to push it hard to get it to move.

Red light on!

Any second now, shuffle ... shuffle ... shuffle.

The light outside was now good enough to see the bush flashing past ... *I hope we are dropped in the right place!*

Green light on ... *this is it boys.* The gut tightened.

Le Beau, standing immediately behind Beamish, gave his corporal a reassuring tap on the helmet.

GO! GO! GO!

Spinning into space ... waiting for the tug of the parachute. Crack ... is it open? Look up, look down ... mushrooming parachutes all around. Fook ... the container! Beamish snapped the quick-release hooks and the CSPEP fell away, the weight of it reaching the end of the rope, banged through his body. The early morning was dead still, no wind to speak of.

The first round cracked past Beamish's head, disappearing up through his parachute. The shock of hearing the shot pass by, jolted Beamish. Below him, he could see men scurrying through the bush ... *there's not supposed to be any fook'n gooks here! My God! They are everywhere ... running like ants, shooting at us!* Green tracer lifted from trees below, popping around the chutes. *The bloody Blue Jobs have dropped us in the wrong place!*

As he pulled down on the lift-webs, the chute began a gentle glide, it was perfect, the container hit the ground and a split second later so did Beamish, as gentle a landing as ever ... *what a way to start!* He thumbed open the quick-release box and unsnapped the container ... *Rifle okay, radio okay, I'm okay,* ... looking around ... *Kratzman and Le Beau all okay ... good!* He instinctively swung around looking for Penga.

'Switch on!' he grunted at the other two.

'Did you see those gooks on the way down?'

'Yes Corp, they seemed to be running to the east,' replied Kratzman, ramming a belt into the MAG.

The troop regrouped as fast as they could. The people on the ground that had been shooting at them seemed to have disappeared. Van Deventer was talking earnestly into his radio, the only word that Beamish overheard was 'compromised' ... *Yeh, that would be right! Fook'd before we've even begun!*

The men were ordered to unpack the containers. Parachutes and helmets were piled up to be recovered later. The weight of the Bergen packs with the amount of extra equipment and provisions was huge. The men staggered under the weight. Beamish needed help to get to his feet.

Van Deventer finished his radio message and called Beamish over.

'Beamish, there were not supposed to be any FRELIMO within fifty kilometres of here. We will wait for more instructions ... in the meantime we carry on as planned.'

'Yes Sur.'

'If we have been compromised twelve hours before our mission is due to commence, then we are fucked to put it mildly,' whispered LCpl Eric Parnell to Beamish. All Beamish could do was nod his agreement.

Finally all thirty-two men dropped from the Daks were assembled and Van Deventer called them into a tight group, 'Okay listen up. We have been dropped in the right place from what I can see ... that vlei line to our west is this one marked on the map.' He pointed to a spot on his map. 'I have spoken to COMOPS and they reckon that we probably dropped on top of some ZANLA gooks on a training mission from Mabalane to our east. That's just bad luck. We have been told to proceed with our mission and ambush the road as planned. Move out in the rehearsed order.'

The men shuffled out into two columns as they had done in rehearsals and moved out. Beamish and his stick were last in the line led by Van Deventer. A Lieutenant, from the Assault Pioneer Troop of Support Commando, led the other column. Beamish did not know him.

The going was painfully slow, the temperature climbing to its forecast maximum of 37°C and the weight of the packs meant that they were completely exhausted after just one hour of walking. Things were made worse by the soft sand they were walking through.

Clouds of Mopani flies descended on the men. They stuck to every bit of moisture, lips, eyes, sweat dripping from foreheads. The men wrapped their face-veils tightly around their eyes and mouths but the flies still got through. Breathing hard under the weight of heavy packs sent the flies into dry mouths and throats, forcing men to cough harshly, spitting to remove the vile taste. Eyes burned from the flies stuck in tearducts. This was the closest thing to purgatory that Beamish could imagine.

Van Deventer was forced to call a halt every half hour as the men could not manage in the harsh conditions. It took five hours to cover the 10km to the main road that they had been tasked to ambush. The men slumped down in the soft sand well away from the road, grateful for a drink of water and a rest. Beamish watched as the men from Support Commando unpacked the claymores and landmines to be set in the road. Once the men had recovered, they were split up into three groups, one group to man the killing ground, the other two, north and south of the ambush site, as stop groups.

Beamish and his two gunners were placed in the group to man the ambush site, the killing ground. Van Deventer went north while Eric Parnell went south. The Support Commando men worked fast, first digging four holes in the road, careful to preserve the lighter top layer. It was hard work as the road surface was well compacted. They ran detonation cord from the fuse in each mine to a central point next to a large anthill. The anthill was covered in vegetation, providing good cover and a view up and down the road. Next, a string of claymores were placed along the side of the road. Each one was disguised under shrubbery cut from the nearby bush. After two hours of feverish activity, the mines were laid and carefully covered. The road was then brushed clean of spoor and all the cables buried. Communications were established with the Stop Groups and a sitrep sent to the RLI rear base at Buffalo Range.

The Support Commando Lieutenant turned out to be Greg Shaw BCR, famous for his various successful demolition missions, destroying bridges and culverts in Mozambique and Zambia. Lt Shaw helped Beamish site his two gunners and they worked out their arcs of fire. There were fifteen men in the ambush position with four MAGs amongst them. Added to the firepower were the four command-detonated landmines and the string of twenty or so claymores.

Positioned at the base of the anthill Beamish set about digging a shallow shell-scrape, relatively easy going as the ground was soft sand graded up from the road. Le Beau and Kratzman were in rocks to Beamish's right.

Nobody had any idea what it was or who it was, they were ambushing. All they knew was, when the ambush was initiated, they were to kill everything they saw.

20

Suburb of Ridgeview, 3km Southwest of the Salisbury City Centre

George Stanbridge and two of his agents had watched Faye Chan place the envelope in the dead-drop behind the sightscreen at the Sunshine Sports Ground. He had fed her with a set of bogus information concerning another attack on the terrorist base in Chimoio. With the help of Jim Winston of SB, they set up elaborate briefing sessions with COMOPs staff. The COMOPS staff were not in on the ruse, they could be forgiven in thinking this was the real thing. They had worked on the basis that ZANLA knew an assassination attempt was coming but Stanbridge worked out a new plan identifying Tongogara's house in Chimoio as the target house. The date set was in one month's time. This was to coincide with a visit by senior Chinese military officials that had already been leaked to the SB by the agent *Zizi*.

The time had come to try and 'turn' Faye Chan. It occurred to Stanbridge that this very smart young woman would see the error of her ways, what choice did she have?

Keeping well out of sight, the CIO men had waited for John Mawere to collect the envelope from the sightscreen and then called Stanbridge on the two-way radio to confirm that the drop was complete.

It was almost dark when Faye got back to the house. She opened the gate and removed the dog's chain. Trudy seemed very agitated, she ran around to the back of the house, barking loudly. The dog only barked like this if there were strangers in the yard or the neighbour's cat or snakes. The house was in darkness. Faye's parents visited friends on a Wednesday night.

'Trudy, stop that barking!' Faye called out. The dog came back around the front of the house but still seemed very unsettled, growling loudly. She knelt down in front of the dog rubbing Trudy's ears, 'It's okay girl, settle down ... time for dinner, I will get your food.'

The front door to the house was never locked; Faye wasn't even sure where the key for the front door was. She pushed the door open and went inside, turning lights on in the house as she moved to the kitchen. Opening the door to the fridge, she took out a packet of half-cooked mince, opened it and poured the contents into the dog's food bowl. An opened tin of dog food was also in the fridge that she added to the mix. There were some leftover vegetables she wanted to mix in with the food, she turned back to open the fridge door.

A gloved hand clamped firmly over her mouth, her head twisted back. At the same time, a powerful arm was wrapped around her waist holding her tightly against her attacker. Her body seemed to convulse in fright, she shook her head violently side to side to try to get free.

'Don't struggle Faye, its only me, George Stanbridge. I think you know why I am here,' said Stanbridge into her ear. She seemed so tiny in his arms, so weak and vulnerable, as if she could break.

Faye stopped writhing, shaking her head slightly in submission. The giant hand remained clamped over her mouth.

'Now I just want to talk to you Faye, I don't want to hurt you in any way. Do you understand Faye? Please don't try to scream, I will let you go.'

She nodded feeling the hand release it's grip slightly. Stanbridge freed her, she spun away, standing panting in front of the fridge. Her eyes glistened with tears at the shock of the sudden attack.

'Sit down Faye, let's have a little chat, shall I make some tea?' asked Stanbridge, pointing her to a chair at the kitchen table.

'What do you want?' she blurted out, moving to the chair, glancing around the room.

'We are quite alone Faye, although a few words into this will bring my people running,' said Stanbridge, indicating the two-way radio in his pocket.

'You can't just come into people's houses like this!' she demanded, quickly regaining her composure.

'That's true Faye, but we both know that you have not exactly been playing the game so to speak. I must say that I am very impressed with how you have conducted your activities. Right under our very noses.'

'I don't know what you are talking about!' she replied, now quite defiant, her eyes flashing her disgust.

'Now come on old girl, I shouldn't have to spell it out. You have been caught red-handed. You could spend the rest of your life in Chikurubi Prison, or worse, be hanged as a spy.'

'I have nothing to say to you,' said Faye, spitting out her words.

'I am here to offer you a deal. I want you to come and work for us. Doing exactly as you are doing, just feeding false information to our enemies,' explained Stanbridge in a soft encouraging voice, removing his gloves and stuffing them in his suit pocket.

'Never … Never, you racist pigs are losing the war, soon our brave freedom fighters will be marching up the streets of Salisbury to victory!'

She shook her fist, her face suddenly flushed with exhilaration.

Stanbridge unwittingly took a step back. Her venomous reaction was quite unexpected.

'Now, that is a bit off, old girl, you know that's not true. You know we are about to take out the ZANLA leadership and then the ZIPRA leadership will follow.'

'We will have a glorious socialist state where the riches of the country are given back to the people. You white colonists will be chased away,' she said triumphantly, her eyes now flashing wildly, her voice strengthening with the power of her conviction.

The viciousness of her rebuke took Stanbridge aback; he was not expecting this reaction at all. This tiny slip of a girl had always seemed quiet and submissive. He was shocked. It was as if he had run into a brick wall.

'Now settle down Faye, lets not get carried away, I am not sure you understand the seriousness of your situation,' replied Stanbridge, trying to stamp his authority on the situation.

'I don't care ... I am prepared to die for the cause. I would never betray my comrades in the bush. There's nothing you can do to me!' She stood up moving towards the kitchen door.

'Sit down Faye!' Stanbridge demanded, moving towards her.

'Leave me alone,' she screamed defiantly, reaching for the door.

Stanbridge lunged for her; she ducked to her left grabbing the empty dog food tin, the jagged lid still attached. As he tried to grab her, she swung the can at him, cutting him across his open hand. Then swinging again backhanded, she tried to cut his face. He lifted his arm to protect himself, taking another deep cut on the wrist. Nowhere near as quick footed as he once was, Stanbridge leapt to catch her, she ducked away from him, moving towards the dining room.

'Stop Faye, don't be stupid!'

Stanbridge grabbed for the Walther PPK in his pocket, lifting it.

'Stop Faye!'

'Shoot me, you white racist ... shoot me!' she yelled on the top of her voice, challenging him.

Stanbridge covered her with the pistol, she did not show any sign of fear, just glaring back at him insolently. His mind was racing as to what to do next.

Faye moved like lightening, she snatched the single brass candlestick holder off the sideboard, and lunged around the table towards him.

The speed of her movement took Stanbridge by surprise, he fired at her ... the bullet burying itself in the dining room wall. She kept coming, swinging the candlestick holder above her head.

'Stop Faye!' screamed Stanbridge.

A strange sound came from her throat like the warning of a lioness, a deep guttural growl ... the unmistakeable sound ... spelling death.

For the first time in his life, George Stanbridge lost control of himself and the situation. He shot the beautiful, brave, defiant Chinese woman in the head. She fell against the table, sliding down onto the parquet flooring. The bullet exploded the back of her skull over the dining room table.

Standing in the middle of the room, Stanbridge was dumbstruck. His chest was heaving from the shock of what had just happened. Blood from his cut hand and arm streamed onto the floor at his feet.

Still holding the pistol out in front of him, Stanbridge approached the body of the dead girl, her face like smooth porcelain, lustrous black hair spread about her face, dead eyes still staring rebelliously up at him.

*

CIO HQ, Livingston Avenue, Salisbury

The team responsible for planning the assassination of the senior ZANLA leadership, sat in their situation room with their radios, telex and other communication equipment. They were in communication with COMOPS HQ in Milton Buildings, the COMOPS Command Dakota, that had only just taken off from New Sarum, Selous Scout HQ at Inkomo Barracks and the RLI fireforce base at Buffalo Range.

The tension in the room was tangible, people speaking in hushed tones, as if afraid to disturb the activities going on many hundreds of kilometres away. Slowly all the sitreps from the operational teams came in. The Selous Scout Flying Column north of Madulo Pan, 12 Troop RLI north of Jorge do Limpopo and 11 Troop south of Mabalane, the Selous Scout teams observing the houses in Jorge do Limpopo and Barragem. The last to report their readiness was the external Admin and Refuelling Area; some 75km due east of Jorge do Limpopo.

All was set.

Everyone was waiting for news of one thing. Where were the three Toyota Landcruisers carrying Tongogara's entourage? To find them, a Lynx with the Becker tracking device was flying high above the road between Chimoio and Jorge do Limpopo and another above the road from Chimoio and Barragem. The most important piece of information was awaited from *Zizi*, the SB agent on the ground. His signal would be absolute confirmation of where Tongogara was going to spend the night.

'Are those radios connecting us with the Air Force working?' asked George Stanbridge, for the umpteenth time.

'Yes Sir, they are working, we have just had a message from the Command Dak, they are crossing the border above the Vumba Mountains,' replied the radioman, patiently answering his boss; everyone knew the pressure he was under.

Stanbridge felt like a lead weight was hanging around his neck. He had banked his reputation on being able to pull off this operation and change the course of the war, or more importantly the course of the political settlement that must surely come. He was on his fourth cup of tea since arriving at his office at first light. He got up to go to the toilet.

'I am going to the loo and then my office, if that radio so much as blinks call me.'

It had been a harrowing twenty four hours for Stanbridge. As he sat down at his desk he took the Walther PPK, the 7.65mm version, he had been given by his father, and placed it carefully in the top drawer of his desk. He lent on his elbows, rubbing his face with his uninjured hand, the other throbbed under a heavy bandage. He felt sick about Faye Chan, it all seemed so unnecessary, but it had to be done. *Why did she react in the way she did? It was all so unnecessary! So much potential lost.*

As Stanbridge sat in quiet contemplation, there was a soft knock at his door. He looked up to see Chief Superintendent Jim Winston, Special Branch, standing there.

'Yes Jim?' said Stanbridge questioningly.

'Bad news, this Faye Chan business George,' stated Winston, concentrating on Stanbridge's face.

'Bloody awful, she would have been a great asset. I still can't believe I shot her. I had no intention ... her reaction was just so aggressive ... like a wild animal,' rambled Stanbridge, obviously still very distressed.

'I have to tell you George … this does not look at all good,' stated Winston blankly, still studying Stanbridge's reaction as all good policemen would.

'What do you mean?' replied Stanbridge indignantly, not happy where this was going.

'All I can say George is that if this operation of yours goes pear-shaped we will be forced to ask you a lot more searching questions. This mole business is upsetting people in high places,' said Winston, his voice flat and unemotional.

Stanbridge did not know what to say … damned if he did … damned if he didn't. His face flushed at the implication.

'Sir … Sir we have a message coming in!' One of the CEO staff had rushed to the door, waving his arm for his boss to follow him.

Stanbridge got up from his chair, suddenly feeling totally exhausted. He brushed past Winston at the door, not trusting himself to say anything more.

By the time Stanbridge entered the Situation Room the message had been received and recorded.

'Is it him, is it *Zizi*?' he asked urgently.

'Yes Sir, he reports that Swallow will be at Barragem at two pm this afternoon for the meeting with the FRELIMO District High Command. He repeated the code word for Barragem twice,' said the radio operator.

'Let me listen to the message,' demanded Stanbridge, wanting to make absolutely sure.

The radio operator ran back the tape and pressed the play button.

A thin voice came over the speaker, whispering seShona into the radio on the other side.

'Comrade Tsorai, this is Comrade Chitofu, please get the children inside at two pm it is going to rain. I repeat … Comrade Chitofu please get the children inside at two pm it is going to rain!'

'That's it! … It's going to rain! … Fantastic … it's going to bloody rain!' Stanbridge danced a little gig. 'We've got the bastards at Barragem. I can hardly believe it, after all this time we have finally got the bastards.' Stanbridge was ecstatic, his staff smiled in collective relief.

'Right … get onto the Scouts and give them the codes for Barragem … Thank God. Tell them ETA two pm. This means that the convoy carrying Tongogara will be on the road directly from Chimoio to Barragem. They will bypass all the ambushes set on the road to Jorge do Limpopo. Send a signal to the RLI at Buffalo Range informing them as well.'

Stanbridge could hardly contain himself.

The telex machine operator began to type up the messages to COMOPS, the Command Dak in the air, the Selous Scouts and RLI. The Command Dak high over Mozambique was the first to acknowledge. The messages in turn were converted into shackle and button codes and transmitted via HF to the teams on the ground.

Sao Jorge do Limpopo, Mozambique, 84km south of Vila Salazar

At first light the Selous Scout Flying Column passed through their start-line at Madulo Pan, a site of a previous successful attack on a ZANLA training base. Many of the men who had participated in that battle could not help but look out to the west as they passed by. Someone said that the parched bones of dead terrorists could still be seen in the dried mud in the pan.

As the column neared Sao Jorge do Limpopo, another 19km further on, the men on the vehicles visibly tensed up, slipping off the safety catches on their Soviet weapons, the loud metallic cracks passed down the line as the heavy machine guns were cocked and ready. The gunners in each of the three Eland 90s shoved a 90mm HE shell into the breech then slapped and locked it in place. This was a crucial phase of the operation for, if the FRELIMO garrison was on its toes, it would end in a massive firefight, the rest of the mission fading into impossibility.

The vehicles steadily approached the outskirts of the town. The two-five at the head of the column slowed down as a lone FRELIMO sentry stepped out into the road. The man must have been guarding the railway siding, he made no attempt to halt the column, instead gazing disinterestedly at the column as it passed by. He returned the wave from the men on the back of the trucks.

Pushing deeper into the village, that had a population of less than a thousand, they reached the turnoff to Mapai. To everyone's complete surprise, the booms at the intersection with the road to Mapai were raised and the sentry boxes empty, in fact the whole area seemed deserted. Captain Walker ordered the column onwards to the south and after a few kilometres pulled them off the road to refuel. The fuel bowsers were then unhitched and concealed in the bush to be collected on the way back. Nobody liked the idea of dragging a tonne of fuel into a firefight. One trailer with Avtur remained with the convoy.

The vehicles grunted back into life and carried on down the remainder of the 60km to the 12 Troop ambush position. Capt Walker was in constant contact with the Command Dak, ticking off each kilometre towards their RV.

At 10am the convoy reached the 12 Troop ambush site. The RLI men had packed up their kit, removed all the explosives from the road and eagerly piled onto the vehicles.

The Flying Column continued unmolested to the outskirts of the village of Mabalane. Each vehicle moved to its pre-designated position according to the carefully rehearsed plan. The other Selous Scouts debussed and set about their nominated tasks. The 12 Troop job was now to protect the vehicles and ensure that there were no surprises.

At first sight, the village appeared deserted. The area was littered with empty beer bottles which indicated that more than one major celebration had taken place in the recent past. One of the important tasks was the destruction of the ZANLA MT yard that contained a neat row of brand new 50-seater Mercedes Benz busses used for transporting CTs from Maputo and Barragem in the south to the Rhodesian border. Capt. Walker ordered that one of the busses be driven onto the road out of town. With sanctions, the chances of finding such a prize in Rhodesia were remote. Delayed charges were set in each of the busses and the other vehicles in the MT yard which included a few Land Rovers and Soviet GAZ trucks.

In the centre of the village was a large building that must have been a community hall or cinema in colonial times. According to the intelligence reports, this building was the main storage for ZANLA arms and ammunition. The Selous Scouts began to clear the building, starting in the basement which turned out to be jam-packed with weapons and equipment. In no time the arms and equipment was being unpacked and a human chain set up to load the newly acquired bus outside.

There was no activity in the village at all. When Capt. Walker reported this to the Command Dak, the news was met with complete disbelief. There should have been an almighty battle going on by now. There were supposed to be well over three thousand ZANLA and FRELIMO at Mabalane.

Delighted with the progress of his mission, Walker entered the building so that he could help with the search for intelligence documents in the offices and store rooms. The upper floor could not be reached from the ground floor but instead via an external concrete staircase. At the top of the staircase was a long passage the length of the building with offices on each side. Half way down the passage was an internal balcony overlooking the hall and cinema below.

Satisfied that his men were doing a great job loading the bus with equipment, Walker climbed the concrete staircase. No movement in the building had been detected. Walker cautiously studied the passage in front of him, his weapon at the ready. There was a faint smell of cigarette smoke but Walker felt that it must be his own men smoking in the floor below. He cautiously entered the passage and with his back to one wall, made his way along. Each office entrance was directly opposite the one across the passage. At the first doorway he carefully looked inside, it was filled with litter and rubbish as was the office on the other side. He moved to the next doorway. As he twisted his head around the doorway, a sudden burst of fire came from the opposite end of the passage. The impact of two rounds spun Walker around as he crashed to the floor, his rifle falling from his hands. With desperate strength, Walker dragged himself back down the passage towards the staircase. More rounds followed him as he went, chipping concrete and brickwork onto the floor. A smear of blood poured from his wounds, as his strength ebbed away. Willing hands grabbed at his webbing and pulled him to safety.

As soon as Walker was clear, his men fired RPG-7 rockets into the passage as well as hurling down M962 fragmentation grenades. A group re-entered the passage running from room to room to make sure the building was clear.

Another burst of fire rang out and a Selous Scout went down, bullet strikes across his back. The CT had been hiding in the roof with a clear field of fire. The wounded man ran back down the passage with his team. At the bottom of the stairs he collapsed and died.

In cold anger, the Selous Scouts bombarded the top floor of the building. One of the Eland 90s was brought in and systematically placed a HE shell through each of the windows, blowing out clouds of dust and rubble with each strike. The explosions brought five ZANLA CTs to the top of the staircase where they were gunned down without mercy.

Helicopter casevac had been called for the wounded Capt Walker and the body of the dead Selous Scout. Capt Walker would never walk again; one of the bullets had severed his spinal column. The vehicles in the convoy were recalled from their positions and preparations were made to leave. No explanation could be found for the fact that two thousand ZANLA insurgents had vanished into thin air!

A detachment of four vehicles and one Eland 90 was sent on further to the south to collect the 11 Troop men, another 22km away. The rest of the flying column needed to secure the escape route to the north. The Selous Scout vehicles fanned out in all-round defence. They expected to have to wait for no more than an hour for the 3 Commando men to be recovered.

*

Massangena, Save River Crossing, Mozambique, 141km northeast of Vila Salazar

Godfrey Nyathi stood in the dirt road on the south bank of the Save River crossing, near the tiny village of Massangena. A jumble of mixed emotions ran through his head as he contemplated the instructions he had received from his SB handlers in Salisbury. He and his escort had left Chimoio exactly as planned. The lead BTR-152s had been despatched well ahead of the Landcruiser convoy and they had successfully cleared the road all the way to the Save, a little less than half way for their long trip south to Aldia de Barragem. Nyathi got his radio message off to SB the night before so the Rhodesians would know that Tongogara was on the move towards Barragem. Each Landcruisers carried a senior leader. They always avoided travelling together in the same vehicles for fear of attack. Tongogara was in the lead vehicle with Nyathi, then Hamadziripi's vehicle with Mhanda's vehicle at the rear.

Nyathi had been able to persuade his boss not to drive himself. It was a long way, over 700km on atrocious roads. Many of the bridges and culverts had been destroyed by the Rhodesians, requiring arduous river crossings. In some cases, it took hours to winch the vehicles through. This had been the case for the past three hours as they had struggled to get all the vehicles across the wide, sandy Save riverbed. Had it been the rainy season, it would have been impossible. Despite the state of the road and the river crossings, the trip had been uneventful without any vehicle breakdowns, not even a flat tyre.

All the vehicles were parked in line on the side of the road; Comrade Tongogara had called for a break to ease their aching bodies from the pummelling from the tortuous road. The men were brewing tea. Ever vigilant, Nyathi had the bodyguard in all-round defence. Tongogara and his officers had retired under a tall thorn acacia tree. The road surface was fine red sand that stretched virtually dead straight for 300km in both directions. The bush was remarkably thick, encroaching near the road, making visibility no more than a few metres. Nyathi was contemplating whether to send the BTRs off ahead again, when he saw dust from vehicles approaching from the south.

'*Chenjerai!* Watch out!' shouted Nyathi, '... everybody into the bush, get off the road!' He ran across to where Tongogara was standing, '*Nyenganyenga* vehicles are approaching from the south, you must take cover in the bush, it could be *Skuz'apo.*'

Tongogara did not question his most trusted aid, he simply signalled his officers to follow him into the bush. Nyathi made his way back to the road and walked towards his men guarding the approach from the south. An RPD gunner had already taken cover in thick bush aiming down the road. The lead BTR's 12.7mm gunner spun his gun to face down the road. The engine was started as a precaution in case a hurried manoeuvre was needed.

'Okay ... every man stay alert, do not open fire unless you are attacked or I call,' screamed Nyathi on the top of his voice so all could hear. The surrounding bush fell into silence; only the sound of the approaching vehicles could be heard. They steadily advanced, engines grinding through the soft patches of sand in the road.

Nyathi lifted his binoculars. The lead vehicle came into focus, it was a FRELIMO BTR-60 painted in the characteristic FRELIMO green. ZANLA had none of these vehicles, they were new, Nyathi had only seen one before at the FRELIMO base in Barragem. The BTR-60 was a formidable machine, eight-wheeled personnel carrier, mounting a KPVT 14.5mm machinegun in a low profile turret plus a PKT 7.62mm coaxial machinegun.

Nyathi relaxed slightly as it was highly unlikely that the Rhodesians could have got their hands on such a vehicle. As the BTR-60 came closer, Nyathi could see that there were four other vehicles in the convoy, all GAZ-66 transport trucks, their backs covered in canvas. Nyathi stepped out into the road and walked towards the approaching vehicle, it was truly intimidating, he could see the 14.5mm gun pointing in his direction. He held up his hand in greeting and the driver of the BTR-60 changed down to slow the vehicle, coming to a halt 20m in front of him. The huge diesel engine rumbled loudly as a man poked his head out of the turret. He was dressed in FRELIMO uniform.

'*Temos uma procura Geral Tongogara,*' demanded the man in Portuguese.

Nyathi shrugged, he had little command of the language.

'We are looking for General Tongogara,' repeated the man, this time in stumbling English.

'We are his escort,' replied Nyathi, suddenly feeling uncomfortable with this unexpected request. 'What do you want?'

As Nyathi answered, the man gestured to the vehicles behind him and armed soldiers started jumping off the transports, the back door of the BTR-60 fell open and more men come out onto the road. Nyathi could not believe his eyes; he searched the faces in front of him to see if these men could be Selous Scouts or SAS masquerading as FRELIMO as they so often did. If they were, he would probably be dead already.

The man in the BTR signalled again, the men ran off into the bush on both sides of the road, an obvious attempt at encirclement.

'Stop!' shouted Nyathi, lifting his rifle at the man in the turret. 'Tell your men to stand still.'

The man in the BTR simply dropped back inside and the vehicle began to inch forward, the 14.5mm gun was now clearly taking aim at Nyathi, standing completely alone in the middle of the road. The massive vehicle drove up to only two metres in front of Nyathi who stood his ground. The man again stood up out of the turret.

'We are here to take over the escort of Comrade Tongogara. We are under the orders of the FRELIMO high command,' yelled the man down at Nyathi.

'What is all of this?' commanded a voice from the bush behind Nyathi. He turned to see General Tongogara walking out onto the road. The General, with a Tokarev pistol in a holster at his waist, still had his arm in a sling. He stopped next to Nyathi. 'Who are you and what is your business?' asked Tongogara in a steady voice.

'I am Colonel Ramirez, and I have orders to take General Tongogara to Maputo. Is that you Comrade?' asked the man.

'Yes, I am Tongogara. Under whose orders Comrade?' enquired Tongogara casually, unfazed by this sudden turn of events. As he spoke, Mhanda and Hamadziripi, stepped out of the bush, both carried AKs.

'My orders are from General Joaquim Chissano himself, Comrade,' replied the man confidently.

'It is true, Comrade General,' said Peter Hamadziripi from behind.

Tongogara swung around to face Hamadziripi, his face suddenly changed, menacing.

'What is the meaning of this Hamadziripi?'

'Comrade General do not be alarmed, we were contacted by Comrade Mugabe before we left Chimoio to say that the Rhodesians were going to try to ambush you in Aldia de Barragem. We did not tell you because we feared that the information would be leaked. It is the *Dare de Chimurenga* who fear for your life, it is they that requested FRELIMO to send an escort.' Hamadziripi raced through the words, aware of Tongogara's threatening stare.

'You could have spoken to me alone Comrade, to warn me,' said Tongogara, taking a step towards Hamadziripi. Nyathi sensed the change of tone in his commander's voice, tightened his grip on his AKM.

'It was not possible Comrade, the radio message came in the last minutes before we left,' replied Hamadziripi, his face now bathed in sweat. He was clearly nervous, but then he was always nervous speaking to the General, who he knew disliked him intensely.

'It is true Comrade General,' added Felix Mhanda, lending support to his friend.

Now Tongogara became agitated. 'Nyathi!'

'Yes *Nyenganyenga.*'

'Get on the radio, call Maputo and ask for confirmation of these orders. Use the emergency codes you have been given.'

Nyathi turned on his heel to run towards the Landcruiser with the radio.

'It is not necessary Comrade General, my orders are very clear. Please get into the back of my vehicle,' insisted the Colonel in the turret. Three FRELIMO troops stepped forward.

Nyathi stopped in his tracks when he saw the sudden movement. In one fluid motion, he lifted his rifle and pumped bullets into the three men, he corrected his aim at the man in the turret who reacted too slowly. At the range of only a few metres, Nyathi took his head off.

Mhanda and Hamadziripi stood in shock as the FRELIMO men were cut down around them. They both dived into the dust on the side of the road and began to crawl away.

Running towards his General, Nyathi grabbed at his good arm, yanking him off the road into the bush. The ZANLA BTR-152 opened up with the 12.7mm, bullets ripped into the FRELIMO vehicle that was too heavily armoured to penetrate, but enough to panic the driver into shoving the vehicle into reverse. It ploughed back into the GAZ truck behind it. The ZANLA men, all in good cover, started shooting at the FRELIMO soldiers who were unprepared for the shock shooting of their commander. Some returned fire. A running battle began as the ZANLA men picked off their targets, chasing the FRELIMO soldiers through the bush.

Nyathi had his General face down in the dirt. Lying on top of him, he fired into the FRELIMO men milling around. He looked down at the man ... *I can kill Tongogara now ... nobody will ever know!*

A whole lifetime can be changed irrevocably by what happens in a split second ... Godfrey Nyathi had the power to do what the whole Rhodesian military establishment had failed to do. In that defining moment, he decided that he could not kill this man ... this was the only man he had met amongst the revolutionary forces who had any hope of leading the new Zimbabwe nation ... if that ever came to pass.

Nyathi, in that instant, ... changed history.

The 14.5mm on the BTR-60 opened up at the ZANLA vehicles, the powerful rounds easily penetrating the much thinner armour on the BTR-152. It exploded into flames, igniting the unspent rounds inside. The smaller vehicle exploded outwards like a balloon, flames jetting up through the open hatch.

In sheer panic the FRELIMO detachment broke off the battle and ran off to the south, back the way they had come. Some threw down their weapons and held their hands in the air, '*Não attire! ... Não attire!*' they shouted, 'Don't shoot!'

'Do not move General,' shouted Nyathi as he leapt to his feet. Dodging through the trees, Nyathi ran towards the BTR-60 that was still pumping rounds left and right into the surrounding bush. The powerful, high velocity bullets, were literally chopping down trees.

Approaching from the blind spot behind the vehicle, Nyathi ran up the rear ramp into the vehicle firing his AKM as he went. The only men in the vehicle were the driver and the gunner in the turret, they stood no chance, he cut them down.

Outside, the gunfire stopped. Men were screaming from their wounds.

As Nyathi stepped out the back of the BTR-60, the full enormity of the destruction confronted him. FRELIMO bodies lay everywhere, his own men had been incinerated in their BTR-152 which was still burning fiercely. Thick smoke hung in the air; there was no breeze, trees next to the road exploded into flame as the sap in their bark reached ignition temperature.

Nyathi began shouting orders for his men to regroup. The few FRELIMO that had surrendered were sitting in the road, their arms still in the air, babbling in Portuguese. It was clear, from what he could make out, that the FRELIMO men were convinced these men were Rhodesians that had ambushed them.

Slowly the ZANLA men regrouped, miraculously, the only two men killed had been in the BTR-152, one other man was slightly wounded. FRELIMO had fared much worse. When all the bodies had been piled into the back of one of the GAZ-66 trucks, they counted twenty-two in number.

'Where are those two traitors, Nyathi?' asked Tongogara quietly.

'The men are searching for them *Nyenganyenga*. Do you think that this was part of a plot to kill you?'

'There is no doubt in my mind. That bullshit about a signal from Mugabe ...' said Tongogara, then breaking into a soft laugh, shaking his head with incredulity, '... The last thing Mugabe would want is to save my life. I wouldn't be surprised if Mugabe told the Rhodesians my travel plans ... to let them do his dirty business for him.'

Tongogara was now laughing out loud, partly from the ridiculous situation and partly the nervous shock from the desperate battle that had raged around him.

At that point, Felix Mhanda was led out onto the road, held by two of Nyathi's men.

'Ah Mhanda, my friend and Comrade ... I am sure you have something you a want to tell me,' laughed Tongogara, with a hint of weariness in his voice. Mhanda was not given a chance to answer. Nyathi was already tying a rope around his feet. The rope was tossed over a tree branch and Mhanda was upended, dangling upside down from a tree.

'Mhanda, you will give me a list of plotters ...'

The man pissed himself, urine running down his stomach, over his face, down his hanging arms, pooling in the soft sand below his outstretched fingers. The FRELIMO men under guard, sitting in the dirt nearby, started jabbering when they saw the man strung up, now convinced this was to be their fate.

'Please Comrade General ... I know nothing of any plot ... it was Hamadziripi ... it was him,' squealed Mhanda.

'Oh well, it looks like we are going to have to do this the hard way ... Nyathi,' instructed Tongogara, resignedly, indicating to Nyathi that it was now his task. Nyathi slipped his hunting knife out of its scabbard and moved towards the man. Mhanda lifted his hands in a vain attempt to protect his stomach. He began babbling out names, 'Muzenda, Mujuru, Moyo, Ushewokunze ...' Nyathi pushed Mhanda's hands aside, then, with the dexterity of a surgeon, he neatly inserted the knife just below the bellybutton and cut a six-inch gash about an inch deep.

Mhanda's scream cut through the air, ringing in the brain like a crashing cymbal.

The men witnessing Mhanda's torture averted their eyes. Blood spurted from the wound, and ran down his body like a cascading stream, covering his face, filling his mouth. The scream was cut off as the man was forced to spit the blood out of his mouth, only to fill again.

In the distance, the distinctive sound of approaching helicopters cracked through the air ...

Peter Hamadziripi heard the scream as he ran for his life through the bush. He knew that it was his friend Felix Mhanda ... all was lost ... his only hope was to escape. If Tongogara was to capture him, his death would be slow and excruciating ... he ran on ... his mind numb with terror.

As Hamadziripi crashed through the bush in disorientated terror, a lioness, the alpha female of her pride, lifted her head disturbed from her afternoon siesta. Her ears flicked as she zeroed into the sound, sniffing at the air. The gunfire from the battle only 4kms away had not disturbed the pride in the slightest, they were used to gunfire. This new sound gave all the indications of distress ... the rest of her clan watched her movements intently, responding instantly as she sprang to her feet. More in curiosity than intent, the lioness padded off in the direction of the sound ...

*

Aldia de Barragem Mozambique, 284km south east of Vila Salazar

Tucked under the thick acacia bush in the Limpopo riverbed, C/Sgt Dennis Kumpher wrote down the message as it came in, carefully checking each letter and number as it was repeated. He then took out his own copy of the codes, decoded the message and handed it to Capt. Schultz.

'It's going to rain! It's us!' whispered Schultz, his voice tinged with excitement. Kumpher nodded gravely. It was their job to kill the ZANLA leadership and change the course of the war. The enormity of their mission suddenly struck home, all their training and preparation over many years, had come down to this one moment. Schultz crawled out from under the bush towards the OP where Ngwenya lay half covered in sand.

'Any developments Cephas?' he whispered.

'Nothing, just a guard of four men same as before, nobody has arrived or left,' replied Ngwenya.

'It's our target Cephas, it's up to us. We can expect activity any minute.' Schultz looked down at his watch; it was 1300hrs, H-hour in three hours!

21

Aldia de Barragem Mozambique, 284km south east of Vila Salazar

Almost to the exact minute the radio message from COMOPS reached Schultz and his Selous Scouts, a convoy of vehicles approached the ZANLA house north of Aldia de Barragem. Sgt Cephas Ngwenya was still on OP when a cloud of dust appeared in the distance, heralding the approach of vehicles. As they came into view, Ngwenya noted the lead vehicle was a BTR-152 mounting a 12.7mm machine gun, then three white Landcruisers. This was exactly what they had been told to expect. The vehicles slowed down as they turned into the driveway, then came to a halt in the shade of a huge *Nkwankwa*[121] tree next to the house. The BTR with the machinegun carried on around the house and parked in front of the veranda. Four men climbed out of each of the Landcruisers and made their way into the house. It all happened too fast and they were too far away for Ngwenya to make a positive identification.

The sound of the convoy arriving had alerted Schultz, who crawled up next to Ngwenya in their hide. They counted six men in the BTR, the twelve men from the Landcruisers, plus the four guards they had already seen, made twenty-two in total.

Ngwenya considered the odds ... *only four Selous Scouts, twenty-two gooks, that's about right!* Initially they had thought that they would be able to attack the target at last light but the arrival of so many of the enemy meant that a daylight attack was now totally impossible.

'I am going to send a sitrep Cephas. You stay in place,' Schultz murmured and slithered off in the sand.

As Ngwenya watched intently through his binoculars, the leader of the ZANLA men gave instructions to the men to check the perimeter of the Portuguese colonial compound. He himself went to check all the outbuildings, including a large corrugated iron shed that once would have housed tractors, farm implements and the servant's quarters. The outbuildings were derelict, most of the roof and the windows and doorframes had been ripped out. There was nothing left of what must have been a splendid garden, just a few shrivelled shrubs and the remains of a rockery. Once he had completed his inspection, the leader walked down to the river that was over 800m wide at that point. The water flowed strongly in the main stream, well below what it would do during the rainy season.

The ZANLA leader sat down in the soft sand on the riverbank under an enormous Wild Fig tree, *umKhiwane,* and looked out over the Limpopo. Ngwenya watched as the man scanned the bush across the river, and the wide dry riverbed in front of him ...

Ngwenya recoiled; it was as if the man knew what he was looking for! He <u>buried his head</u> in the sand, lying dead still.

121 White-stem thorn.

The other ZANLA men reluctantly shuffled about the perimeter of the house that was largely swept clean of any grass cover, just bone-dry sand and pebbles. The heat and flies were insufferable, the men looked and behaved exhausted. Completing their cursory search, the ZANLA men collected in the shade of the veranda. Loud conversation carried to where Ngwenya lay hidden. Their leader stood up from where he had been sitting, shouting at the men to keep quiet; there was a meeting going on inside.

The leader called to his men to begin the evening meal. Climbing up the stairs onto the veranda, the leader joked with his men.

'Whose turn is it to cook?'

'Tsumba, Comrade', said a man pointing to the youngest man in the group.

'Ah, Tsumba, you will make your wife happy one day because you can cook.'

'Aie Comrade, Tsumba will likely be someone's wife,' laughed the man to the great amusement of the others.

The laughter on the veranda carried to Ngwenya hiding in the riverbed. He could make out what they were saying because they were speaking loudly in seShona.

*

Road between Aldia de Barragem and Mabalane, 250km south of Vila Salazar

'Hello Zero, Hello Zero ... this is Blue41 do you read,' came a call from the Lynx, 7,000ft AGL above the road between Aldia de Barragem and Mabalane calling COMOPS TAC HQ aboard the Command Dak.

'Blue41, Zero, we copy you fives,' replied the Command Dak instantly.

'Roger, Zero, I am picking up a radio signal from the target Swallow at ...' the Lynx pilot gave a map reference. The Lynx carried Becker homing equipment.

'Blue41, standby.'

There was total consternation in the Command Dak as the COMOPS commander checked all the details. It was impossible; they had a report from the Selous Scouts that they had the target vehicles visual at Aldia de Barragem.

'Blue41, Zero, do you have the vehicle visual ... Over?'

'Negative I am too high, do you want me to take a look?'

'Roger, take a look.'

'Blue41, copied.'

Nobody spoke as the seconds ticked by. The pilot needed to drop altitude to get a visual identification of the vehicle giving off the tracking signal.

'Have the CIO reported any other vehicles with their tracking device?' the Commander asked, serious concern in his voice.

'Negative,' the officer on the command net replied.

'Fuck, what can this be then?'

The radio from the Lynx lit up again, 'Zero, Blue41 ... Roger I have two vehicles visual, travelling north, they are white Landcruisers, and I estimate thirty-five clicks south of Mabalane ... Over.'

'Fuck! Fuck! Fuck!' the COMOPS Commander burst out. 'Tell Blue41 to keep the vehicles visual ... we will get back to him.' The COMOPS Commander, a Brigadier, rounded on the radio operators, 'Get a message to the CIO confirming they only have one vehicle with a tracking device. Tell them what we have here ... How far are those vehicles from the RLI ambush site?'

'I estimate no more that fifteen clicks Sir,' came the reply.

'For fuck sakes. I don't believe this! Get a message to that RLI call-sign, what is it, 31, to take out those vehicles.' The Brigadier's voice was almost at a scream. 'How long will it be before those vehicles get to 31's position?'

'It's only a guess Sir, but maybe fifteen to twenty minutes.'

'I just don't fucking believe this. Who do we have on 31?'

'Lieutenant Greg Shaw from Support Commando and elements of Three Commando Sir.'

'Get him on the air ... NOW!'

In the ambush position commanded by Lt Greg Shaw, they had received a radio message from COMOPS TAC HQ aboard the Command Dak to stand down. They were told that the target was not expected in their sector and they were told not to attack any vehicles on the road until they were given further instructions.

Cpl Arthur Beamish and the men were pulled back from the road well out of sight.

'Looks like another lemon *Caporal*,' commented Le Beau as he bent over his gas cooker to brew up some tea.

'Fook'n COMOPS couldn't organise a piss-up in a brewery,' replied Beamish nodding his head in agreement.

'Ow are we going to get out *Caporal*?' asked Le Beau in a rare case of attempted conversation.

'We are supposed to be picked up by Selous Scout vehicles early tomorrow,' replied Beamish distractedly.

'So who were we supposed to ambush anyway Corp?' pressed Kratzman. 'Are they not coming any more?'

'How the fook am I to know, we are all members of the mushroom club ... they keep us in the dark and feed us shit,' grunted Beamish, happy to repeat his favourite saying that he felt described the army perfectly.

'Yes, I know Corp but you must have some idea?' asked Kratzman, not giving up.

'Fook'n hell Yank leave it alone ... I don't know and I don't want to know ... when we are told to take out someone in the ambush we will find out then ... now leave me alone for fook sakes!'

All three VHF radios burst into life as the Command Dak called them.

'31, 31, 31 ... Zero ... do you copy?'

Lt Shaw responded instantly, 'Zero, 31 copy you fives.'

'You have two vehicles approaching your loc from the south, two white Landcruisers, take them out, I say again ... take them out ... do you copy?'

At that very second, Eric Parnell in the stop group to the south called to confirm he had vehicles approaching at speed.

'Beamish, get your men into position!' screamed Shaw as he took off towards the anthill and his explosives. There was a mad scramble as the men grabbed rifles and kit and ran the hundred metres towards the road.

'31, 31Bravo, target is through my position, confirm two Landcruisers,' called Parnell.

Lt Shaw reached the anthill as the first Landcruiser sped past. He clamped down on the trigger just as the second Landcruiser entered the killing ground. The road underneath the vehicle erupted into a vertical pillar of dirt and smoke, launching it skyward, simultaneously being struck from the side by millions of steel pellets from the claymores strung along the side of the road. The Landcruiser began a barrel roll in mid-air before coming back to earth bonnet first, then, still travelling at seventy kilometres an hour, began to bounce end over end, doors flung open, the occupants hurled out like rag dolls into the dusty road.

Slowing down because of the explosion behind it, the first vehicle arrived at Lt Van Deventer's stop position. It was attacked by MAG and rifle fire causing it to veer off the road into a tree where it disintegrated into a fireball, followed by loud explosions as the ammunition and ordinance it was carrying blew up.

Beamish and his men did not get the opportunity to fire off one round. The Lynx swooped down low over their position, '31, Blue 41, you are requested to collect the bodies for ID ... Over.'

'Corporal Beamish, bring your stick, come with me ... the rest of you cover us,' called Shaw, getting up to run into the road. The Landcruiser had come to rest a good 50m away; it looked like it had been carrying a driver and three passengers.

'31, 31 ... Blue 41, you have vehicles approaching from the north, I count six, three are BTR troop carriers ...' called the Lynx pilot matter-of-factly, as if commenting on how pleasant the weather was this time of year.

'Beamish, collect those bodies ... quickly man,' ordered Shaw pointing at the bodies lying in the road. He then called Van Deventer, '31Alpha, do you have those vehicles visual ... Over?'

'Roger, I can see their dust approaching, maybe three clicks ... Over.' The road was dead straight and the countryside as flat as a pancake, the dust from the approaching convoy lifted high into the late afternoon sky.

'31Alpha, 31 ... do not engage unless you are fired upon. I say again ... do not engage unless you are fired upon,' called Shaw urgently, Van Deventer could be hopelessly outnumbered and too far away from Shaw and Beamish for them to provide support.

'31Alpha, copied.'

'31Bravo, 31.' Shaw called Parnell's stop group. Parnell acknowledged instantly.

'Roger, 31Bravo, RV at my loc, do you copy ... Over.' Shaw knew he needed to consolidate his call-signs, things could get out of hand.

'31Bravo, copied, we are moving now.'

By this time, Beamish and his stick had dragged the four bodies off the road. The description 'bodies' was not strictly true as one was still alive, albeit seriously banged up. Shaw pulled a folded sheet of paper out of his combat jacket. It had grainy photographs of ten men printed on it, he held the paper against each of the four faces.

Not one match!

'Okay pull these bodies into the bush and take up your positions in the ambush,' Shaw instructed Beamish and his men.

'31, 31Alpha, vehicles one click away ... Over.' Van Deventer called an urgent warning. The dust from the convoy was now visible from the ambush site.

The approaching convoy of vehicles could see the burning Landcruiser ahead of them and they slowed down. The two leading BTRs had 12.7mm machine guns mounted above the cab and they could be seen spinning them from side to side, covering both sides of the road. The burning vehicle spread flames to the surrounding trees that ignited in plumes of fire as the tinder-dry leaves and bark exploded. The fire raced down the side of the road, covering the area in thick acrid smoke, making it difficult to see. The oncoming convoy disappeared behind the curtain of smoke.

Van Deventer and his men stayed in their position as they heard the vehicles come to a stop. Shouted instructions carried over the loudly idling diesel engines. The smoke was too thick to see through, flames crackled loudly. The intense heat from the burning vehicle could be felt from across the road.

Then out of the smoke, a sweepline of FRELIMO troops came into view. They were following behind two BTRs that were creeping side by side, slowly down the road.

The sweepline was going to walk right through Van Deventer's position. Van Deventer had two Support Commando men manning a 88mm (3.5 inch) anti-tank rocket launcher. They had already loaded a missile and were aiming it through the smoke. The M20A1B1 rocket launcher, acquired from the Portuguese, was a two-piece smoothbore weapon of the open-tube type. They were fired by an electrical firing mechanism with a magneto, that provided the current, located in the trigger grip.

The number two man on the rocket glanced across at Van Deventer who gave him a thumbs up. The man tapped his partner firmly on the shoulder and the rocket instantly launched. A jet of hot gasses burst out from the rear of the launcher as the rocket flew out, travelling the fifty metres to the nearest BTR in half a second, entering through the grill in front of the engine, blowing the engine up through the steel bonnet. The impact and explosion knocked the 12.7mm gunner off his weapon throwing him back into the crew compartment.

Turning the machinegun, the gunner in the second BTR opened up into the smoke, raking the bush on both sides of the road. The FRELIMO sweepline went to ground and added their fire.

Van Deventer's position soon became untenable, the heavy machinegun cutting down trees and branches all around. It was impossible to return fire accurately. The men with the 88mm rocket were unable to reload the launcher, they were pinned down.

'Let's get out of here!' Van Deventer called to his stop group, as he began to crawl backwards away from the road. The men needed no second thought; the withering gunfire whistled only centimetres above their heads.

The FRELIMO sweepline, realising that they were opposed by only a small number of men, began to skirmish forward. They dodged from tree to tree, diving into cover and returning fire. The BTR 12.7 gunner zeroed in on where the Rhodesians were hiding and started to lay down more accurate fire. The driver moved off the road into a better position.

Van Deventer was trapped, they could not cut and run.

'31, 31, 31Alpha, we are taking heavy fire, we are pinned down ... we need support ... Over.'

High above in the Command Dak, the Brigadier was pulling his hair out. The Lynx had reported that both vehicles had been successfully taken out, but that the men on the ground had not identified any ZANLA leaders. It was possible that they had been travelling in the first, incinerated Landcruiser. Then Van Deventer's predicament came through on the Battle Command Net frequency.

'31Alpha, 31 ... stand by, we will come forward to your loc,' replied Shaw. He then turned to Beamish. 'Beamish, 31Alpha is in shit up the road. Take the crew with the eighty-eight mill with you, get across the road and try and flank the bastards. We will move up this side of the road to provide support.' At that moment, Parnell and his stick came jogging back through the bush. 'I'll take 31Bravo with me.'

'Yes Sur,' was all Beamish could manage, the war up the road sounded bad. The thump of the heavy machinegun sent shivers through the spine.'

'Hello Zero, Hello Zero, this is 31 ... request air support, Over.' Shaw called the Command Dak for help ... they were going to need it.

Racing across the road with his two gunners and the two-man crew of the anti-tank rocket, Beamish could clearly see the raging bush fire; a slight kink in the road obscured the BTR firing at Van Deventer. Once into the bush they moved forward at a fast walking pace, a gunner on each side and the rocket crew behind.

On the opposite side of the road, Shaw had brought his 60mm mortar into action, the well-practiced crew were starting to drop shells in support of Van Deventer. Van Deventer could be heard on the radio providing corrections, 'left fifty, add one fifty ... add one hundred ...'

It did not take long for Beamish to see the BTR through the trees; it had pulled off the road pointing into the bush, its gun firing steadily. The BTR was open-topped with the 12.7mm mounted on a bracket just behind the cab. A turret did not protect the gunner from behind; Beamish could just see the top of his head through the trees.

The bushfire was spreading towards down the side of the road. Smoke filled the air and the lack of breeze made it worse.

'Can you get a shot at that thing?' asked Beamish of the Support Commando men.

'No Corp, we need to get closer, there's too many trees in the way.'

'We need to get it to come to us. Le Beau ... Yank shoot at that BTR ... try and get the gunner,' instructed Beamish. 'You two get that bloody thing ready.'

Both gunners opened up at the back of the BTR. The effect was immediate. The sound of the rounds hitting the rear of the vehicle, and some whistling over the top was enough to spook the gunner, who stopped shooting and ducked inside. The driver slammed the vehicle into reverse and started pulling back out into the road. The MAG rounds could not penetrate the 9mm thick metal skin.

'Come on boys,' Beamish called to the men with the rocket, as he rushed to the edge of the road. The rocket was already in the launcher; the operator knelt down next to a tree. The BTR was no more than 60m away, reversing up the road. Both MAGs hammered away, a front left tyre burst, causing the vehicle to veer broadside on, presenting the rocket crew with a bigger target.

WHOOSH ... the rocket ignited ... travelled the short distance, striking the BTR just below the closed hatch on the driver's side. The BTR exploded, a jet of flame shot back into the crew compartment incinerating the 12.7 gunner. They must have been carrying spare fuel because a ball of flame lifted out of the back of the vehicle as the diesel reached ignition temperature.

Beamish and his RLI men shouted out in spontaneous triumph.

The FRELIMO sweepline could not see the explosion of the second BTR, instead pressing their attack on Van Deventer who was still defending his position valiantly.

'31, 31 this is Yellow Leader, do you read?' An air force pilot was calling Lt Shaw. The call came through clearly on Beamish's radio. There was no response from Shaw. Gunfire across the road increased in intensity as Shaw and Parnell entered the fray.

The air force pilot called again. He was orbiting at 25,000ft and could see the burning vehicle and the bushfire spreading in the western side of the road.

'Yellow Leader, 31Charlie, reading you fives,' replied Beamish.

'Roger, 31Charlie, can you call me in?'

'Yellow Leader, Charlie Tangos to my east and to my north, 31 ... 31Alpha and 31Bravo are in contact. I am uncertain of their position ... Over.'

There was a pause as the pilot consulted his briefing notes, working out who these call-signs were. The radio call-signs and a summary of the orders were strapped to his thigh.

It was then than Lt Shaw, 31, came back on the air. He confirmed the position of the enemy, but added, 'Yellow Leader, I cannot call you in, I am pinned down, I will mark FLOT on your command ... Over.'

'Roger, all 31 call-signs mark FLOT on my call,' called the pilot, Yellow Leader. '31Charlie, you call me in, I am attacking east to west, do you copy?'

'31Charlie, copied,' snapped back Beamish. He had never called in Hunters before. The sound of the jets flying above carried above the gunfire.

'Roger, all 31 call-signs ... standby ... standby ... mark FLOT ... mark FLOT.'

Beamish tossed out a smoke grenade, its bright red colour contrasting with the smoke from the bushfire.

'Roger, I have you all visual ... 31Charlie, confirm CTs to the north.'

'31Charlie, confirmed CTs one hundred and fifty metres to the north,' called Beamish, the adrenaline coursing through his body, bringing the scene in front of him into sharp focus.

Two Hawker Hunters from Yellow Section peeled off and dived towards their target. The pilot could see the three fizzing smoke grenades clearly and the FRELIMO troops moving through the bush to the north.

One behind the other, at 500ft, the Hunters screamed over, strafing the ground with their four 30mm Aden cannons, exactly where Beamish had indicated. Dust lifted into the air as the explosive heads detonated, to devastating effect.

The FRELIMO troops in the path of the air attack where annihilated, their bodies shredded by the withering cannon fire. Those that survived, broke in panic, running to the north. Wounded men were screaming in pain. The jets passed overhead, climbing steeply back into the ice blue sky, Beamish could see them clearly, sun glinting off the cockpit canopies.

'All 31 call-signs, stay in your positions. We will take another run,' called Yellow Leader.

FRELIMO men appeared in the bush across the road, they were looking left and right, as if contemplating crossing over.

'Confirm gooks visual across the road, twelve o'clock,' hissed Beamish. He glanced at the two gunners, including the two rocket men, who now had their rifles in their hands.

A screaming roar rolled across the bush as the Hunters returned, their cannons firing, cutting a swathe through the trees. The FRELIMO soldiers across the road from Beamish, decided now was their chance to make a break for it; they came sprinting across the road directly towards Beamish's stick. None of them made it, all seven died in a hail of MAG and rifle fire. Their bodies lay sprawled in the road.

As quickly as the Hunters had arrived, they left ...

There was no point trying to hunt down the remainder of the FRELIMO men. The focus now was on escape.

22

Aldia de Barragem Mozambique, 284km south east of Vila Salazar

As Ngwenya and Schultz watched in total surprise, the members of the guard inexplicably fired up the BTR and drove out of the compound, leaving behind the three white Landcruisers. They could not believe their eyes. The men in the bodyguard had cooked themselves a meal then packed up all their kit, loaded the vehicles, and left.

'Did you see anyone come out of the house?' Schultz asked Ngwenya, his binoculars in his eyes.

'No, but then we can't see what's happening on the other side of the house,' replied Ngwenya.

'But the Landcruisers are still here ... the target must still be inside. Have you seen any women at all? Tongogara is supposed to have a girlfriend in this town,' whispered Schultz earnestly.

'Negative ... maybe the escort has gone to fetch her.'

'That's possible ...' Schultz was now deep in thought. 'Right ... it's now or never, I think it's dark enough.'

Their target was being handed to them on a plate!

The four Selous Scouts crept out of the thick undergrowth in the riverbed, dusted themselves off and then proceeded down the approach road to the house. In the early evening, they looked like any group of FRELIMO soldiers returning from a patrol. The house stood alone, well away from neighbouring properties. The Selous Scouts used the outbuildings to mask their approach to the main house. This allowed them to get within twenty metres of the back door without being seen. They stopped for a few minutes to make absolutely sure that they had not been detected and to check that no hidden guard had been posted.

A light was on in the kitchen and from what they could see; another light was on in the dining room. The rest of the house was in darkness. The electricity network in the area had long since collapsed so the light could only be from gas or paraffin lamps.

Schultz studied the ground, scanning everything in minute detail. He had survived thus far through meticulous attention to detail. It was important to make sure there were no obstacles on the way in and on the escape route out, nothing that could make a noise or cause an injury. Then, signalling his men, he ran silently across the open ground to the back door. Ngwenya was right behind him with his pack containing the bunker-bombs. They crouched down next to the back door, hearts beating hard. Taking a few moments to get their breathing back under control, Schultz signalled the other two.

Seals and Kumpher crossed the open ground, taking position on the opposite side of the door.

The back door was a stable-door with the top half standing open; a full-length mosquito screen covered the whole doorway. The screen was torn in half. The air was alive with mosquitos, being so close to the only source of permanent water for hundreds of kilometres. They buzzed around the men's faces biting into every bit of exposed skin. Loud conversation could be heard coming from inside the house, unmistakably seShona. *The ZANLA men are still here!*

Gently opening his pack, Ngwenya withdrew a bunker bomb fitted with a delayed fuse. Schultz signalled for him to wait, instead reaching up to the mosquito screen to see if it was latched. Schultz's own improvised plan was to try to snatch one of the senior FRELIMO or ZANLA men, this was a major intelligence gathering opportunity. Blowing them all up with a bunker bomb would defeat that purpose. Plan A: snatch and kill, Plan B: kill.

Schultz carefully pulled the spring-loaded mosquito screen open. It gave off a loud creak on its rusty hinges. The men froze … they waited … Schultz let the screen push back into place. Trying to control their breathing, the four men paused, tension building in their bodies, hearts racing in their chests.

The sound of voices continued from inside the building.

A Fierynecked Nightjar, *Datiwa*, whistled loudly close by, *koo-WEEU, koo-WIririri*. Hearts missed a beat in fright. Each man sat in stunned silence trying to get their breathing back under control. The Nightjar, also called the Litanybird, had a call that set to words says, *good lord deliver us … good lord deliver us*.

The only other way into the house was through the front door, but the noise of climbing onto the concrete veranda and opening the door would be just as problematic.

Ngwenya went through the rehearsals in his mind. The other option was to hurl the bunker bombs through the windows and then rush in to finish off the occupants. Schultz had always been clear that he would prefer to do the killing as silently as possible to aid their escape. *There is, after all, a Brigade of FRELIMO within five kilometres* – Ngwenya worked through the options in his mind. The voices inside continued talking, their tone unaltered, just too soft for Ngwenya to make out exactly what they were saying.

Making a decision to continue with Plan A, Schultz signalled to Ngwenya.

'*Gogodza*, knock knock … *Pamusoroi!* … Excuse me!' Ngwenya called through the back door. '*Ndiani anoda chikafu?* … Who wants some food?'

Ngwenya waited … there was no response … *this is bloody strange*! The voices inside carried on as before. *Maybe the are pissed and can't hear!*

Schultz drew his men's attention again with hand signals. He pointed at the door, showed three fingers, *on the count of three!* He placed his hand on the screen door and jerked it open, the snapped movement actually made no sound at all. Then flipping open the latch to the stable door they were inside the darkened kitchen.

Seals and Kumpher stayed outside to protect the escape route.

The inside of the kitchen showed years of neglect, paint peeling off the walls, cracked floor and wall tiles, the sink was covered in rust. The fridge door stood open, broken on its hinges. It was a large rambling house, the dinning room was down a long dark passage. Signalling again, Schultz entered the passage, placing each step carefully, his rubber soled 'clandestine boots' silent on the concrete floor. Ngwenya followed, his AK47 at the ready.

The double door to the dining room stood open bathing that part of the passage in soft light. The voices were much louder now, Ngwenya could now make out the conversation, it sounded like a discussion in a bar ... *this just does not stack up!*

Every instinct was telling him to stop Schultz and get out of the house.

*

CIO HQ, Livingston Avenue, Salisbury

The tension in the Situation Room in CIO HQ had reached crisis proportions. The call from the COMOPS TAC HQ aboard the Command Dak had everyone rattled. The RLI had ambushed two Landcruisers on the road between Barragem and Mabalane, but nobody could confirm the identity of the passengers. The last message from Schultz and his Sierra call-sign had said that they were going in on their target. The other Sierra call-sign at Jorge do Limpopo had reported no movement at the house they had been watching and had already been recovered by the Selous Scout Flying Column.

'Do we have confirmation from the Lynx that the vehicles were both completely destroyed in the ambush?' Stanbridge asked his radioman for the third time.

'Yes Sir, the one was seen burning; nobody escaped, while the RLI recovered four bodies from the other. No targets on the list were ID'd.'

'Damn, but one of them had our transmitter in it! The bastards may have switched vehicles,' stammered Stanbridge, the shock in his voice palpable. 'Did Schultz confirm that they had Landcruisers visual at the house in Barragem?'

'Yes Sir, he reported three.'

'This does not make any sense at all. Our man never reported any changes in the plan did he?' said Stanbridge thinking aloud. '*Zizi* reported the convoy on its way to Barragem.'

In his mind's eye, Stanbridge could see his life-long career going up in smoke if the ZANLA leadership were not in that house in Barragem ... they had banked everything on this one opportunity. The carefully arranged disinformation fed to Faye Chan, the information spread by their spy in the ZANLA leadership, the diversionary attacks ... *Tongogara and his gang just have to be in that house!*

*

Aldia de Barragem Mozambique, 284km south east of Vila Salazar

Crouched down low next to the doorway to the dining room, Captain *Tsere* Schultz slipped a G-60 'flash-bang' from a pouch under his left arm. Like Audie Murphy, he pulled the pin out with his teeth, then holding the stun grenade with his right hand, he planned to roll the grenade backhanded into the room. The talking inside the room continued without interruption.

Schultz felt a light tap on his shoulder. He flashed his head around to see Cephas Ngwenya shaking his head slowly from side to side ... *something is desperately wrong!*

The talking in the dining room stopped abruptly.

The Selous Scouts froze, every muscle tight as a guitar string, breath held in the lungs.

'That would be Captain Chris Schultz, wouldn't it be?' said a voice from inside the room. The voice had a posh English Public School accent.

Who is this? Furtive glances passed between the Selous Scouts, too shocked to move.

'Captain Schultz, I am going to ask you to lay down your weapons. I know this is a hackneyed phrase but you are completely surrounded, I can assure you that there is no escape.'

'Who the fuck are you?' blurted out Schultz, his mind racing to assimilate what was going on. He did not want to stick his head into the dining room in case it got shot off.

'I am Major George Cornwell of Seven Troop, twenty-two SAS, my good fellow. In the room behind you is Sergeant Green and with him are three SAS troopers, there are some men in here with me and they are all the way around the house on the outside,' replied the voice.

The number of questions that raced through Schultz's mind was beyond belief; the circumstances were completely out of control, like a terrifying nightmare where nothing makes sense.

'I must ask you again ... put down your weapons and come inside the room,' said this man Cornwell, more demandingly.

From behind the Selous Scouts, back down the passage, came another voice, 'Nice and easy me old son, if any of you move a muscle I'll be forced to spoil your day,' said the new voice in a strong Yorkshire accent. A bright torchlight filled the passage and it was clear that they had no choice but to comply.

'I have a grenade in my hand with the pin pulled; I will throw it into the room. Leave us alone!' said Schultz defiantly.

'Be my guest old fruit, we half expected you to have thrown it already,' replied the Pom with the fancy accent. '... You were hoping to make a high-level capture!'

Footsteps came down the passage; Ngwenya saw the approaching silhouettes of three men with rifles raised in the shoulder.

'Well, well, well, so here we have the famous Captain Chris Schultz, Silver Cross of Rhodesia ... good evening t' you, Sur,' said one of the men. 'Now lets just slip that pin back into the grenade shall we.' The man took the pin out of his hand and pushed it back into place, at the same time taking the grenade out of his grip.

Speechless, the two Selous Scouts were efficiently relieved of their weapons and pushed unceremoniously into the dining room. The room was empty except for a large wooden table with a man sitting on the only other piece of furniture, a wooden bar stool. Three other men in parachute smocks and webbing flanked him. Sitting in the middle of the table was a tape recorder with one of the reels still turning. The whole seShona conversation had been played on the tape recorder.

'So you can see, we have been expecting you Captain,' said the Englishman gently.

Schultz's eyes flashed at the SAS troopers behind the man. Their weapons were held lightly in their arms but there was no question that they were alert and meant business. The other SAS men stood behind him.

Seals and Kumpher were brusquely manhandled into the room, grumbling their objection.

'I am afraid we have very little time, so I can't engage in chit chat Captain,' smiled the SAS Major disarmingly. 'Our brass were anxious that the ZANLA leadership, Tongogara in particular, not be killed. They have great plans for him you know.'

Schultz did not respond, intent instead on buying time to assimilate the situation.

'Now we could have simply booby trapped the house and blown you to smithereens, but we chose not to,' said the Major.

Still no response came from Schultz.

'In a few moments a very large helicopter will come skimming in over the trees and our friends from the Senior Service will whisk us back to our ship offshore. When that happens I have no doubt that our FRELIMO friends will become agitated and come looking about.' The Major now had a broad smile on his face, quite obviously enjoying himself.

'Why didn't you kill us?' asked Schultz, defiance in his voice.

'We wanted to send you a message, or more accurately, 22-SAS wants to send you a message. The message is simply this ... we have been tasked to protect Tongogara for the time being. He is at present being entertained aboard HMS Intrepid in the Mozambique Channel. We will return him to his normal duties when the dust has settled, so to speak.'

'Nobody will believe me,' replied Schultz.

'That may be the case, but it is important that you relay this message to your boss. We don't want any unnecessary bloodshed,' stated the SAS man emphatically, striking the table with the flat of his hand.

The loud, WHUMP ... WHUMP of a large helicopter could be heard in the distance, speedily approaching.

'Ah, there they are now, excellent timings, as always,' declared the Major, standing up. 'We will wish you adieu Captain, and the best of luck. I would skedaddle out of here directly if I was you.'

The helicopter clattered outside, flaring into the LZ that the SAS men had marked with flares; dust from its rotors entered the house through the broken windows. The SAS men swiftly departed the room. The Major walked up to Schultz proffering his hand, Schultz instinctively took it and the two men shook hands.

The Major leaned forward, 'When all this is over Captain, give me a call, I can offer you a job … plenty of excitement, meet strange and exotic people … and kill them.' The man threw his head back and laughed, a loud infectious laugh, that forced a begrudging smile from Schultz.

Outside the Royal Navy Westland Sea King helicopter, spun back to full power, its enormous bulk lifted into the night sky, disappearing to the east.

All Schultz could think was … *this war is totally fucked!*

The shocked and disconsolate Selous Scout team, melted into the bush, as they made their way to their pick-up point. Nobody spoke … each alone with his thoughts … Sgt. Cephas Ngwenya contemplated for the first time that this war could not be won! *These men with big helicopters, where did they come from?*

23

Mozambique, 30km south of Vila Salazar

The Selous Scout Flying Column picked up Lt Shaw, Van Deventer, Beamish and the other men in their ambush team. Despite the fierce firefight with FRELIMO, nobody was injured. They drove back into the small town of Mabalane at three in the morning. Beamish and his two gunners found themselves squashed into a Unimog Pig, with Eric Parnell and his stick. It was so uncomfortable that it became necessary for everyone inside to stand up and hold onto the side as the vehicle jolted and bounced along.

The men were allowed off the vehicle for a few minutes when they arrived in Mabalane so that everyone could take a leak and snatch something to eat. It was a pitch-dark night, with the moon and stars obscured by high cloud. 2nd Lt Van Deventer was in the other vehicle with Lt Shaw from Support Commando and his men.

It was perfectly quiet, except for the sound of a dog barking somewhere in the distance. The town had no streetlights and all the surrounding houses were in darkness. The locals had either run into the bush or were hiding in their houses terrified of what the invaders from the north could do to them.

With the casevac of Capt. Walker, a Selous Scout Colour Sergeant had taken command of the flying column, while the most senior rank amongst the RLI was Lt Shaw. He sat with the Selous Scout man discussing the plan for exiting the country. Beamish, Parnell and Van Deventer were listening in. A Lieutenant from the Armoured Car Regiment was in charge of the Eland 90s.

'Okay Sir,' said the Colour Sergeant addressing Shaw, as the group huddled around a map laid out on the ground. 'The plan is to drive straight back up the road, fight through Jorge do Limpopo if we have to, then cross the border at the same place we entered to the east of Vila Salazar.' He traced the route on the map using a penlight torch and a stick he was holding. 'We know this road well, so we can expect that it will take about four hours to the powerlines and then another four hours to get through the bush to the border.'

'Are we expecting any opposition Colour?' asked Shaw.

'We didn't get any on the way in, which was strange as both ZANLA and FRELIMO have large garrisons at Jorge do Limpopo and Mapai,' replied the Selous Scout matter-of-factly. 'We have plenty of firepower plus the Blue Jobs should be around to provide air support.'

'Looks pretty straightforward, let's hope the bastards haven't put any landmines in the road. They must know we are here,' stated Shaw.

'That is one thing, but I am more worried about their tanks. They are supposed to have a few up here somewhere. We don't have anything to stop a tank other than the Elands.'

'My 90mm gun will sort out any of those T-54s if they are around Colour,' chipped in the Lieutenant from the Armoured Car Regiment.

'Let's hope you see him before he sees you … Sir,' said the Selous Scout. 'Okay … lets move out in ten minutes … same convoy order as on the way in. It's a hundred and thirty five clicks to Jorge do Limpopo, I would like to get there before first light.'

There was no room for debate. The Selous Scout folded his map and disappeared into the night.

The vehicles all started up and the lead Eland 90 moved out into the road, Beamish's vehicle ended up second from the rear, with an Eland 90 behind them. With no breeze, the cold night air was thick with gritty dust that seemed to get into the mouth despite the face-veil. It was impossible to look forward into the dust, so Beamish stood at the back of the vehicle holding onto the roll-bar, cursing the army in his mind.

The truck had a crew of four Selous Scouts including the driver. Mounted at the rear were two MAGs. A captured 12.7mm machinegun was mounted on top of the cab facing forward, protected by steel plate on either side. With Beamish, his two gunners and Parnell's stick, there were seven RLI men, plus the four Selous Scouts made a total of eleven.

Driving through the cold darkness, the passage of the convoy was marked by tiny red lights shining at the rear of each vehicle. Without headlights the driver could not see the road surface, he just focused on the red light in front of him, concentrating hard at maintaining his following distance. He could not avoid holes or obstructions. The result was violent lurching left and right as the truck bounced and gyrated over the rough road, throwing the passengers around viciously in the back. The convoy was travelling at close to 60km/hr. making matters much worse. The Selous Scout driver had insisted that the RLI passengers strap in, with only the Selous Scout men manning the guns. Beamish had told him to 'Fook off.' The driver merely shrugged … *if you want to become a human missile if we hit a tin, be my guest.*

The convoy left Mabalane without incident, drove the short distance to Jorge do Limpopo at a steady pace, without any sign of ZANLA or FRELIMO. In fact, they saw nobody at all. The trip through the town of Jorge do Limpopo was also uneventful. The small town was, for all intents and purposes, the last hurdle on the way back to Rhodesia. There were no other towns to pass through other than the tiny hamlet at Madulo Pan.

As they reached the 30km point, just short of the powerlines the men visibly relaxed … nearly home.

Home … it was a powerful thought. Beamish, for the first time, had come to terms with the fact that Rhodesia was his home … that is where he belonged.

*

COMOPS TAC HQ aboard the Command Dak, 10,000ft AGL 50km southeast of Vila Salazar

The message from the Selous Scout call-sign at the ambush site near Aldia de Barragem had been alarming to say the least. All it said was that the mission had been compromised and that the Flying Column should expect an ambush as it exited Mozambique. It was still dark outside; the Dak had only been on station for a few minutes having flown from New Sarum Air Force base in Salisbury. The message had come in on the HF net via Selous Scout HQ at Andre Rabie Barracks.

As he sat at his post in the Command Dak, the Brigadier thought about whether he should raise the alarm. The latest sitrep from the Flying Column reported 8km to the turn-off at the powerlines, less than 40km to the border. As he looked out the window, the first sign of the morning appeared on the horizon.

'Call the Flying Column ... warn them of a potential ambush,' he said.

The message never got through.

*

CIO HQ, Livingston Avenue, Salisbury

George Stanbridge held the transcribed message from the Selous Scout team at Aldia de Barragem. The word 'compromised' stood out like a flashing red light, as if a screeching siren was going off in his head. Without saying a word, Stanbridge excused himself from the operations room and walked down the passage to his office.

He lifted the telephone receiver and dialled a number, willing the old phone to go faster.

With only one ring on the other side, the phone was picked up.

'Broken spear,' was all Stanbridge said, repeating it again, 'broken spear.'

The phone went dead.

1,000km to the south a radio message blared in the headphones of the pilot of a Beechcraft King Air B100. The pilot called the Lansaria Airport[122] control tower to activate the flight plan that he had submitted the day before. The co-pilot called two burly looking men who were standing next to the wing, who immediately climbed on board. The door was clamped shut and the two 533 kW Garrett AiResearch TPE-331 engines began to whine. The aircraft bumped along the uneven taxiway to the end of runway 06 Left and took off to the northeast.

The aircraft registration had the familiar G- prefix for aircraft registered in the UK ... its flight plan said Charles Prince[123] airport Salisbury ...

Stanbridge left his office, took the lift to the ground floor and walked purposefully through the carpark. A BMW 2500 drove slowly down Livingston Avenue, it pulled to a halt when the driver saw Stanbridge wave from the pavement. He got into the back seat and the car sped off, turning into Lomagundi Road ... the road to Charles Prince Airport.

---

122 Airport, mainly light aircraft and civilian operators, 29km northwest of Johannesburg.
123 Formally named Mt Hampden airport, built under the Empire Air Training Scheme in World War II.

The driver turned to George Stanbridge and in a posh English accent said, 'I am sorry it had to end this way George ... as they say ... all good things ...'

George Stanbridge sat back into the seat and looked out at the houses with manicured gardens flashing past ... the Jacaranda were in flower, carpeting the pavements with their lavender blossoms ... *thank God for the old school tie*, he reflected ... Each kilometre took him away from his home ... his country ... it was all over.

*

Mozambique, 22km south of Vila Salazar

At 5am, the early morning light appeared in the east. The convoy drove on. Beamish had no idea where they were or how close they were to the border ... he just wanted it to be over. It was freezing cold; every muscle ached from being bashed around in the back of the truck. The vibration played havoc with the bladder. Anyone needing to take a piss had to do so out the back door, precariously hanging onto the rear roll-bar with one hand.

The light steadily improved until the vehicle in front was clearly visible. Mercifully, an early morning breeze sucked the dust off the road, but made it much colder. A shivering Beamish looked around at the men and weapons, all covered in a fine red dust, making them almost unrecognisable.

A loud thudding bang echoed over the convoy. The vehicle ahead, a Four-Five, turned off the road into the bush on the left, while Beamish's went right, pushing over a tree as it did so. The radios burst into life.

'Ambush right ... ambush right,' someone was calling. Another loud explosion split the morning, a whining shell passed overhead. More explosions followed in quick succession, a very heavy calibre machinegun was firing. As Beamish watched, the Eland 90 behind accelerated into the bush, passing their vehicle, crashing through the trees.

All the vehicles had pulled off the road; the well-rehearsed ambush routine was being executed. In the bush left and right of the road, the convoy pushed forward together. The radio was alive with calls as the vehicles in the front of the convoy took on the ambushers.

Small arms and machinegun fire erupted ahead. Stray rounds passed over the vehicle, buzzing and whining as they went. Beamish ducked back into the vehicle, sitting down next to Le Beau, pushing his rifle through the metal port in the side of the vehicle ... *fookin hell!*

The Selous Scout standing next to Beamish opened up with the MAG ... 'Gooks left ... Gooks left,' he shouted.

His mate on the 12.7 above the cab twisted the barrel around and added his fire. The noise was ear splitting in the confined space. Hot shell casings from the MAG fell onto Beamish's arm making him yelp in pain. Le Beau opened fire with his MAG, the barrel pushed through a gun port in the side of the vehicle. In an ambush the idea is to shoot off as many rounds as possible, it did not matter that they weren't aimed at anything. Kratzman joined in with his gun. More hot shell casings flew at Beamish, MAGs, only inches from each of his arms.

'Stop firing ... Stop firing,' screamed Beamish, his voice drowned out by the sound of three MAGs and a 12.7 firing at the same time. Le Beau was oblivious to Beamish's burning arms. Beamish took off his combat cap and slapped Le Beau with it, trying to get him to stop, the pain was killing him. Le Beau looked at him blankly, thinking that Beamish was urging him on, he kept firing, Beamish resorting to trying to bat the casings away as they flew at him. He thought of standing up, but the distinctive sound of bullets hitting the outside of the vehicle put paid to that.

It was impossible to see what was going on outside the vehicle, all that Beamish could see were trees scraping past outside, the Selous Scout standing up next to him stopped to refill his ammunition box. The ammo boxes had belts for the MAG already loaded into them, so it was just a case of dropping a new box into position, lifting the belt out and slapping it into the breach.

Beamish's vehicle suddenly stopped. The Selous Scout next to him grunted. Blood burst from his chest, spraying over Beamish. The man slumped down onto the floor of the truck. A grinding metallically sound of the engine starter-motor, carried to the back of the vehicle. The driver desperately tried to restart the vehicle; a burning smell filled the air as the starter-motor burnt itself out.

The other Selous Scout behind Beamish on the MAG bellowed at the driver, 'Pudding is down, Pudding is down, we need a casevac.'

Pudding must be the nickname for the wounded man.

The driver reached for the HF radio to call the convoy commander.

'Oscar1, Oscar1, Oscar14 ... do you read.'

No response.

He called again, nothing.

'Try the big means,' someone shouted.

Beamish swung around in the confined space to see if he could help the stricken man, but he was wedged in the tiny space between the row of seats and the back doors. Bullets were still flying over the top of the vehicle.

'We are sitting ducks ... we can't stay here,' screamed the Selous Scout behind Beamish.

'I am almost out of ammo,' called the man on 12.7.

'The engine's fucked, we must have taken a round through the engine or radiator,' replied the driver, concern in his voice.

All the other vehicles in the convoy had disappeared into the bush ahead.

'I can't see any gooks at the moment, but it won't take them long to find us,' said the Selous Scout on the MAG.

The driver made the call, 'Okay everyone out ... all-round defence ... Go!'

The rear door was flung open and the wounded man Pudding fell out into the dirt before anyone could catch him. Everyone jumped out except the man on the 12.7; he was calling over and over again on the radio.

The Selous Scout gunner went to work on Pudding who was looking in very bad shape. The round must have hit him in the back and then exited through his chest. He was sucking for air, blood bubbling out of his mouth.

'Whose in charge here,' asked Beamish examining the Selous Scouts who all looked exactly the same in FRELIMO uniforms, thick black camo-cream, bushy beards, combat caps clamped over long hair.

'I am,' said the Driver.

'Well, what's the plan?' asked Beamish urgently, Eric Parnell stood next to him, also interested to find out. Their briefing had not extended to this eventuality.

'It's best to stay with the vehicle, it's easier to find us from the air, plus we have spare ammo, water and the radio equipment,' said the Driver.

'Yes but it makes a fook'n big target for the gooks as well,' replied Beamish, now thinking hard about what to do.

'You won't believe this,' called out the man still inside the truck, 'the only people I can raise on the big means is Vila Salazar!'

'We may have to string a dipole[124], we might be in a blank spot. The Command Dak probably isn't up yet,' replied the Driver.

'There isn't time to start stringing dipoles up,' exclaimed Beamish.

'Pudding's had it,' moaned the Selous Scout working on the wounded man. 'He had no chance … I did everything I could.'

Beamish looked down at the all too familiar sight of torn first field dressings, drips, drip kits and … blood.

Nobody responded, just looking down at the dead man, his combat cap now covering his face. The Selous Scouts showed no outward emotion, they were all business.

Kratzman's MAG burst into life. Everyone dived into the dirt.

'I got him … he is over there to the west,' shouted Kratzman. A lone, disorientated, FRELIMO cadre had stumbled into their position.

Beamish had dived down next to the Selous Scout driver. 'Look, we can't stay here, this place is going to be crawling with gooks in no time.'

'Now they will be! … Fuck, you RLI types have no idea, why shoot one gook and give our position away!'

Beamish didn't answer.

'What's your name?' asked the Selous Scout abruptly. He wasn't interested in Beamish's rank, he could have been a colonel, it would have made no difference.

'Beamish. That's Parnell,' replied Beamish, pointing to where Eric Parnell had taken cover.

'You can call me Jack. What frequency have you got your A63 set on?'

'130.60 … J60.'

'Change it to the battle command net frequency … 132.20, code L20. That way when they come looking for us we will all be on the same frequency, you better tell your other stick commander.'

'Okay,' replied Beamish, starting to realize just how switched on these

---

[124] A dipole antenna is a radio antenna with a centre-fed driven element. It consists of two metal conductors of rod or wire, in this case, strung between trees or between the vehicle and a tree. The radio frequency voltage is applied to the antenna at the centre, between the two conductors.

Selous Scouts were. There was no way these men were going to take orders from Beamish.

'The first thing we need to figure out is exactly where we are. I know we are well north of Jorge do Limpopo, but I wasn't map reading while I was driving ...' The man looked around. 'The road would be to our west maybe only a few hundred metres,' added Selous Scout Jack, mostly to himself. He really wasn't interested in seeking Beamish's opinion.

Jack studied the broken truck, his dead comrade, and the RLI men, obviously deep in thought ... summing up the situation. 'Well one thing's for sure we are not short of firepower, our gunner, plus your two Beamish, and another there,' he said pointing to Eric Parnell's gunner. That makes four MAGs amongst the ten of us ...'

'How far is it to the border?' asked Beamish, dreading the answer.

The man didn't need to consult the map. 'Twenty-two clicks give or take, to the border ... in a straight line, but that would be directly through a nest of FRELIMO at Malvernia.'

The implications did not bear thinking about ... *twenty-two clicks with half the FRELIMO army chasing us ...*

Beamish instinctively looked to the sky ... *where are the bloody Blue Jobs?* There was a strong burning rubber smell in the air. To the north, two pillars of smoke lifted high into the morning sky. A fire was also burning to the east. The VHF radios remained silent.

Selous Scout Jack saw him look up. 'Don't worry Beamish, they will figure out we are missing and come looking. We won't have to walk twenty-two clicks.' Then he turned to all the men who had been attentively listening to the conversation with Beamish, 'Okay, people ... fill your water bottles from the jerry-cans ... gunners fill your belts from the box of rounds in the truck. Get rid of excess weight ... carry water, ammo, radio batteries and one tin of bully beef. Throw everything else into the truck.' Addressing the man in the truck, 'Spike! ... Load up the TR48'. Turning to the man who had attended to Pudding, his arms covered in blood, 'Gonzo![125] ... Take a gun.' Then turning once again to the RLI men, 'We move out in twenty minutes ... Gonzo, wrap Pudding in a bivy, and bury him over near that tree, cut a mark into the tree so we can find it again later ... somebody help him. I'm going to booby-trap the truck.'

The men followed Jack's instructions without question; there was no doubt who was in charge. The men went about their business. Eric Parnell helped Gonzo dig his shallow grave, while Selous Scout Jack rigged a POMZ across the back doors of the Pig, with two AP mines in the soft sand immediately in front of the back doors, in exactly the position a person would have to stand to open them. The men were ready in the allotted time, all studying Jack intently for his next set of instructions ... they instinctively knew that their survival was now in this man's hands.

Instead of addressing the men as a group, Jack spoke to Beamish so all could hear. This was his way of indicating that he saw Beamish as the 2IC in

125 Chilapalapa, rat.

this escapade.

'Okay, Beamish, we will make our way to the road so that we can pinpoint our position. Once that is established, we will move across country to by-pass Malvernia, then make our way to the border fence. It shouldn't take more than a few hours for the Blue Jobs to find us … or the Flying Column will double back. I will take the lead with Gonzo, then your stick Parnell, Beamish and your gunners at the back with Spike. Turn off your radios, I'll leave mine on …' Then turning to make his final point, he addressed all the men, '… you people move quietly if you want to stay alive!'

It was only 6:30am and the heat was already building. What Selous Scout Jack had not shared was that, once FRELIMO found the burnt-out truck, following the spoor of ten men through the bush was a piece of cake!

24

Mozambique, 19km south of Vila Salazar

The fact that the Selous Scout Flying column had met no resistance on the way into Mozambique or on the way out, was for one simple reason, FRELIMO and ZANLA knew they were coming. They had laid a carefully planned trap, 19km south of Malvernia. The trap was set at the intersection with the 500kV powerlines running from Cahora Bassa to South Africa.

The trap included two T-54B tanks and about 1,000 FRELIMO and ZANLA troops. The tanks had been positioned in heavy bush close to the turnoff at the powerlines, facing south down the road. The troops were dug in on both sides of the road and along the cut line underneath the powerlines. In the early hours of the morning, as the Flying Column approached the turnoff, the two tanks initiated the ambush.

The inexperience of the tank crews was the saving grace. The first round missed the Eland 90 at the head of the column, by inches, while the second round took out the third vehicle in the column, a Four-Five, killing all the occupants. The vehicle had been literally torn apart like a hyena on a carcass. The Eland 90 crew at the head of the column finished off one of the tanks, while the other tank had spun around and escaped to the north. The two destroyed vehicles were still burning an hour later. The column had taken heavy fire from RPG and machineguns but they had forced their way through the ambush, along the cut line under the powerlines. Their well-rehearsed anti-ambush drill had flanked the enemy position, saving the day.

Once clear of the ambush, the Selous Scout in charge of the column took stock and discovered that Selous Scout Jack's vehicle was missing (Oscar14). There was no way they could return to run the gauntlet. They reported the missing vehicle to COMOPS TAC HQ aboard the Command Dak and to Selous Scout HQ at Andre Rabie Barracks. The air force scrambled a Lynx that had been waiting at Mbalauta. Two G-cars were repositioned to Vila Salazar to be as close as possible for an extraction, and a Hunter section was asked to loiter at 25,000ft. The Brigadier in the Command Dak also called New Sarum to put two Canberras on immediate standby, armed with Alpha bombs, in case they were needed.

Everyone knew that Selous Scout Jack, Oscar14, plus Beamish and his detachment, 31Charlie, of the RLI were still alive as their HF message had been forwarded by 2RR at Vila Salazar.

They needed to be extracted.

*

Mozambique, 18km southeast of Vila Salazar

Selous Scout Jack and Beamish could see the cutline for the powerlines and two giant steel pylons. Jack had changed his mind about moving towards the road. He figured that the powerlines were the route home anyway and he did not want to cross the road and give the enemy their spoor to follow. It had been less than an hour's slow walk to the powerlines and the men were still relatively fresh. Now they could get an accurate fix on their position.

Beamish crouched next to Jack with his map in his hand and they agreed the grid reference. Jack also had an aerial photograph that showed the pylons. Each pylon had a number stencilled on it so they could match the two up. Part of the planning had been to record the pylon numbers for exactly this eventuality.

A distant thudding bang cut the air.

'Gooks have found our truck,' commented Jack nonchalantly. 'That means, once they have wiped the shit out of their eyes they will come looking for us.'

The radios lit up on the battle net. 'Oscar14, Zero, do you copy?' The Command Dak was calling.

'Zero, Oscar14, reading you fives.'

'Confirm your loc.'

'Zero we are at ... I have pylon number ... immediately to my north.' Jack read out the map reference in clear, there was no time to code things up, time was of the essence.

'Roger, Oscar14, standby for uplift in figures two zero.'

'Oscar14 copied.'

All the men had heard the radio message ... the feeling of relief, of knowing that the helicopters were coming, was indescribable. The men smiled at each other.

'Beamish, you wait here, I want to go forward to see if there is a suitable LZ on the cutline,' whispered Jack. He melted into the bush before Beamish could reply.

Beamish had the men lying down in tight all-round defence, their feet almost touching. Both his gunners facing back the way they had come. The tree cover was reasonably dense overhead while the ground was mostly sand with isolated tufts of grass, mainly under the shade of the trees. It was hot, well over 37°C. The strong smell of burning still filled the air.

Gonzo got to his feet.

'What are you doing?' asked Beamish.

'I'm going back on our spoor to lay a POMZ,' replied Gonzo. He didn't need permission. He too disappeared into the bush.

'Don't shoot that bastard when he comes back,' commented Beamish to no one in particular.

The minutes ticked by. Beamish looked at his watch, only ten minutes before the helicopters were due to arrive ... *please be quick.*

'Here comes Gonzo,' said Kratzman. 'He's runnin like a bat out of hell.'

Beamish whipped around to see the approaching Selous Scout, he had his head down with his rifle at the high port, his kit bouncing on his waist.

He arrived completely out of breath, sliding onto the ground next to Beamish.

'Maybe twenty gooks on our spoor ... I only just had enough time to set the POMZ ... we should hear it any second,' puffed Gonzo, sucking in air with a combination of surprise and exertion.

'Fook,' replied Beamish, looking back towards the powerlines ... *where the fook is Jack?*

The POMZ AP mine consists of a small TNT explosive charge inside a hollow cylindrical cast-iron fragmentation sleeve. The sleeve has large fragments cast into the outside and is open at the bottom to accept the insertion of a wooden mounting stake, which leaves the explosive head about 20cm above ground. On top is a weather cap, covering a fuse well, initiated with a tripwire fuse. The effective radius of the mine is often quoted as 4m, but a small number of large fragments may be lethal at ranges far exceeding that.

A loud thumping rumble rolled through the bush.

'Make that nineteen ...' said Gonzo.

The distinctive clattering sound of helicopters drifted on the breeze.

On the edge of the cutline, Jack popped a green smoke grenade.

At least two hundred ZANLA cadres had also heard the approaching helicopters. The hissing smoke grenade gave them something to shoot at.

The air literally filled with lead. The cutline under the powerlines was at least 300m wide so the rifle fire was not accurate, but it sounded like Da Nang on a bad day.

'Oscar14, Blue 1, do you read,' called the helicopter pilot.

Jack was leopard crawling back through the bush towards Beamish, he didn't answer.

'Blue 1, 31Charlie, copy you fives, we are taking heavy fire from our north ... we are fifty metres to the south of the green smoke ... Over.' Beamish took out his map, unfolded it and laid it out on the ground, shoving sand on the edges to hold it down. The map unfolded in this way could be seen easily from the air.

The two helicopters flew directly over Beamish's position at no more than 200ft, one behind the other. The FRELIMO follow-up group saw them coming and opened up with their AKs.

'31Charlie, I have you visual ... Shit ...'

The pilot had not counted on being fired at. Both helicopters rolled into a wider orbit. Then a 12.7mm opened up from the ZANLA position on the cutline. The green tracer raced across the sky towards the helicopters, forcing them away.

'31Charlie, Blue 1, we cannot get in to pick you up. You need to move to your east ... maybe three clicks there is a clearing for an LZ.' The helicopters moved further to the east, away from the 12.7.

The Lynx arrived overhead. The 12.7 started banging away at him.

'Okay, everybody up, we have to move,' shouted Beamish. 'We need to move further up the powerlines ... run.'

The men took off headlong into the bush, running for their lives. Being so far back from the cutline, they could not be seen from the other side. The fact that the helicopters had flown off to the east gave the CTs a target to aim at.

Beamish could not hear the Lynx calling in the Hunter strike, as it was on a different frequency. The Hunters came in from the east along the line of the powerlines and pounded the cutline. Each dropped a fran canister, throwing petroleum gel over the gunners on the 12.7 and the tightly grouped ZANLA cadres.

The escaping men ran for all they were worth, adrenaline carrying them on despite the intense heat. The MAG gunners breathed hard, the weight of the gun and the soft sand taking its toll. Dropping back, Beamish kept pace with them.

'Come on lads … not far to go …'

Running in the sand was like treacle; it seemed to suck at their rubber-soled boots making them feel heavier and heavier with every step.

… *2km to the LZ* …

Stray rounds started to crack over their heads … *someone is shooting at us!*

Beamish hoped that Jack had overheard the instructions from the helicopter pilot and was making his way to the LZ.

More rounds flew over … they seemed closer.

'Come on lads … we have some gooks chasing us,' shouted Beamish. The men didn't respond, just doggedly putting one foot in front of another, their run now a laboured shuffle, their boots dragging in the sand. Sweat soaked their clothing, filling their eyes … making them sting.

… *1km to the LZ* …

The helicopters came into view through the trees; tightly orbiting the LZ … *come on lads … we are so close.* They ran on.

… *200m to the LZ* …

Eric Parnell got to the clearing first. Removing his combat cap, he waved frantically at the helicopters. He did not want to throw smoke and give their position away.

One of the helicopters dived out of its orbit, flaring blades whipping up dust and loose grass; it almost disappeared in the long grass, only its spinning blades visible. The chosen LZ was in the middle of a dry vlei, covered in thick pampas grass almost shoulder height. Eric glanced back at Beamish who was struggling behind him.

'GO Eric,' shouted Beamish. 'GO man, get the hell out of here.' Beamish waved frantically towards the helicopter, bending over with his hands on his knees to catch his breath.

Parnell's stick jumped into the pampas grass, their rifles held above their shoulders as they struggled to push through, moving almost in slow motion. They disappeared from view as the grass swallowed them up. Out flew the helicopter, its nose pointing downwards as the pilot clawed back into the air … away it went. The next helicopter was already landing, taking the same spot, now flattened by the blades from the previous helicopter.

Beamish looked at the two Selous Scouts standing behind him, Gonzo and Spike.

'You two go … we will wait for Jack.'

They hesitated, looking back into the bush as if willing Jack to appear.

'Go for fook sakes … GO,' screamed Beamish pointing towards the helicopter.

They went, jumping through the thick grass, following the path made by Parnell and his stick.

They made it. Out flew the helicopter ... engines racing, dust and grass flying ... the choppertech, crouching over his guns waved at Beamish. Away they flew, nose pointed towards Rhodesia and home.

... Home ...

Silence returned, just the familiar faint engine note of the Lynx in the distance, as it climbed back to altitude.

Beamish turning back to look at his two gunners, they both grinned back at him ... they knew they would be last out ... *that was Beamish.*

Where the fook is Jack?

'We will probably only have to wait a few minutes, the border's only twenty-two kilometres away,' said Beamish, trying to sound confident. He would dearly have wanted to be on that first helicopter ... he was glad Eric would be safe.

'Oscar14, 31Charlie ... do you copy,' called Beamish.

'Roger, 31Charlie I am at the edge of the LZ ... where are you?' asked Jack.

Before Beamish could answer, all hell broke loose.

A band of CTs had been running up inside the bush on the south side of the powerlines. They had been following the spoor left by the escaping RLI and Selous Scouts ... it wasn't difficult.

As soon as they saw Jack, they opened up at him. He dived into the thick pampas grass in the vlei; there was nowhere else for him to go. Beamish could not see anything to shoot at; the gunfire was to his north.

'Lads, follow me into this grass. We will hide until the chopper gets back.'

All three pushed into the grass, it was dry and dusty, making the nose twitch, wanting to sneeze.

'Jack, we are inside the vlei in the long grass,' whispered Beamish into the radio.

'So am I ... just stay put ... the choppers will be back any second,' came the hushed reply.

The band of ZANLA CTs stood studying the vlei. It was at least 200m across. The matted reeds were an impenetrable barrier, it looked like a field of dry sugarcane. The RLI men could hear them talking to each other. It was clear they were deciding what to do. It did not take long.

Three Chinese stick grenades were thrown into the vlei.

THUD ... THUD ... THUD.

The Rhodesians all lay flat on their stomachs, hands over their heads. Dust and dirt were thrown up from the explosions, close to where they were hiding ... *fook ... I hope these pricks don't have white phos!*

The grenades were followed by a sustained burst of RPD machinegun fire. The voices became more animated as the CTs threw around a few more ideas. Burning the grass had to be an option ... and so it was.

The faint crackle carried to the RLI men as the tinder dry grass started to burn. The smell of burning grass filled the air, smoke billowed up, churning black, lifting burning cinders with the intense heat of the updraft.

The three RLI men were lying only inches from each other. The noise of the popping and sizzling fire meant that Beamish had to speak loudly.

'We are going to have to make a run for it. Either that or fry to death. Better a bullet than the fire,' stated Beamish resignedly.

An AK47 opened up to their left; it was Jack as he tried to cover his own escape. Beamish took out a green smoke grenade and threw it with all his strength to his right … to try and create a diversion … to give the CTs something to shoot at.

'Le Beau, shoot at where you heard those voices … we will take off, you follow … we will cover you,' instructed Beamish. 'Go.'

The thick black smoke swirled to over 2,000ft. The helicopters returning from Vila Salazar could see it almost as soon as they took off. Only a few minutes of flying time brought helicopters over the burning vlei. The lead pilot saw the ZANLA CTs hiding on the edge of the vlei; it was obvious what had happened. He turned his head to look at the choppertech; he shrugged, *what was there to say?*

Banking hard, the Alouette turned and dropped altitude. The twin .303 Brownings rattled and vibrated as the gunner directed fire towards the CT position, hunched over his gun, eyes fixed to the gun-sight. Bullet strikes lifted spurts of dirt and dust as the gunner 'walked' his machineguns towards the CTs. A man spun around and fell. His comrades broke and ran, chased by the deadly fire as they went.

The second helicopter turned towards the vlei. A green smoke grenade was burning brightly in the middle, the deadly bushfire was racing towards it. As the pilot studied the vlei, men could be seen jumping through the grass ahead of the flames, falling, getting back to the feet, pushing hard through the barrier of the thick, tangled reeds. A man held the MAG to his shoulder and fired back through the flames.

The pilot flared for his landing, as close to the escaping men as possible, he had no idea how many were waiting on the ground for him. The smoke enveloped the helicopter, the spinning blades only making the fire spread more fiercely, like a giant fan.

Beamish saw the helicopter through the smoke, the tech crouched behind the gun, his face hidden by the intercom mask. Bullets were flying everywhere as the CTs took aim at the helicopter, zipping, buzzing, biting at the air, as if the air itself was alive.

'Come on lads!' urged Beamish to his two gunners. All movement was in laboured slow motion; as if the reeds were gripping claws holding them back. It seemed impossible to cross the short gap to the helicopter as it sat on the ground, only its blades visible above the reeds.

Their MAGs, resting on the shoulder strap, acted as a drag-anchor as the two gunners tried to push through the barrier. Kratzman, in desperation, lifted the gun above his head, even his enormous strength was hardly enough. Le Beau, being so short, had no chance; he was like a fly in a spider-web, pulling and spinning but going nowhere, the fire flicking at his shirt. He screamed in desperation, the helicopter was so close and yet so far.

Beamish got to the helicopter first, throwing in his pack and rifle. Selous Scout Jack was there too, he ran around the helicopter to climb into the front seat. Then Kratzman came, his MAG above his head, his blackened face bathed in sweat. He tossed his gun into the helicopter and dived back into the grass after Le Beau.

'Le Beau ... Le Beau!' screamed Kratzman in desperation.

The roaring bushfire was now everywhere, ferociously encroaching; the heat was like an open furnace. Smoke filled his lungs until he could scream no more, coughing, spluttering, choking. It was impossible to see the little Frenchman, just a savage black sea of burning reeds.

By the grace of God, Kratzman tripped and fell over the Frenchman who lay in the grass, overcome by the smoke and fire. He bent down and lifted the small man onto his shoulder in a fireman's lift, using his spare hand to scoop up Le Beau's gun. Still bullets zipped and whistled overhead.

Kratzman, with Le Beau slumped senseless over his shoulders, appeared through the smoke in front of the helicopter. Beamish ran forward, taking the gun. Staggering from the heat and his smoke-filled lungs, Kratzman found the strength to hurl Le Beau into the helicopter. Beamish jumped in, pulling at Kratzman's shirt as the big man threw himself headfirst through the door.

The helicopter, the most beautiful thing in the world, lifted out of the clinging vlei, Kratzman's legs still dangling in space.

The fire closed in over the LZ, burning it to nothing.

Beamish sat on the bench seat next to the choppertech, Le Beau lay on the floor, coughing in spasms as he tried to clear his raw chest. Kratzman hauled himself up onto the seat, retrieved his gun from the floor and sat in silence looking out at the bush flying past below.

Taking out a water bottle, Beamish held it to Le Beau's lips to try and relieve his distress. He splashed water over his face, Le Beau looked up, his expression showing his appreciation. Another coughing spasm racked his chest as he threw up, his body shaking in shock.

Glancing up, Beamish looked at Selous Scout Jack sitting opposite him, a broad grin on his face. He seemed as relaxed as if he were watching cricket, Jack turned to look out the door as the helicopter made its desperate treetop escape from Mozambique.

Beamish said a silent prayer ... *these fookin Blue Jobs are good ... man they are good!*

A feeling of overwhelming relief washed over Beamish, he closed his eyes and rested his head against the rear bulkhead ... allowing the loud whining clatter of the helicopter to fill his mind. *We are going home ...* it was a powerful realisation that struck Beamish ... *Rhodesia is my home ...*

The Alouette engine note changed.

Glancing up from his reverie, Beamish saw the pilot's hands racing across his instruments. He was talking to the tech waving his left hand. Turning to look at the tech, the pilot whipped off his mask.

'There's a problem … fuel starvation … we may have taken a few rounds in the fuel tank,' he shouted. Looking out to the west, Malvernia was clearly visible, only 3km away.

The pilot waved his left hand again, this time twirling it around in a circular motion. The helicopter was now swiftly losing altitude, the bush coming up at them. There was no preparation.

'BRACE!' screamed the pilot.

The helicopter hit the ground hard; throwing the men around inside, Kratzman was thrown out, rolling in the dust. The still spinning blades, whacked at the trees, sending wood splinters and chunks of bark into a vortex. Pieces of wood hit Beamish in his face opening a cut above his forehead.

'Get out … get out!' shouted the choppertech as the engine stopped, the blades lay bent and broken.

Looking up, Beamish saw the other helicopter appear overhead. It was already coming in to land. The pilot and tech were speaking to each other, pointing at the other helicopter. Waving at Beamish, the pilot indicating that they should move to the where the helicopter was landing. Once again, dust was flying everywhere.

'You go,' Beamish shouted at the pilot and his tech, '… take Le Beau …' he pointed at the Frenchman who was sitting helplessly on the ground, still coughing convulsively. 'You go too,' he said to Selous Scout Jack.

Blood was filing Beamish's eyes as he brushed it away with his hand. It was sticky … there was no pain.

'No … I will wait with you Beamish,' said Jack, his face still smiling. He had a first-field dressing in his hand, wiping at Beamish's face.

'We can deal with that later …' said Beamish, brushing Jack's hand away.

Beamish had the presence of mind to ask Kratzman to take Le Beau's spare belts. Kratzman and the choppertech lifted Le Beau under the arms and supported him across to the waiting helicopter. It was impossible for Le Beau to speak; he coughed in spasms, spittle running down his chin, his chest heaving in convulsions. He waved with his hands, indicating that he was okay to stay.

'Bugger off Le Beau, … make sure the beers are cold for when we get back,' shouted Beamish above the screaming engine.

The FRELIMO garrison at Malvernia to the west had seen the helicopter come down and they organised into a sweep towards the crash site. They started with 82mm mortars.

The sudden activity in Malvernia alerting the 2RR boys at Vila Salazar, Afonso scanned the town with the television camera.

A 14.5mm machinegun, opened up in the direction of the helicopters, the gunner could not see the target but he could see the dust kicked up by the spinning blades.

Up the Alouette went, carrying the two airmen and Le Beau. Heavy gunfire chased it across the sky as it banked to the east, staying at treetop level. Beamish watched it disappear through the trees …

Mortars were dropping onto Beamish's position.

'We need to move closer to the border, we can't stay here, the Freds will come looking ...' said Beamish to the remaining two men, 'the fence can't be more than two clicks.'

The other two nodded, it was as good a plan as any ... there was no knowing how long the helicopter would be.

Beamish lifted his handset to call the Lynx at 6,000ft above them. The 14.5mm was taking pot shots at it ... the sound of the enormous rounds flying overhead sent a chill down the spine.

'Blue 3, 31Charlie, do you read?'

'31Charlie, reading you fives ... you have gooks to your southwest ... maybe four hundred metres.'

'Roger, Blue 3, we are moving to the fence.'

... 1.7km from safety ...

'Copied ... I will try to slow them down.'

Then another voice broke over the VHF net.

'Beamish this is 74, you Pommie bastard.' It was Captain John at Vila Salazar. He had recognised Beamish's Lancastrian accent.

'Come on lad's ... let's get to the fence,' said Beamish, his voice strained with the shock of the past few minutes.

It was only a few metres before the first FRELIMO cadres saw them.

'RUN,' was all Beamish could think to say. This was not a time to take on a vastly superior force. They took off, running towards the border fence; with no idea what they were going to do when they got there.

... 1.5km to safety ...

Gunfire intensified, bullets whipped through the trees above their heads. The CTs could not shoot accurately and chase them at the same time. They just sprayed the bush with rounds hoping for a strike.

The Lynx turned onto an attack run.

The pilot could see Beamish and his men running through the bush towards the fence, FRELIMO closing in on them from the south. The 14.5m started firing as soon as the Lynx dropped onto its attack dive.

At 1,400m, the Lynx was within the effective range of the weapon. Shells spun past the cockpit, the pilot did not flinch, lining up the FRELIMO soldiers on the ground, at 600ft he opened up with the twin Brownings mounted above the cockpit and at 300ft he dropped two fran canisters.

An explosive shell passed through the windscreen, missed the pilot by inches and lodged in the rear engine. The 14.5mm anti-aircraft round could penetrate 20mm of steel, enough to destroy the aircraft engine.

The sudden loss of power, as the pilot tried to pull up, was too much. The brave pilot, had no time to recover, he was too low ... he went straight into the ground. The aircraft disintegrating into a fireball as the fuel and ordinance exploded.

'74 ... 74, 31Charlie, fire mission,' shouted Beamish into the handpiece. He was out of breath from running through the bush, he knew if he did not get support they were done for. They would die trapped against the border fence.

... 1km to safety ...

'31Charlie, 74, ... target ident,' came the reply from 2RR Mortar Platoon.

'I am to your east ... maybe a thousand metres ... we are trying to get to the fence ... I need your support ... now?' Beamish knew he was going to have to call the mortars directly onto his position and pray that they survived.

Afonso had watched the Lynx crash on the TV screen. He could see the tracer rounds from the 14.5mm still firing.

The first 2RR mortar bombs were aimed at the 14.5mm that had not moved since its attack on the Lynx. Accurate fire suppressed the heavy machinegun. Then 2RR corrected onto a bearing towards Beamish's estimated position. Captain John was shouting instructions into the field telephone. All eight tubes were dropping bombs, one after the other, as fast as they could.

... 700m to safety ...

The whistle of mortars filled the air, the first rounds were close, within 50m.

'Keep moving lads,' hissed Beamish. Selous Scout Jack and Jim Kratzman simply stared ahead of them, blocking out what was going on around them. Mortar shrapnel whistled through the trees, slivers of wood and debris fell from the sky.

The fence came into sight; Beamish got the men down into cover in a shallow drainage culvert dug next to the track. As he looked down the track towards Malvernia, the old border gates were clearly visible only a few hundred metres away.

'Don't shoot,' Beamish hissed. 'We will need to take as many with us as possible ... this is it boys ...'

He lifted the radio hand-piece again and whispered,'74 ... I am at the fence about four hundred metres east of the gates.'

The mortar fire stopped.

A truck engine started up from across the border.

The fence was only metres away from Beamish and his men. FRELIMO soldiers appeared through the bush. They were cautious, looking carefully through the bush, uncertain of where the Rhodesians were hiding. They advanced slowly, chattering loudly to each other, pointing at the fence.

'Steady boys,' whispered Beamish. The three men took aim at the approaching troops ...

The engine noise from across the border, changed note as the driver raced through the gears. Beamish could not look around, concentrating on the approaching enemy.

Eight muted thuds rolled across the bush from the west ... then another eight. The bush in front of Beamish dissolved in smoke as the 2RR mortar-men laid down a barrage of smoke bombs.

The three Rhodesians opened up on the FRELIMO men, only a few metres away. In an instant, it was all smoke, bullets and confusion. It was impossible to miss, Kratzman ran through a belt of a hundred rounds in a flash, traversing his gun left and right.

Across the border Slade's *Mama Weer All Crazee Now*[126], blared across no-man's land.

> *I don't want to drink my whisky like you do*
> *I don't need to spend my money but still do ...*
>
> *... I said Mama but we're all crazy now*
> *I said Mama but we're all crazy now ...*

As Beamish snuck a look towards the border gates, an armoured Four-Five, travelling at full speed crashed into the gates. A man on top of the cab was spraying MAG rounds in front of him.

More smoke bombs fell, covering the whole area in a grey haze that made the air taste like acrid talcum powder.

> *... I said Mama but we're all crazy now*
> *I said Mama but we're all crazy now ...*

'It's fookin 2RR, come on lads,' shouted Beamish as he broke cover, sprinting down the road towards the truck that now seemed to be wedged against the gatepost.

... 200m ... to safety ...

Selous Scout Jack overtook Beamish on the sprint, firing his AK as he ran, Kratzman had the gun up over his shoulder, his giant strides sounded like an elephant as he thumped along the compacted road, the MAG belts around his neck slapping against his chest.

More smoke fell, now added to by the 81mm HE rounds aimed further into the town.

> *... I said Mama but we're all crazy now*
> *I said Mama but we're all crazy now ...*

The noise was incredible as the FRELIMO garrison went into a shooting frenzy; the truck crashing into the gates was like a stick had being thrust into a hornet's nest.

The wound on Beamish's forehead opened up again. Blood filled his eyes as he ran for safety. Sweat and blood burned, obscuring his vision. He couldn't wipe it away ... just focusing on the Four-Five. He could hear the big man pounding along behind him, the sound of his heavy breathing ... *come on Yank!*

... 100m to safety ...

Beamish's world seemed to snap into slow motion ... the red stinging haze in his eyes ... the truck looming up ... *so close ... 25m to safety ...*

... Guns firing ... smoke ... the noise was like a flood through the brain, numbing all feeling ... hands at the back doors to the truck ... screaming ...

126 Written by Jim Lea and Noddy Holder. Polydor Records 1972

lifting ... pulling him in.

A loud grunt from behind, Jim collapsed onto his knees, only metres from the back of the truck.

Jim ...

The haze made it impossible to see, just flickering shadows as men shouted, calling out frenzied instructions ... the doors slammed shut and the truck began to reverse ... rocking wildly as the driver fought for control. The gates were torn off their hinges dragged behind the truck, preventing it accelerating in the thick sand. Rounds struck the sides like a million hammers at once.

'Beamish ... it's me John, we've got you ...' screamed Captain John through the deafening cacophony.

Jim ...

A hand wiped at his forehead, it stung like hell ... his head suddenly feeling like it was going to split open ... a shooting pain behind the eyes. Somebody threw water over his head.

> *Don't stop now a c-'mon*
> *Another drop now c-'mon*
> *I wanna lot now so c-'mon*

'Your man's been hit Beamish ... don't worry the Doc has got him,' shouted Captain John, his mouth only inches from Beamish's ear. He could hear the voice but everything else was blurred.

A hand wiped at Beamish's forehead again, the pain made his eyes shut tightly.

The truck ... diesel engine rattling and vibrating ... brakes screeching to a halt ... back doors flung open ... Hands pulling and lifting again.

The thudding zing of mortar fire continued, an MAG was firing.

Jim ... being carried towards a building ...

> *... I said Mama but we're all crazy now*
> *I said Mama but we're all crazy now ...*

The music stopped.

All sound stopped ... as if on cue.

Sitting on a camp chair on the veranda, Beamish looked down at the young medic working on Jim. Selous Scout Jack was holding a drip; dressings were being pulled apart by the 2RR men, desperate to help.

'What's your name son?' asked Beamish of the medic everyone called 'Doc'.

'Williams ...' replied the Doc.

'Is he going to make it?'

Williams looked like he was twelve years old, thin arms, hands like a concert pianist. The young man looked up at Beamish, the look on his face white as a sheet, marked with defeat, shock and pain.

'He's gone Corporal Beamish … he's gone.'

And when it's time for leaving Mozambique
To say goodbye to sand and sea
You turn around to take a final peek
And you see why it's so unique to be
Among the lovely people living free
… in sunny Mozambique[127].

So many men had died …

Arthur Beamish struggled up from the chair and walked on unsteady legs down the steps of the veranda into the bright sunlight. The 2RR men watched him go, a lonely forlorn figure, covered in blood, his filthy tattered uniform stuck to his sweat drenched back, rifle held at his side.

He looked up into the cloudless blue sky that stretched from horizon to horizon … It was suddenly perfectly quiet, as if the world was taking a breath.

Despite the warm morning sun, Beamish shivered. He looked down at his left hand, it was shaking … he watched it as if it was somehow removed … not part of him.

A Swainson's Francolin, *Horwe*, called out harshly, penetratingly, from the bush outside the minefield … *krrraa … krrraa … krrraa*.

Taking a deep breath, Beamish drank in the distinctive evocative scent of the African bush in the early morning.

He closed his eyes … letting the comforting sun beat on his face … the sun so merciless yet so reassuring, promising hope and renewal.

His thoughts returned to Jock McIntyre, Penga Marais, Le Beau D'aubigne … and Jim Kratzman … all of a sudden he felt completely alone … The world seemed to be closing in on him … all his toughness and bravado washed away.

'Once more unto the breach, dear friends, once more,' said Captain John, who had walked out behind him. 'This is your lot in life Beamish, … you are a soldier son.'

Beamish had no knowledge of Shakespeare. He turned to look at Captain John whose shining eyes were smiling at him.

'Think of all the things you are missing out on? … You could always go back to England … and drive a bus or something,' quipped Captain John flippantly.

As the two men stood looking down the sandy road towards Mbalauta, a lone Kudu bull strode proudly out into the road. His magnificent, twirling horns reflected the sunlight, a thick mane of black hair hung at his throat, the grey coat shone. He turned his head to look at the soldiers, unafraid, confident and assured.

Watching the antelope move silently off into the bush, Beamish was once again struck by the glorious enormity of it all, the African wilderness … the endless open space … where a man's birth is not an unyielding debilitating

127 Bob Dylan and Jacques Levy, supra, *Mozambique*.

burden ... where a man can feel truly alive ... where he can make something of himself.

This was something worth fighting for ...

...Beamish turned to Captain John and smiled, 'There is nothing for me in England ... this is my home now ...'

The morning quiet was interrupted by the loud, echoing banging of Mafuta on the iron railway line ... calling the men to breakfast.

'*Nyamazaans ... skaafu ... skaafu ... bareka!*[128]'

---

128 Chilapalapa, '... Animals (term of endearment), food is ready, come on, hurry up!'

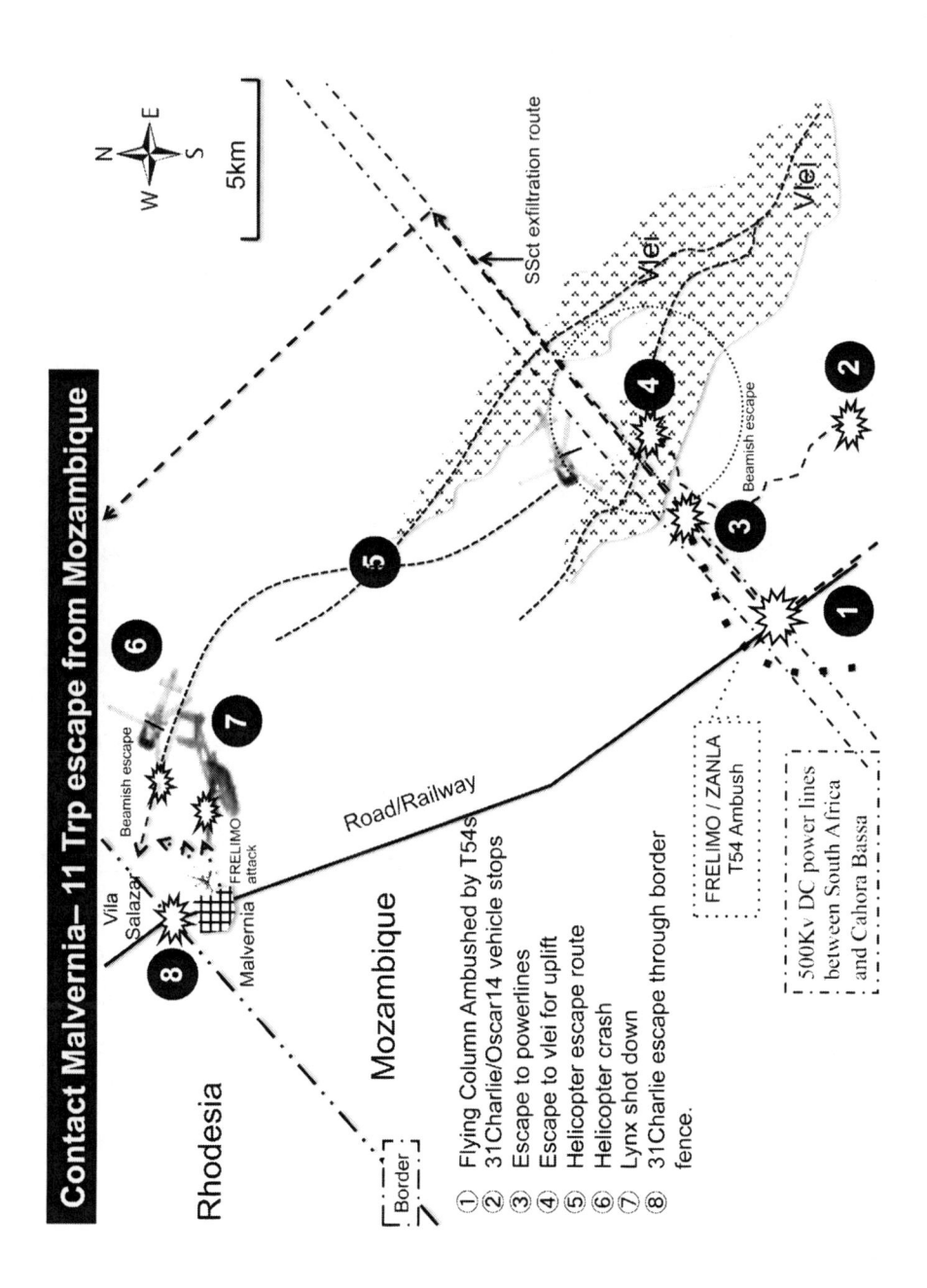

Contact Malvernia – 11 Trp escape from Mozambique

1. Flying Column Ambushed by T54s
2. 31Charlie/Oscar14 vehicle stops
3. Escape to powerlines
4. Escape to vlei for uplift
5. Helicopter escape route
6. Helicopter crash
7. Lynx shot down
8. 31Charlie escape through border fence.

FRELIMO / ZANLA T54 Ambush

500Kv DC power lines between South Africa and Cahora Bassa

Rhodesia
Mozambique
Vila Salazar
Malvernia
SSct exfiltration route
Beamish escape
Road/Railway
Border

335

25

Mozambique Channel, 332 nautical miles due east of Maputo

The giant engines churned the sea into froth as HMS Intrepid, amphibious assault ship, cruised through the turquoise ocean of the Mozambique Channel. Godfrey Nyathi stood next to the huge steel doors on the hanger deck as the crew winched a Sea King out onto the landing ramp.

He felt out of place in his Chinese khaki fatigues. The sailors avoided him, and nobody spoke to him other than a naval officer called Wright. An armed soldier in camouflage uniform, who said that he was a Royal Marine, escorted him from place to place on the ship.

During his torture, Felix Mhanda had given a list of names, nineteen when Nyathi counted them up afterwards. Tongogara was distressed to hear many of the names, men he liked and trusted. FRELIMO were really only innocent bystanders, fed a bunch of lies to get their support for Tongogara's assassination. They had no idea what they were doing. There was going to be some serious fall-out that Tongogara was going to have to sort out.

Nyathi did not kill Mhanda, instead leaving him hanging just above the ground so that the vultures, hyenas and jackals could get him. They had not been able to find Hamadziripi in the bush and they did not have time to spend hours searching for him.

As Nyathi stood looking out to sea, General Josiah Tongogara walked out of the hanger, also escorted by an armed Marine.

'Nyathi ... they are taking us back ... the danger has passed,' said Tongogara in seShona, a rare smile on his face. He seemed happy and relaxed. Nyathi did not answer, just nodded his understanding.

Another, much smaller man, appeared, flanked by Captain Zhang Youxia of the PLA. The small man was dressed neatly in a dark steel-grey Chinese *Sun Yat-sen* suit, with turn-down military-style collar, four patch pockets and five centre-front buttons.

The four pockets were said to represent the Four Cardinal Principles cited in the classic *Book of Changes*[129] and understood by the Chinese as fundamental principles of conduct: propriety, justice, honesty and a sense of shame. The five centre-front buttons were said to represent the five powers of the constitution of the Republic; Executive, Legislative, Judicial, Examination and Control. The three cuff-buttons were to symbolise the Three Principles of the People; nationalism, democracy and the people's livelihood or socialism.

The small man had no idea of the symbolic significance of his uniform, nor did he subscribe to its philosophical principles.

'Nyathi, let me introduce you to the Great Crocodile of the Zezuru nation. Meet Comrade Robert Mugabe,' stated Tongogara expansively.

---

[129] The *I Ching* or *Book of Changes* is one of the oldest of the Chinese classical texts. The book contains a divination system comparable to European Middle Ages geomancy or the West African *Ifa* system; in modern East Asia, it is still widely used for this purpose.

He emphasised the words 'Great Crocodile', the fact that he had not said 'Zimbabwean nation' was an obvious, very deliberate affront.

Then, turning to the little man, Tongogara said, 'Comrade, this is the brave cadre who saved my life from those rebellious pigs, Hamadziripi and Mhanda.'

Mugabe stood forward.

Nyathi recoiled. The man, a head shorter, was a picture of anger and resentment. It was as if a dark malevolent spirit was hovering above his head. The man glanced at Tongogara, pure hatred in his eyes.

Robert Mugabe offered his hand in silence. Nyathi instinctively reached for it, the shock of the touch sending a shiver down his spine. It was as if the man had reached into his soul. Despite the heat of the day, the hand was cold as ice, clammy, like a corpse.

Nyathi shook the hand; it gave no response, as if it was dead. The feel of Mugabe's hand was blood-curdling. Nyathi felt an involuntary shiver. Mugabe would not meet his eyes, staring past him, his eyes like black coals, devoid of feeling.

The image of the great, cold-blooded heartless crocodile, who's only instinct is to kill, to hide unseen, to strike without mercy ... the ultimate tyrant of the African bush, struck Nyathi like a hammer-blow.

Godfrey Nyathi knew at that instant that this man could not be allowed to rule his nation ... he had seen for the first time in his life, the face of pure, unadulterated, overpowering evil ...

Postscript

Whether there was a spy or a group of spies in the Rhodesian CIO and COMOPS is moot. In his book *Winds of Destruction*[130], Group Captain P. J. H. Petter-Bowyer, himself a member of COMOPS, refers to a briefing from General Peter Walls that a spy was working in COMOPS. The warning, he said, had been received from the CIO. The leaders of COMOPS, in turn, were concerned that spies were active in the CIO and stopped briefing the CIO on their plans and objectives. Petter-Bowyer in a thinly veiled accusation states, '… selected operations were launched earlier than these agencies (CIO) expected. Every time this was done, we gained maximum surprise because no forewarning to the enemy had been possible via the unknown mole …' Petter-Bowyer expressed the opinion that he did not think Ken Flower, the head of CIO, was the spy but instead accused his deputy.

Moorcroft and McLaughlin[131] in their book on the Rhodesian War confirm the active relationship between the CIO and MI6 and the leaking by the British of information to ZANLA in Mozambique. They also state that a spy was discovered in the CIO quoted as a 'very senior member of the Rhodesian security elite.' These writers mentioned no names, but they expressed the view that it was not Ken Flower.

Ken Flower, the head of the CIO at independence, was asked by the new Mugabe Government to carry on heading the CIO. The intriguing element in the hiring of Flower was, of course, his switching of allegiances. His critics, who had labelled Flower as the 'doublest' of all double agents, viewed this as vindication.

In his book *See You in November*[132] Peter Stiff quoted the CIO agent in Zambia, Alan *Taffy* Brice, as saying, '… Britain's secret services had been tipped off about … my mission, almost certainly by someone in the CIO. Knowledge of my existence was restricted to a select few … There is little doubt that MI6 had a direct and long standing pipeline into Rhodesian Intelligence through a senior officer.' Brice was referring to a plan to use him in a plot to assassinate Mugabe in London before the Lancaster House peace talks.

Josiah Tongogara is purported to have died in a car accident on Boxing Day 1979, only four months before the achievement of his great ambition, the freedom of his people and the independence of his country. He was 41 years old.

Tongogara had attended a meeting with the President of Mozambique, Samora Machel in Maputo on Christmas Eve. This meeting was an attempt by Tongogara to make his peace with the Mozambican President, who still harboured a grudge against Tongogara for the murder, in 1975, of his close

---

130 *Winds of Destruction* (2005), 30° South Publishers at 351.
131 *The Rhodesian War a Military History*, Pen & Sword (2008) at 122 -123.
132 *See You in November*, Peter Stiff, Galago (1985), page 298.

friend, Herbert Chitepo. In that meeting, Tongogara reiterated his innocence.

The official story is that the Landcruiser in which Tongogara was travelling overturned while trying to overtake a FRELIMO lorry that was towing a long trailer. As the vehicle tried to overtake, the trailer swung out, side-swiping the Landcruiser. Tongogara was killed instantly. He was sitting in the left hand front seat next to the driver. No other passengers were seriously injured in the accident, in fact they all walked away unscathed[133].

Josiah Tungamirai[134], the ZANLA High Command's Political Commissar, relates that on the night of the fatality, he and Tongogara had been travelling with others in two vehicles from Maputo to Chimoio. Tungamirai said he was in the front vehicle. It was dark and the roads were bad. Tungamirai's car passed a military vehicle that had been carelessly abandoned, with no warning signs, at the side of the road. After that, he could no longer see the headlights of the following car in his rear view mirror. Eventually he turned back and they found Tongogara's car had struck the abandoned vehicle. Tongogara was sitting in the front passenger seat. Tungamirai said that he had struggled to lift Tongogara out of the wrecked car. He said that as he was doing so, Tongogara heaved a huge sigh and died in his arms.

Members of Tongogara's escort disappeared soon after the accident. One account states that a member of the escort was detained in a Mozambican jail where he managed to smuggle out a message. The message said that Tongogara had been shot in the stomach and axed in the head whilst asleep in his quarters. His stomach had been cut open to remove the bullets and the mutilations were made to appear like road accident injuries[135].

It is no secret that, in 1979, Josiah Tongogara was the most popular man in Zimbabwe, overshadowing Robert Mugabe. He was vehemently opposed to communism and Mugabe's plan of setting up a one-party state once in power and banning all political opposition. Many expected him to be the first president of Zimbabwe, with Robert Mugabe, head of ZANU, as prime minister.

In *Winds of Destruction*[136] Petter-Bowyer refers to a conversation over dinner with the ZIPRA leadership, Dumiso Dabengwa and Lookout Masuku in early 1980. He states that these men were extremely disturbed by the death of Tongogara as they saw him as a man to be trusted. They described a meeting in London between themselves, Tongogara and Tungamirai, where a strategy was devised to be implemented if Mugabe or Nkomo walked out of the Lancaster House peace talks. In that meeting Tongogara had made it clear that the war could not be allowed to continue and if the political leaders

133 *Re-Living the Second Chimurenga*, Fay Chung, Nordic Africa Institute (2006) at 139.
134 After independence, Tungamirai was commander of the Air Force and later served as Minister of State for Indigenization and Empowerment. Tungamirai was flown to a South African hospital after complications from a kidney transplant. He died there on 25 August 2005. After Josiah Tungamirai's death, his widow Pamela Tungamirai claimed that he had been poisoned.
135 *See You in November*, Peter Stiff, Galago (1985), page 300.
136 *Winds of Destruction* (2005), supra at 378 -379.

failed their people, then a military triumvirate made up of ZIPRA, ZANLA and the Rhodesia forces must take power. He spelled out a plan as follows:

- The military triumvirate would be set up, initially in London, then to be moved to Salisbury, under the leadership of General Peter Walls (who at that point had not been consulted by Tongogara). The first task was to ensure separation of forces.
- After a period of planning, the integration of the military forces.
- A 100-seat Parliament, as the basis of a Government of national unity, would be set up to rule for a period of 5 years. The Executive Governor would be Sir Humphrey Gibbs who had the respect all parties including the British. Over the period of 5 years, the processes of government would be created including the drafting of a constitution, after which elections would be held.
- No British interference was to be tolerated.

Mugabe did walk out of the Lancaster House peace talks but he was forced to return to the table after President Samora Machel of Mozambique warned him that he would remove his support and all ZANLA soldiers from his country. Tongogara was never in a position to initiate his plan.

Dabengwa and Masuku were both of the opinion that Josiah Tungamirai had leaked Tongogara's strategy to Mugabe who had then set in motion the assassination. They claimed an agent was recruited from East Germany who arranged the car accident. Enos Nkala paid him in US Dollars at the Maputo Airport[137] on behalf of Mugabe's leadership team.

In an article in the Zimbabwean[138], *Zimbabwe Democracy Now* spokeswoman Ethel Moyo said that there was widespread suspicion of foul play. She quotes the United States Central Intelligence Agency who said that Mugabe, who regarded Tongogara as a potential political rival due to his ambition, popularity and decisive style, could have killed him.

Ian Smith insisted in his memoirs that Tongogara's 'own people' killed him and that he had disclosed at Lancaster House that Tongogara was under threat. 'I made a point of discussing his death with our police commissioner and head of Special Branch, and both assured me that Tongogara had been assassinated,' Smith wrote.

A retired detective in the Law and Order Section of the former British South African Police (now Zimbabwe Republic Police) said photographs of Tongogara's body showed three wounds, consistent with gunshots to his upper torso. The official undertaker's statement was not a formal autopsy report, and as such, was dismissed by all but ZANU.[139] The undertaker, Mr Ken Stokes of Mashford & Sons of Salisbury, had flown to Mozambique to collect the body and return it to Rhodesia for burial at the request of the

---

137 After independenace Nkala held various ministeries including Finance, Defence and Home Affairs.
138 *The Zimbabwean*, 12 December 2009.
139 Ethel Moyo, *The Zimbabwean*, supra.

British Embassy in Maputo. Mr Stokes is reported as saying, 'The injuries are consistent with a car accident.'[140] No official post-mortem was requested.

Another theory is that the Rhodesian SAS killed Tongogara. If that were so, it seems inconceivable that the truth would not have come out after so many years. Plus the obvious point, that if it were the SAS, there would have been no survivors to the car accident.

Enos Nkala, one of the founders of ZANU, in his memoirs reveals that he believed Tongogara was killed (if Petter-Bowyer's meeting with Dabengwa and Masuku is to be believed, he was part of the plot). He stated that two days after Tongogara's death, the US Embassy in Zambia issued a statement saying; 'Almost no one in Lusaka accepts Mugabe's assurance that Tongogara died accidentally'. He stated further that, 'When (our) ambassador told the Soviet Ambassador the news, the (latter) immediately charged *inside job*.'[141]

What sort of President would Josiah Tongogara have been? We can only imagine. He may well have been a worse dictator and more violently oppressive than Mugabe. His track-record in brutally putting down the Nhari and Vashandi Rebellions may have foreshadowed what was to come ... but then ... maybe not ...

Benjamin Takavarasha paid a haunting tribute to Josiah Tongogara at the anniversary of his death in 2011.

> *The vultures hail and cheer the brave hunter on, till his prey to hand,*
> *Whence him their easier prey;*
> *Crocodile tears overflowing, his prey all their own,*
> *Feasting by his corpse, his name they hail no more.*

---

140 Stiff, supra, at 300.
141 The Zimbabwean, 23 August 2006.

COCKY LOBIN OVER GERMANY
Daryl Sahli

YOUNG MEN FLYING BIG MACHINES INTO INCREDIBLE DANGER. COMPELLING, CHILLING, PART STORY, PART HISTORY, ALWAYS REAL!

It is March 1944, the Battle of Berlin has ground to a halt, both sides battered to submission. Bomber Command gathers itself for the next assault. This story follows a bomber crew from 44 (Rhodesia) Squadron who have completed their 15th mission, only half way through their tour. Follow the routine of their lives, their living conditions, the parties and the commitment of the dedicated ground crews and support staff. The squadron has lost more than half its number in only a few months, the chances of survival now seem impossible. These are young men from the four corners of the Empire, from the wild bush-land of Rhodesia, the endless bitterly cold rolling plains of Canada, the hot and desolate centre of Australia and the squalor of bombed English cities. These men were thrust together by force of circumstance, forged in battle, their relationship based on mutual reliance and determination … to see it through … come what may.

The bombers face a ferocious, determined and well organised enemy. On the next mission they face the latest in night fighting and radar technology, the odds are stacked against them as never before. The Lancaster Cocky Lobin, C-Charlie, must carry her crew through a withering aerial battle, radar predicted flak, fast and well armed night-fighters and the weather. This is a fight to the death … a test, for men barely out of their teens, like no other.

Due for Release in 2013

Winner of the Bronze Award in the Military/Wartime Fiction category in the 2012 Independent Publisher (IPPY) Book Awards in the United States.

A DESPERATE COLONIAL STRUGGLE ON A CONTINENT TORN BY WAR

Set in an almost forgotten guerrilla war in what is now called Zimbabwe during the 1970s, this is a journey into the world of young men fighting and dying at the behest of their political masters. The strain of having to survive close-quarter skirmishes preoccupy the combatants, who helplessly find themselves caught up in a conflict spinning out of control.

Mike Smith, an insecure nineteen-year old national serviceman, is immersed in a bloody insurgency witnessing horrors that seem too much for a young man to have to bear.

Tongerai Chabanga, a commander of the liberation movement, must withstand political pressure from his leaders outside the country to prosecute the war in a manner he disagrees with. At the same time, he is faced with the atrocities perpetrated of a depraved Soviet Spetznaz military advisor who threatens to undo the work he has done.

CPSIA information can be obtained
at www.ICGtesting.com
Printed in the USA
LVOW12s0325270617
539400LV00002B/446/P